ONWARDS AND UPWARDS

Danny and Maxie Maws think the world of each other. As a milkman and a nanny, making ends meet is a constant juggling act – not helped by their mothers who are sworn enemies – but they are happy together and that's all that matters, until their flashy new neighbours convince Danny he is not giving Maxie the sort of life she deserves. Afraid of losing her, Danny embarks on a series of disastrous money-making schemes, getting himself into deeper and deeper trouble – and then Maxie begins to face a few troubles of her own...

ONWARDS AND UPWARDS

ONWARDS AND UPWARDS

by

Lynda Page

Magna Large Print Books
Long Preston, North Yorkshire,
BD23 4ND, England.

British Library Cataloguing in Publication Data.

Page, Lynda
    Onwards and upwards.

    A catalogue record of this book is
    available from the British Library

    ISBN   978-0-7505-2646-3

First published in Great Britain in 2006 by Headline Book Publishing

Published in Large Print 2007 by arrangement with Headline Book Publishing Ltd.

Magna Large Print is an imprint of Library Magna Books Ltd.

Printed and bound in Great Britain by
T.J. (International) Ltd., Cornwall, PL28 8RW

For Eileen and Frank Embleton.

It frightens me to count the number of years
we have been friends.

I love you both.

Acknowledgements

To all the readers of my books – you keep me
doing what I love doing best.
Thank you.

CHAPTER ONE

Nineteen thousand, seven hundred and forty-six pounds, seventeen shillings and fourpence. The figures danced tantalisingly before the dark brown eyes of twenty-three-year-old Daniel Maws. A man with this kind of money to his name was a rich man indeed, set up for life. At today's hourly rates of pay for the kind of job he was employed to do, it would take at least twenty years for him to earn such an enormous amount. There were so many things a huge windfall such as this could buy him. A big house with a large garden in a good area; a smart car parked in the sweeping, well-tended drive; a business of his own which would support this new lifestyle after the winnings ran out. And still there'd be more than enough left over for them to take a luxury holiday somewhere exotic like Torquay or Bournemouth for a week – no, a fortnight. They'd take real leather luggage with them, not imitation, packed solid with the cut of clothes people of means wore when staying in first-class hotels. He'd be able to make his mother's and mother-in-law's lives easier too, but most important to him, he'd be able to offer his beloved wife of six months, Max-ina, the kind of lifestyle working-class types like themselves usually only dreamed about, regard-less of the fact he had never heard Maxie even hint that she was anything other than happy with the life they had already.

The pools official was coming towards him now, the precious cheque clutched in his hand, as simultaneously rapturous applause and cheers erupted from the large crowd who'd gathered to witness this momentous occasion. Danny was in no doubt they were all envious of him. His heart pounded in anticipation. He held out his hand in readiness to receive his life-changing award and realised his arm was being vigorously shaken. Jerking round his head, he was most surprised to see a pair of beady eyes glaring back at him. What was Mrs Watkins, one of his customers, doing at this prestigious affair, and especially dressed as she was?

Before he could enquire she blurted, 'A' yer *ever* gonna deliver me milk today? My old man's moaning for his cuppa. He's a grumpy old bugger at the best of times first thing, but without his milky brew he's worse than a madman with an axe in his head.' She paused long enough to screw up her old face quizzically. 'And what yer holding yer hand out like that for? And why've yer got that silly grin on yer face? Yer look like a village idiot, so you do.'

The life-changing cheque, the portly official about to hand it to him, and the cheering crowd around vanished in a moment. Cruelly snatched from his delicious daydream back into the realms of reality, a shamefaced Danny mumbled, 'Eh? Oh, I was er … er… Look, I'm sorry, Mrs Watkins, for the delay today but you see...'

'Oh, don't bother me with yer excuses, lad, just deliver me bottle of milk and bring peace to me house. In fact, I'll help meself as at the pace you're going this morning it'll be lunchtime before anyone in this street gets their breakfast.' She pulled a bottle of sterilised milk out of a full crate, then wagging a warning finger at him, added, 'In all fairness, I know yer've only been in this job a week but I'd watch it, lad, if I was you, 'cos folks in this street are starting to grumble about yer time-keeping. It only takes one to decide they've had enough and make a complaint to the dairy, and you'll have had yer chips. Thirty years Sid Clapper had the round before you and never once was he late, hail, rain or shine, from the day he started. Air raids never stopped him neither during the war. And yer never caught *him* reading the newspaper on duty,' she said, flashing a scathing glance at the copy of the *Daily Sketch* that Danny had open across his knees.

He watched the wizened old woman scuttle off up the street towards her shabby terrace house, her sparse salt-and-pepper hair scraped back under a holey blue hairnet, faded pink fleecey dressing gown pulled tight around her shrivelled body. She kicked the door shut behind her with one disintegrating slipper.

Danny privately conceded that for the first few days in his new job his customers had received their daily delivery later than they should have while he'd been getting to grips with his new responsibilities, but today's delay wasn't entirely down to him. Machinery that sealed the foil tops on the filled bottles had broken down during the night and the couple of hours lost while the night-duty mechanic fixed it had meant all the milkmen had been late leaving this morning.

His eyes settled again on the bold headline in his newspaper. He gave a despondent sigh. Judging by the photograph, the balding, beaming, smartly dressed and extremely lucky man who had won the pools' jackpot the previous Saturday didn't look to be so much in need of the windfall as Danny was himself. According to the accompanying article, he was the owner of a prosperous plumbing business, so he was already well off anyway. Money came to money, it seemed to Danny. Not that he begrudged the man his good fortune, far from it. Danny was generous by nature and liked to see people make good, most especially working-class types like himself. But if the truism was accurate, then he and Maxie, despite both working hard, were destined to live out their lives scratting from one pay day to the next. Nevertheless, he was happy with the life he had, and if it continued just as it was it wouldn't bother Danny in the slightest. All the riches in the world wouldn't make up for it if he ever lost his Maxie.

A gust of chilly early-morning wind whipping through the open sides of the milk float made him shudder, and also served to remind him where he was and what he was supposed to be doing. If he didn't get a move on he would most certainly start to annoy the customers and then demotion to his old job back inside the dairy, or worse still the sack, were strong possibilities. Folding up the newspaper, he put it in his haversack along with his lunch box, pushing it under his seat.

The street he was delivering on rose quite steeply for a hundred or so yards, then levelled out

16

before rising steeply again. Pressing his foot down hard on the accelerator pedal to get as much power as he could into the engine, he coaxed the electric vehicle along. He had only travelled half-way up the incline when his attention was caught by a young woman. It was obvious from her dishevelled appearance and the fact that her thick hand-knitted jumper was inside out that she had dressed hurriedly that morning. She was pushing a dilapidated and cumbersome Silver Cross coach pram with one hand while urgently flagging him down with the other. He brought the float to a halt alongside her. She didn't look at all happy and Danny felt certain he knew the reason why.

'Yer late today, Milky,' she snapped at him. 'In fact, yer've bin late every day since you took over from the last one. I'm Mrs White from number sixty-nine. You should have delivered to me ages ago. I've not been able to give my Ronnie his bottle 'cos I've no milk to fill it with nor to put on his Farley's rusk. The poor little blighter's starving and it's no good me trying to explain to him that he'll have to wait 'cos the milky ain't shown yet, 'cos at six months old, well, he don't understand, does he?'

Danny cast a look at the grubby baby propped up inside the pram, his chubby face smeared with criss-cross grimy tear tracks and dried mucus under his button nose. Their eyes locked and Danny felt it must surely be his imagination that the child was staring at him accusingly, as if blaming him entirely for his own hungry state. Dragging his eyes from the child, Danny looked back at Mrs White apologetically. 'Look, I'm

17

sorry I've been late since I took over this round, but I promise I'll do my best to make sure it doesn't happen again.'

'It better hadn't 'cos I'm warning yer – I'll have to put in a complaint to the dairy. I'll help meself to me two pints,' she said, letting go of the pram handle to lean over and grab hold of two bottles of pasteurised from the crate nearest to her. Turning back to the pram to put the bottles inside and hurry home to feed her baby, she let out a terrified shriek. Simultaneously the two bottles slipped from her hands to crash to the ground, sending glass and milk scattering all ways.

At her shout Danny automatically stuck his head out of the cab to see what had caused her outburst and his eyes popped open to witness the pram careering off down the road, gathering momentum as it went, the propped-up baby inside screaming hysterically at its sudden alienation from his mother. Without further ado Danny leaped out of his cab and pelted after the pram, losing his cap which rolled into a puddle in a gutter but just managing to grab hold of the handle before the pram collided with a parked Transit van at the bottom of the hill.

The rhythmic jangling of bottles then caught his attention and he jerked round his head, his jaw dropping open in horror to see the milk float, travelling backwards and veering dangerously from side to side, go sailing past him. Seconds later it came to a crashing halt against a lamp post, dashing the stacked crates of full and empty milk bottles to smithereens against the cobbled road. A white river of milk swirled in the gutter.

18

Staring open-mouthed at the chaos around him and very aware of the repercussions this was going to cause, Danny was oblivious to the street's inhabitants spilling out into the street to see what all the commotion was about.

An hysterical Mrs White arrived to grab her still wailing baby out of its pram and clutch him protectively to her. 'Oh, yer saved me baby, Milky!' she cried. 'Oh, thank you, thank you. I don't know what the hell I was thinking of, not putting the brake on the pram before I let go of the handle. Oh, my Ronnie could've bin killed! Yer a hero, Milky, yer really are.' It was only then that the state of the float registered with her. Pulling a face, she grumbled, 'Oh, no. This means I'll have to traipse all the way down the shop to get me milk this morning, and that old bat that runs it charges a penny a pint more than you do.'

A while later an ashamed Danny was facing his very angry dairy manager.

'Of all the stupid things to do! Not putting the brake on the float, and on a hill like you was on... I had high hopes of you, Maws, I really had.' Wilf Stibbins, a small, rotund man with thin greying hair cut in a short back and sides, horn-rimmed spectacles clamped high on the bridge of his misshapen nose, paused just long enough to shake his head ruefully and take a deep breath before continuing his lecture.

'Look at the state of you,' he snapped, giving Danny a disgusted glance. 'You're a disgrace to this dairy. And where's your cap? Caps are to be worn at all times, you know that. I really felt you

19

had the makings of a top-notch roundsman, Maws, I really did. I took a gamble, with you being on the young side for such a responsible job, but I was positive I was doing the right thing in promoting you above several others, all champing at the bit to get Sid's round when he retired.

'Yer've let me down badly, lad, you really have. Barely a week in the job and already you've caused the firm untold costs. Whether the float is salvageable remains to be seen, not to mention the lost revenue. It was practically full. The owner isn't going to be very happy when I explain this to him. Well, I don't think I need tell you how serious this matter is, Maws. It grieves me to do it as you've been a good employee over the years you've worked here but in the circumstances I have no alternative...'

Danny's heart sank like a stone, fearing what was coming. Working at the dairy had been his one and only job since leaving school at fifteen. His much-loved late father had been a milkman, and like most sons hereabouts Danny had automatically followed in his footsteps. Providing the local community with their daily milk was not everyone's choice of profession, not that it wasn't perceived as a decent job but primarily because of the early-morning start which in reality meant the middle of the night. Getting up at three to start at four didn't bother Danny, though. His philosophy was, sooner start, sooner finished. Eight years he'd waited to land a roundsman's position. He'd been elated when he'd finally been granted it, and hell-bent on proving his worth so that when a bigger round came up, bringing a bigger wage with it, he'd be in line to land it. And now, within less than a week...

A vision of his wife flashed before Danny then. She meant everything to him. He loved Maxina with every ounce of his being; failing her in any way distressed him above all things. Maxie had been so proud of him when he had broken the news of his promotion to her. She wasn't going to be very proud of him now, was she? And the loss of the extra thirty shillings a week, plus the chance of good tips at Christmas, was going to put paid to all the plans they'd had. He vehemently prayed his punishment for this morning's catastrophe was going to be only demotion back inside the dairy, not dismissal; at least that way he wouldn't be going home to tell Maxie her husband was un-employed. But he feared his prayer would not be answered. The destruction of company property, whatever the cause, was almost top of the list of sackable offences. He took a deep breath, preparing to hear the worst.

Just then the telephone on Wilf's desk burst shrilly into life and the dairy manager glared mur-derously at it. 'If this is another bloody customer from your round, calling to complain they haven't received their delivery this morning, I'll ... I'll...'

Snatching up the receiver he barked into it, 'Stibbins, dairy manager.' As he listened to his caller his face took on a look of shocked surprise. 'Oh!' he blustered. 'Oh, er ... I see... Did he really?... Well, yes, I agree, it is a very heroic action... A medal! Well, I think that's going a little too... Oh, you think it's the least he deserves?... Yes, yes, you have my word he'll be rewarded for

21

his bravery... What! You expect the dairy to compensate you for the penny extra you had to pay for milk from the local shop! Well, of all the ... er ... er ... yes, of course we will. Glad you think so highly of us, madam. Good day to you too.'

Replacing the receiver, he snorted disgustedly. 'I can't believe the nerve of that woman! From what she's just said it seems to me it's her forgetfulness you've to thank for landing up in all this trouble. In the circumstances it's her who should be offering to compensate the dairy for the trouble she's caused today, not the other way around.'

Then he eyed Danny fixedly. 'Well, Maws, it seems you're rather the local hero. Why didn't you tell me how the float came to be damaged?' But before Danny could make any sort of response, as had been the case from the moment he had arrived in the office for this dressing down, his boss continued. 'Well, this changes matters. It most certainly does. It wouldn't look good for the dairy to dismiss one of its employees for saving a child's life, now would it? Once I've explained to him, I'm sure Mr Wilson will see it that way too. Look ... er ... just finish your shift by helping to clean the dairy down.' Wilf stood up, took off his white overall, unhooked his suit jacket from the coat stand behind him and pulled it on. 'I'd better go and update Mr Wilson on what's happened. Off you go then. Oh, and Maws ... next time you decide to play Superman, take a second to secure the hand brake on your float first.'

CHAPTER TWO

As Danny hurried out of his boss's office, mortally relieved he wasn't going to lose his job thanks to Mrs White's taking the trouble to telephone, albeit for an obvious motive, in the dining room of a large detached house at the affluent end of the Glenfield Road on the outskirts of the city, his wife was staring at her employer, dumbfounded by the devastating news that had just been casually delivered. Finding her voice at last, Maxina Maws, a pleasant-faced twenty three year old with long dark brown hair pulled tidily up into a pony tail, said in a shocked voice: 'The whole family is moving to Newcastle at the end of next week?'

Tossing back her mane of ash-blonde hair, Sally Carson, a stunningly attractive older woman with a perfect English rose complexion, took another sip of her percolated coffee before responding. 'Yes, it's all rather exciting, isn't it? Doctor Carson has accepted a partnership in a practice in a village just outside the city. I'm not sure how I'll adapt to country life but one has to make sacrifices for the sake of one's husband's career. And, of course, it will be far better for Felicity to be raised in the country away from all this grime and fog.'

Her face took on a dreamy expression. 'Oh, Maxie dear, you should see the house we're moving into! A proper country cottage with a thatched roof and climbing roses round the door. The only pity of it all is that I can't ask you to come with us since you're married. Such a shame. Felicity will miss you dreadfully, she's so attached to you. Still, children are very adaptable and I'm told she'll soon become attached to her new nanny. She came across as a nice enough woman when we interviewed her so I feel lucky she's agreed to work for us. Miss Dawson is much older than you, Maxie dear, but has come highly recommended. Of course, now Felicity has about reached school age it's more of a housekeeper's position that Miss Dawson will be taking up with us.'

She paused and looked a mite sheepishly at Maxie. 'I should have told you before about our plans, shouldn't I? Duncan kept telling me I should, but I worried I would lose you before I was ready to. You can appreciate that, can't you, Maxie? Besides, you'll have no trouble securing yourself another position. It'll be your choice entirely who you'll go to next. You'll be fought over, I've no doubt. I will, of course, give you an excellent reference. You've been an absolute treasure, and I shall make certain any potential employer is left in no doubt of that.'

She drained her cup before pushing back her Schreiber dining chair, gracefully standing up and rearranging her smart full grey-checked skirt which she had teamed with a pale pink twin set. Fingering her expensive pearl necklace, she said, 'Well, I must get on. So much to organise and so little time. What is that saying Mrs Baker is always

24

coming out with ... well, amongst so many others. She has a penchant for quoting them and I haven't a clue what they all mean.' She paused for a moment then exclaimed, 'Onwards and upwards! Yes, that's the one. Most apt in this case, don't you think, Maxie dear? This partnership for Doctor Carson is most certainly a move in the right direction for us. Now, you need to be getting on with preparing Felicity's lunch so I won't keep you. Oh, I suppose I ought to tell Mrs Baker too now I've informed you. Can you send her in to see me when you come across her?'

Winnie Baker, the Carsons' daily, was emptying a galvanised bucket of dirty suds into the large pot sink when Maxie entered the kitchen. The roly-poly middle-aged woman, a stained wraparound apron pulled tight around her large girth, made to make a chirpy comment to the young nanny she'd grown fond of during the time they had worked together, but the look on Maxie's face had her asking worriedly instead, 'Someone died, gel?'

'Pardon, Mrs B? Oh, no, I've just heard something upsetting, that's all. Mrs Carson wants to see you straight away.'

The daily's worried look vanished to be replaced by a smile. 'Oh, yes, it's pay day. I hope she's remembered to pay me for the extra time I did on Monday afternoon, clearing up after the guests she had staying over the weekend.'

Maxie thoughtfully watched the older woman bustle off, wondering how Winnie Baker was going to receive the news that after next weekend she'd be looking for new employment.

Preparing her charge's lunch temporarily forgotten, Maxie folded her arms and leaned back against the sink. After leaving college, working for the Carsons had been her one and only job. She had been delighted to secure it against all the others just as well qualified as herself who had been interviewed for the position. Would her next job be as enjoyable? The Carsons had proved to be the type who appreciated that those they employed were skilled at what they did, and largely left them to it. Maxie derived great satisfaction from knowing that she had played a major part in turning the newly born Felicity into the unpretentious, thoughtful but also fun-loving five year old she had developed into.

As the time had drawn nearer to Felicity starting school and no other children had appeared, Maxie had wondered how her responsibilities in the household would change. If the Carsons would expect her to undertake more of a housekeeper's role and, if that were the case, how she actually felt about her primary duties not being a nanny's any longer. She enjoyed the nurturing of children, viewed it as her vocation in life, but regardless didn't like the thought of leaving the Carsons' employment. She had decided that when the time came, she would settle for what they offered her. Their leaving for pastures new had never entered her head. Sally Carson might see her own life as going onwards and upwards but at right this minute Maxie perceived hers doing just the opposite.

Winnie came bustling back in, interrupting her thoughts. The older woman was clearly angered

26

by the news she had just received.

'Well, of all the bloody nerve!' she snapped fiercely. 'Gets given yer pay and thanked for what yer've done in one breath, and in the next told that as of the end of next week yer on the scrap heap, without so much as a by your leave.' Snatching up a cleaning cloth, she began vigorously wiping an already clean kitchen table. 'Her ladyship musta known fer weeks about all this. She could have let us in on it, so we had more warning. She's not a bad sort is Mrs Carson on the whole, compared to some I've given me services to, but she can show a selfish streak at times. Fancy admitting she didn't tell us about their plans before in case we staff upped sticks and left her high and dry, with no one to fanny around after her before she was ready to let us go!'

A defiant glint suddenly sparked in her eyes and she stopped what she was doing to stare at Maxie. 'Well, *I'll* teach her a lesson for making a monkey out of me, and hopefully she'll think twice before she does 'ote like this again. Since he's retired my husband's been on at me to cut down me hours 'cos on the pension he gets from the Post Office for his fifty-year service we can manage quite well. Out of loyalty to Mrs Carson I wouldn't agree. Still, she ain't shown us no loyalty by giving us decent notice of her intentions, has she, so I don't owe her any now. I'm gonna give my old man his wish, but I'm going one better and cutting out me hours completely!' Flinging back her head, she announced, 'As of this minute, I'm retired.'

Maxie watched, stunned, as she waddled off to collect her shabby black coat from the utility

27

room just off the kitchen, pulled it on then swung her large black handbag into the crook of her arm. Walking back to the younger woman, Winnie smiled warmly at her. 'Well, ta-ra, me old duck.'

'You're really leaving, right this minute, Mrs B?' Maxie said, aghast.

'I don't say things I don't mean, Maxie lovey. I'm really upset by what her ladyship's done. It's 1967, not 1927. The days of us menials having to take on the chin what our superiors dish out to us, putting up and shutting up, are long over, thank God. In all the years I've worked for her, Mrs Carson has never once had cause to complain about me work. I've even come in many a time on a Sunday to help her and the good doctor when they've had visitors. She should have known, after all this time, I wasn't the sort to leave her high and dry. The least she owed me was decent warning I was about to lose me job, to give me time to get another. How does she know you and me ain't reliant on our pay to settle the rent, and if we don't get another job quick could risk eviction?'

Maxie sighed. Winnie Baker had a point.

'I've enjoyed working alongside you,' she continued. 'Some nannies I've been on staff with in jobs felt they was so superior they couldn't even bring themselves to talk to the likes of a skivvy, but you ain't bin high-faluting at all. I shall miss yer, ducky. I really wish you well for yer future. And you ain't got n'ote to worry about over getting another position, not with your credentials. You'll be snapped up. If yer ever round my way in future, pop in for a cuppa. There'll

28

always be a welcome for you at my hearth. Well, it'll seem strange me not having to get up at the crack of dawn every morning except Sunday in future, but I'll get used to it.' She leaned forward and gave Maxie an unexpected peck on the cheek before turning away and bustling out.

A presence by her side made Maxie jump then. She looked down to see a pretty child smiling up at her. A surge of guilt swamped her. She'd been so consumed by the devastating news this young girl's mother had delivered a short while ago, and Winnie Baker's abrupt departure, that all thoughts of her charge had flown from Maxie's mind. She knelt down to Felicity's level and took her small hands in hers. 'You've finished the colouring, have you?'

The child nodded.

'Well, if you go and wash your hands then sit at the nursery table, I'll have your lunch waiting for you.'

As she watched Felicity skip happily off a great sense of loss filled Maxie. In a few days' time she would no longer have anything to do with this child she had become so fond of. It felt to Maxie as if she was suffering a bereavement.

CHAPTER THREE

Immediately Maxie walked through the back door at just after six that evening, Danny stopped what he was doing and went across to her, giving her a peck on the cheek and a hug. 'Dinner's about ready to dish up. There's a pot of tea mashed so get your coat off and go and sit at the table, I'll bring you one through.'

Maxie smiled warmly at him. She and Danny had known each other forever, it seemed, having been introduced to each other while still in their prams by their respective mothers who'd moved in at the same time next door to each other, where they still lived, in a street not far from where Danny and Maxie lived now. Despite their opposite genders the children had quickly become inseparable, finding in each other everything they needed in a friend so that they never bothered making others. As their deep friendship turned to love with adulthood, neither felt the need to test the water with other members of the opposite sex. Marriage seemed the natural progression for them.

At five foot ten, with a thatch of mousy hair and rough-hewn features that, although far from unattractive, would never claim a second look from any other good-looking woman but Maxie, Danny was the 'wouldn't hurt a fly' sort, a steady, reliable, trustworthy man, just the type to suit the honest, steady, trustworthy woman Maxie was herself. Their ambitions were modest. They just wanted to have enough money coming in to pay for the necessities, with a little extra on top for the odd night out or piece of clothing.

'I'm a lucky woman, Daniel Maws. I wonder how many women get this sort of treatment from their husbands?'

'Well, in all fairness I can only do what I do 'cos of the timing of my shifts. If I worked factory shifts, for instance, then this afternoon I wouldn't have been able to take a look at that noise that was coming from the sidecar and fix it so we can have a spin on Sunday.'

'Oh, if you've fixed it then it was nothing serious like we feared?'

'A mudguard had come loose and that's what the rattling was, so you can start planning where you want to go. Oh, and it was the sausages you wanted cooking for dinner tonight, not the mutton chops?'

She tutted and with an amused twinkle in her eyes, said, 'I knew you weren't really listening to me last night when you asked me. Lucky for you, you picked right. The sausages would be off by tomorrow.' She gave him another peck on his cheek. 'Come on, I'll give you a hand by mashing the spuds.'

A few minutes later, as they sat opposite each other enjoying their meal from second-hand plates they had picked up from the market while building their bottom drawer together, Maxie asked her husband, 'How did work go today?'

He'd never lied, or even embroidered the truth

to her in any way before, and hadn't any intention of doing so even if it meant he risked looking a mite foolish for forgetting to secure the float. Maxie's eyes were riveted on him as he proceeded to relate the events of that morning.

After he had finished Maxie exclaimed, 'Oh, Danny, I'm so proud of you!' Then, while he looked at her bemused, she started laughing.

'What do you find so funny?'

Wiping tears of mirth from her eyes, she giggled. 'Oh, I would love to have seen your face when that float crashed.'

'It's not funny, Maxie,' he scolded her. 'I could have got the sack if Mrs White hadn't telephoned and explained how it all happened, even if her main reason for doing so was to ask for a refund of the extra she then had to pay for her pint.'

'Some cheek she's got, doing that. Folk never cease to amaze me. But at least her greed saved you from taking the blame for what happened, so we should be grateful for that.' Maxie's face assumed a serious expression. 'I'm really glad you never got the sack, Danny, because ... well, you see ... I did.'

He gawped at her, thinking he must have heard her wrong. Maxie would never do anything that would warrant her getting sacked, surely. She was too honest and conscientious. 'Did you just tell me you got sacked?'

'Well, not the sack exactly, but given my notice.'

'If this is some sort of joke, Maxie, call me thick but I can't see the funny side.'

'It's no joke, Danny. The Carsons are leaving the area. Doctor Carson's accepted a partnership

32

and is going to a village somewhere near Newcastle. Mrs Carson described the cottage they're moving into. It sounds idyllic, Danny. It's going to be a much better environment for Felicity to grow up in, with all that fresh air. Oh, but, Danny... Winnie Baker was so angry with Mrs Carson for not giving her decent warning about their plans that she walked out and isn't going back. Mrs Carson was livid when she found out and I left her frantically telephoning around to see if she could hire a temporary daily to cover Mrs B's duties before the move next weekend.'

He looked genuinely grieved. 'Oh, Maxie, I know how much you loved that job. You'll miss Felicity dreadfully, won't you? But you'll soon be snapped up once you let it be known you're on the market.'

She pushed away her empty plate and smiled appreciatively at him. 'That's what everyone keeps telling me. I just hope it's the case. Miss Milligan should be able to help me like she did with getting my job with the Carsons.'

He looked bemused. 'Miss Milligan? Oh, yes, the lady who runs the nanny agency in town. I'm sure she will.'

Just then the front door knocker sounded loudly. They looked at each other. People they knew usually called around the back.

'Probably a salesman or suchlike. I'll go while you finish your dinner,' Maxie told Danny, getting up.

She wasn't given chance to greet her caller as, immediately she opened the door, the fashionably dressed petite young woman facing her jubilantly exclaimed, 'Oh, thank God! I was beginning to think we were the only people of our age in this area. You don't know how relieved I am to find we're not after all. Gail Barclay,' she introduced herself. 'Me and Terry moved into number one day before yesterday and all I've seen in the street since is old people shuffling up and down.' She noticed Maxie glance quizzically at the cup she was holding in her hand. 'Oh, I don't really want any sugar. It's just that I don't know a living soul around here. It's an excuse to knock on doors in the hope of finding just what I have now, and that's someone my age I can introduce myself to. Well, it could have taken forever, couldn't it, for you and me to bump into each other in the street? I've never been one for letting the grass grow under my feet. My mother's always telling me that you have to go out and get what you want or you could die of old age waiting for it to come to you. Look, you and your better half, that's assuming you have got a better half, should come over for drinks and then we can introduce ourselves properly and you can tell us where we go to have fun around here. See you in a minute.'

With that she hurried off, leaving Maxie staring blankly after her.

Danny was just putting the last forkful of food into his mouth when she reached him.

'Well, it seems a couple of around our age have moved into Mrs Green's old house after she left it to go into the old people's home,' Maxie said to him as she gathered together dirty crockery. 'We've been invited over. Tonight. Now, in fact.

They want our advice about local amenities and such like.'

After the day he'd had, going out socialising was the last thing Danny felt like doing, and he suspected that after her own devastating news Maxie didn't in truth feel like it either, but regardless he said, 'Well, we should do our best to welcome them to the street.'

As soon as they knocked on the door of number one, fifteen minutes later, it swung open and they were both ushered inside by Gail Barclay.

Maxie, who had hurriedly changed her plain working attire for a pale blue, knee-length shift dress, her hair now loose and flowing past her shoulders, was quite happy and comfortable with her own appearance but nevertheless admired the expensive-looking black hipster trousers and open-necked green silk shirt that Gail had on. Stacked packing boxes lined the walls of the hall-way and they had to manoeuvre their way past them as they followed her into the living room.

This house was much larger than the one Maxie and Danny occupied, being three-bedroomed against their own tiny two, and Maxie was amazed by the size of the living room compared to their own which hardly had enough space to accommodate their 1930s-style three-piece suite, oak gate-legged dining table and a few other bits of furniture. Here the fitted beige carpet appeared in good condition as did the wallpaper, albeit the flower pattern was very dated. The Maws' own furniture was all second-hand, or third in some cases, but the furniture in this room was obvi-

35

ously brand new and the latest in design. Maxie recognised the dining suite to be G-Plan only because she'd seen it advertised in a magazine she'd been thumbing through in the dentist's waiting room.

As she quickly glanced around – doing what she felt it was expected of her to do – her face took on a distant expression. Not being the materialistic type, she wasn't in the least envious of their neighbours for their large house or the over-furnished rooms, just relieved she didn't have the task of cleaning a place this size.

As he himself took in his surroundings, looking round admiringly as he felt was expected of him by his new neighbours, Danny caught sight of Maxie's face and completely misconstrued her expression, believing she regretted that a place like this was beyond their means.

Maxie meanwhile was thinking that she must say the right things to her hostess. Little did she realise that her well-intentioned remarks and the tone in which she spoke them would send a wave of inadequacy flooding through her husband.

'It's a lovely house, Gail. I'd give my eye teeth to live in a place like this. I could only ever dream of owning furniture like you've got.'

Danny was then commandeered by his host. Terry Nelson was not much taller than Gail, but what he lacked in stature he made up for in self-assurance. Puffing out his chest importantly, he said to Danny, 'So, what's your pleasure, mate? You name it, I've got it.'

As he followed his host over to a bar in the corner, a freestanding piece of furniture the front

36

of which was padded with red plastic, to Danny's amazement he saw that it was stacked with bottles of every spirit imaginable, some he had never even heard of.

Gail meanwhile gave a disdainful snort at Maxie's enthusiastic appraisal of her house. 'This, lovely! Really?' Then she slapped Maxie playfully on the arm. 'Oh, you're just being nice. It's a dump, isn't it? If I have to look at that hideous flowered wallpaper in here for much longer, I'll go potty. The bedrooms are worse, if that's possible. We only took the rental on because we were desperate. The agent wasn't very honest with us about the state it's in. Good decorative order, he told us. Maybe an old lady might think so but it's not what I call in good order. And it hasn't any form of central heating whatsoever. Well, I don't call coal fires downstairs and single-bar electric fires in the bedrooms central heating. I haven't had time to get hold of that agent since we arrived but you can be assured that, when I do, he will definitely be getting a piece of my mind.'

'Why were you so desperate for a house that you hadn't time to view any?' Maxie asked her.

'Because of Terry's promotion. We're from Coventry originally. The company he works for has opened a new branch here on Gallowtree Gate and the man they had lined up to manage it decided at the last minute he didn't want the job after all. So they offered it to Terry. Bit of a back-handed promotion but he should have been given the job in the first place. As they were in a hole he had them over a barrel so he got himself a bigger wage than they were originally going to pay. Serves them right!

'Anyway, we only had a week to sort everything out so no time to come and view anything, just did it all by telephone. We'd no option but to take the first vacant property we were offered or else pay a fortune to stay in a hotel and an obscene amount for storage of our furniture.'

She flashed a glance at Terry who was busy pouring drinks for himself and Danny. 'Typical men, looking after themselves. Excuse me,' she called across, 'mine's a sweet Martini.' She looked at Maxie enquiringly. 'What will you have ... oh, I don't even know your name yet?'

'Maxina Maws. Maxie. And my husband's name is Danny.'

Gail looked at her, bemused. 'Maxina? I haven't heard that name before. Is it foreign?'

Maxie laughed. 'No, it's just a combination of two names my parents couldn't decide between. My dad wanted to call me Tina, my mother Maxine. So they settled on Maxina.'

'Mmm, it's nice. I like it. Make that two Martinis,' Gail called across to Terry. 'Large ones.'

'Oh, I'd sooner have coffee or tea, please, Gail.'

She looked appalled. 'Why on earth would you want tea or coffee when a proper drink is on offer?'

'Well, I've work in the morning.'

'You work? Oh!' Gail looked most put out. 'That's a blow, I was hoping you'd show me around town tomorrow. You could take a day off, though, couldn't you? Everyone has an upset stomach at some time.'

Conscientious Maxie wasn't in the habit of

38

taking time off work unless it was absolutely un-
avoidable. 'I would be delighted to show you
around town on Saturday afternoon, if you're
free,' she offered, and having astutely realised by
now that Gail was the sort of woman who liked to
get her own way, hurriedly added so that the topic
wasn't pursued, 'You don't work yourself, then?'

Gail gave a scoffing laugh. 'Why should I when
His Nibs can afford to keep me? I was secretary
to the managing director of a plastics factory, but
gave that up when I moved in with Terry nine
months ago.'

Maxie looked at her in surprise. 'Oh, so you're
not married then?'

'Good Lord, no.' Gail eyed her hard. 'Not one
of the prim and proper type who labels what
we're doing "living in sin", are you?'

How other people conducted their lives was
their own business so long as it didn't greatly
affect her own, was Maxie's opinion. 'Not at all.
I'm just surprised you're not as you and Terry
look very married, if you understand me.'

'Well, we are, all but for a bit of paper. Anyway,
marriage is an outdated institution that's easy to
get into but damn' hard to get out of. I love Terry
right this minute, but who knows how I'll feel
about him when I get up tomorrow morning?
What if someone better came along next week
and I wasn't free to pursue him? I can't see the
point in marriage myself, not unless you intend
having kids, which I never do.' Gail physically
shuddered, a look of utter disgust flooding her
face. 'Just the thought of something alien growing
inside me makes me feel sick ... I get a rash if I

39

come within fifty yards of one of those awful, smelly, noisy creatures.'

Maxie inwardly smiled as she wondered what Gail's reaction would be to the announcement that she herself looked after awful, smelly, noisy creatures for a living, and immensely enjoyed what she did. 'It will be helpful for you to know some local details. The dustbin men call on Tuesday...'

Over by the bar, as he poured out the drinks, Terry was asking Danny, 'So where are the trendiest places to go to for fun in this town?'

Danny pulled a thoughtful face. 'There's a lot of good clubs, I understand. One of the lads at work is always going on about the good times he has at a night club called the Adam and Eve. And ... er ... oh, yes, Bradley's ... no, sorry, Bailey's. And there's the Palais on Humberstone Gate...'

Terry handed Danny a chunky glass tumbler with yellow and orange daisies painted around it, full to the brim with Bacardi and a splash of Coke. 'Great! We'll make up a foursome on Friday night. Which do you recommend we try first?'

Danny looked doubtfully at the glass in his hand. His request for a small lager had fallen on deaf ears. He was not a spirits drinker but would somehow have to stomach this so as not to offend his host. Taking a tentative sip and trying not to grimace as the near neat alcohol burned his throat, he said, 'I can't, I'm afraid. Maxie and me have never really been into that sort of thing.'

Terry stopped what he was doing and gawped at him. 'Well, what *do* you do for fun then?'

Danny's face lit up. 'All sorts. Ten-pin bowling.

The pictures... Westerns are our favourite. We go down the local occasionally on a Saturday night, if we feel like it. And we enjoy going for a spin on a Sunday afternoon.'

Up until then Terry had been staring aghast at Danny as he listed the Maws' ideas of fun, but when Danny mentioned they liked to ride out on a Sunday his own face grew more animated. 'You've a car, have you? What make? Mine's a Volvo P1800, two-door coupé, top speed a hundred and five miles an hour. It's the white one parked outside. Paid extra for a sun visor and a Philips radio. Bought it after my promotion as a treat to myself.'

'You've a Volvo P1800?' Danny enthused. 'With a sun roof and radio ... really? We hope to have a car one day but it won't be of that calibre. We're not really bothered what make it is so long as it's reliable.'

Terry's impressed expression had changed to one of bemusement. 'Well, if you've not got a car, what exactly do you go for a spin in then?'

'Our motorbike and sidecar,' Danny told him proudly.

Terry cocked an eyebrow at him. 'Am I right then in assuming you're the sort that go camping for your holidays?'

'Yes, we do. We go as often as we can. Leicester-shire has some beautiful countryside, and there's loads of places to pitch a tent like Swithland Woods and the back of Bradgate Park. We've also been to the Derbyshire Dales, Wales, Devon... We're off to the Lake District next bank holiday for a couple of days. We'd like to do Scotland

41

sometime but we'd really need a newer bike for such a distance as the one we have belonged to my dad and it's thirty years old. Some parts of it are past replacing if they go again.' He eyed Terry keenly. 'You aren't campers too, are you?'

'Absolutely not,' Terry said scornfully. 'I can't think of a worse way to relax. My idea of a holiday is plenty of drink under a blazing sun while watching half-naked women parading before me.' His face took on a superior expression. 'I get top discount on my holidays because I'm branch manager for a national travel agent's. A crowd of us went to Benidorm in June. We had such a blast! Nicknamed ourselves *The Cool Cats on Tour.*' A broad grin split his face. 'I can't remember much about that holiday, I was smashed most of the time. The drink there is so cheap, and treble the measure you get here. Talking of drinks, I'd better take Gail's to her before she starts creating blue murder.'

'About damned time,' she snapped at Terry as she took her drink from him.

Maxie thanked him politely for hers and dubiously looked down at the reddish-brown liquid.

'So,' said Terry to Danny, 'what did you say you do for a living?'

'I'm a milkman,' he replied proudly.

Maxie missed the look that passed between Terry and Gail as she was taking a sip of her drink, her eyes momentarily shutting in shock as the strong liquid stung the back of her throat. She enjoyed a social drink when she and Danny occasionally dropped into the local. Her preference there was for sweet Woodpecker cider. This

42

was the first Martini she had ever tasted and she didn't like it. Privately she wondered how on earth she was going to get through the rest of the evening without upsetting her new neighbours.

Danny, though, hadn't missed the look Terry and Gail exchanged when he announced his job. It could only be interpreted as derogatory. He was in no doubt that because Terry was management, and he a mere worker, this couple viewed him as being beneath them. They were nothing but snobs. Then he noticed Terry silently motion Gail to join him in the next room.

Maxie looked puzzled as they went out and whispered to Danny, 'Where have they gone?' Before he could respond she continued, 'I can't drink this, it's making me feel sick, but I'll have to, won't I, or it'll look rude?'

He flashed a look around. Spotting a potted rubber plant over by the door through which Gail and Terry had disappeared, he took the tumbler from her and shot over, meaning to empty it on to the soil and save his wife the agony of drinking it. As he reached the doorway and made to do the deed, his host's voice became audible. What was being said froze Danny rigid.

'Get rid, Gail. He's a flipping milkman, for God's sake. Drives round in a motorbike and sidecar. Goes camping for his holidays. He looked at me like I'd got two heads when I told him we went to Benidorm last June. I don't think he's ever heard of the place, let alone knows it's in Spain. I've my reputation to think of and I'm not going to attract the right kind in this town if we're seen to be knocking about with the likes of

43

them two ... especially *him*. Take more care who you invite over in future.'

'Oh, but she seems all right, Terry,' Gail said sulkily.

'Ah, come off it, Gail. If she's got that much about her, how come she's saddled herself with a boring little fart like him? Mind you, thinking about it, *you* were living with a loser – men's outfitter's assistant, wasn't he? – until I came along and swept you off your feet. Showed you what fun you could have.' His voice took on a sardonic tone then. 'Pity I'm attached to you at the moment, my sweet, or I could have taken up the challenge there myself. She could do with a lesson on how to dress herself more fashionably, and a new hair style wouldn't go amiss, but she's not a bad-looking chick.'

Gail's tone turned ugly. 'You make one move towards her, or any other female, Terry Nelson, and I warn you, you'll be in hospital praying they can stitch your *manly tackle* back on. That's no idle threat either, I mean it.'

He laughed. 'I would never dare cross you, my love. Just keeping you on your toes. Now get them out of here before any more of my drink is wasted on them. Eh, and get on to the agent first thing tomorrow and chivvy him up. We need to move pronto to a house and area more suitable to a man in my position.'

Danny had never felt so humiliated in his life. An overwhelming desire to get himself and Maxie away from these awful people consumed him. Hurrying across to her, he urged, 'Time we went.'

She looked shocked. 'Oh, but we've only been

44

here at the most ten minutes. It would be so rude of us to...'

Just then their hosts returned. Before they could speak, Danny put in: 'We'd best be off. You must have a lot to do, only having just moved in, and we don't want to hinder you.' He put both his and Maxie's tumblers down on the dining table then took his bemused wife's arm. 'Nice to have met you. Come on, Maxie.'

Back home, as soon as Danny closed the door after them, she turned on him. 'What on earth got into you? That was really rude of us, leaving like that! What must Gail and Terry be thinking of us?'

He knew exactly what their new neighbours thought of them, especially himself, but he wasn't going to upset Maxie by telling her. His mind raced frantically for a plausible way to excuse his behaviour. 'Well, er ... er ... it's just that when we moved in here the constant stream of neighbours dropping in to wish us well got on our nerves, didn't it, and it took us three times as long to get unpacked and settled in than it would have done if they'd just left us alone.'

She frowned at him quizzically. 'People calling on us to welcome us to the street never got on my nerves, nor do I remember you ever saying they got on yours. You gladly made as many pots of tea as I did, and nor did you complain about the homemade cakes they brought with them. Anyway, Gail invited us over, so we never called on spec.'

'Yes ... well ... look, I didn't really like them, Maxie.'

She gawped at him. 'I don't know how you can say that when we hardly had time to get to know them. Why don't you like them, Danny?'

He gave a shrug. 'Just don't.' He sighed. 'Look, can't we just drop this? I urgently need the lav. Put the kettle on and I'll mash us a cuppa when I get back.'

With that he disappeared out of the back door.

Maxie stared after him, totally bemused. She had a strong suspicion he did not urgently need the toilet but had just used that by way of an excuse to get away from her, in the hope that when he returned this subject would be forgotten. But she couldn't forget it. Her husband was a man who would sit patiently for hours listening to an old lady whittle on about her ailments, secretly bored rigid but suffering silently sooner than risk upsetting her. His actions tonight in making it blatantly obvious he was desperate to get away from their new neighbours were totally out of character. She racked her brains for an explanation but couldn't think of a plausible one. As far as she was aware, Terry and Gail had been the perfect host and hostess.

Then a thought struck her. Today's events must have left Danny feeling shocked. The dairy should really reward him in some way, though she doubted they would. And, of course, the worrying fact that in several days she would be jobless could have affected him more than he had let on to her. They could survive, with careful management, on his wage alone now he'd been promoted, but his pay didn't actually increase until he'd proved his worth over a month's trial

46

period and he'd still three weeks of that to go yet. His uncharacteristic behaviour must be due to worry that they would not be able to meet their bills unless she landed a job straight away. But Danny knew her better than anyone, even her own mother, and he must be aware that should a suitable nannying position not present itself, she would take any job offered until one did come up.

When he returned she would allay his fears as to their financial situation. Another thing she must do as soon as possible was somehow excuse Danny's behaviour to their new neighbours and hope she could quash any bad feeling that might have developed between them.

She caught sight of the stack of dirty pots in the sink. In their haste to fulfil Gail's invitation, clearing up after dinner had been abandoned. After filling the kettle for their pot of tea, she rolled up her sleeves to set about the washing up.

Danny meanwhile was sitting in the near pitch dark, elbows on his knees, head resting in his hands, staring blankly at the rotting wooden door of the dank, icy-cold outside lavatory where an assortment of insects had made their home in the abundance of cracks and crevices in the crumbling walls.

The humiliation of being branded boring, sneered at for not holding down a management position, had wounded him more deeply than anything he could remember, but it was not uppermost in his mind.

No man was more proud of the woman by his side than Danny on the day Maxie became his life-long partner. Whatever mood she was in, whatever her state of dress, she looked beautiful to him and he adored her with all his being. She had never given him any reason to doubt in the slightest that she was not happy with him the way he was; she'd always seemed content with the life-style they could afford; but in the future would she start to look at him as Terry had tonight, as a lowly milkman and a boring one at that?

He had witnessed that expression on Maxie's face when she had seen the expensive modern furniture in their new neighbours' house, heard the longing tone in her voice when she had pro-claimed to their hostess what she herself would give to live in a spacious house like theirs. Had tonight sowed seeds of regret within Maxie that she had settled for the likes of him when she could have looked around for a wealthier man to give her a far brighter future than he had any prospect of enjoying as matters stood? But far worse than that, he'd heard another man claim he was attracted to Danny's wife and, save for the fact that he was attached to another at the moment, would have tried his luck with her. The thought of his Maxie in another's arms drove Danny crazy. He would go to any lengths to stop that happening.

He knew that if he wasn't to live every day of the rest of his life fearing he could lose his beloved wife to another man, he needed to give her every reason not to look in another man's direction. How he would go about this he had no clue at the moment, but one thing he was aware of: there was no time to waste if he didn't wish to risk his deepest fears coming true.

Later that night Maxie lay in bed listening to the gentle rhythmic breathing of her husband. He'd acted most strangely when he had returned from the out house. There had been something different about him. She couldn't put her finger on it but Danny was most certainly not himself. On his return, before she could say a word to him, he had rushed across to her, wrapped his arms tightly around her and told her in an urgent manner that from now on things were going to be very different. Immediately afterwards he'd announced that he was going to bed as he was tired.

She could well appreciate he was exhausted after what had transpired earlier today, but what he had meant by things being different from now on she hadn't a clue. Different in what way? She was happy with the way their life was and what the future held for them, and had no reason to doubt Danny felt likewise. Then she realised she had more than likely misconstrued what he had said. Pulling the covers up closely around her, she closed her eyes and soon drifted off.

Danny, though, was far from the blissful release of sleep. His mind was too full of how he was going to instigate the changes he needed to make to keep this woman beside him. Funding the sort of lifestyle Terry provided for Gail would take money he hadn't got. A better paid job was beyond his reach, he wasn't qualified to do anything other than manual work in the milk industry, so he'd be wasting his time trying to secure himself a better-paying job than he had now. At the dairy, further promotion to a better paid round was not going to come his way until he'd proved his worth on the one he had. And besides, it had taken eight years for him to be given the chance of that so there was no telling when or if his next promotion would arrive.

His thoughts veered wildly, each fresh avenue he explored proving to be a dead end, then suddenly came to a thudding halt as a way to enhance his income occurred to him. He could have slapped himself for not thinking of it before. He could get a part-time job! Exact finishing times were unpredictable in his line of work but usually he was away by two o'clock and then he was free to do what he liked for the rest of the afternoon. There must be a firm in the area that needed a man like himself who was willing to do anything. Tomorrow afternoon he would begin his search.

CHAPTER FOUR

Next afternoon four o'clock found a despondent Danny staring at the Jobs Vacant cards displayed in a local corner shop. This was the twelfth shop in the vicinity he'd tried. There were plenty of firms looking for part-time workers of all descriptions, from leaflet deliverers to manual labourers on building sites, but the pay they were offering was a pittance, would go hardly any way to improve their standard of living. It seemed his idea that a part-time job was the answer to his problem was not such a good one after all. So what did he do now?

Then he caught sight of a card he hadn't noticed before and his heart soared. 'Part-time petrol pump attendant wanted between the hours of two in the afternoon and eight in the evening.' The garage offering the job was on the Hinckley Road which wasn't far from the dairy or where they lived, so it was very convenient. The hourly rate wasn't great but better than all the others offered for part-time work. Quickly doing a calculation in his head, Danny worked out that this job would bring him in another six pounds a week on top of the ten he was already receiving. That regular extra amount would go a long way towards him achieving his goal. He just had to hope that the job was still available and that the owner liked the look of him.

Kicking up his heels, he raced off.

A good while later a jubilant Danny rushed through the back door to find a very anxious Maxie waiting for him. She was so glad to see him she did not notice the excited state he was in.

'Oh, Danny!' she exclaimed in relief. 'Where have you been? I got home from work at lunchtime like I always do on Saturday and made a sandwich for you to eat before we went to do the weekly shopping together and ... well, it's gone five now and I was just about to go to the telephone box and call the hospital. I was worried you'd had an accident on your shift this morning and the dairy forgot to inform me.'

'Ah, yes, well, I'm sorry about that. Look, I have to make this quick, I'm expected back.'

'Back? Back where?'

'At the garage.'

'Garage? What garage?'

'The one where I'm working.'

Maxie looked stunned. 'You've left the dairy?'

'No. I'm working part-time at the garage. Petrol pump attendant. Two 'til eight. Mr Gilbert, the owner, has been showing me my duties. Since his last part-timer left he hasn't been able to find anyone with the right credentials to take their place so he's been covering it himself. The poor old bloke is about on his knees. He told me his wife is threatening to leave him if she doesn't see more of him. I told him I could start today. Well, it's the least I can do.'

Her mouth was opening and closing fish-like. 'But ... but ... I don't understand? Why have you gone and got yourself a part-time job?'

He placed his hands on her arms, leaning over to kiss the top of her head. 'Because the extra money will help me give you the kind of life you deserve, Maxie. There's so much I want to do for you. Like, buy a little car for our trips out. It'd be much more comfortable for you, wouldn't it, than that draughty old sidecar? Then new furniture for the house, the sort you admired over at the new neighbours'. Plus a bigger house to put it all in. And I want to take you out regular to nice places ... restaurants, dancing, anywhere you want to go.' An urgent expression filled his face. 'Look, I'm sorry. I really have to get back as I told Mr Gilbert I'd be as quick as I can. I should be home about eight-thirty.'

'But ... but ... you've had no dinner.'

'Keep it hot on the stove for me and I'll have it when I get home.'

With that he shot out of the door, leaving her staring blankly after him.

Fifteen minutes later Ada Billings was surprised at first to see who her caller was before her homely middle-aged face creased into a happy welcoming smile.

'Hello, me duck. Don't usually get the pleasure of your company on a Sat'day evening. Danny not with you?' There was disappointment in her voice. 'Oh, but he usually pops his head around the door to say hello to me before he goes in to see *her* next door.'

Maxie sat herself down in the shabby armchair opposite the one her mother was sitting in and unbuttoned her coat. 'Mam, don't be like that.

53

She is his mother.'

Ada pulled a disdainful expression. 'Yes, and shame for him she is. He's a nice lad is Danny.'

'You used to think his mother was nice until... What did happen between you and Danny's mother, Mam? What was bad enough to stop you having anything to do with each other for the last ten years?'

Ada folded her arms under her matronly bosom, lips tight. 'Ask *her.*'

Maxie tutted in annoyance. After it became apparent that the two close friends, both by then sadly widowed, had fallen out, their offspring had been trying their level best to unearth the cause so they could get the pair of them to make up, but to absolutely no avail. Before whatever had transpired to cause the pair to fall out, the two women had been best friends, virtually inseparable. Maxie and Danny had come to the conclusion that it must have been something more than the usual tiff to have caused their respective mothers to alienate themselves from each other so completely and, as the years had passed, to grow to despise one another to such an extent that they couldn't bear to be in the same room together. But regardless of their own differences, both women nevertheless had a deep fondness for each other's offspring. They had encouraged the relationship and couldn't have been more delighted on the day Danny and Maxie married.

On the day itself both mothers were on their best behaviour, refusing to let their private feud hamper their children's big day. They kept out of each other's way, only coming together for the wedding photographs while still standing as far apart as possible.

After the marriage a routine was quickly established by the young couple to keep peace with their respective mothers. Tuesday evening they visited Maxie's mother Ada, Thursday Danny's mother Kathleen. Each woman came separately for tea on the occasional Saturday. Once a month they would take one of the mothers for a ride out for the afternoon in the countryside, the other woman the following month.

Both Maxie and Danny longed to have their mothers sharing their table together, happy banter flowing as it had before the rift had driven them apart, but things had now reached a stage where they had given up hope of ever bringing about a reconciliation and had stopped trying.

'So why has Danny not popped his head round the door to say hello to me before he's gone into his mother's?' Ada demanded.

'He's not in with her.' Maxie gave a heavy sigh. 'Oh, Mam, I don't know what's going on.'

At her tone, Ada frowned quizzically at her daughter. 'You two had a row? Most unusual if you have. In fact, I don't think you've ever had one before – or not to my knowledge. But before you answer me, I've a feeling a cup of tea is called for. Hold yer horses while I mash one,' she said, getting up.

Usually Maxie would have offered to do it but today her mind was elsewhere.

Minutes later her mother returned carrying a tray set with the tea things which she placed on a small table beside her chair. 'I'll leave it to mash

55

for a minute.' Having settled herself back into her armchair, she clasped her hands in her lap and gave her daughter her full attention. 'Now, what do yer mean, you've no idea what's going on?'

'Well, I don't, Mam. Danny's acting really strangely.'

'Strangely? How exactly?'

'Just not like himself.'

'Since when?'

'Well, since ... well, actually, since we got an invite yesterday evening from the new neighbours who've moved into Mrs Green's old house.'

'Did anything happen while you were there?'

'Not that I know of.'

Ada pursed her lips. 'And how is he acting strangely?'

Maxie exhaled sharply. 'Well, we'd been at the new neighbours' about ten minutes and been given drinks. We were all getting on really well when suddenly Danny insisted we ought to go. I was so embarrassed! He was really rude and I dread to think what the new people thought of us. I must go and apologise... But anyway, as soon as we got home I asked him what on earth he was playing at. He said he just didn't like them. Well, I don't see how he could have decided that as we'd hardly been there ten minutes. But I couldn't question him any further because he disappeared off to the toilet and was gone ages. I was just about to go and ask if he was all right when he came back, flung his arms around me and gave me a big hug. He said from now on everything was going to be different, then immediately went off to bed.

'Today I finished at my normal time for a Saturday, expecting him home about the same time as me, but he never showed. By five I was frantic, thinking he must have had an accident and the dairy had forgotten to tell me. I was about to go and telephone the Royal to ask if he'd been brought in when he burst through the door, saying he'd got himself a part-time job as a petrol attendant and with the money was going to buy me all the things I deserved and take me out regular to nice places.'

'Well, that's very commendable of Danny, being prepared to work hard to buy things for his wife.'

Maxie stared at her in surprise. 'You approve, Mam?'

Her tone of voice firm, Ada said, 'If that's what Danny wants to do for you then you must show your support for him, Maxie.'

'But I can't show my support because I *don't* support what he's doing. He'll kill himself, Mam. His work at the dairy is hard graft, lifting all those heavy crates when he loads his float then racing around delivering the milk as quick as he can. After that he has to unload the float and wash it down before he's finished. It's a nine-hour shift, six days a week, and now he's agreed to work at the garage each day from two 'til eight. If he's working all those hours, when am I going to see him? I can't understand why he's suddenly got it into his head he has to buy me nice things and take me out to expensive places. As soon as he gets home tonight, I'm going to demand he stops this nonsense.'

'No, you mustn't,' Ada told her firmly. 'Whatever you do, you mustn't ever put a stop to your husband wanting to better your lives, however much you may think his way of doing it is wrong. Danny's not acting strangely, he's acting like a man who wants the best for his family and is willing to work extra hard to get that. You must never, ever show a lack of faith in him.' She leaned forward and in a pleading tone now added, 'Please, Maxie, if ever you listen to yer mother's advice, make that time now. Please don't make the same mistake I did.'

Maxie was staring at her. 'What mistake, Mam?'

'Eh? Oh, nothing, lovey. It was a slip of the tongue. Oh, that tea should be mashed by now.' She gave her full attention to pouring it out. 'Did I bring the milk in? Oh, yes. Er... I forgot the biscuits. Fetch the tin, please, dear. It's in its usual place.'

Maxie knew her mother had made no slip of the tongue. She had made a mistake in the past, and that mistake was bad enough for her to plead with her daughter now not to make the same one. But how could Maxie avoid doing it when she didn't know what exactly her mother had done? 'The biscuits can wait, Mam. Now what mistake did you make that you desperately don't want me to repeat?'

Teapot poised in mid-air, Ada stared blindly at her for several long moments before heaving a deep sigh. Putting the teapot back down on the tray, she clasped her hands in her lap, sighed

58

heavily again and said in a trembling voice, 'The doctors said your father's death was caused by his heart being weakened from a bout of pneumonia he'd suffered as a child. But I know better. *I* killed your father, Maxie.'

She gasped in shock. 'What! What do you mean, you killed my dad?'

'Not physically, lovey. But I know it was really a broken heart yer dad died from, and it was me that broke it. What I didn't do years before lay behind him going to an early grave.'

Maxie was looking at her in bewilderment. 'Just what didn't you do for my dad, Mam?'

'Show my faith in him the one time he asked me to. And because I didn't he lost faith in himself, lost his self-worth. Just about the worst thing one human being can do to another is to make them feel worthless.' Ada took a deep breath, her eyes looking distant. 'I fell hook, line and sinker for your dad the first time I was introduced to him. He was a mate of me friend's boyfriend. I was sixteen at the time. Cyril was different from all the other lads I knew roundabouts. He showed proper respect for a woman, not acting like she was second class to himself. Cyril fell for me too. He told me I was his soul-mate and we were destined to meet. It wasn't long before we were talking of marriage.

'We'd only just decided on an engagement date when I found out I was expecting you. A bit of hanky-panky on the canal bank one night got out of hand as can happen when yer in love but too young to handle yer emotions. When I told Cyril I was expecting, I'd no doubt he'd do the gentlemanly thing. Two weeks later we were married by special licence and set up house in a tiny terrace we found to rent off Tindell Street. It wasn't up to much but we made it habitable enough with the help of cast-offs from family and friends. We were like two pigs in muck, we were so happy together!

'Yer dad seemed to like his job well enough, at Dunlop in the moulding shop. His wage weren't great but we could just about manage on it. I was happy playing housewife. I've never really told yer much about my side of the family, Maxie, just let you think they was good folk when in truth they weren't. Me dad was a waster, I can't ever remember him doing a decent day's work, and me poor mam was dogged by ill health so we kids practically raised ourselves. I wanted n'ote more for meself than to be married to a decent type of man and have a place of me own, and I'd more than got me wish when I married yer dad. The only part of me wish I never got granted was that after you arrived, no more children came along.

'Yer dad was a good man, Maxie. He always handed me his unopened pay packet every week to dish out as I felt fit, and most weeks I managed to hand him back a pound, some weeks a bit more. He seemed content. He never abused drink or me or you in any way whatsoever, and never looked in another woman's direction that I'm aware of.

'We'd been married about six years when one day, totally out of the blue, yer dad told me that he wanted to pack in his job to go into business for himself. It seemed it'd been a lifelong dream of his to open a hardware shop and he would have done it before then if we'd not had to bring forward our wedding. He'd had to spend what savings he had on that and setting up house. Since we'd married he'd been putting past as much as he could each week out of what I gave him as pocket money and now he felt he had enough to get him off to a good start. He'd done his homework. The nearest hardware shop to us was a good bus ride away so there was definitely a need for one in our area. People were doing lots of repair jobs around the house for themselves instead of waiting years for the landlord to oblige, and they couldn't afford to get expensive tradesmen in. Cyril told me he planned to sell everything from the tiniest screw to paraffin for heaters. He also told me that if the shop did well, he would open a second in another area.

'Well, I just about blew a gasket. Called him a stupid fool, a brainless clot, you name it, to be thinking of giving up a regular weekly wage when he had a family to provide for. He had responsibilities, I said. He wasn't a single man who could please himself what he did. I accused him of holding out on me because if he had money saved, there were things we all desperately needed, things for the house, far more important things to spend his money on than squandering it like I was certain he was about to. Cyril tried his hardest to explain to me that this business idea had great potential and could be the making of us but I wouldn't hear him out. All I pictured was us losing our home and all the nice things in it that we'd managed to collect over the years and then landing on the streets, up to our eyeballs in debt. I wasn't having that, not for anything I wasn't.

'I flatly refused to give yer dad my blessing on his plan, wouldn't budge an inch. Cyril being the man he was, he wouldn't go ahead without my backing and I knew that. So we all got our new shoes and clothes, I got a new mattress to replace the moth-eaten old flock one, and we had our first ever holiday at the seaside, staying in a boarding house. Yer dad never mentioned going on his own again, and as far as I was concerned I'd saved us from a fate worse than death.

'It was a conversation a couple of years later that brought home to me just what I'd done to my husband. A neighbour was bragging her own man had been promoted to foreman and as he worked in the same department as yer dad did, I asked Cyril when he came home that night why he hadn't applied for the job as the extra money it brought with it each week would have made such a difference to us.' Ada paused, lowering her head, her voice a husky whisper now. 'What he replied made my blood run cold. He said, "If my wife feels I'm not capable of running a shop successfully to provide for my family, then what chance have I of my bosses believing I'm fit to oversee a department of twenty men?"'

Ada gave a loud sniff and raised her head, tears glinting in her eyes. 'It was then I saw how old he looked, and shrunken, as if he'd lost his purpose in life. And it struck me then that after I'd flatly refused to allow him to go ahead with pursuing his dream, things between us had never been the same. Cyril was distant with me. I suddenly realised I couldn't remember the last time he'd laughed. I realised that through my own selfishness I'd not only prevented what I thought was a foolhardy plan, but by what I'd said to yer dad, and how I'd said it, I'd made him feel a fool for even considering he could run a shop and provide for us all. But by then the damage was done and it was too late to put it right.'

She heaved a great sigh. 'What I should have done when yer dad came to me with his plan was be glad he was trying to make life better for us. I should have offered him my support as a wife and let him know that if the worst happened and the business failed, we'd deal with it together.' She gave a wan smile. 'If those close to you can't show they've faith in you, then who can, eh, lovey?'

Leaning forward, she eyed her daughter earnestly. 'Maxie, learn by my mistake. Don't make Danny feel stupid for him wanting to do his best by you, in the best way he knows how. Give him credit for knowing what he's capable of and what he's not, like I should have done yer dad. When you see him tonight, let him know he's got you behind him and you're proud of him for what he's doing. I'm proud of my son-in-law and I shall let him know I am the next time I see him.'

Maxie felt like she'd been hit with a sledgehammer. She'd never had any idea her mother carried such a burden of guilt over what she felt was her own part in her husband's early death. That confession, Maxie knew, had taken her a lot. She wouldn't have wanted to risk lessening Maxie's respect for her. There was no danger of it, though. She would learn from her mother's mistake.

Maxie smiled tenderly at her. 'I still can't understand why Danny should suddenly feel he needs to do all this for me when he knows I'm quite happy to wait. If we never had enough money for fancy things then it wouldn't be the end of the world for me. I've got what I want most and that's Danny himself. I strongly disagree with the burden he's taking on and I'm worried he'll make himself ill, but I'll shove that all aside, Mam, and show him I'm proud of him and that he has my support.' She leaned over and laid her hand gently on her mother's knee. 'Thank you for stopping me from making a big mistake. And, Mam...'

Ada stopped her by holding up a warning hand. 'I know you're going to tell me not to blame myself for the part I played in your father's early death. Maybe what I did had nothing to do with it. But then again, maybe it did. I'll never know, will I? At least I haven't got to worry about you heading down the same path.' She put a bright smile on her face and said cheerily, 'Now, after all that talking I'm parched so let's have that tea then you can tell me what's happened to you since I saw yer last.'

Before she made her way home, not feeling it right not to, Maxie called in to say hello to her mother-in-law. As always the matronly woman whom Maxie loved nearly as much as she did her own mother looked pleased to see who her caller was.

'Oh, what a lovely surprise, ducky. Danny not with you?'

Maxie had already decided that it was not her place to tell her mother-in-law what he was up to, that was for Danny to do himself. How Kathy perceived her daughter-in-law was important to Maxie and she did not want Danny's mother even remotely thinking that she had turned into a materialistic woman, pushing her husband into taking a part-time job in order to fund expensive luxuries and nights out.

'He's not with me because he's busy,' she replied, which was not a lie because he was.

Kathy looked knowing. 'His dad was forever fixing that bike. It always seems to need some sort of work, doesn't it, ducky? Still, it gets you about and Danny loves tinkering with it, just like his dad did. So what brings you here then?'

'Oh, I needed to see my mam about something.' She saw the expectant look in Kathy's eyes and knew her mother-in-law wanted to be told what it was. After all, she was family. 'I got my notice...'

'Yer notice!' Kathy interjected, aghast. 'What on earth did you do that was so bad they sacked yer? 'Cos I can't think of a thing you'd do meself.'

'Oh, I wasn't sacked, Mrs Maws. The family are moving to Newcastle.'

'Oh, I see. So it's reassurance you're needing, ducky. Well, I'll tell you what I'm sure...' she pulled a tight face before continuing '...*her* next door told yer. You'll have no trouble getting a new job, not with your credentials. You'll be snapped up, I've no doubt. Now, cuppa tea?'

Maxie was awash with it but regardless accepted her mother-in-law's offer so as not to offend her.

Tea mashed, they spent a very pleasant half-hour in congenial chit-chat before Maxie excused herself to return home.

Maxie greeted her husband that evening at just after eight-thirty with a welcoming smile, a hug and a hot dinner which she gave him on a tray in front of the fire. Sitting down in the chair opposite, she looked hard at Danny. He seemed tired. Well, he must be exhausted as he'd been up since three that morning and been on the go non-stop ever since. She wanted to ask him what on earth he thought he was playing at, jeopardising his health for a few pounds more when they weren't going to make their marriage any happier, but her mother's story tonight and her warning advice prevented that.

Forcing a look of keen interest to her face, Maxie asked, 'So how did it go at the garage?'

Danny was piling his fork with cottage pie. A surge of panic rushed through him as he looked across at her. Lying to his wife was sacrilege to Danny, but to tell her the truth about the way his first stint at the garage had gone would not help in his desperate quest to convince her he was not the dull no-hoper Terry had cruelly branded him as, but a man who could prove his worth and provide a prosperous future for her.

The job had not been as easy as he had thought it was going to be. Trade was steady and he'd not had time between satisfying one customer for a sit down before another car had rolled on to the forecourt, wanting service. The pumps were not at all easy to operate either. A heavy handle at the side had to be turned quickly to start the petrol flowing. The numbers on the dial above, showing the amount of petrol being dispensed and its cost, seemed to Danny to speed furiously round and several times he had misjudged, stopping the dispensing operation just after the number of gallons requested by the customer had been reached. This had proved costly to him as he was to find out at the end of his shift when Mr Gilbert had returned at eight to lock and cash up.

'You're short by four shillings and eightpence,' his new boss had informed him as he had checked the cash against the till's tally-roll and the number of gallons dispensed by the three pumps on the forecourt.

'I can explain that,' Danny had replied. 'In fairness, Mr Gilbert, you did only show me once how to use the pumps. After you'd left it took me a few attempts to judge when to stop them. Occasionally I went over the amount the customer asked for, mostly by just a penny or twopence but once or twice by a shilling. Well, the customers all refused to pay the difference even though the petrol was in their tanks.'

Mr Gilbert, a big burly man with a profuse grey beard and shrewd little eyes, had looked at him hard on hearing this. 'Well, lad, it's been a costly way for you to learn, ain't it? I trust that from now on you'll be an expert. I shall deduct the four shillings and eightpence from your wage at the end of the week.'

Despite this dismaying news, Danny was already making plans as to how his wage from the garage was going to be spent when he got it at the end of the week. He supposed he couldn't in all fairness expect his boss to bear the cost of his mistakes and vowed not to make any more or he'd end up owing Mr Gilbert more than he was earning and, worse than that, be left looking a fool in Maxie's eyes when he couldn't produce the extra money he'd promised.

Now, ignoring his scruples over telling a lie, he replied lightly, 'Piece of cake. Nothing to it. I was thinking that on Saturday you could go and get yourself a nice dress, a decent one from a proper dress shop, then in the evening we could go out to a club or ... somewhere nice anyway.'

Maxie could think of far better things to spend this extra money on than wasting it on a shop-bought dress for herself when she was perfectly capable of making her own on her Singer treadle as she did most of her other clothes. The roof on the sidecar leaked badly when it rained and needed replacing; the pattern on the lino in the kitchen was worn away in parts and holes were beginning to appear; the list was endless. Neither did she at all fancy spending an evening in a heaving night club, deafened by music she hadn't any fondness for, and dancing to her was not just a case of flinging your arms around and jiggling all over as everybody seemed to do these days. Women her own age might see her as a square fuddy-duddy, but jumping up and down to the latest chart toppers had never held any interest or excitement for Maxie. She much preferred middle-of-the-road type ballads sung by artists such as Frank Sinatra, Dean Martin, Frank Ifield, Kathy Kirby, plus anything in the genre known as Country and Western. She had a yearning to learn ballroom dancing, a pursuit they hadn't taken up as yet as they'd not had money to spare for the expensive evening attire needed, but hopefully in the future they might. Danny was well aware of her likes and dislikes so Maxie was surprised he was suggesting this form of recreation. She'd always believed he enjoyed the same things that she did.

She was about to query his suggested venue for their night out when her mother's advice of earlier that evening came to mind and instead she said, 'If you want to go clubbing then I'll look forward to it.' Then another thought struck her. 'But aren't you working at the garage on Saturday evening?'

His food now finished, Danny put his empty tray down on the floor to the side of him and slapped his hand to his forehead to show how stupid he felt. 'Oh, damn, I'd forgotten.' Then his face brightened. 'But only 'til eight. We can still go out. I've heard the chaps at work talking in the canteen. Apparently the discos don't start filling up until after ten, and they don't shut 'til one.'

But you'll be dead on your feet, having worked all those hours, Maxie thought to herself. To bear this out, she noticed the way his eyelids were drooping now. It was barely nine o'clock. If Danny was falling asleep this early after one day at his part-time job, how exhausted was he going to be by the end of the week? Because of his early start they usually went to bed, except for Saturday night, no later than ten-thirty, and he would take an hour's nap each day after he'd arrived home from his shift and eaten his lunch. His extra job at the garage was going to prevent him from having that rest in the afternoon. Oh, well, he was insisting on doing this, and as her mother advised going along with his wishes, Maxie felt she had no choice.

She got up, went over to him and placed one hand gently on his shoulder to rouse him. 'You look beat, sweetheart. Why don't you have an early night?' On a Sunday Danny always got up first and made breakfast for her, bringing it up to her in bed along with the paper, unless they had planned to go out for the day and then they both got up together. They hadn't made any plan for a whole day out tomorrow so she would let him have a late lie in and take him breakfast in bed for a change.

When she told him of her plan Danny emphatically refused to co-operate. Maxie remained unaware that the last thing he wanted was for her to see him as weak in any way. Shoving his fatigue aside, he got up, picked up his tray and went off into the kitchen to wash up and make his wife a cup of tea, leaving her sighing in frustration.

CHAPTER FIVE

The following Saturday evening Maxie was sitting at the dining table with her chin resting in her hands, staring blindly across the room. Upstairs hung her new dress, the one Danny had vehemently insisted she buy herself despite the fact that the money to pay for it wasn't going to be in his pocket until this evening when Mr Gilbert gave him his wages. Maxie had funded it out of her own wages.

It was a lovely dress, a fitted sleeveless shift made from black wool jersey, edged around the arm-holes and knee-length hemline with a broad band of contrasting white material. It did suit her and she felt nice in it. But she wasn't at all comfortable about what she herself felt was the obscene amount she had paid for it, despite the fact it wasn't the most expensive dress she'd viewed by far. Nevertheless, three pounds, nineteen shillings and eleven-pence was double their weekly food bill and she could have made the dress herself for not much more than ten shillings and it would have looked just as good on her. Nor did she feel comfortable about the fact that she had bought herself something while Danny had nothing new.

Apart from putting on her dress, she was ready to go out as soon as Danny had eaten the dinner she had prepared him, which was keeping hot in the oven, and had washed and changed himself. In

71

truth, Maxie didn't want to go out, and especially not somewhere she was sure would prove to be purgatory to her.

Her week at work had been far more arduous than normal due to the fact that Sally Carson had not been able to find a replacement for Winnie, despite even stooping so low as to try to bribe the dailies of friends, and therefore had roped in Maxie to help with the general cleaning. She had felt morally obliged to help her employer out with this on top of her normal duties of tending to her charge. Trying to dust and polish furniture, vacuum carpets and keep Felicity occupied, while several removals men had also been in the process of crating up china and household goods in readiness for the move at the weekend, had been no mean feat. Somehow she had managed and Sally Carson had rewarded her efforts with a two-pound box of Dairy Milk chocolates – in fact, as fond as she was of these Maxie would sooner have been given the money they'd cost instead – plus a very glowing reference which would leave no prospective employer in any doubt that she was perfect nanny material.

Saying goodbye to a family of whom she had become very fond during her five years with them, most especially Felicity, had proved extremely difficult. It was all credit to Maxie that she'd managed to stem her tears until she had reached home where she had broken down and sobbed convulsively. First thing Monday morning she would embark on her search for a new position though she wasn't particularly looking forward to the interview stage of the proceedings, to having her abilities and character come under scrutiny as she had upon leaving college and first applying for jobs.

And as if finding a suitable new position for herself and keeping a wage coming in wasn't enough of a concern, Maxie also had the worry of her husband.

Taking on this part-time job was proving too much for Danny, despite his insistence that he was coping, no problems. But to her mind no man could physically sustain working a fifteen-hour day, and strenuous work at that, with no physical ill effect, no matter how young and fit they were. Was he so naive as to think she hadn't noticed he had to fight to keep awake when he finally got home in the evening, or that as the week had progressed she hadn't noticed his level of fatigue had risen? In his drive to secure all the wonderful things he said he was going to buy – the new car, furniture, expensive clothes, bigger house – he hadn't seemed to give any thought to the fact that this week they had hardly seen each other.

She hated returning home of an evening to an empty house, Danny not there to greet her, and no dinner made ready to dish up. She missed the catch-up chats they used to have as they ate their meal, continuing afterwards while they sat together watching an interesting programme on their flickering second-hand black-and-white television, or while he read his newspaper and she her current book. Nowadays Danny barely managed to muster the energy to eat his food, let alone sustain a conversation. Since he'd taken on this extra work they hadn't actually eaten a meal together. Their sex life was suffering too. But he seemed hell-bent on doing what he was, and she had no choice but to grin and bear it if she didn't want to risk making him feel small.

And on top of all this was Maxie's worry over their new neighbours. On her way home from work in the week she had knocked on the door of number one, first to offer her apologies for the abrupt departure Danny had precipitated, and secondly to offer to escort Gail around the town the following Saturday afternoon. But on opening the door and seeing who her visitor was, Gail had acted in a very offhand way. Maxie's apology for their abrupt departure was briefly dismissed and her offer to act as escort round the town rudely refused. It had been obvious to Maxie that Gail's excuse that she hadn't time to chat further as she was busy was a lie; her whole attitude betrayed it. As Maxie had returned from her shopping trip to town this afternoon she had spotted Gail and Terry about to get into their car. She had called over to them and waved, but they had totally ignored her when she knew they had heard and seen her.

It had been blatantly obvious that the new neighbours wanted nothing to do with her and Maxie couldn't attribute this merely to Danny and her leaving their house so soon after they'd arrived. There must be another reason for their attitude but Maxie couldn't for the life of her think what it was.

She glanced up at the clock. Danny would be home soon. She rose and went to check his dinner wasn't spoiling.

74

The man cradling Maxie in his arms was obviously well set up, judging by the cut of his clothes, and he was strikingly good-looking. Maxie herself, dressed in an expensive strapless evening gown, her hair perfectly styled, was gazing up at him, face bathed in adoration.

'I can give you your heart's desire,' the man was saying to her. 'Get rid of that millstone round your neck. A woman like you should never have settled for the likes of a milkman, for Christ's sake! Come with me to my car and I'll take you away from your mundane life, give you the luxury you deserve. Come on, Maxie, come with me now...'

Danny attempted to yell to her not to go with this man but to give her husband another chance. He found he couldn't speak. Then he tried to run and stop the man taking his beloved wife away from him, but his legs wouldn't move. When he looked down he saw he was wearing his milkman's white coat and his legs were tightly chained to two heavy milk churns.

A voice close by was calling his name and he felt his arm being shaken. He jerked up his head and it took him several seconds to focus his eyes. When he did he saw an angry-faced Mr Gilbert looming over him.

'You were asleep, lad,' he boomed accusingly.

His brain still fuddled from the nightmare he'd just experienced, Danny blurted out, 'No, I wasn't asleep, Mr Gilbert, just resting my eyes.'

Joe Gilbert gave a disdainful snort. 'That's asleep in my book. Look, lad, it's not working out, is it?'

Danny gawped as the meaning behind his boss's words registered with him. 'Well, it's my first week, Mr Gilbert. Everyone has mishaps when they start a new job, don't they?'

'I grant yer, lad, most do, but it's the number of mishaps you've had and the severity of them that concern me. First there was the trouble you had misjudging the pumps. On yer second shift you somehow managed to jam the pump handle in the on position and the tank you were filling overflowed, to gush out all over my forecourt. The night after that you put two-star petrol in a car that took four-star, and to say the customer wasn't happy is putting it mildly. The night after that, I admit, nothing appeared to go wrong unless I'm still to discover it. Then last night you let a customer drive away without paying. She fobbed you off with the oldest trick in the book, saying she'd left her purse at home and would return later with the money. If we ever see that money then I'll shave off my beard – and my beard is my pride and joy so you can be certain I know without a doubt I'm on a safe bet there. Now tonight I find you asleep...

'It's obvious to me your full concentration isn't on this job. You already have a full-time occupation with yer milk round and by the time you come here you're tired. You know, I was dubious about taking you on when you told me you were delivering milk, but you convinced me you were up to it. If you are hell-bent on working extra then my advice to you is to find something that doesn't require the level of concentration this job does. Gardening or something.'

Joe Gilbert's well-intentioned suggestion was no consolation to Danny. He had seen that sort of work offered in shop windows during his search and the hourly pay was a third what he was getting here. His desire to provide his wife with a bright future and stop another man tempting her away with what he could offer her, seemed to be disintegrating in a puff of smoke.

The panic he'd experienced in his dream a minute or so ago returned with a vengeance. 'Please, Mr Gilbert, give me another chance,' pleaded Danny. 'I've learned by my mistakes, honest, and they won't happen again.'

'You're a good lad, Danny, and I believe you mean what you say. But you've already got a full-time job, and adding another practically full-time on top is too much for the most able of men to cope with. A lesser man than you wouldn't have lasted the week, so I admire the fact you did and are willing to stick it out. Whatever you need the extra money for it must be important to you, that's all I can say. If it's any consolation the mishaps you've suffered, well, they've happened to most other forecourt attendants when they first start and are getting to grips with things. Though not usually all in the same week!'

Joe Gilbert put his hand in his pocket and pulled out a five-pound note. 'I'm being generous, giving you this. Truth be told, the amount I could deduct from your pay for mistakes made more than covers the wages you've earned, but at least your being here has stopped my wife nagging me for a week. I've spent some time with her which is worth five pounds to me.' He put the money in the top pocket of Danny's jacket. 'Best of luck, lad. I really hope you find summat more suitable. Now off you go so I can get on with cashing up and locking up, and get off back home myself.'

It was a very subdued Danny, head bowed and hands buried deep in his pockets, who made his way slowly towards home. Maxie would be waiting for him there, wearing the new dress he'd insisted she buy ready for the exciting night out he'd promised her. How was he going to break the news to her that he had just about enough to pay for the dress and not much more after all his extra labours? He wasn't getting his quest to prove his worth to her off to a very good start.

Why, oh, why did that woman have to knock on their door last week? It had led to his overhearing how others perceived him, and swiftly from that to the realisation he could lose Maxie if he didn't give her reason never to regret marrying him. But then, if he hadn't overheard Terry he would still be happily oblivious, carrying on the way he always had, totally unaware of the ticking bomb that could explode at any time and blow apart his marriage. Danny might only be a milkman but he was not stupid, and only a stupid man would choose to ignore what he'd learned and not bother to put up a fight to save the most important thing in the world to him.

Danny was passing the local pub which caught his eye. He hadn't come up with an excuse yet to explain to Maxie why he wouldn't be returning to the garage. He looked down the street. Their house was a three-minute walk away at most. He needed a bit longer than that to come up with a plausible story. Maybe a pint of beer would help.

The Charles Napier was packed to bursting with local residents enjoying a Saturday evening out. Men propped up the bar while their women-folk put the world to rights around the tables, their only interaction with their men occurring when further drinks were required. The landlord had yet to relent and install a juke box. In a corner the chipped ivory keys of a badly tuned piano were being mercilessly hammered by the sausage-like fingers of a well-padded woman whose skills left much to be desired. At the moment several people were looking in her direction, puzzled as they struggled to decipher just what tune she was playing. This pub was also a place the younger generation used as a starting-off point. Having joined their mates here, they promptly went off to find themselves a more suitable venue, one that didn't try to pretend the Swinging Sixties had never happened.

Danny manoeuvred his way to the bar and joined several others vying for the attention of the two harassed barmaids. It felt strange to him to be here without Maxie. He felt guilty that she was at home waiting for him but shoved this aside, remembering the reason he had come here in the first place and the problem to which he needed to give urgent attention.

He felt a nudge in his side and automatically turned his head to see Andy Plant, a colleague from work. Andy worked in the bottle-sterilising department.

Despite being the same age, the two men were miles apart in their outlook on life. Fun-loving

Andy counted his weekend a failure if he hadn't drunk himself stupid along with his mates and had at least one shag from an obliging female. He considered the far more principled, quietly dressed and shackled Danny a positive square.

'Hiya, Danny,' he piped up now, then looked hard at him. 'God, mate, you look knackered!' He gave a sniff, then leaned closer to Danny and sniffed again. 'Is that petrol I smell on yer? Jesus, yer reek of it. Had a bath in it, have yer?'

Danny said the first thing that came into his head. 'Er... I was helping a mate fix his car.'

'Oh, yer know a bit about cars, do yer? That's handy to know 'cos when I have trouble with mine, I'll know who to call on. Thought it was just old motorbikes you were into? Me granddad used to have a motorbike and sidecar like the one you've got, but he had to give it up when he met me gran 'cos she refused to be seen dead in it. Obviously your wife don't mind looking a prat when yer go out in it.'

Danny reeled from this fresh blow. Did Maxie secretly feel an idiot, being driven around in the sidecar, but hadn't said anything so as not to hurt his feelings? She knew that bike and sidecar had belonged to his late father and were precious to him. They were also the only means of transportation they could afford. But if Maxie felt like that about them... His urgent need to do better by her was rekindled – not that Andy needed to know it. 'My wife enjoys travelling in the sidecar. Says it's exhilarating,' he snapped to save face.

'Really? Well, each to their own, I suppose. Anyway, don't often see you in here, and

80

'specially not without the missus. She let you off the leash for once?'

Already smarting from the other derogatory remark this man had made, Danny's eyes darkened angrily. 'Maxie does *not* have me tied to her apron strings. She's not that kind of woman. I've just called in for a quick pint after helping a mate fix his car then I'm off home to collect her. We're going out dancing tonight.'

'Dancing?' Andy said, surprised. 'Didn't think you was into that sort of thing. Where are you off to then? We're all going to the Ilrondo tonight.'

Danny had never heard of the place. It sounded Italian or Spanish, and he wasn't sure if it was the name of a fancy new restaurant or something else. Not wanting to look ill informed he said, 'I hope you have a good time.'

'Bloody right we will! John Mayall and his Bluesbreakers are playing tonight. There's a bird that goes there every Sat'day who's had her eye on me for a while. I've decided tonight's her lucky night ... well, unless 'ote better is on offer. What do yer think of me new get up? Groovy, ain't it?'

Danny flashed a glance over his mate's red flared trousers, bright yellow jacket and emerald green shirt with a long pointed collar. On his feet were black Cuban-heeled boots which added an inch and a half to his five foot six. Danny had never felt the need to bring attention to himself by wearing such bright clashing colours, favouring quieter blues and browns which Maxie said he always looked smart in. Diplomatically he replied, 'You'll certainly be noticed.'

Andy grinned. 'That's the idea – and by the

gels, I hope.' He pulled a face. 'Have ter watch it these days as there's some queer folk around, if yer understand me. Pint of lager, you gorgeous creature,' he said to the barmaid, smiling at her winningly, to which she responded with a look that said: I wouldn't touch you with a barge pole. Andy missed it as he'd turned his full attention back to Danny. 'What about you?' he asked as he pulled a wad of notes from his pocket and peeled off a pound.

He noticed Danny's eyes riveted on the cash in his hand, and grinned. 'N'ote as good as the feeling of having plenty of cash to spend, is there?' Then he laughed as he put the wad back in his pocket. 'Well, not that you'd know, you being a married man. A man loses all rights to his own money when he shackles himself. Loses his rights to everything, in fact. I ain't gonna bother with all that nonsense unless I find meself a rich bird. Oh, and she's gotta be good-looking obviously. Thanks, gorgeous,' he said to the barmaid as she placed his pint in front of him. Handing her his money, he said, 'Another of the same for me mucker as I think he's forgot what he came in here for.' Then he noticed Danny was looking puzzled. 'Giving the brain cells an outing, are yer, Danny boy?'

'What? Oh, er ... well, I didn't realise the pay for working in the sterilising department was so good, judging by the amount you're carrying on you tonight.'

Andy looked at him as though he'd suddenly grown another head. 'Are you as green as yer are cabbage-looking? None of this,' he said, patting his jacket pocket, 'is from me job. *They* don't pay you enough to buy yer own pot to piss in!'

'Oh, you've a part-time job then?' Danny asked keenly, his hopes soaring, thinking that if it paid that well, and hopefully they had some vacancies, he might be lucky himself.

Andy sniggered. 'I suppose you could call it that ... in a manner of speaking.'

Danny looked confused. 'I'm sorry?'

Andy ruefully shook his head. 'You really haven't got a clue, have yer, Danny boy? I supplement me wages by buying and selling stuff.'

'And the shop pays you that much?'

'Shop! You really ain't on the same planet as the rest of us, are yer, mate? I don't work for no shop, I work for meself. Buy and sell 'ote I can get hold of. Well, what me contact can get hold of, I should say.'

Danny felt stupid for not realising that no shop paid their assistants enough to account for the stack of notes Andy had on him. 'Oh, I see. And buying and selling stuff is really that profitable, is it?' His mind was working overtime. Maybe what Andy did was the answer to his own financial problem. 'Er ... do you mind me asking how you get hold of the stuff you sell?'

Andy looked at him warily. 'Why?'

'Oh ... well ... you see, I'm looking for ways to earn some extra meself.'

'Oh, wife after a new suite, is she?'

Danny flashed him a brief smile. 'Something like that.'

'Well, don't you make enough coppers on the *old orange?*'

83

Danny shook his head. 'What others do is their business but I don't go near that myself.'

'Why not?' asked Andy accusingly.

'Because to my mind flogging bottles of orange juice that've been ... well, earmarked for chucking away, is risky. It might make anyone who bought it ill, especially kids.'

'N'ote wrong with the stuff,' Andy scoffed. 'Nobody I've ever sold it to has ever complained that drinking it made 'em ill, and neither have any of the other lads who are involved in it. Anyway, what you're forgetting is that the people who buy orange juice from us can't normally afford to buy it unless we flog it on the cheap.'

'Yes, well, that may be so but I'm still not comfortable doing it. Anyway, if I wanted in then it'd be less for the rest of you to squabble over, wouldn't it?'

'Yeah, well, I s'pose you have a point there.' Andy took a long draught from his lager while looking at Danny hard for several long seconds. 'I might be able to put some of my non-dairy stuff your way. Sometimes I get offered more than I can take.'

His companion's interest lit his eyes. 'Oh, that would be good of you. I'd appreciate it very much.' Then a worrying thought struck him. Danny might be naive in some ways but he wasn't exactly dense. 'Er ... this stuff. Is it legal?'

'Of course it's fucking kosher,' Andy retaliated. 'I might have a liking for making a fast buck but I ain't gonna land meself in jail, no chance.'

Danny looked ashamed. 'Sorry if you felt I was insinuating something.'

'Yeah, well, better watch yer mouth in future. The stuff I get hold of is all bankrupt stock, fire-damaged and such like.'

'Er ... can I just ask you ... well, when you get it, what sort of stuff is it and where do you sell it?'

Andy gave a fed-up sigh. 'Look, mate, if I wanted an apprentice I'd have took one on. Where d'yer think I sell the bloody stuff? To anyone who'll buy it. Mostly housewives. They're always looking for a bargain. I get offered all sorts, household stuff mostly. The sort of stuff people are always on the look out for, and cheaper than they can get it anywhere else.'

'Er ... do you think you could consider me when you next get offered more than you can take then, Andy?'

He gave a nonchalant shrug. 'I suppose I could. Eh, but what I've told you ain't to be made common knowledge. My business is mine, understand me?'

'Yes, of course, Andy, goes without saying.'

'I might be able to put some tea towels your way now, if yer want 'em. They'll cost you a tanner each and you can sell them for a shilling.'

Danny's heart raced. A hundred per cent profit sounded good to him. 'Oh, yes, most definitely, thank you.'

'I'll give yer ten pounds' worth then, shall I?'

'Oh? Er...' He hadn't got ten pounds that wasn't spoken for already. But he had five and in his excitement at the prospect of making some money towards his cause, he temporarily forgot that this was to replace the money for the dress he'd insisted Maxie buy herself. 'Ten's too much for me just now, but I can manage five.'

'Five it is then. 'Course, for me trouble I'll need a cut. Shall we say ten per cent?'

Danny realised he must have been an idiot to think Andy would help him out for free. Well, he supposed ninety per cent was still an excellent profit. 'Yes, of course.'

Andy spat on his hand and held it out to him. 'We've a deal then.'

He tried not to show his distaste as he shook Andy's spit-smeared hand to seal their bargain.

After downing his pint, Danny made the rest of his way home with a spring in his step. Judging by the amount in Andy's pocket he felt positive his own quest was on its way upward after its drastic nose-dive earlier this evening.

He was just about to enter the back door when he stopped short, realising that he'd still not for-mulated an excuse to give Maxie. Before he could engage his brain the door was thrown open and she cried, 'Oh, Danny, I'm so glad to see you. I was getting frantic. It's gone half-nine. Where have you been? Your dinner's nearly ruined.' She grabbed his arm and pulled him inside. Then she gave a sniff. 'You stink of petrol and ... is that drink too?'

'Er ... well ... after what happened tonight, I called in for a pint on my way home. I should have come back first, I'm sorry, Maxie, but you see ... you see...' His mind was whirling madly.

'Well, Danny? What happened tonight that was so bad you needed a drink before you came home?'

'Well ... you see ... you see...' Then despite his

qualms of conscience, in his need not to devalue himself in Maxie's eyes, he told a lie. 'He wasn't a nice man, wasn't Mr Gilbert. He'd no intention of keeping me on, just wanted me to cover for him this week as he'd another man starting on Monday, someone experienced. When he came to give me my pay tonight he made all these things up that he said I'd done, made out they'd cost him, and said I should be grateful he wasn't charging me.'

Maxie was staring at him in disbelief. 'Oh, Danny, to use you that way! But it's awful. He can't get away with what he's done to you, surely?'

Danny gulped, feeling beads of sweat forming on his brow to trickle down his neck. 'There's nothing I can do.' He lunged toward her and took her tightly in his arms. 'Look, I promised you life was going to be different for us and it is, Maxie, believe me it is,' he said earnestly.

Temporarily forgetting her mother's advice, she made to tell him that she was perfectly happy with life the way it had been before he began this crusade. 'Danny...'

Terrified of hearing she didn't believe he was capable of making life any better for her, he cut her short with, 'All those things I promised I was going to get you, I will. This is just a temporary setback, Maxie.' He really should tell her about his deal with Andy but wanted to make sure it was all kosher and he really was going to make money from it first. 'I'll look for another part-time job on Monday. Obviously we'll have to postpone our night out tonight. I'm so sorry to disappoint you but I'll make it up to you next

Saturday for definite. Now I'd better go and get changed out of these clothes and have a wash.'

With that he hurried off upstairs.

Maxie stared after him and gave a deep sigh. She felt so hurt that Mr Gilbert had taken her husband on under false pretences and, after all his hard work this week, cast him off so callously. It wasn't fair. She felt a great desire to go and see the man herself, demand he pay her husband what was rightly his, and give him a piece of her mind for using Danny as he had. But as the owner, what he said went; Danny was right, there was nothing to be done. Workers these days were at the mercy of their employers, with very few laws to protect them. And then there was the matter of the three pounds, nineteen shillings and elevenpence she had spent on the dress instead of the housekeeping. With Danny not able to refund it, next week was going to prove a struggle for them financially. But she would manage somehow with what money they did have. The only consolation for Maxie was that she had been spared the purgatory of spending four hours in a night club, for this week at least.

Going into the kitchen, she took his dinner out of the oven and put it on the table, then set about mashing a pot of tea. Tea brewed and ready to pour out, it struck her that Danny had been gone longer than it should have taken him to wash and change, and come to think of it, she couldn't hear any movement from upstairs. Going to investigate, she found him fully clothed, flat out and dead asleep on their bed. Exhaustion had got the better of him. As gently as she could, she eased off his clothes and pulled the bedclothes up over him. She stood looking down at him, a tender smile on her face. How she loved this man. And although she was bewildered about why he'd suddenly felt he had to provide all those material things for her, he must love her to want to look after her like that.

Quietly she let herself out of the bedroom and went back downstairs.

Danny slept soundly until four o'clock the next afternoon. When he finally awoke Maxie just happened to be in the bedroom checking on him, as she had done numerous times that day.

Yawning loudly, he stretched himself and smiled up at her. 'Oh, that was a good sleep I had, Maxie.'

'I should think it was. You've been in bed over eighteen hours.'

'What!' he exclaimed, mortified, struggling to sit up. 'But why didn't you wake me? We were going out for a spin this afternoon.'

'Because you obviously needed that or you wouldn't have slept so long.' And they hadn't any spare money to put petrol in the tank due to yesterday's events, though not wanting to remind him of this, she thoughtfully added, 'I was glad we never went out today because I had some darning to do.'

Well, when I achieve my ambition you'll never have to darn again. Rich men's wives don't have to because they have the money to replace worn items instead of having to make do and mend, thought Danny.

CHAPTER SIX

As Danny was driving his float out of the dairy yard at five-thirty the following morning to begin his deliveries, over the whirling sound of the electric motor he heard his name being called. Thinking he'd forgotten something, he brought the float to an abrupt halt and stuck his head out of the open side to see who wanted him.

It was Andy. 'Oi! Bring yer float to the back of my car. It's the brown Rover three-litre with the bash in the wing, parked in the car park.' He took a quick look around to check no one was observing them, and when he was satisfied everyone else was occupied with their own duties, urged, 'Well, get a move on before someone spots us.'

The staff car park was at the side of the dairy and no windows overlooked it. Andy had the boot of the car open by the time Danny brought his float to a halt beside it. Taking out a large cardboard box, he heaved it on to the floor to the side of Danny, just managing to wedge it into the tight space.

'Are these the tea towels you promised to get me?' Danny asked.

As he closed his car boot Andy flashed a look of derision at him. 'Well, what the bleddy hell else do you think it is?'

'Well, it's just that we're on work premises and...'

'Bleddy safer than doing business at home before my beady-eyed brother who'd beat me up for his share if he knew what I did in private. Less he knows the better. Eh, and mek sure no one here spots this box and starts asking questions. The boss won't tek kindly to you using a dairy vehicle to transport non-dairy goods. Me fiver,' he urged, holding out his hand. 'Come on, hurry up.'

Thankfully Danny had brought it with him. Fishing it out of his pocket, he leaned over and handed it to Andy who quickly stuffed it in his own then immediately legged it back to his work station before he was missed.

Danny leaned over to open the box far enough to pull out one of the tea towels which he examined. Not that he knew much about the quality of tea towels, that was Maxie's department, but these looked all right to him. Soon he would have a wad of cash just like Andy had had on him on Saturday night, but his profit was going to be put to far better use than spent on enjoying himself. All he had to do now was decide where best to sell the tea towels. His mother and Maxie's were always on the look out for a bargain. They each had a part-time job, as dinner lady and early-morning office cleaner respectively, which even supplemented by a widow's pension didn't leave much over after the bills had been settled. He would give them a couple of tea towels each as he could under no circumstances charge them. But their neighbours and his own would surely be interested... That's where he would make his start.

'Maws!'

Hearing his name being bellowed, Danny shot his head out of his cab to look back and see Wilf Stibbins heading towards him. The manager didn't look happy.

'What the hell are you still doing on the premises? And in the car park too!'

Hurriedly shoving the tea towels back in the box and praying his boss didn't get close enough to spot it wedged there beside him, Danny shouted back, 'Oh ... er ... took a wrong turning, Mr Stibbins.'

The reply to this was even angrier. 'Get that float out of here before my telephone starts ringing off its hook with complaints from moaning women saying their milk ain't on their doorstep.'

Danny didn't need telling again.

At just after seven-thirty he was hurrying back to his float to empty his hand crate of used bottles and refill it with full ones ready to deliver to his next set of houses, and to take a second to check his sheet and remind himself what customer had what as he hadn't yet memorised exact orders, this being only his second week as a roundsman, when a woman arrived breathlessly beside him, a young male child of about three, naked except for a grubby holey vest, in tow. It was Mrs Orton from number three, the house at the bottom of the road which he'd delivered to a short while ago.

Danny was pleased with himself for remembering her name, but immediately worried he'd somehow missed her delivery and asked, 'I left your right order, didn't I, Mrs Orton?'

'Oh, yes, Milky … look, I can't keep calling yer Milky. What is yer name?'

He told her.

'Well, Danny, I forgot to leave a note when I left my money out last Friday morning to tell yer I wanted to up me order from one pint of green top to two a day, for the time being. Me mother-in-law's decided to park herself on us for a couple of weeks while she recovers from a sprained ankle. Silly bat reckons she tripped in the street but I think she's made it up so she can have me fetching and carrying for her for as long as she can spin it out. She can certainly get around when she thinks I ain't looking. I know for a fact the biscuit tin was full of Arrowroots when I popped around to the shops and when I got back it was half-empty. Anyway, have you any spare on you today? And from tomorrow I want two 'til further notice.'

Milkmen always carried a few spare so as to meet such requests. Smiling at her, Danny told her to help herself while he took his delivery sheet out of his pocket and made a note of her change of requirements.

After thanking him and making to depart, she noticed a child's bare backside sticking out from the open side of the cab and, recognising it as her own son's, she erupted. 'Billy! I told you to stay inside while Mammy did her errand.' Then, realising the child was engrossed in pulling out the contents of a box, she exclaimed, 'And just what are you up to, you little tyke?' Rushing over to him, she grabbed hold of his arm and yanked him to her while looking at Danny apologetically. 'Kids! I dunno, turn yer back for one minute and they're into all sorts.'

Then, her own curiosity getting the better of her, she flashed a look towards the box whose contents had intrigued her son so much. 'Oh!' she exclaimed. 'Are them tea towels?' She let go of her son and scooped a towel out of the box, holding it up for close examination. 'This looks all right. I could do with a couple of new 'uns. Mine are hardly fit to use as dusters. Selling 'em, are yer? How much?' Just then a door opening caught her attention. Turning around, she addressed the neighbour who was just about to bend down and collect her delivery of milk. 'Eh, Marge, interested in tea towels?'

'Might be, depends how much?' she responded, a look of interest on her face.

As an intrigued Marge came over to join them, Mrs Orton asked Danny, 'Well, how much then?'

'Er ... a shilling each,' he said cautiously.

'A shilling, eh? Cheaper than the market. They're asking one and six. And it's cheaper than that suitcase chappy who comes round. I'll have two. Hang on while I run back and get me purse.' Grabbing her son in one hand and clutching her bottle of milk and two tea towels in the other, Mrs Orton hurried off.

'Yeah, I'll have two an' all,' said Marge. 'And I'll tek another two for me mother at that price.' She spotted another woman emerging from her house, dressed for outdoors, clutching a gondola shopping bag. 'Oi, Dot!' she called over. 'Interested in cheap tea towels?'

It seemed to Danny that he was suddenly surrounded by women who appeared to be coming from all over, fighting with each other to claim their cheap tea towels before they lost out. Coins were being thrust at him from all sides and the next he knew the box was empty and some women had to go away disappointed.

He couldn't believe what had just happened. In such a short space of time he'd made himself a profit of five pounds, and could have made more if he'd had the stock. He'd not even been given time to take out the ones for his own family before the vultures had descended. As soon as he got back to the dairy he'd collar Andy and buy another load from him to sell in another street on his round tomorrow, and the first thing he'd do then was take out what he wanted for his own family. But if today was anything to go by, then this week he'd not only be able to refund Maxie her dress money but also fund a good night out at the weekend plus put some aside towards a new suite or suchlike. And he hadn't needed to knacker himself in the process. More importantly, if Maxie had started to doubt his ability to provide for her, then when he told her of his success today it was bound to quash any doubts she may still harbour.

Then an idea struck him. He wouldn't tell her what had happened today. He would wait until the weekend and surprise her by giving her all the proceeds of his successful new venture. That would make a real impact on her.

Later that morning, dressed as presentably as she

could in a plain blue box-pleated knee-length skirt, matching jacket and white blouse, her long brown hair clipped tidily back at the base of her neck, Maxie entered the premises of the agency she had used to secure her position with the Carsons five years ago.

The last time she had visited the agency an elderly woman, an ex-nanny herself, had operated it from a small office situated above Bellman's wool shop on the Gallowtree Gate. It was therefore surprising for Maxie to see that the room she entered now had been knocked through to encompass another much larger office next to it, and the one desk where Miss Milligan had sat with her one filing cabinet beside her had now given way to several new desks and cabinets. All the work stations were staffed by women in their early-twenties, each dealing with female clients sitting at the other side of their desks. Several women were seated on a row of chairs beside Maxie, filling in application forms. The agency had certainly expanded since she was last here, but what concerned Maxie most was that it obviously wasn't just herself who was looking for a nannying position.

'Can I help you?' A mini-skirted blonde, her face plastered in makeup though she couldn't have been much older than sixteen, called over to her from the reception desk.

Maxie approached it. 'I'd like an appointment to see Miss Milligan, please,' she responded, flashing a smile at the girl.

The receptionist looked blankly at her. 'Who? We ain't got no Miss Milligan working here. Oh,

96

you mean the old biddy Mrs Bishoplees took over the agency from last year?' She picked up a printed form from a pile on her desk, attached it to a clipboard then handed it to Maxie. 'Fill that out and someone will see yer when it's your turn.'

It was two and a half hours later before Maxie was finally called over.

She seated herself on a chair before the woman who had summoned her. The fashionably dressed, heavily made up woman took her form from her and, without looking at it, beamed brightly at Maxie. In a gushing tone she said, 'Welcome to the agency! My name is Thelma Wilson. Now, how may I help you?' She then immediately held up her hand. 'No, don't tell me. I'm an expert in taking one look at any of our clients and knowing immediately what position they're after. You look the efficient solicitor's secretary to me. I'm right, aren't I?'

'Well, actually, no, you're not,' Maxie told her.

The woman looked stunned that she could possibly have made a mistake. 'Oh! Well, a personal assistant then?'

Maxie shook her head. 'Nanny.'

'Nanny? Oh, Mrs Bishoplees decided to drop that side of the business six months after she bought the agency. There isn't so much call for nannies these days, not like there used to be. We just handle office placements here now.'

'Oh, I see,' Maxie said, disappointed. 'Do you know of an agency that does handle nannies, please?'

'There isn't one in Leicester, as far as I know. Plenty of other competing agencies offering office work, first to fill the vacancy gets the fee... I'm sure you know how it works. But I'm not aware of them handling domestic positions. Sure I can't interest you in office work instead?'

Maxie flashed her a brief smile. 'No, thanks.'

'I couldn't help overhearing,' piped up a woman sitting at a desk nearby. 'There is a nanny agency I know of...'

'Oh?' Maxie eyed her keenly.

'It's based in London but their service covers the whole country. I know because I used to work in the office next door. I was friendly with a girl who worked there before I had to move up here because of my husband's job. Anyway, I'm sure they advertise their services in *The Lady* magazine.'

Maxie politely thanked her for this information although she didn't relish the thought of having to travel all the way to London in order to secure herself a position one hundred miles away in her home town. Miss Milligan had prided herself on the fact that she thoroughly interviewed prospective employers, and only when she was personally satisfied they were of good sound character and would treat her nannies with the respect they deserved did she take them on to her books. She'd been as thorough with her vetting of the nannies likewise. Maxie felt it was doubtful that this unknown agency would take the time and trouble to visit far-flung employers in their home and vet their suitability, as Miss Milligan had done.

'It might be worth a look in the *Leicester Mercury*,' Thelma Wilson suggested. 'You never know, people wanting a nanny in Leicester might

98

try that avenue first before having to pay out extortionate rates to a London agency.'

Maxie smiled gratefully at her. 'Yes, I'll try the *Mercury*, thank you.'

Back at the dairy, after offloading, hosing down the float and putting it on charge ready for the next day's business, Danny went in search of Andy, hoping he hadn't already finished his shift. Finding him nowhere around and thinking he would have to wait until the next day to ask for more stock, thankfully he spotted his quarry making his way out of the large iron gates. He caught up with Andy as he was unlocking his car.

'Glad I've caught you,' Danny said as he reached him. 'Any chance of some more tea towels? I've got rid of all the ones you gave me already.'

Andy looked impressed. 'Really? Bleddy hell, Danny boy, you've surprised me. Didn't think you was the selling type. Just shows yer can't judge a book by its cover, eh? Those tea towels I gave you were some of the load I bought from me contact and couldn't be bothered to sell meself. I had the last lot off him so unless he's picked up any more I doubt you'll be in luck. I might see him tonight down the pub and ask if he's picked up any new stock.'

Danny's disappointment was readily apparent. 'Oh! Only might?'

'Well, depends if I feel like going. If I do, and if me contact shows, and if he's managed to see *his* contacts and bought anything off them, do you want including?'

Danny said without hesitation, 'Oh, yes, please.'

99

'Right, well, gimme yer dosh then. This business is all cash on delivery, and as I'm taking delivery on your behalf I need yer cash up front.'

'Yes, I see.' Danny fished in his pocket, pulling out a handful of silver coins from his day's trading. While an increasingly frustrated Andy looked on, he carefully counted out five pounds' worth into his mate's hand.

Andy looked at him with disdain. 'You'll never get rich in this game at this rate, Danny boy. Nor is my ten per cent of five pounds really meking what I'm doing for yer worth me while.'

Danny looked at him blankly. 'I'm sorry, I don't understand what you're getting at?'

'Oh, for Christ's sake! Yer need to speculate to accumulate if yer want to make more than a bit of pocket money now and again.'

Danny certainly did if he was to achieve his ultimate aim. Buoyed up by his success this morning, he fished in his pocket and pulled out the rest of his cash, which was his original stake. He handed it all over to Andy. 'Right, I'll have ten pounds' worth of whatever you get this time.'

Andy grinned. 'That's more like it!'

Arriving home at just before two, Danny found the house empty and presumed Maxie was attending interviews for a new position. Having eaten the chicken paste sandwich she had left ready for him before she went out herself, he settled back into his armchair to have a short nap. Once he was refreshed he would see what jobs needed doing around the house.

A while later he was roused from his slumbers

by the sound of the back door opening and shutting. He'd been having a lovely dream. In it the car he'd been driving had been the sporty kind, bright red with a roll-back roof. Maxie had been beside him, expensively dressed in a tasteful cocktail dress, a diamond necklace and matching earrings. They had just left their mansion house and she was accompanying him on his rounds of the string of shops he owned... Danny was so charged by his success of this morning that at this moment he felt anything was possible.

Yawning and stretching, he arrived in the kitchen just as Maxie was turning on the stove to heat the kettle.

Damping down a great desire to inform her of his success today in order to give her a bigger surprise at the end of the week, he asked, 'How did you get on?'

She flashed him a brief smile. 'Not as well as I'd hoped. Miss Milligan has retired and sold her agency to a Mrs Bishoplees who only caters for office staff. There isn't another agency in Leicester that deals with nannies and the only other one anyone knew of is in London.'

He looked confused. 'So you've to go all the way down to London to find out if anyone here in Leicester wants a nanny?'

'Stupid, isn't it, but that's the way it seems. I'm worried that this state of affairs has come about because there's not so much call for nannies as there used to be, and then I'll be fighting with all the other qualified girls for the few jobs that are on offer. I will go to see this agency in London but only as a last resort. I'm going to try the jobs section in the *Leicester Mercury* first.'

A while later, Danny was cleaning the tappets of the motorbike's engine, with a view to presenting the vehicle as well-maintained and roadworthy to a potential future buyer as soon as he had funds in hand to purchase the four-wheeled variety of transport he meant them to have. He laid down the tappet and the sandpaper he was cleaning it with on the newspaper spread in front of him on the dining table and glanced across at Maxie who was sitting opposite him, scanning the jobs section.

'Lots to apply for then, is there?'

She looked worried. 'Not as many as I'd have liked. Nannies seem to come under the section covering domestic staff. There's lots of people looking for cleaners and cooks, mostly part-time, but I've only found four that want an actual full-time nanny at the moment. Two aren't suitable for me as they're miles from where we live. Still, two is better than nothing, isn't it?' The first one doesn't say much,' she said, reading out the advert to him. '"Urgently required: experienced qualified nanny for four-year-old boy. Apply to Mrs Reece, Hilltop House, 86 Letchworth Road." Big detached houses they are up there and you've got to have money to live in them, so hopefully the wage offered will be decent. And it's in walking distance, so if I am successful that would be handy.

'The other one reads, "Caring person, with relevant qualifications and experience preferred, to look after dependant. Apply: Mrs Gibson, 24 Meadowhurst Road." Well, that road is off

Letchworth Road and the houses aren't so big but they're still detached and you'd still have to have money to live in one, so hopefully they'll be offering a decent wage too. I shall write off for an interview with both of them straight away and hope that at least they'll see me.' She put an optimistic smile on her face. 'And there might be someone else advertising for a nanny in tomorrow night's paper.'

It was very apparent to Danny how disappointing today had proved to his wife and he wanted to tell her that, judging by his success, in future they wouldn't need her wage so badly then she could have the choice of whether she worked or not. But common sense told him that he was going to have to do much better than today, and regularly, before he could start making such elaborate claims. He vowed that he would do better and wouldn't rest until he was absolutely certain Maxie was in no doubt she would never find a better man than she already had.

CHAPTER SEVEN

Maxie took a look around the room she had been shown into. She could only describe it as good quality gone shabby. There was no evidence of any children in the room, a stray toy, feeding bottle, discarded item of clothing or dummy, but then that didn't surprise her as people who could afford nannies usually had no-go areas in their home that they reserved for adult occupancy only. She therefore assumed the child she was being interviewed to care for was in the nursery and would be introduced to her at a later stage, if her interviewer thought it suitable to do so.

'Tea?' enquired Mrs Gibson, sitting on the faded chintz-covered armchair opposite Maxie's. She was a tiny woman, sparrow-like, with hands and feet no bigger than a child's. Her voice was bird-like too, high-pitched and fluting. Maxie guessed she was in her late-thirties. She was wearing a plain brown, calf-length straight skirt and a beige blouse fastened high at the neck, over which she wore a beige cardigan. No jewellery except for a plain thin wedding band.

Very neat, prim and proper, Mrs Gibson did not seem to have the aura of motherhood about her in any way whatsoever, but Maxie reminded herself that it would be wrong of her to make any firm judgements about her prospective employer after only being in her company for a couple of minutes. She smiled politely back.

'Yes, please.'

'Milk? Sugar?'

'Yes to both, please.'

Passing Maxie a delicate rose-patterned china cup and saucer, the cup only half-filled with Earl Grey tea, the woman said in her squeaky voice, 'You're much younger than I was expecting. Still, as long as you have the relevant qualifications to do the job, that's what counts, isn't it?'

Maxie hurriedly placed her cup on the occasional table to the side of her and handed a long brown envelope over to Mrs Gibson. 'I passed all my exams with distinction, Mrs Gibson. Inside the envelope are my certificates and a reference from my last employer.'

Mrs Gibson accepted the envelope and placed it to the side of her. 'I'll read them later. I have to say, you look a very presentable young lady with a lovely manner about you. I have a feeling you're going to suit very well. It was gratifying to read in your letter to me that you had been with your last employer for five years and that your employment was only terminated because they moved out of the area. They must have been very happy with your work and conduct if you were with them all that time. Our last help was with us for several years and we were extremely happy with her but illness forced her to retire last week. You're our first applicant and let's hope you're our last.

'Well, your hours of work will be eight-thirty to six o'clock, Monday to Friday, and until one o'clock on Saturday. My husband and I don't go out socialising very often but if we should, then it would just be for the occasional evening and of course we would provide a taxi home for you. Now, a little about your charge and then I'll take you to meet her. She can be a bit trying at times but I'm sure you're used to that in your line of work. She likes to be read to and does enjoy a good chat, but she sleeps a lot so I suggest you bring plenty of reading material of your own with you, or your knitting or whatever. I manage a charity shop in aid of spastic children in town and work there most days, but I'll see to her breakfast before I go out in the morning and her dinner in the evening. All I will require you to see to is her lunch. Something light ... a boiled egg and thinly sliced bread and butter, that sort of thing. Her injections have to be given every three hours and she has an assortment of tablets to be given at regular intervals, but I shall arrange for the doctor to call on the morning you start so he can instruct you about her medication.'

Maxie frowned. Medication? She wasn't qualified to give medication apart from an occasional aspirin when absolutely necessary. She had helped nurse Felicity through the normal childhood coughs and colds, regular tummy upsets after eating too much sweet stuff, and a terrible bout of measles, but if this child was on medication then she was obviously very sick which the advert had mentioned nothing about. Before she could question Mrs Gibson, however, the woman had stood up and was making her way across the room, saying, 'Well, time introductions were made. I have a feeling you two are going to get on famously.'

Obediently, Maxie followed her out of the room and up the stairs that opened on to a wide landing. Standing before a door, Mrs Gibson turned to her and said quietly, 'She might be sleeping. I'd better go in first and check so she doesn't get a shock. Have to be careful with her heart condition, you see. I'll call you when it's safe to come in.' Opening the door, she slipped inside and pushed it to behind her.

Maxie stared worriedly at the closed door. Heart condition?

The door opened and Mrs Gibson reappeared. 'She's awake and looking forward to meeting you. Come on in, dear.'

The room she followed Mrs Gibson into was gloomy as the curtains were drawn and Maxie had a job to see where she was going. Moments later she realised she was standing beside a double bed and had to blink several times to confirm that she wasn't mistaken in what she was seeing. But it was no illusion. Propped up on pillows in the middle of the bed was a wizened old woman in a pink bed jacket over a thick cotton nightdress. She was staring back at Maxie keenly.

'I apologise for the lack of light in here,' Mrs Gibson was saying, 'but too much of it hurts Mother's eyes. When she's being read to we have a special lamp that can be adjusted so the light is concentrated only on the page being read. Oh, and I forgot to mention she's completely deaf in one ear and her hearing in the other isn't so good, so when you talk to her you'll have to speak very loudly.'

Dragging her eyes away from the old woman in

the bed, Maxie turned to look at Mrs Gibson. 'I'm sorry, there's been some mistake.'

'What's that, I can't hear her?' piped up the old woman in a reedy voice, cupping one hand to her ear.

'Just a minute, Mother,' Mrs Gibson shouted back at her then looked at Maxie, frowning in bewilderment. 'Mistake?'

Maxie took a deep breath. 'May I ask if you're under the impression that I'm a nurse, Mrs Gibson?'

'Well, yes, of course.'

'I'm not a nurse, Mrs Gibson, I'm a nanny.'

The other woman looked stunned. 'A nanny! Well, why on earth did you apply for a qualified nurse's position?'

'I didn't. Well, I hadn't realised I had. Your advertisement was under the section for domestic situations covering nannies and such like, not the nursing section.'

'Well, aren't you going to introduce me to my new nurse, Hilary?' shouted the old woman.

'She's not a nurse, Mother, she's a nanny,' Hilary Gibson loudly informed her.

'Nanny?' She looked puzzled. 'Am I not a bit old for one of those?'

'Just a little, Mother.'

Then, to Maxie's surprise, Hilary Gibson started laughing. 'Oh, dear, this is most amusing. My husband will surely find it so too when I tell him this evening. Oh, but it's not funny really, is it, dear? What a waste of time this has been for you! I can only apologise. My husband will certainly put the *Leicester Mercury* in their place over this mistake. We'll expect our advertisement to be reinserted at no extra charge, and under the right section this time.' A look of regret filled her face. 'Oh, such a shame you aren't a nurse. I feel you'd have suited us very well. Again I do apologise for this error and for wasting your time.'

Back out on the street, reunited with her brown envelope, Maxie took a moment to afford herself a brief smile. Mrs Gibson had been right, the situation had its comic side. She took a look at her wrist watch. She had an hour to kill before she was due for her appointment with Mrs Reece, but at least from the advertisement she knew that this interview was definitely for a nanny to a four-year-old boy.

The Western Park was a ten-minute walk away and boasted an imposing Victorian pavilion housing a café. Maxie decided she would while away her time over a cup of coffee in the café and gaze out of its windows on to the splendid flower beds that were the pride and joy of the park's team of gardeners.

Just under an hour later, standing inside the pillared entrance to the imposing residence of the Reeces, Maxie gazed around her with awe. There was no doubt in her mind that the people she was about to be interviewed by were extremely wealthy. Well, they had to be to live in a house like this. Despite her qualifications and her own confidence that she was more than able to do any nannying job, she worried that her education and background would not be good enough for the likes of these people. But, regardless, she felt morally obliged to turn up for her interview, though she strongly suspected it would not be a long one.

Taking a deep breath, her head held high, she lifted the heavy brass knocker on the Tudor-style oak door. It seemed to Maxie that she'd hardly brought it down against its brass knocker plate to announce her arrival when the door burst open and a glamorous, fur-clad woman in her late-thirties proclaimed: 'Thank goodness you're punctual! Come along in,' she ordered Maxie.

Standing in the wide, thickly carpeted hall, leaving the front door open, the woman whipped the brown envelope Maxie was holding from her hand, pulling out the contents which she quickly scanned.

'That all seems to be in order,' she said, thrusting it back at Maxie. 'Wages are four pounds a week, inclusive. Day off on Sunday unless Mr Reece and I have arrangements. If so we'll expect you to be flexible. Two weeks' holiday a year at a mutually agreed date. Uniform to be worn at all times on duty. Friendships, male or female, to be conducted away from the house. All meals are provided by Cook. You'll find your room on the top floor next to hers and the bathroom is shared between you. Cook's bath night is Tuesday so you're at liberty to make yours any other night. Also she does appreciate the bathroom being left as you find it after use. She doesn't appreciate any interference in the running of her kitchen whatsoever.

'Now, I can't think of anything else, but what I haven't covered will have to be dealt with when I return on Monday afternoon.' A car was heard to draw up on the drive. 'That's my taxi.' She pointed across to a heavy-looking crocodile-skin suitcase and matching vanity case by the sweeping staircase. 'Bring my luggage out for me.' She was about to hurry out when she stopped short and added, 'Oh, I nearly forgot. You'll find Sebastian in the nursery. You'll have to make your own introductions, I haven't the time.'

Maxie had been staring wide-eyed at Mrs Reece during the whole of this tirade. She couldn't believe this woman had asked no questions of her, taken no time to check out her qualifications or references to prove they were not forged in any way, and was now quite happy to go off wherever she was bound without even asking Maxie if the job suited her. Most astounding of all to Maxie was the fact that she was leaving her four-year-old son with a complete stranger. Maxie could have been a murderer, for all Mrs Reece knew. 'Excuse me, Mrs Reece.'

On her way out of the front door, she spun around and snapped, 'Whatever it is, it will have to wait. I've to meet my husband at the station at a quarter to four, and unless I want his bad mood to spoil this whole weekend then it's in my own best interests to be there on time. He can't abide lateness, whatever the reason.'

'But it can't wait, Mrs Reece.'

'Oh, for goodness' sake, make it quick then,' she snapped, even more irritated.

So Maxie came straight to the point. 'I'm afraid I can't accept the job, Mrs Reece.'

At Maxie's announcement a look of utter confusion flooded her face. 'Can't accept it! What do

111

you mean, you can't accept it? You're an unemployed nanny, aren't you, and the wage I'm offering I am assured is the going rate. And what better conditions could you hope for than what are offered to you here?'

'Well, I can't live in for a start, Mrs Reece.'

'What! Don't be absurd. All nannies live in.'

'Well, I don't, Mrs Reece. I'm married, you see.'

'Married!' She glared at Maxie. 'Nannies don't marry! They're like nuns and matrons, married to their profession.' She flashed a look at her wrist watch 'Oh, gosh, look at the time!' She flapped her hand dismissively. 'We'll discuss this when I get back.'

She made to turn and hurry off to board her waiting taxi but Maxie shot after her, waylaying her just as she was about to be helped aboard by the driver. 'Mrs Reece, this job is not for me. Thank you for offering it to me but good day.'

With that she strode off down the drive, leaving a furious Mrs Reece shouting after her. 'Come back! I said, come back, you hear? You can't do this to me, you can't!'

Later that evening as Maxie and Danny shared their meal he was laughing hard as she finished her tale of the misunderstanding with Mrs Gibson, then staring at her appalled as she told him about Mrs Reece.

'No?' he was intermittently saying between mouthfuls of cauliflower cheese accompanied by a thick slice of corned beef. 'No, she never! Mrs Reece really was going to leave her son in your charge when she'd hardly spent five minutes with you and her poor boy hadn't met you at all? I can't understand how her mind must work.'

Maxie looked across the table at him tenderly. She had missed his company dreadfully last week when he'd been labouring hard at his ill-fated part-time job. She was so glad to have him back again, sharing a meal with her and chatting about daily events. 'When I told her I didn't want her job, she couldn't believe I might even consider turning down such a good offer. I've no doubt working for the likes of her would have been hell.' Maxie's face took on a wistful expression. 'I'm just glad I wasn't introduced to the little boy.'

Danny didn't need to ask why. To his wife, all children were precious treasures who needed showering with love and protection, and judging by what she had told him about the boy's mother it was doubtful he received either from her. At least Maxie hadn't had a chance to form any sort of attachment to him, though that wouldn't stop her secretly hoping that a loving, caring nanny was found for Sebastian who would become a substitute mother to him.

'Well, it's back to the *Mercury* for me,' she continued. 'I got a copy on my way home.' She smiled at her husband encouragingly. 'Anyway, enough about my day, how was yours?'

Today had proved another disappointment to Danny, as had every day since Tuesday when he'd gone into work fired up with enthusiasm and excitement to see what fresh merchandise Andy had secured for them both from his contact the previous night. To Danny's chagrin he had found out that Andy had not reported for work, and as the week had worn on and there was still no sign of Andy returning his despondency had deepened. All he could think of was those four days of lost opportunity. Just what the reason was for Andy's absence he'd no idea, and nor it seemed had anyone else. No one had heard from him. But as Andy was the only person who could help him achieve his ambition, all Danny could do was wait patiently until he returned.

Of course, this was leaving him with the terrible problem of funding their promised night out tomorrow night. His weekly two pounds pocket money from his wage just about covered a cheap night out for them at the pictures or ten-pin bowling, petrol for the motorbike for a trip out on a Sunday afternoon, and just about enough left over for his own incidentals during the week. Maxie chipped in with whatever she had spare from her housekeeping but that wasn't always possible for her, depending what expenses she was facing. But he couldn't let her down again. The night out he'd promised must take place, but at the moment how he was going to pay for it he hadn't a clue. He prayed for a miracle. There was also the fact that he hadn't as yet refunded the money that she'd laid out on her dress. He was just grateful that Maxie hadn't mentioned this fact and hoped she wouldn't until he was in funds again.

Planting a bright smile on his face, he replied, 'I'm starting to remember which of my customers has what each day, and I actually finished my round sooner than I've done since I started.

'Course, the boss made sure I was kept busy 'til the end of my shift helping the lads in the swilling area, rinsing the filthy bottles before they go into the sterilising machine. Some people just can't be bothered to do it before they put them out on the doorsteps for return. There's some dirty buggers around, Maxie, believe me. One of the bottles that came back today had pee in it, can you believe?'

She shuddered in disgust. 'Animals have better habits than some people. I'm glad that you're doing well. Mr Stibbins will have no reason not to pass you after your trial period and give you the round permanently.'

Since last week Danny hadn't mentioned their proposed night out and she did need to clarify with him if it was still on or not in order to prepare herself. She was hoping she might dissuade him by arguing that she had no wage coming in this week and they were having to manage just on his.

'Danny, are we still going out tomorrow night? Only until I get a job I've no money coming in and I don't mind if...'

'Maxie, I promised you a good night out,' he interjected. 'You shall have one.'

His answer was not the one she had been hoping for and in her disappointment she missed the worried look that her question had sparked in his eyes.

There were three 'Nanny Wanted' advertisements in that evening's *Mercury* but all were for addresses in villages in the shires that she'd be unable to get to. What was advertised, though,

115

was a place for a person with experience of children in a private nursery, covering for a staff member who was off temporarily due to illness. The address was on the London Road, a journey involving two separate buses each way. But it was a job that Maxie did have the necessary skills for and if she was successful the pay would help out their finances until she secured herself a full-time nanny's position.

Maxie fetched her writing pad and a fountain pen and set about writing a letter of application to post the next morning.

CHAPTER EIGHT

Sleep evaded Danny that night. His mind was far too busy desperately trying to fathom a way to pay for the big night out without damaging his credibility with Maxie. In his burning need to prove himself to her, he had pig-headedly not seized the opportunity to postpone their night out when she had reminded him of their financial state. As matters stood now there was only one avenue open to him that he could think of and that was to hope that Andy was back at work next morning. Danny could then tell him he wanted to reduce the amount Andy was to spend with his contact on Danny's behalf and ask to have the remainder of the money returned to him as he had urgent need of it. He just prayed it wasn't too late and Andy had already done the business.

Andy's shift started at six and, despite the fact that Danny was supposed to leave the dairy to begin his deliveries at five-thirty, he used every excuse he could think of to delay his own departure. Finally, at six-twenty he could delay no longer. Andy was not going to resolve his problem. There was still no sign of him. In a last desperate attempt he had waylaid several of Andy's colleagues in the sterilising department to ask if they knew where he lived but the closest he got to an address was that it was a flat somewhere on the Fosse Road. Fosse Road was at least half a mile long, and jostling for space on the busy thorough-fare were a cinema, several factories, a church, at least three pubs, a hotel and several rows of shops as well as numerous terraces of houses, some of them converted into flats. It could take days of calling on spec to find the flat Andy lived in.

Danny was left with no other choice but to break the news to Maxie that he couldn't honour his promise. He should have had the sense to wait until he'd actually got the money in his hand to pay for it before making such a pledge. If he was letting her down on just one night out, what hope had he of carrying out his promise to give her a better life?

It was a wretchedly despondent Danny who finally set off in his float to begin his deliveries.

Later that morning, Diane Yardley was looking at him in concern. 'You all right, Danny? God, but you look like doom itself this morning.' She gave a laugh. 'The sight of me in my curlers ain't that frightening, is it?'

'Eh? Oh, no, Mrs Yardley. 'I've … er … just got a bit of a thick head.'

'Well, if that's how you look with just a bit of a thick head, I'd hate ter see you with a raging migraine. Couple of Aspro help?'

A couple of headache tablets was not the cure he needed for his ailment so much as a couple of fivers, or tenners preferably. 'Thanks for the offer, Mrs Yardley, but my headache's not that bad.'

'If yer sure.' She fished her purse out of her pinafore pocket, taking out a ten-shilling note which she handed to him.

He counted out her change from the brown

leather money bag slung over his shoulder and, giving it to her, said, 'Cheerio, then, Mrs Yardley. I'll see you next week.'

She made to shut her door when a thought struck and she called after him. 'Oh, yer won't forget to mark me down as paid up in yer book, will yer? Only I noticed you ain't done it.' Then she quickly added, 'Not that I don't trust yer but I like to keep these things right, to be on the safe side.'

He stopped and turned to face her, delving in his pocket for his book. As it wasn't there he realised he must have left it behind in the float. 'Sorry, Mrs Yardley, I've left my book in the milk float but I promise you I'll mark you down as paid as soon as I get back to it.'

He found his book on the floor by the driver's seat. In his preoccupied state he'd not noticed it had fallen out of the pocket of his white uniform. Keeping his promise to Mrs Yardley, he slipped into the driver's seat, opened the book to the page showing her address and made to put a tick in the paid-in-full column at the side of her details. Then he froze like stone as suddenly the answer to his prayers, the miracle he'd been praying for, presented itself to him.

It lay inside his money bag.

All he would have to do was borrow enough to pay for tonight out of his customers' payments, marking them down as non-payers, and then return the money as soon as he could from his profits via his dealings with Andy, marking his customers down then as having paid up. Ten pounds should be enough. Four pounds refund to Maxie for her dress, and the rest to give her a night out she would remember. Oh, it was so simple! Why hadn't he thought of it before?

A door opening close by caught his attention and he looked across to see the sorry sight of Mrs Bean emerging from her house. The folks he delivered to on his round were not the most affluent but neither were they the poorest people the city of Leicester boasted, but Mrs Bean was without a doubt the most destitute resident of this street. At seventy-eight, childless and a widow for over twenty-five years, plagued with arthritis too, Mrs Bean was unable to undertake any kind of work to supplement her paltry widow's pension. From what Danny had glimpsed of her dire living conditions when collecting her dues, it had seemed to him the landlord had overlooked, whether conveniently or not, any type of modernisation or the most basic repairs when it came to this particular tenant's house. Danny had also noticed that her possessions were very few and those she did have looked extremely old and battered. Mrs Bean's order from Danny was for a bottle of sterilised milk every three days. She carefully eked it out yet according to his book she had never missed a single payment.

Spotting Danny sitting in the float, she shuffled across to him. Smiling her cheery toothless grin, she said, 'Morning, lovey. You'll find me money wrapped in a piece of paper under the stone by me doorstep. I was hanging on to give it to yer meself but yer later than normal this morning and if I'd hung on any longer the butcher might have run out of sausages and then I wouldn't get one for me dinner tomorrow. Ta-ra now, ducky.'

As Danny watched Mrs Bean slowly shuffle her way down the street a terrible feeling of shame flooded his being. However bad local people's financial status was, most of them managed to fund a piece of the cheapest cut of beef for their Sunday dinner. All Mrs Bean could afford was one sausage. Was he seriously contemplating stealing – because when all was said and done it *was* stealing even if he did intend paying all he'd 'borrowed' back – from the likes of that poor old soul who, despite having to go without, always made sure her milk bill was paid? Had he really been going to use her money and that of her neighbours, not because he was starving but to fund a night out?

He felt disgusted with himself. He had never been so desperately committed to achieve any-thing in his whole life as he was to proving himself to Maxie, but beyond that were his own honesty and integrity. It would be easy for him to 'borrow' the money and there was little chance anyone would find out for the short period he intended to keep it, but he'd never be able to hide his guilt at what he had done and Maxie would soon sense something was not right with him and demand to know what it was. He'd end up telling her, and then how could he ever expect her to be proud of the man she had married, a thief as well as one who lacked the basic ability to provide a good life for his wife? No, if he was to live with his conscience even in the short term he knew he had to come clean with Maxie, tell her he hadn't the funds after all to take her out tonight and prepare himself to meet the consequences.

Due to his late start and distractedness while doing his round he was an hour later than he should have been arriving back at the dairy. By the time he'd handed in his money bag and book to the office clerk, unloaded the float, hosed it down and put it on to charge, it was almost half-past two when he walked out of the entrance gates.

Normally Danny would be looking forward to getting home, but more especially so on a Saturday, eagerly anticipating spending the rest of the weekend with his wife. Today he dreaded facing her and the fifteen-minute journey from the dairy to his house took him twice as long.

Outside the back door, consumed by a terrible feeling of foreboding, Danny took several deep breaths which did little to calm his trepidation. Regardless, he knew he had to face Maxie sometime and could not delay the inevitable any longer. Grasping the door knob, he turned it and went inside.

There was no evidence that she was home. No music, no kettle singing on the stove, no movement upstairs. The house was deadly silent, an empty feeling to it. Had Maxie not waited for him to accompany her to town to do the weekend shopping? Then he spotted a note on the kitchen table. He picked it up. Maxie had been asked by a desperate neighbour to watch her children for her while she ran an urgent errand. She had made a cheese sandwich for Danny which was on a plate with a tea cloth over it in the pantry. The neighbour had said she'd be no longer than an hour so Maxie should be back by two-thirty. Danny looked at his wrist watch. It was now ten-past three. Either the neighbour's errand had taken longer than she'd thought or she had returned and Maxie was having a chat with her. Either way he'd received a temporary reprieve from his ordeal.

It was twenty-past six by the time Maxie finally came flying through the door. 'Oh, I'm so sorry, Danny, I thought I'd never get away,' she cried as she stripped off her coat and hooked it on the back of the door.

Danny had been unable to concentrate on anything during his long wait, sitting ramrod straight on a chair at the dining table, listening for the sound of the back door opening. The trepidation he'd been suffering when he'd first arrived home had now built up to fever pitch. With a sick feeling of fear swirling in his stomach, he forced himself to rise and go to greet Maxie.

From his stance in the kitchen doorway he found her tipping potatoes into the sink. Sensing his presence, she turned to smile across at him. 'You found my note and the sandwich I left you?'

He nodded.

'Today of all days Carol's mother had to trip over and break her ankle. I'd planned to spend the whole afternoon getting myself ready for our night out. Still, these things happen, don't they? It won't take me long to get ready once we've had our egg and chips. Thankfully I did the weekend shopping this morning since I wasn't at work myself. While I was out I posted my application for that job at the nursery, so keep your fingers crossed they'll think I'm worth seeing.'

Still busily updating Danny, she turned back to resume peeling the potatoes. 'I took Carol's children to the park and they had a whale of a time on the swings and roundabout and paddling in the pool. Hopefully I've tired them out and Carol and Keith can relax tonight after the shock of today. The hospital have kept her mother in for a few days. I hope you don't mind as I know it's your mam's turn to visit us tomorrow ... I'm sure she'll understand when I explain to her ... but I've told Carol I'll look after the children again in the afternoon so she and Keith can visit her mother.' She flashed a look at him. 'You don't mind do you, Danny?' When she still received no response, she frowned at him. 'Danny, are you all right?'

He was far from all right, but regardless managed to croak, 'Yeah, yeah ... 'course I'm all right. And, no, 'course I don't mind if you baby-sit Carol's children tomorrow afternoon.' He was aware that the time had come for him to divulge what he needed to. Swallowing hard, he took a deep breath. 'Er... Maxie?'

She turned her head to look across at him. 'Yes, Danny?'

'Er... Well, er ... I ... er ... er...' Then his nerve suddenly failed him. He was unable to bring himself to tell Maxie the truth, see the look of disappointment in her eyes revealing him as the failure he was. 'I thought that while you were cooking tea I'd go and have a wash and shave,' he said lightly.

With that he rushed over to pick up the kettle of hot water then hurried off up the stairs.

Maxie sighed. She had hoped that Danny might have changed his mind about taking her to a night club tonight but it seemed that her wish

124

hadn't been granted and she had no choice but to make the best of it.

During the next two hours, several times Danny desperately tried to summon up the courage to confront his wife with his news, but each time at the last moment he couldn't go on. Now, himself smartly dressed in his best suit, Danny was blindly pacing the back room, waiting for Maxie to come down the stairs and join him. He knew he could procrastinate no longer. What he had to say was unforgivable as it was. He'd stupidly made it even worse by the fact he had let her go ahead and get herself all dressed up.

Then his heart almost stopped as he heard her footsteps descending the stairs, and suddenly she was before him, smiling.

'Well, will I do?' she asked him, giving a twirl.

His eyes drank her in. God, but she looked beautiful. That black dress, simple and classy in design ... well, she looked positively stunning. Any man would be proud to have her hanging on his arm.

'You ... oh, Maxie, you look fabulous!'

She smiled happily at this compliment. 'Well, you don't look half bad yourself, Mr Maws.' She picked up her coat from the arm of the chair where she had put it earlier. 'Did you lock the back door?'

He nodded.

'Well then, shall we go?'

His heart was hammering painfully, his legs felt weak. He wished vehemently that a bolt of lightning would strike him dead, anything to put off having to face what he could no longer avoid. But he knew he was never going to be that lucky.

Taking a deep breath and steeling himself, he blurted, 'Maxie ... look, Maxie ... I er ... well, I have something to...'

Just then an almighty thump resounded on the back door and a muffled voice was heard to shout: 'What the hell is yer back door locked for? Let me in! Oi, Maxie, Danny! Can you hear me? Let me in.'

Maxie frowned in bewilderment. 'What on earth is my mother doing here? She knows you're taking me out tonight.' With that she rushed off to answer her mother's summons.

On opening the back door Maxie was stunned by the sight that greeted her. Ada was standing there dressed in her nightdress and dressing gown, feet in slippers, a hairnet covering her rollered hair, large bulging black handbag clutched under one arm.

Before Maxie could say a word, she pushed past her to enter the kitchen, saying, 'Oh, ducky, get the kettle on and mash me a cuppa. Even better, have you a drop of brandy, whisky ... anything alcoholic will do. My God, I need it. Oh, it were awful, lovey. I thought World War Three had started.' By this time Ada was in the back room easing herself into an armchair. Maxie, who had followed her through, was now standing beside Danny and they were both staring at her in surprise.

'I see *she's* not here yet. I expect *she* will be any minute, though.'

'She?' queried Maxie. Then the penny dropped. 'You mean, Danny's mother? Mam, what on earth has happened?'

Just then the back door was heard to burst open

again and the next they knew Danny's mother, dressed identically to Ada in dressing gown, night-dress and slippers, rollered hair encased under a blue hairnet, clutching her large handbag under her arm, was easing herself down into the arm-chair opposite her former best friend, now arch enemy. 'Oh, God, I thought me end had come! Get us a cuppa, will yer, Danny, Maxie? Better still, something medicinal.' She glared across at Ada. 'I see you've already made yerself at home. I suppose you were hoping I'd been finished off?'

Ada glared back equally as nastily. 'For your information, Kathleen Maws, I was on me way round yours to check up on yer, but I heard yer shouting blue murder so I knew you was all right.'

'I was not shouting blue murder,' she vehemently denied. 'If I was shouting at all, it was 'cos of shock.'

'About what?' both Danny and Maxie asked in unison.

'Well...' they both began.

'Look, just one of you tell us,' ordered Danny.

'I will,' said Ada. 'As I was here first.' And before Kathy could remonstrate she launched into the tale. 'For months now I've been telling that landlord's agent when he's called for the rent that there's peculiar noises coming from the attic.'

'So have I!' erupted Kathy.

Ignoring her, Ada continued, 'He kept saying he'd send someone round to have a look into it.'

'He kept telling me that too,' Kathy interrupted again.

Still ignoring her, Ada pressed on. 'But did he

127

hell as like send anyone round! Well, tonight I was just making meself a cuppa to settle down with in front of the telly to watch me evening programmes, when all hell let loose.'

'I was in the kitchen, too, making me cuppa before me evening programmes started. I thought a bomb had gone off, I really did,' put in Kathy.

Ada snorted disdainfully at her before continuing. 'Such a loud crash it was. Dust and muck everywhere...'

'Mam, please get to the point,' urged Maxie. 'What caused this loud crash?'

'Well, I'm not too sure, ducky. I wasn't going to wait around and find out in case the whole house collapsed with me in it. I just grabbed me bag, which thankfully was on me kitchen table, and made a run for it.'

'Me too,' said Kathy. 'And I ain't setting foot back inside my house until I'm convinced it's safe to.'

'Me neither,' declared Ada resolutely.

Both Danny and Maxie were well aware that neither of these women was easily frightened. They would not be sitting here, dressed as they were, and especially not in the same room, if the situation they had both found themselves in had not been potentially life-threatening. Both Danny and Maxie were mortally relieved that their mothers were safe and unharmed. Danny, though, was even more relieved – in fact, 'relief' was not a strong enough word to describe how he was feeling – because he had been granted his miracle. He never would have asked for it to be delivered to him in this guise, though. He was caught between extreme anger with the landlord for putting his mother and mother-in-law's lives in danger due to his lax attitude towards his tenants' welfare – and wanting to thank him profusely for saving Danny from his own dreadful predicament.

'I'd better go round and see what I can find out,' he told them.

'Just be careful,' warned his mother.

'Yes, don't do 'ote foolhardy,' ordered his mother-in-law.

'If yer can see a way to get me some clothes, I'd be grateful,' added Kathy.

'Me too,' Ada followed up.

As soon as he'd gone off, Ada clapped a hand to her mouth and proclaimed in remorse, 'Oh, lovey, you and Danny was going out tonight! He was taking you somewhere special, you told me. Oh, of all the nights for this to happen! And you do look smashing in yer new dress.'

'Yes, yer do,' agreed Kathy. 'Just beautiful you look, like one of them models in the magazines. And my Danny looked so handsome in his suit. Look, when he gets back you could still go out.'

'Yes, yer mustn't let what's happened to us ruin yer evening, Maxie lovey,' insisted Ada.

Maxie couldn't believe they were both expecting her and Danny to swan happily off and enjoy themselves, not only after what had just befallen them but more especially since it would entail leaving them alone together under the same roof. There was no telling what they might find on their return.

She smiled at them. 'Me and Danny can go out another Saturday night. I'll switch the television

129

on for you and go and mash you both a cuppa.'

Maxie went off into the kitchen to the sounds of the two women squabbling over which programme they wanted to watch.

It was well over an hour before Danny returned, during which time Maxie had played constant peacemaker while the two women continually passed sniping comments between themselves. Danny looked like someone had thrown a bag of cement over him. He had a deep tear in his trouser leg, obviously where it had caught on something sharp.

'Well, was it a bomb?' Kathy demanded.

He shook his head. 'From what I can gather it seems the beam going through the adjoining houses, which held up both water tanks in the attics, was so rotted from age it gave way. Both full tanks came crashing down through the attic floor, then the bedroom floor, and down into the back rooms. Good job you were both out of there at the time, that's all I can say.'

'Oh, my God!' uttered Maxie. 'You could both have been killed.'

'Well, thankfully your love of a cuppa to watch the telly with seems to have saved you both,' said Danny. 'Anyway, Mr Galloway, your next door neighbour, Mam, came in with me to find out what had happened and once we'd worked it out he went off to see the landlord's agent and inform him he must deal with it. 'Course, Mr Galloway's worried about his own house now and that the same thing could happen to him. In fact, all the neighbours round you are demanding an inspection to put their minds at rest. I managed to get

130

you both some clothes out of your wardrobes but everything I got needs a good wash, I'm afraid, the mess has gone everywhere. Mrs Galloway lent me a suitcase to put them all in. It's in the kitchen.' He looked warily at them both. 'It looks like you're staying with us while the landlord sorts all this out, doesn't it?'

The women scowled at each other.

'Well, I bags the spare bedroom, being's I was here first,' Ada got in.

'I've as much right to that bedroom as you have, whether you got here first or not,' Kathy snapped back at her.

'It's my bed that's in there, I gave it to 'em when they got married,' said a defiant Ada.

'It might be your bed frame but it's my mattress that's on it. I gave 'em it when they got married,' Kathy spat back.

Maxie took a deep breath. 'Well, as we've only got one spare bedroom...'

Before she could finish both mothers erupted: 'I'm not sharing a bedroom with *her!*'

Maxie and Danny looked at each other, then back at their respective mothers.

'The front room would double as a makeshift bedroom but we've no money to buy a bed for it ... borrowing one at such short notice, even if someone we know has one spare, will take a while to work out. Then there's the problem of getting it here.' In an attempt to make a joke, Maxie said, 'Which of you is going down in the cellar then?'

The look they both gave her told her they didn't find the joke in the least funny.

'Well, shall I toss a coin to see which of you is

sleeping on the sofa?' Danny diplomatically suggested.

'I'm not sleeping on no sofa, not with my back,'
snapped Kathy. 'And 'specially not your sofa
where several springs have gone.'

'I've got a back too,' snapped Ada. 'And it's
worse than yours.'

'It damned well is not!' cried Kathy. 'I'm a
martyr to my back, everyone knows that.'

Maxie threw up her hands in frustration. 'Look,
it seems to me that in the circumstances you've
no choice but to share the spare bed. I'll go and
make it up. Danny, would you come and help
me, please?'

'Yeah, sure,' he said, knowing that Maxie had
asked him so they could both make their escape.

Before she left the room she smiled warmly at
both mothers. 'I'll mash us all another nice
cuppa when I come down, and then I'll wash all
your clothes through to dry overnight on the
drying cradles so you've both something clean to
wear in the morning.'

'I'll mash that cuppa,' offered Ada.

'I was just going to offer to do that,' Kathy
hissed at her.

Maxie and Danny hurried off to leave them to
it.

Upstairs in the spare bedroom, as they made up
the bed ready for their unexpected guests, Maxie
asked Danny, 'How long do you think it will take
the landlord to do the repairs?'

He gave a helpless shrug. 'Your guess is as good
as mine. Looks like we're in for a rough ride for
a while.'

She sighed. 'Seems so. The way those two are with each other, you'd never guess they used to be the best of friends, would you? Whatever it was that caused the falling out must have been bad. Both our mams are wonderful people, Danny, except when they're together, that is. I can't imagine either of them doing something against the other that was so awful it caused this feud.' She paused and looked tenderly at him across the bed. 'Look, Danny, I know how much you were looking forward to going out tonight, and I know what's happened to our mothers is no fault of ours, but all the same this has put a damper on things.'

He purposely billowed the sheet they were laying out so it flew over his head and she couldn't see the guilty look that filled his eyes when he responded. 'Well, I am disappointed as I was really looking forward to giving you a night out you'd not forget in a hurry, but at least our mothers are safe and sound. As things were it could have been a lot worse, couldn't it? We'll go out...' He just stopped himself from making a firm commitment and possibly repeating the terrible situation he had found himself in today. He'd learned a hard lesson. Next time he promised Maxie something, he'd make sure he had the money to back up his promise first. 'Well, as soon as we can safely leave that pair alone for a few hours.'

Maxie sighed in relief. Their mothers' plight, as serious as it was, had in its way done her a big favour by saving her – for the time being, at any rate – from a night out that would have been hell for her.

CHAPTER NINE

Danny couldn't believe his eyes on Monday morning as he was driving his loaded float past the entrance to the sterilising department. Andy was coming out, dragging behind him a low-loading flat cart full of crates of cleaned bottles ready for refilling.

Bringing the float to an abrupt halt, Danny got out and dashed across to him. 'You all right?' he asked him in concern.

Andy's face puckered. 'I am now. Thought I was a goner, though, I really did. I ate a bad pie, didn't I? When yer've had a skinful yer don't notice if summat yer eating's off, do yer? I tell yer, that's the last time I go to that bleddy chip shop on King Richard's Road. That pie they sold me musta been weeks old to do what it did to me. Talk about thinking yer gonna lose yer bowels... Anyway, I'm glad I've seen yer 'cos I've got us some tins. Go down really well do tins. You'll have no trouble getting rid of them.'

'Tins?' queried Danny.

'Yer know, them things you open with a tin opener?' Andy responded mockingly.

'I know what tins are, Andy. Tins of what, though?'

He shrugged. 'I dunno.'

'You don't? Why?'

'Well, 'cos the tins I got us ain't got any labels

on, that's why.'

'Oh! Well, how am I supposed to sell them if I don't know what's in them?'

'You don't need to know what's in 'em. Housewives snap yer hand off for cheap tins.' He gave a laugh. 'And they get an extra bonus 'cos it gives 'em a nice surprise when they open them.'

Danny looked doubtful. 'I'm not sure I'm happy about selling stuff I'm not sure of, if you get my drift. Might be best if I gave it a miss this time round, Andy.'

'Too late, I've already bought them for yer. Ten quids' worth, same price as the tea towels at a tanner each. They're in the back of me car ready for you to stack on the back of your float this morning. If you budge up all yer milk crates you should get them on. I've been looking out for yer this morning, hoping I'd catch yer.'

'Four hundred tins?' gasped Danny.

'God, you're quick,' Andy said, impressed. 'That's exactly how many you've got. See how honest I am? When yer sell them for a shilling each, you'll have made ten pounds' profit.'

It sounded good to Danny as that would mean he had twenty pounds in the pot, which wasn't a bad return on his original five. All the same, Andy might be happy selling mystery tins but Danny didn't feel comfortable with it. He felt in a way it would be deceiving his customers. For all he knew the tins could be full of water.

'If I don't sell them all today, what do I do with the ones I've left over?'

'That's your problem, mate, not mine. Look, if yer gonna continue being involved in this yer've

135

gotta get yer act together, start using yer brains. Drop by your house on yer way back to the dairy after yer deliveries this morning and store what's left over in yer outhouse. Sell what's left from the sidecar on yer motorbike.'

Danny felt stupid for not thinking of that himself. 'Oh, yes, I could, I suppose. But look, before I try and sell them, I'd like to open one of them up first so at least I can tell the housewives what they're buying.'

Andy gave a frustrated sigh. 'God strewth, give me strength! What is it with you, eh? It's those that buys' own choice whether they hand over their money to you for what you've got. If they don't like what's in the tins when they open 'em then it's their own fault for buying, not yours. They've no comeback on you.' Despite his explanation he could tell by Danny's expression that he was still not happy. Andy delved in his pocket and pulled out a Swiss Army knife, levering out the tin opener appendage. 'Oh, if it makes you happy we'll open one to check what's inside. But one of yours, okay?' He flashed a look up and down the yard and, seeing the coast was clear, ordered Danny: 'Bring yer float around to the car park and meet me there.'

Several minutes later both of them peered at the contents of an opened tin.

'It looks ter me like the tin of Irish stew I had for me dinner last night,' said a chuffed Andy. 'Our luck's in, mate, these'll go down a treat.'

Despite the fact that he helped Maxie cook their meals, she was the one who prepared things beforehand and Danny had to accept Andy's word that the tins contained Irish stew. They did appear to contain meat.

'Right, let's get these boxes loaded on yer float before we're caught,' Andy instructed him.

At seven o'clock that morning Maxie arrived downstairs to find both mothers bustling around the kitchen. As soon as they sensed her presence they pushed and shoved each other out of the way to get to her first.

Ada won. 'Sit yerself down at the table,' she ordered her daughter. 'I've made yer breakfast. Fried egg and fried bread.' She snatched up the teapot just before Kathy did and began pouring out a cup of tea for Maxie.

'I've made yer breakfast too,' piped up Kathy. 'Porridge, nice and thick, and I've saved the cream from the top of the milk for yer to put on it.' She flashed Ada a dark scowl. 'Porridge is a far better breakfast than greasy fried egg and bread.'

'And you call that stuff you've cobbled together porridge, do yer?' Ada snarled back. 'Looks more like concrete to me. Anyway, she's my daughter and I know what's best for her, if yer don't mind.'

'But I do mind. You might have gave birth to Maxie but she's my daughter-in-law and has been as good as a birth daughter to me, so I think I know what's best for her too.'

The last thing Maxie wanted at this time of the morning was two warring women giving her a headache. 'Mother! Mrs Maws!' she said, holding up a warning hand. Despite the prospect of either breakfast failing to appeal to her one little bit as her preferred start to the day was buttered toast,

137

she said, 'I appreciate what you've both made me. I'll have the porridge first, then the fried egg and bread.' Then, carefully choosing her words so as not to offend either of them, she added, 'I really don't expect you to make my breakfast for me. You have to get off to work yourselves.'

'Well, ducky, while I'm here I don't expect to be waited on,' said Ada.

'No, me neither,' said Kathy.

Maxie smiled warmly at them both. 'Did you both sleep well?' As soon as she had asked the question she could have kicked herself, steeling herself for the response she knew she was more than likely to get.

Ada flashed a scowl in Kathy's direction. 'Considering *she* snores like a pig, I did.'

'I do not snore! But I can assure *you*, Ada Billings, you toss and turn worse than a boat on the high seas in a force-nine gale. I spent half the night with no covers on me 'cos they were wrapped tightly around *your* fat body.'

'Er ... did you say you'd both cooked me breakfast?' interjected Maxie, hoping to defuse the situation.

Both women bustled off to be the first to fetch what they had cooked for her.

Maxie could not get out of eating every last scrap. Both of them sat watching her while they drank several cups of tea each, but thankfully no bickering took place so she was allowed to eat her meal in peace. As soon as she pushed her empty plate away and thanked them for the delicious food, they both rose, announcing they'd be late for work and would see her again when they returned about two.

For six hours at least Maxie would be spared their squabbling and she meant to savour every moment because it promised to start again as soon as they returned from work.

Much later that morning, Danny felt he fully appreciated what an ear of corn must feel like when a plague of locusts launched an attack on it. Once word got out he was carrying tins of Irish stew at a knock-down price, women of all shapes, sizes and ages swooped on him drove-like. Before he knew it, they were swarming back to their respective houses all armed with their precious cargo and his pockets were bulging with the coins they had thrust at him. All he was left with out of his original four hundred was two tins. Despite his dazed state, his mind was still functioning clearly enough for him to know that he was onto a winner through his association with Andy. At this rate he'd soon be able to start funding in earnest the kind of life he desperately wanted to give Maxie. As soon as he got home tonight he'd refund her the four pounds for her new dress, and the sixteen pounds he had left he'd give to Andy for his next load of stuff.

But Danny had received his quota of luck for that day. Andy was stunned by the news that he'd sold all but two of his tins, but hadn't as yet made a start on selling his own. He wouldn't be seeking out his contact until he did and there was no saying how long it would take him to offload his own tins. Danny therefore had no choice but to bide his time and hope that Andy sold the stuff as quickly as he himself had. Regardless of this setback, he was still elated from his success of that morning and jauntily made his way home, the money for his next deal safely weighing down his pockets. He meant to hide it away until Andy said the word to him to hand it over. Walking through the back door of his house, he stopped short as the sounds of a heated exchange coming from the back room hit him full force. His mother and mother-in-law were arguing, again.

Marching through, he found them wagging fingers at each other across the dining table. 'Mother, Mrs Billings, what on earth is going on?' he demanded.

They were so involved in their exchange neither of them had heard Danny enter. At the sound of his voice they both stopped mid-flow and looked startled.

'Oh, hello, Danny,' they said in unison. 'Cuppa tea coming up.'

They both began to scramble up to be the first to make his tea.

Danny stopped them by saying, 'I'll make us all a cuppa. You were both ... well, er ... arguing when I came in. Is there anything wrong?'

It was Kathy who got in first. 'I'll say there's summat wrong. *She* stole my handbag this morning.'

'I did not steal your handbag,' Ada shot back at her. 'It was you that stole mine. I took yours because you'd already gone off to work with mine so I picked up the one that was left.'

'Well, as you went out before me that's not true, is it?'

'If you remember right, you left the house before I did.'

'Well, they both look the same, it would be an easy mistake to make,' said Danny tactfully.

'Both look the same!' Ada snapped at him, insulted. 'They look nothing like the same. Mine's leather, not cheap plastic rubbish.'

'Eh, mine's leather too,' Kathy erupted. 'How dare you accuse me of owning cheap rubbish?'

'Well, they're both black, that's what I meant,' said Danny. 'Look, you've got your own hand-bags back now, haven't you, so no harm done. Where's Maxie?' he asked, not that he didn't want to know but in a bid to change the subject.

They both shrugged.

'Dunno,' said Ada. 'I got home first and she wasn't here. She's probably out job hunting.'

More than likely made her escape before you two got home from work, Danny thought. But she probably was out job hunting. Looking over the cards in shop windows on the off chance someone might have advertised for the services of a nanny.

Just then the back door was heard to open and Maxie rushed in, a wide beam of delight on her face. 'Well, you're looking at a working woman again,' she announced to them all. 'I got the job I wrote after at the nursery. The owner received my application letter first thing this morning and despatched a telegram to ask me down for immediate interview. I start tomorrow! It's only temporary but at least it's a job while I find myself a permanent one.'

The pride Danny felt in his wife was apparent

141

in his face, but before he could express his congratulations Kathy piped up.

'Well, this calls for a special meal. I shall pop down the butcher's and get a nice bit of shin beef for a stew. And I'll make my special dumplings...'

Ada pulled a mocking face. 'Call that a special meal, do yer? *I* shall go to the butcher's and get us a pork chop each *and* make my secret-recipe apple sauce to accompany it. And of course everyone knows my roast spuds are just the best in Leicester...'

Maxie knew without doubt another argument was brewing. Smiling sweetly at them both, she said, 'Thank you for the offers but dinner tonight is already planned. We're having mince, carrots and mashed potatoes. And,' she added, *'I'm* cooking it.'

Both women knew they'd been thwarted and there was nothing they could do about it without risk of upsetting Maxie, which they wouldn't do.

'There is something that needs discussing,' said Ada. 'Money for our keep while we're here with you?'

'Yes, I was just going to mention that but *she* stole my thunder,' said Kathy.

'We couldn't take any money off you,' insisted Danny.

'No, we couldn't,' agreed Maxie. 'Things will be a bit tight but we'll manage.'

'Oh, hark at the Rothschilds,' said Ada. 'Three pounds a week from each of us seems fair to me.'

'And me,' said Kathy. 'And if it's not enough, you must tell us.'

'Yes, you must,' said Ada.

Danny and Maxie were both struck dumb, and not because without their mothers' contribution to the housekeeping, it would in fact be a great struggle for them to manage. What surprised them most was the fact that both women were agreed on something for once.

CHAPTER TEN

The following Friday afternoon Maxie ran one hand over her face in frustration. On Tuesday morning she had arrived promptly at the nursery, fired with enthusiasm to start her job, and was especially looking forward to meeting all the children and doing her best for them. At the interview conducted by the owner she had been led to believe that here the welfare of the children was paramount, the best equipment was provided to cater for their every need, and the rest of the staff were warm and friendly. In fact, the reality was far from anything she had been led to expect and as the days had worn on Maxie had grown increasingly despondent and worried about the goings on at her temporary place of work.

The owner of the nursery, Mrs Naomi Maidenhead, a stunningly attractive woman in her late-thirties whose immaculate appearance told all who met her that she was a woman of means, only showed her face first thing in the morning when the children arrived. She left soon after their parents or guardians had departed. Where she went or what she did during this time Maxie had no idea. She returned just before the children were collected at six o'clock.

Miss Freda Green, the senior nursery nurse, a thin, sharp-featured, humourless woman in her early-fifties, gave the impression of believing that

144

children were an inconvenience who should be seen and not heard. She only did the bare minimum towards their care and also had a habit of disappearing for long periods, leaving Maxie to cope on her own.

If there was any other member of staff employed, apart from the one she was covering for temporarily, then Maxie had not seen hide nor hair of them and certainly no reference had been made to them within her earshot.

The twenty-five children whose parents paid dearly for their daily care were far from a joy to look after, though this wasn't their fault. Without adequate numbers of staff to oversee their care and supervise the stimulation all young children require to aid their development, most of the time they were left to their own devices, fighting with each other or crying from frustrated boredom. Several were now whimpering miserably because their nappies needed changing.

Maxie did her best to provide all the children with as much care and motivation as she could, but was fighting a losing battle here. There were other matters that deeply bothered her regarding the running of this establishment and she felt it her duty towards the children to voice these concerns.

Trying to soothe a younger child who had banged his head on the bars of the playpen he was imprisoned inside, while at the same time gently scolding an older one for doing his best to destroy a three-wheeler trike, Maxie noticed her immediate superior had returned. It was very apparent exactly what she had been doing during her absence as she was bleary-eyed, stifling yawns and her dress looked rumpled. She'd been sleeping.

Placing the now soothed child back in the playpen in front of a pile of wooden bricks, in the hope they would occupy it for at least a few minutes before it started screaming for attention again, Maxie went across to her superior.

She smiled politely at the older woman. 'Miss Green, I'd like a word, please.'

The senior nurse flashed a superior look at her underling. 'It'll have to wait. It's time to get the children tidied up before they're collected. You really should have started to do that by now.'

Maxie couldn't believe the impudence of the woman. Fighting hard to restrain her rising temper she said, 'With due respect, Miss Green, I can't manage to sort out all these children by myself.'

'While Mrs Maidenhead isn't on the premises I am in charge and I had some urgent matters to see to in the office,' she informed Maxie in a superior tone of voice.

'Miss Green, I know I've only been here four days but it seems to me that two members of staff is not nearly enough to look after all these children properly. Well, one member of staff really as I'm left on my own quite a lot ... most of the time, in fact.'

Just then Mrs Maidenhead entered, her smart leather court shoes clattering purposefully across the floor as she approached them. She gave a swift glance around the room then brought her eyes to rest on her two employees, speaking loudly to be heard over the din the children were creating. 'Why haven't you made a start on getting them ready for collection?'

'It seems, Mrs Maidenhead, that the temporary staff member you've hired doesn't seem willing to pull her weight,' responded Miss Green. 'I was just about to give her a ticking off when you arrived.'

Maxie stared at her in disbelief. 'That is most unfair, Miss Green. I have more than pulled my weight in the four days I've been here, and you know I have.' She gave her full attention to the owner of the nursery. 'Mrs Maidenhead, I was just saying to Miss Green that it's my opinion you need at least five staff members on duty all the time to supervise the number of children you take in. Most of the time they're just left to their own devices because I'm running around changing nappies, wiping noses, breaking up squabbles and comforting those that are upset. They hardly get any individual care.'

While she had the owner's attention Maxie felt she should take this opportunity to voice all her concerns. 'I'm also worried that most of the children aren't getting enough to eat at dinner-time. There are so many who are too young to feed themselves and if Miss Green and I can't help because we're otherwise engaged, well, they go hungry. And then there's the food that's served to them... Mrs Barber who comes in to cook ... well, she's not very particular about her personal hygiene. She looks and smells like she hasn't had a wash for weeks or a change of clothes for days. When I went into the kitchen to fetch one of the

147

children a drink while she was cooking their dinner this morning, she was smoking a cigarette and letting the ash fall into the pan of mince. And then there's the mince itself. Well, it was more fat and gristle than meat! And the vegetables were far from fresh...'

'Have you anything else you wish to get off your chest, Mrs Maws?' Mrs Maidenhead asked quietly.

'No, I think that's all for now.'

'I appreciate you telling me your concerns, Mrs Maws, but as I've never received any complaints whatsoever from my clients in all of the ten years I've been running my business, all I can assume is that the people who bring their children here are more than happy with the service I offer them.' She handed both women a brown envelope and said to Maxie, 'I haven't included your pay for tomorrow morning but that will be added to next week's pay packet. Now, ladies, I'll remind you that you have less than an hour to make these children respectable and gathered ready in the collection room. I also have a prospective new client arriving at seven this evening so I'd like everything in this room shipshape and Bristol fashion for her inspection. Oh, Miss Green, make sure all the old toys are put away out of sight and the new ones laid out, and vice versa before the children arrive tomorrow.' She smiled at them both. 'I'll leave you to it.'

With that she marched out.

Maxie stared after her. New toys? The ones the children were given to entertain them were all well used, very basic and far from enough to go round them all. Obviously the new toys were kept just for impressing potential clients. It seemed to Maxie also that prospective clients were purposely given their tour of inspection out of business hours so they would have no choice but to believe Mrs Maidenhead's version of how well taken care of her charges were.

Maxie feared that the people who entrusted the care of their children to the nursery had no idea just how little attention their precious offspring were in fact receiving. It wasn't very likely the children themselves could convey this to their parents.

True, Maxie was only working here on a temporary basis. Soon enough she would leave, either because the permanent member of staff she was covering for was well enough to resume her duties or because Maxie herself had secured a nanny's position, but that still left her with the uneasy knowledge of the neglect children suffered in Mrs Maidenhead's establishment. Her own love and respect for the innocent defenceless mites prevented her from turning her back on them. Quite how she was going to tackle this dilemma she did not know, but she knew she had to or she would not be able to live with herself.

In a whirl of activity for Maxie, Miss Green's contribution barely registering, an hour later all the children had been disrobed of the blue or pink smocks put on them each day to protect their clothes, nappies changed where necessary, had hands and faces wiped with a flannel, been dressed in their outdoor clothes and were now gathered together in an outer room ready for collection. After poking her head around the door to ensure everything was to her satisfaction, Mrs Maidenhead hooked it open to allow the parents gathered outside in the entrance hall to collect their children.

Standing by the wall beside Miss Green, Maxie watched the swarm of people enter, search hurriedly around to spot their own particular child or children, rush over and scoop them up.

A woman close to Maxie, hugging her two-year-old son protectively to her, was saying to him, 'Had a good day, darling? Played games with all the other children, have you? Enjoyed your daily visit to the park today in the sunshine? I hope you've been a good boy, Johnny.' She looked at Miss Green questioningly. 'I hope he ate all his dinner up. He can be a faddy eater.'

'Every morsel, Mrs Harper,' she responded cordially. 'I personally assisted Johnny myself.'

Mrs Harper smiled tenderly at her son and affectionately kissed his forehead. 'He's tired out, bless him, after all the fun he's had today. I do miss not having him with me at home but I know it's best for him to have lots of other children to play with and do the things you're trained to do in respect of a child's development. I want my son to have the best start in life I can give him. I'd better get him home. See you tomorrow then.'

Maxie watched thoughtfully as she began to weave her way through the crowd of other women to make her way out. Fun! Johnny's day had been more fraught than fun as he'd vied with the other children for her attention and his share of the toys. And what was this about his daily visit

150

to the park? Since she had started the weather had been sunny and warm but the children hadn't been taken outside into the fresh air in any way whatsoever. That poor woman had no idea that her precious child was imprisoned for most of the day in a playpen, squabbling with the other mites alongside him over the few toys they were allowed except for dinnertime when the younger children were put in high chairs, Maxie herself running between them all to try to make sure each had their fill. Miss Green sternly supervised the older children who sat around a table.

It was wrong that Johnny's mother was being deceived as she was. Like everyone was who brought their children here. Maxie knew that if she didn't enlighten these people then they would continue to be oblivious.

Heedless that she was about to put her own job in jeopardy, she called out to Johnny's mother: 'Excuse me, Mrs Harper. Have you got a minute?' Then, raising her voice, she addressed the rest of the gathering. 'Excuse me, but have you all got a minute?'

A bewildered Miss Green hissed at her, 'What are you doing?'

'Miss Green, these people need to know that their children are not being properly cared for here. It's a disgrace what goes on. These children can't stand up for themselves, but I can stand up for them.'

Miss Green looked taken aback for a moment then, seemingly forgetting she had an audience, her eyes darkened warningly. One bony hand gripped Maxie's arm vice-like. In a low voice she snarled, 'I'm not going to stand by and let you ruin what we've got here. No harm comes to the children so what's your problem?'

'No good comes to them either, does it?'

Her lip curled. 'Mrs Maidenhead said you were the quiet sort, old-fashioned in your outlook, the sort to be told what to do and get on with it. Not the sort who likes to cause problems.'

'And Mrs Maidenhead's right, that's just what I am like, but I'm also not the sort to stand by and say nothing when I see something isn't right. And what's going on here is definitely not right as you well know, Miss Green.'

'Now you look here...' she hissed.

'No, you look here, Miss Green. It's obvious to me that Mrs Maidenhead is only in this business for the money. And as for you, well, you don't even like children so why you chose a profession looking after them is beyond me. But then, you don't exactly do much looking after them, do you, so I suppose it's an easy living for you.'

Spinning back to face the gathering in the room who were all staring at her, waiting to know why she had summoned their attention, Maxie took a deep breath about to address them when Mrs Maidenhead's voice called out from the doorway.

'What's going on in here?'

One of the mothers turned to look at the proprietor. 'That's what we're waiting to find out. Your young nursery nurse asked us all if we had a minute so I presume she has something to tell us.'

'It's all right, Mrs Maidenhead,' called Miss Green, shoving herself in front of Maxie. 'There's

152

been a misunderstanding but it's all sorted now.' She addressed the parents. 'We'll see you all in the morning. Good evening.'

'No, please wait!' shouted Maxie, struggling to be heard above the growing hubbub of the children while side-stepping Miss Green and moving to position herself in the middle of the crowd. 'You all need to know what's going on here.'

'Going on?' one of the mothers demanded, looking worried. 'Just what do you mean?'

'Yes, what do you mean?' another piped up.

'Mrs Maws, I'd like to speak to you in my office – now!' Naomi Maidenhead shouted across to Maxie, obviously concerned that her new employee was about to divulge matters regarding the running of her establishment that she preferred did not become common knowledge.

Ignoring her, Maxie once again addressed the crowd. 'I feel it's my duty to inform you all that your children are not being looked after while they're here – well, not in the way you've been led to believe.'

'Don't listen to her,' Naomi Maidenhead erupted, her eyes blazing. 'She's ... she's lied her way into a job here. I've just discovered she's from another nursery that wants to bad mouth me so you'll take your business to them.'

'That's not true,' Maxie insisted. 'I'm a fully qualified nanny and came here to help temporarily while a member of staff who's broken her leg recovers. I'm looking for a permanent position in my own line of work. Now, did you all know that Miss Green and I are the only staff members looking after all these children?'

The parents looked mystified by this, all shaking their heads.

'You told me, Mrs Maidenhead, that you employed six qualified nursery nurses to look after the children,' said Mrs Harper to her.

'Well, if Mrs Maidenhead does then the other four have not been on duty while I've been here,' said Maxie. 'You all need to know that the younger children are kept in playpens all day while the older ones are left to fight between themselves for the few toys they're allowed. As Miss Green is not present in the nursery most of the time, I've been left to deal with all the children's needs on my own. While I've been here the children have not been taken out for fresh air every day, something it would be impossible to do with just the two of us anyway. As for the food they're given to eat ... well, it's not of the quality I suspect you think they're getting.'

Mrs Harper spun round to face Mrs Maidenhead. 'Is this true?' she demanded.

Before she could respond, Maxie reared back her head and said with quiet conviction, 'All of this is true, I swear it.'

The concerned parents stared at Mrs Maidenhead, their expressions reflecting contempt and anger.

'My Johnny is no longer coming here, Mrs Maidenhead,' Mrs Harper announced.

'My Janet neither,' said another mother.

Mrs Harper looked gratefully at Maxie. 'Thank you for having the guts to tell us all this.'

With Miss Green looking on in amazement they all started trooping out, Mrs Maidenhead being unceremoniously pushed aside with looks of scorn by the parents who passed her by.

As soon as the last one had departed, Naomi Maidenhead spat furiously, 'You bitch! You've ruined me.'

Maxie looked at her, appalled. 'Have you no thought at all for the poor children whose lives you've made miserable while they've been in your care, Mrs Maidenhead? I'm just thankful your other nursery nurse broke her leg and I came here or I dread to think how many more would have suffered while you ran your business in such a disgraceful way.'

The other woman knew she was beaten. Clenching her fists, face incensed, she hissed, 'Remove yourself from my premises. Now!'

Maxie wanted nothing more than to do that. With head held high, she left the nursery for good.

The whole experience had deeply distressed her but she had no regrets at all about the way she had acted. It was Mrs Maidenhead's clients' choice whether they continued to use her services or not, now they were fully aware of the facts. Maxie did feel for them, though, since they now faced having to find a replacement nursery for their precious children and would feel anxious for quite a while about any new establishment thanks to Naomi Maidenhead's lies and greed.

Maxie herself was now unemployed again but knew without doubt that Danny would fully support her actions.

As soon as she opened the back door of her house the sound of raised voices met her. Her mother and mother-in-law were going at it hammer and tongs again. After what had just transpired she just wanted a cup of tea in peace and quiet, which was obviously the last thing she was going to have here. There was a café on the King Richard's Road. It was a good walk away and wasn't the most salubrious of places; in fact it was known by the locals as Greasy Lil's despite the fact that the owner was a little fat Greek gentleman called Mr Adonis, but she could go there for a mug of tea and mull over what had transpired today before she had to relate it all to her family. She made to depart then stopped as realisation struck her. This was her home after all. By acting as they were, their two mothers were treating her and Danny with disrespect. It was wrong that they were making Maxie feel her own home was no longer a sanctuary through their selfish behaviour. Well, she had had enough. With uncharacteristic aggression she barged into the back room and demanded, 'What on earth is going on with you two now?'

At Maxie's sudden entrance and sharp tone of voice they both froze.

It was Kathy who spoke first. '*She's* hidden the bag of new wool I bought yesterday. I'm going to make you that lovely cable twin set I got the pattern for out of *Woman's Weekly* last week. I had to buy new pins too 'cos all mine are under the rubble in my house and they're in the bag with the wool. I know *she's* your mother, Maxie, but she's spiteful, so she is, 'cos she knows I want to get cracking on it.'

'I've done no such thing!' Ada erupted. 'I keep

156

telling *her* that but she won't listen to me. It's *her* that's hidden *my* bag of new wool and pins I bought yesterday for Danny's new jumper, 'cos she knows I wanted to make a start on it today. It's *her* that's spiteful.'

'Oh, for goodness' sake, neither of you has done what you've each accused the other of,' Maxie crossly informed them both. 'Because it was me that moved the bags. I put them in the cupboard under the stairs because you'd both left them on the sofa and I had to move them before I could sit down last night. I did tell you what I was doing but at the time you were both squabbling over whether we were watching *Dr Kildare* or *Emergency Ward 10* on the television, regardless of what Danny or me wanted.'

They both stared at her for a moment, shamefaced.

'Er ... have you had a good day, lovey?' Ada asked meekly.

'Yes, have yer?' asked Kathy, equally as humbly.

'No, I've damned well not,' Maxie snapped crossly back.

She rarely showed anger, or even mild annoyance, and they were taken aback to see it now.

'And it didn't help coming in to what I did,' Maxie continued. She gave a deep frustrated sigh. 'Look, Danny and I love you dearly and you're both welcome in our house for as long as you need to be, but have you any idea what it's been like for us since you moved in? It's like living in a war zone. We're both constantly treading on egg shells because we're worried about saying the slightest thing that might spark you two off. When you're

157

both in the house, which is most of the time apart from when you're out at work or off shopping, if you manage to go ten minutes without glaring at each other, passing a snide comment or erupting into a full-scale row over ... well, anything, which is to say nothing ... then we're lucky.' She suddenly stopped her diatribe and asked them, 'Where's Danny?'

'Oh, er ... he's gone over to check if any progress has been made on the repairs to our houses,' said a subdued Ada.

'Oh, used that as an excuse, has he, to get away from you two?' Maxie sharply responded. She gave another fed-up sigh. 'Look, you're both lovely people and you used to be the best of friends. Neither Danny nor I can work out just what one of you did to the other that's caused such bad feeling between you.

'Now we've been patient all the time this has been going on and done our best to accommodate you both so as not to worsen the situation, but I've had enough and I'm positive Danny has too. Obviously you have nowhere else to go while your landlord gets the repairs done so you're going to have to find a way to live peacefully together while you're here.' She eyed them both pleadingly. 'Can't you just forget about the past and kiss and make up?'

Kathy flashed Ada a stony glare. 'Well, I might consider it, if she apologises to me and begs me forgiveness.'

'What!' Ada exclaimed. '*Me* beg *your* forgiveness? It's you that should be begging for mine after what you did to me...'

158

'Stop it!' Maxie erupted. 'Will one of you please tell me what was the cause of all this?'

They both sniffed haughtily at each other, then, folding their arms under their bosom, turned their backs, proclaiming, 'Ask *her.*'

Maxie gave a groan of frustration. 'That's what you both always say whenever we ask you. We're so fed up we don't want to bother anymore. Look, I'm not asking, I'm telling you – I have to know what's behind this. Mother, you tell me.'

'Why should it be me?' Ada was pouting like a child.

'Oh, for goodness' sake! You tell me then, Mrs Maws?'

'Why should it be me?' Kathy said huffily. '*She* knows what *she* did, so it should be *her.*'

Ada spun round to face her. 'You mean, you know what you did, so it should be you!'

'Stop it! Just stop it,' Maxie cried. 'You're both acting like children. Mother, I'm asking you what happened. Please afford me the courtesy of telling me. If I knew just what it was, maybe we could finally sort it out even if that does mean one of you climbing down off your high horse and apologising for whatever it was you did.'

Ada stared blindly at her, her mouth opening and closing fish-like. 'Well ... er ... well ... it was ... er...' Her face set defiantly. 'I can't bring meself to, Maxie. You'll have to ask *her.*'

Maxie's temper snapped. 'All right. Either you tell me, Mrs Maws, or I warn you, I'll personally pack all your bags and wave you both off.'

'You wouldn't?' gasped Ada.

'You wouldn't?' exclaimed Kathy.

'I would,' she said with conviction. 'I've warned you, I've had enough. So one last time. Mrs Maws, tell me what's behind your feud.'

Kathy gulped. 'Well ... it was like this ... er...' Her voice trailed off and she stared at Maxie blankly.

Then the truth suddenly hit her. 'Neither of you even remembers what caused all this, do you?'

Shamefaced, Ada looked down to study her feet. 'Well, truth be told, no, I don't, ducky.' She lifted her head and cast a glance at her enemy. 'So you'll have to do the honours.'

Equally as shamefaced, Kathy said, 'I'm afraid I can't 'cos for the life of me, I don't remember either. Time sort of dulls yer memory, doesn't it?'

'Mmm, it does,' agreed Ada.

Maxie stared at them both incredulously. 'So let me get this straight. Just over ten years ago you two had a tiff over something and blamed each other. When no one apologised you stubbornly let the situation fester 'til it reached the stage it's at now, where you can't stand the sight of each other.' She shook her head. 'I can't believe this, I really can't.' She walked over to a dining chair and sank down on it, her face wreathed in utter disbelief. 'You've wasted ten years of friendship and put me and Danny through hell over something that couldn't be that bad at all else you'd both have remembered it vividly.'

The other women stared at each other, tight-faced.

'Well, it musta bin summat we disagreed on,' said Ada defensively.

'Yes, musta bin,' agreed Kathy, and gave a deep

sigh. 'What, though? I mean, it's not like we fell out very often before that, was it?'

'No,' said Ada. 'No, we didn't. Hardly at all, in fact.'

'Then it's *got* to be something really trivial that's just been allowed to get out of hand,' said Maxie.

Both the mothers looked deeply embarrassed.

It was Ada who spoke first. 'If we was kids, our parents would bang our heads together, wouldn't they, eh, Kathy? Then send us to bed with no dinner.'

She nodded. 'They most certainly would, *and* give us a pasting for good measure. Oh, Ada, we've bin stupid clots, ain't we, gel?'

'We certainly have. Oh, Kathy, I ain't half missed yer friendship!'

'Me yours too, Ada. All these years I've felt me right arm's bin missing without you by me side.'

The women took a step forward and hugged each other tightly.

'Friends again, eh, gel?' Kathy asked Ada.

'Oh, yes, please. Most definitely.'

'Want a cuppa?' Kathy asked Ada.

'I do, most certainly, so we can toast our renewed friendship. But you sit down and I'll mash us all one.'

'No,' Kathy insisted, 'you sit down while I do us the honour.'

'Both of you sit down,' ordered Maxie, rising. 'You've a lot of making up to do, *I'll* make the tea.'

A few minutes later Danny popped his head tentatively around the back door. Spotting Maxie alone he whispered, 'Is it safe to come in or are they still at loggerheads?'

She smiled across at him. 'It's safe.'

He entered, shutting the back door behind him. 'They'd argue about anything those two, Maxie. I don't know how much more I can stand. I'm beginning to dread coming home.'

'Well, you don't need to anymore.'

He looked puzzled. 'I don't?'

She grinned. 'They've made amends. Best of friends from now on.' And added as an afterthought, 'Hopefully.'

The relief on his face was clear to see. 'Really, Maxie? Really?'

'Yes, really.'

She proceeded to update him. He was as surprised as she had been. 'You mean, they've been sworn enemies all these years but neither of them can remember who or what caused the feud in the first place? I don't believe it, I really don't! Oh, but what a relief it's all over.' Kissing her cheek, he took the tray of tea things from her. 'I'll take these through, then I'll help you get dinner on the go.'

'Oh, goodness, yes, dinner. With all this going on I forgot we all want feeding. My mother said she was going to make a pie with those tins of Irish stew without the labels on she found in your pack-up bag the other day when she was emptying it for you, but she obviously forgot. We'll have a pie tomorrow. I'll do cauliflower cheese and mash tonight. Quick, hot and filling. Er ... you never did say where you got those tins from, Danny?'

Fearing a repetition of his failure over the garage

162

job, Danny hadn't as yet enlightened Maxie about his arrangement with Andy; besides, he wanted to wait until he could utterly surprise her by handing her a wad of money, telling her to go and pay cash for whatever she wanted and that there would be more to come at regular intervals.

'Didn't I? Oh, I'm sure I did,' he replied evasively. 'Oh, goodness, better take this tea through before it gets cold. Now those two aren't having a go at each other, they might start on me instead.'

For Maxie and Danny it was a sight worth beholding to see their mothers sitting side by side on the settee, talking and laughing amicably together like they used to.

They both looked expectantly at Danny when he came in, followed by Maxie.

'Any news on our houses, son?' his mother asked.

'Well, the workmen are in. I saw their tools lying around through the back-room window and their tea-making things in the kitchen, but it's hard to tell whether any actual progress has been made. I know I took both sets of keys with me but I didn't think it wise to go inside in case I disturbed anything and the houses fell down on top of me. I'll pop over again in a few days and see if I can catch the foreman, get an update from him and maybe have more to report.'

'Oh, well,' said Ada. 'No rush to go home, is there, Kathy?'

'No, Ada lovey. We're quite cosy here, ain't we?' She looked at Maxie and Danny. 'It's nice, the four of us, ain't it?'

Maxie and Danny flashed a meaningful glance

163

at each other. 'Mmm,' they mouthed.

'Oh, ducky, when you arrived home you said you'd had a bad day, and it must have been some bad day to put you in the mood you was in then,' said Ada to Maxie. 'She had a right go at us, didn't she, Kathy?'

'Oh, yes, she did that. I'm glad yer did, though, ducky,' she added, smiling. 'Onwards and up-wards for me and Ada from now on.'

'Oh, yes, most certainly,' agreed Ada. 'So, lovey, what did make you such a crosspatch today?'

Danny looked quizzically at her. 'You were in a bad mood, Maxie? That's not like you. What upset you then?'

After taking a deep breath, she related what had transpired at the nursery that day. As she relayed her tale they all sat looking at her, interjecting now and again with, 'Oh, no!' 'Them poor little mites.' 'She never! What, really?'

When she had finally finished Danny put his arms around her, pulling her close. 'You did the right thing, sweetheart.'

'Bloody right she did,' said a fuming Ada. 'That Mrs Maidenhead wants stringing up for treating those poor kiddies like that.'

'That Miss Green sounds like a right little Hitler. She wants stringing up alongside her boss,' said an equally angry Kathy. 'But at least you can sleep soundly at night, ducky, knowing that from now on those kiddies will be being better served somewhere that will treat 'em how they should be treated.'

'Yes, well, I feel for those kiddies, 'course I do, but I'm not very happy you've been run ragged

164

for the last four days trying to do the work of five,' said Danny to his wife.

How he wished he was in a position to tell his beloved they didn't need her wage to survive on, that they could manage more than adequately on what he alone was bringing in. But he was working on that. If he could just build his sideline up to bring him in a regular amount each week...

When he had approached Andy again this morning, to ask when he was seeing his man, Andy had laughed at him, flippantly asking what all the rush was as he himself hadn't had chance to spend what he'd made on his tins yet. He was in no hurry but might pop down the pub his contact frequented tonight; then again he might not as it was Friday and he was meeting his mates to go dancing, see what talent was on offer that his wad of cash would impress.

It was leaving Danny feeling very frustrated. Every day since he'd offloaded his tins the housewives had been asking him if he'd anything else. He'd plenty of customers and nothing to sell them. It was ludicrous. He was never going to achieve his aim at this rate and then his worst nightmare could come to fruition. In his mind's eye he saw Maxie, a look of contempt in her eyes, walking out of their house with a packed suitcase into the arms of another man, one she could respect and admire and who would provide properly for her, unlike Danny as matters stood. He vehemently hoped that Andy would see fit to do business with his contact tonight before he went off to enjoy himself then Danny would come another step nearer to achieving his goal.

He realised Maxie was speaking to him. 'Sorry?' he said to her.

'You were miles away, Danny, and you've got an awfully worried look on your face. Look, I know me not having a job again is bound to be worrying you...'

He stopped her by pressing his fingers to her lips, and before he could stop himself had reaffirmed his ambitious promise to her. 'Maxie, you stop worrying. I made you a promise that I was going to make your life better and it's not an idle one. Sometimes things don't happen as quickly as I'd like, that's all. Oh, that reminds me, I haven't given you the money for your dress. It's upstairs. Next time I go up I'll get it for you.' That made him feel better. At least he'd fulfilled one of his promises to her. Now he needed to make good on the other, or he dreaded the consequences.

CHAPTER ELEVEN

Danny's customers in the area of terraced streets he delivered in were mostly made up of house-wives and widow-women of varying ages, shapes and sizes, plus a scattering of widowers, elderly spinsters or bachelors. Most customers were very pleasant, some dour, and the odd self-important type a bit clipped in their attitude towards trades-men like Danny. On the whole, though, they were a nice bunch of people to deal with. But there was one customer he particularly dreaded having personal contact with.

A vulgarly dressed, hard-faced woman in her early-forties, the locals had nicknamed her Elsie Tanner behind her back after the brash, loud-mouthed, trouble-making character in the tele-vision series *Coronation Street*. Bernice Frasier, as she was really called, was not the sort who shrank from speaking her mind, whether invited to or not, and her milder-natured neighbours avoided her company as much as possible. Her relation-ship with her husband, a slob of a man who was a lorry driver by trade when he wasn't keeping the local pub in profit, was tempestuous to say the least. Violent rows erupted virtually daily between them, constantly shattering the peace of their long-suffering neighbours. And if the two older family members weren't bad enough, adding to their neighbours' problems were the two Frasier

167

offspring, both male, in their early-twenties, leather-jacketed and with long greasy hair. Each lad was as obnoxious as their parents. Well aware how annoying it was for those roundabout they would sit for hours outside in the street, revving up their motorbikes. Bernice's elaborate excuses for avoiding settlement of weekly bills were worthy of publication in the *Pay Dodger's Manual*. Apart from her debts to the coal merchant, bread man, provisions delivery man, off licence, news-agent and several tally men, at the moment she was four weeks behind with her milk bill.

Finding no money left out for him under the un-rinsed, stinking milk bottles outside the Frasiers' back door, Danny took a deep breath to steel him-self before he gave it a tentative knock. He wasn't expecting his summons to be answered and nearly jumped out of his skin when the door swung open. Bernice was revealed in all her glory, bleached blonde hair sticking up wildly. She was dressed in a grubby turquoise Bri Nylon negligee that re-vealed more than it concealed, a Park Drive dang-ling from her mouth. She leaned nonchalantly on the door frame, giving him the once over.

'Well, if it's not our handsome young milky. So, what canna do fer you today?' She took the cigar-ette from her mouth and ran her tongue seductively over her top lip while giving him a provocative leer. 'Old man's out so if yer wanna come in, I'm sure I can teach you a thing or two.'

He was left in no doubt just what she was refer-ring to. Regardless of the fact that he would never, ever betray Maxie, the thought of physical contact with this woman, even accidentally touching her hand, utterly revolted him. She had, though, managed to embarrass him. 'Er ... well ... er ... I've come to collect your dues, Mrs Frasier.'

She looked surprised. 'Dues? And what dues would they be then?'

She knew very well what dues he was referring to. Nevertheless he gave her a smile and said politely, 'Your milk bill, Mrs Frasier.'

'Oh, me milk bill. Well, I thought you might like to settle that for me, by way of compensation.'

He looked taken aback. 'Sorry, Mrs Frasier? Compensation? Compensation for what?'

She smirked at him condescendingly. 'Oh, playing it all innocent, I see. Well, let me jog yer memory.' She put her hand in her pocket and pulled out a scrap of bright yellow paper with red lettering on it. She waved it at him. 'Recognise this?'

He shook his head. 'No.'

She thrust her face close to his and said, 'Well, yer should, 'cos it was stuck to the bottom of one of them labelless tins I bought cheap off yer a few days ago.' She reared back her head. 'Irish stew? Was it fucking hell as like! It was dog meat. Good quality dog meat, mind, not the type folks around here can afford. It had meaty chunks and rich jelly, like the advert on the telly says, and it fooled me at first 'til I found this bit of label stuck to the bottom of the tin when I went to throw it away.' While Danny stared at her as what she was telling him registered, she took a long drag of her cigarette. 'My old man's not the sweetest-natured in the world. I wonder what he'll say when he finds out what he actually had for his dinner twice this week? More to the point, how he'll act.

Got a hefty punch has my old man, and he doesn't need much of an excuse to use it. Then, of course, there's the rest of the folks who bought those tins off yer.'

An ashen-faced Danny insisted, 'I was told it was Irish stew, Mrs Frasier, honest I was.'

She sneered at him. 'So you say. Mind you, you don't strike me as the usual sort that flogs off stuff on the side. But then, I suppose looks can be deceiving, can't they? You'd never tek me for a mother of two lads in their twenties, would yer now? Anyway, I take it you agree to my offer. Toodaloo then.'

As she kicked shut the door behind her, Bernice grinned to herself. That chance discovery of a piece of label stuck to the bottom of the tin she had bought off Danny had resulted in a double triumph for her. First, she had found a way to settle her outstanding milk bill. Secondly, and far more satisfying, she had a measure of sweet revenge on her husband, payback for all the nasty things he had done to her over the years. Of course, in future, she wasn't going to splash out on the best quality dog food he'd enjoyed this week but would buy a cheaper variety. The way he gobbled his food down, he'd never notice the difference. She would, though, and revel in her secret.

Danny meanwhile was staring blindly at the Frasiers' rotting back door. He couldn't believe that he had unwittingly sold dog food in the guise of Irish stew to all those people. He felt sick at the thought. He ought to try and discover them all, hope they hadn't partaken of the tin's contents yet and think of an excuse to buy them back. But then, like Mrs Frasier, there was a strong possibility the tin's contents had already been used and what would their reaction be when they discovered the truth? They would hardly take it kindly. They could all band together and lynch him. He had no choice but to give in to Bernice Frasier's blackmail and hope she kept her mouth shut. At least he'd known for definite the tea towels were tea towels when he'd sold them. In future he would not sell anything that he wasn't absolutely positive of. He hoped Andy hadn't yet sold all his stock of tins. Danny would seek him out urgently and inform him what he'd discovered. Then another terrible thought struck him. The two tins he hadn't sold were in the cupboard at home. As soon as he returned he needed to dispose of them before the worst happened.

During the rest of his deliveries that morning it was a very subdued Danny who greeted his customers, barely able to look them in the eye. He couldn't wait to get back to the depot and break the news to Andy.

A while later he stared stupefied at a man standing before him. 'I'm sorry, Mr Mahon, did you say that Andy's ... left?'

Gilbert Mahon looked stolidly at Danny over the top of his half-moon glasses. 'Not left, Danny, he's bin sacked. He's had it coming to him for a long time. Lazy beggar he was! Always disappearing off for ages on some excuse or other, usually for a crafty fag or to chat up the office gels. When he did condescend to do some work, snail's pace describes it. He swanned in here this morning, half an hour late, still dressed in the clothes he'd

171

obviously gone out in last night, reeking of booze and looking like death warmed up. It was obvious we were going to get even less work out of him than we usually do. The boss told him to collect his cards from the office and sling his hook.'

Danny felt his world crumbling around him. He was sorry to hear Andy had lost his job, but then if what Gilbert Mahon had said about his attitude was true he deserved what he'd got. But paramount in Danny's mind was his complete dependency on Andy to further his own cause.

'You've gone pale, lad,' Gilbert Mahon said. 'This news has obviously upset yer. I didn't realise Andy was such a friend of yours. It surprises me, mind, as I wouldn't have thought he was your sort at all. Jack-the-lad type is Andy while you ... well, you're the steady sort that's good to his mother and can be wholly relied upon. We was all sorry to see you leave this department when you got moved up into deliveries. If yer fancy giving up yer round and coming back inside, we'd be glad of yer back in here, no hesitation.'

'Thanks, Mr Mahon, I'll bear that in mind,' Danny said weakly. 'Er ... I don't suppose you know where Andy lives, do you?'

'You asked me that the other day and I said I didn't then. Must be important since yer so desperate to see him. Owe yer money, does he? If he does, fat chance you have of getting it back! His parting words to us as he left this morning were he was glad he'd been finished as he was thinking of going with a couple of his mates to Blackpool to try their luck up there. This had made his mind up for him. He was going off home to pack

172

up and heading up there today, he reckoned.'

Danny's world crashed about him then. He needed Andy to secure stock for him. What was he going to do now? After saying a polite goodbye to Gilbert Mahon, a very distracted Danny left the dairy.

Maxie, meanwhile, having spent a pleasant morning buying the weekend shopping accompanied by her mother and mother-in-law – both getting along famously together after so long as enemies – realised as they chatted and laughed together while putting the groceries away that she had forgotten to call into the newsagent's on their way back to pick up a *Leicester Mercury*. Not wanting to miss any opportunity to secure herself work, she left the two others discussing local issues, in particular a close neighbour with a penchant for keeping several cats who preferred to use the neighbours' yards as a toilet rather than her own, and went off to buy one.

Mrs Kendrick, the wife of the newsagent, was a cheery-faced, bustling, middle-aged woman who felt it was her duty to know as much of the private business of her customers as she could glean, either from them or from others who knew them. She claimed it was so she could advise them what brand of goods would suit them best, but in truth it was to satisfy her own insatiable appetite for gossip. She smiled warmly at Maxie as she took the money from her for a newspaper and two bars of Fry's Mint Crème chocolate for Ada and Kathy to enjoy while they watched the television tonight.

'So, how yer getting on in yer new job, Maxie?

173

Nursery, isn't it? I admire yer, I really do. How yer can stand all them screaming kids around yer all day is beyond me. Looking after my two when they was little was enough for me.'

Obviously her mother or mother-in-law had revealed this information to Mrs Kendrick while visiting her shop, more likely than not unintentionally. Maxie needed to watch what she replied to the woman or she would want to probe for further information that Maxie did not want to share with her and the rest of her customers.

'I've left the nursery as it proved too far for me to travel, Mrs Kendrick, so I'm looking for something closer to home.'

'Oh, I see.' She looked thoughtful. 'I'm not sure there's anything in the nannying line in the cards in my window. In fact, I know there's not as I make it my business to know what people are advertising for ... just to make sure nothing I'm not happy with is being displayed in my window, if you see what I mean.'

She then took it upon herself to take the copy of the newspaper from Maxie, laying it on the countertop and thumbing through to the Jobs Vacant section. She ran her finger down a column. 'Oh, look, someone wants a nanny in Thurcaston. One child, aged six months, eight 'til six-thirty while the mother is out at work and every other Saturday morning. Good conditions and pay to be negotiated, it says. Oh, but then, that's miles away from here so no good for you, ducky.'

She began scanning again. 'Plenty for cleaners, gardeners, drivers, a couple for cooks. Oh, here's one! No, that's no good for you either as it's for a

174

live-in nanny. Shame that, it's for an address off the Hinckley Road which would have been ideal for you. You could have walked there.' She scanned her eyes down the column again until she came to the end. Folding up the newspaper, she handed it back to Maxie. 'That's it, I'm afraid. Still, there might be something in on Monday. I'll make sure I keep a copy aside for you.'

Maxie gave a deep sigh. She was beginning to worry that occupations such as the one she had chosen to follow were becoming a thing of the past during the rapidly changing 1960s.

Mrs Kendrick was looking at her thoughtfully. As though she had read Maxie's mind she said, 'Seems ter me, ducky, there ain't so much call for nannies these days as there used ter be. Maybe people ain't quite as wealthy as they used to be and are having to cut their cloth accordingly, or maybe the women who used to feel it right to palm their kiddies off on a stranger have examined their consciences and realised they should be raised by their own mothers. Who knows?

'Anyway, now might be a good time for you to change direction, Maxie. I mean, you're a bright young thing and yer can't say you ain't the reliable sort as I've known yer long enough to be sure you most certainly are. I can't say the same about a lot of other young women of your age, mind. Skirts up to their armpits ... and what is this new thing they're all into now? Flower power? Call themselves happies or hoppies, something like that... And what's all this about free love?'

She pulled an extremely disapproving face. 'They'll soon learn that n'ote in life comes free,

175

there's always a price to pay. I suspect hardly any of 'em have done a decent day's work in their lives, yet they bleat on that the world owes them. The likes of a youngster such as you these days is a rarity, lovey. You've got yer head screwed on. I'm sure you could learn a new trade easy enough.' She broke off to take payment from a customer for a newspaper and a packet of Embassy filter-tipped then continued, 'There's lots of vacancies in the paper for all sorts of things, Maxie, and I happen to know personally that Mr Wallis is looking for an assistant in his greengrocer's shop just down the road. And I noticed the other day when I went past Brucciana's bakery on the West Bridge that they're looking for staff in their factory. You'd get the perk of cheap bread and cakes if yer worked there, I'm sure.'

Neither job appealed to Maxie but regardless she smiled appreciatively. 'I'll have to give your suggestions some serious thought.' Mrs Kendrick did have a point, she supposed. Maybe she should consider looking at other options by way of paid employment.

Having cordially wished Mrs Kendrick good afternoon, Maxie left the shop.

She'd hardly closed the door when a smartly dressed, very good-looking man in his early-thirties approached her.

'Excuse me, I'm sorry to bother you, but could I have a word if you have a moment?' he asked her.

Maxie recognised him as the customer Mrs Kendrick had served during their conversation and wondered what he could possibly want to speak to her about. 'Yes, of course,' she answered,

176

smiling politely at him. 'What can I do for you?'

He looked a little uncomfortable. 'Well, I do hope you'll forgive me, I wasn't intentionally eavesdropping, but I couldn't help overhearing what the woman in the shop was saying to you as I was waiting to be served... I understand you're looking for a job. It's just, I'm looking for someone, you see, and you could be that person.'

Maxie's heart soared and she eyed him expectantly. 'You need a nanny?'

'Well, not exactly. My wife and I have only been married three months. Hopefully we will in the future, though.' He smiled encouragingly at her. 'My name is Matthew Holbrook. I'm an estate agent and I've just opened my own business in between the wool shop and the florist's on the Hinckley Road. It's a gamble I'm taking, opening up in the suburbs and not the city centre, but I feel that if I'm to shine out above the rest I need to tackle things a little differently. I'm sure there's a need for a local estate agent in an area like this one, full of houses and shops and factory premises.

'Well, I'm hoping I've picked on the right area to be in as you can probably tell from my accent that I'm not from Leicester. I've come up here as my wife is a local girl. It was a big wrench for me to move so far away from my own family but my wife's happiness was worth the sacrifice.'

He smiled. 'We had one of those whirlwind romances. I'd been invited to a dinner party and was seated next to Melissa. She'd been staying with a friend who'd been invited and asked if she could bring Melissa with her. We got chatting and found we had a lot in common. I asked her out for a drink the next evening and, well, to cut a long story short, we were married by special licence three weeks later and here I am.' He suddenly paused and smiled in embarrassment. 'I apologise, I got a little carried away in telling you what brought me to Leicester, but I'm still pinching myself that a woman like Melissa actually asked me to marry her! Anyway, back to business...

'I'm positive people will feel far more confident about using an estate agent to sell their properties or rent them out if that agent lives and works in the area themself. I just hope I'm proved right. I've been interviewing for a receptionist to help me man the office as in my line of work I'm out and about quite a lot, and while I'm out could be losing potential business. To be honest, the sort of person I've been interviewing for the position hasn't exactly measured up. I'm looking for someone who I can rely on and trust. I'm getting desperate, and desperate measures call for desperate actions, don't they? I know it isn't really the done thing to approach you like this but after overhearing the lady in the shop sing your praises, and learning you're looking for work, I felt that maybe I was the answer to your problem and you to mine.'

Maxie had only gone out to fetch a newspaper. To find herself being offered a job like this completely knocked her for six. He seemed a nice enough man, open and sincere, someone she felt she could work for very happily. She was flattered he considered her worthy of becoming his assistant. She had to admit his proposition was

178

intriguing her, but there was one huge problem for Maxie that Mr Holbrook hadn't seemed to consider. 'I'm very honoured you think I could be what you're looking for, Mr Holbrook but, you see, I haven't any office experience and so I wouldn't be much use to you.'

'Answering the telephone politely and making appointments doesn't require a qualification in secretarial work. At the moment, as I've only just started up the business, I've been handling all the paperwork on the houses and rentals myself. Hopefully, when the business expands I will need a secretary, but I'll still need a receptionist too. Look, why don't you give it a try for a couple of weeks and see how you get on? What have you to lose?'

As matters stood, nothing. She'd answered the telephone for Mrs Carson on many occasions and taken messages for her when she'd been out. Making appointments couldn't be all that difficult. Maxie smiled warmly at him. 'All right, Mr Holbrook, I will give it a try.'

He looked delighted. Grasping her hand, he shook it firmly. 'Oh, that's great. A big weight off my mind. I'm not a mean man so I'm sure we can come to a mutual agreement on your wages.' Releasing her hand, he said, 'So I'll see you Monday morning at eight-thirty, Miss ... er ... Mrs...'

She grinned broadly at him. 'Maxina Maws. Mrs. I like to be called Maxie. I'll be at your office at eight-thirty on the dot, Mr Holbrook.'

'I'll leave you to enjoy the rest of the weekend then.' He made to depart, then stopped. 'Er ... your first assignment for me. Could you direct me back to the main road? After shutting up shop at lunchtime I thought I'd have a wander round before I went home, just to familiarise myself with some of the streets around here that I haven't had chance to explore yet, and … well … rather embarrassing, but I've managed to get myself lost.'

He started to chuckle and Maxie found herself chuckling along with him until they were both giggling helplessly. It was at just this moment that a very disillusioned Danny came around the corner of the street and froze rigid at the sight of his wife with a very good-looking, smartly dressed man. It seemed obvious to him that Maxie knew this man very well, and his immediate thought was that his worst nightmare had come true. Maxie had met someone who could offer her a better life than Danny himself could. He wanted to rush across to her, beg her not to leave him for this man and to give him a chance to prove himself to her, but his feet wouldn't move.

Meanwhile, Maxie and Matthew managed to control their mirth enough for Maxie to give him the directions he'd requested and for Matthew to go on his way. Maxie then turned to make her own way home, hoping that Danny was back by now as she couldn't wait to tell him her thrilling news. Just then she caught sight of a figure on the corner opposite and, realising it was her husband, without further ado kicked up her heels and dashed across to him.

She was so excited about what she had to tell him that she completely missed the look of total horror on his face at what he felt positive she was about to tell him.

'Oh, Danny,' she blurted out. 'You'll never guess what's just happened. I've been offered a job with that man...' She looked in the direction Matthew had gone in but, seeing no sign of him, returned her attention to Danny. 'Oh, he's gone. I expect he was in a hurry to get home to his wife, they haven't been married long.'

The word 'wife' struck Danny forcibly and before Maxie could say anything else he exclaimed, 'He's married?'

She nodded. 'One of those whirlwind romances, he told me: they were married within three weeks of meeting each other. His wife actually asked him to marry her! It all sounds very romantic. Anyway, Mr Holbrook ... Matthew Holbrook, that's his name ... is an estate agent who's just opened an office on the Hinckley Road. He's been having trouble finding the right person to be his receptionist, and after overhearing a conversation Mrs Kendrick and myself were having while he was waiting to be served, he collared me outside and asked if I'd like to have a try at the job. It's usually very annoying when Mrs Kendrick gossips away like she does but for once I'm glad she stuck her nose into my business. Isn't this great news, Danny?'

Oh, yes, it was the most brilliant news to Danny that he had completely misconstrued the situation he had witnessed. But it had also served to confirm for him that Maxie could meet another man like Holbrook at any time, someone who wasn't newly and happily married, and it could happen anywhere. Fulfilling his own plan was even more urgent now. He needed a replacement

181

for Andy as his middleman. Then it struck him that what he really needed was to find his own contact so he could go straight to them himself, as and when he needed to, and not be reliant on anyone else.

Andy had said he did business in a pub. It was a pity he had never mentioned the man's name as that would have made Danny's search much easier. But then, Andy's contact surely couldn't be the only man in the area selling on bankrupt, fire-damaged or surplus stock? There must be plenty around willing to do business direct with Danny.

He realised Maxie had taken his arm and was propelling him down the street. 'Where are we going?' he asked.

She stopped and looked at him quizzically. 'Where do you think? Home. I can't wait to break my good news to our mothers. I go out for a newspaper and come back with a job! They won't believe it, will they?'

They had just turned the corner into their street when a removals van parked on the opposite side of the road caught their attention.

'Looks like Terry and Gail are moving out,' said Maxie. 'But they've only just moved in. I wonder why they're leaving such a lovely house so soon?' Just then Terry appeared carrying the rubber plant. Maxie called out a greeting to him and gave him a wave. As he hurried off, she looked at her husband askance. 'I know he saw and heard me but he totally ignored me, Danny.'

He had, very blatantly so, and Danny inwardly seethed at the man's rudeness towards his wife. Thank goodness they were leaving the area as

Danny was well aware that both of them, especially Terry, had viewed all who lived in these streets as beneath them. 'Oh, I'm sure he didn't,' he said diplomatically.

'We should go over and offer our help.'

There was no way Danny was voluntarily going to put his wife in such a position again. 'Oh, we'd only get in the way of all those removals men. Anyway, you've some good news to tell our mothers, haven't you?'

'Oh, yes, I have, haven't I?'

Maxie was right, Ada and Kathy did have trouble taking in her news and made her tell her story twice before they were convinced.

'Well, I'll be blowed,' said Ada. 'Just thank goodness you went to the shop when yer did, that's all I can say.'

'He does sound a nice man,' said Kathy. 'Does he want a cleaner or tea lady?' she asked eagerly.

Maxie laughed. 'As soon as he does I'll be sure to recommend you. As long as I'm still working there, of course.'

'Don't be daft,' scolded Ada. ''Course you'll still be working there. Mrs Kendrick was right in her praise of you. Still, I'm yer mother and yer won't listen to me, so you tell yer wife, Danny. She's special, ain't she?'

She certainly was and it worried Danny that other people, and strangers at that, were noticing just how special.

'Well, I hope yer going to take Maxie out tonight to celebrate her good luck?' said Kathy.

His mother was right, Maxie's good fortune was well deserving of celebration but tonight he had been planning on going out by himself so he could begin his search to locate a supplier.

Fearing that Danny would resurrect his desire to take her to a night club, which was the last thing she felt like, Maxie blurted, 'Oh, but we must all celebrate my good luck as a family. We could all go down the local, couldn't we?'

'Well, if you want us to help you celebrate then I'm game,' said a chuffed Ada.

'Yeah, me too,' agreed Kathy, equally as chuffed. 'You all right with that, Danny?'

'Yes, 'course I am,' he fibbed, planting a smile on his face.

'Well, I'll make a start on the dinner so we can get it past early then get ourselves ready to go out,' said Maxie.

'No need,' Ada told her. 'It's all done ready for going in the oven. Me and Kathy did it while you was out.'

Maxie looked gratefully at them both then a thought struck her. 'How did you know I was going to do corned beef hash for us all tonight, we never discussed it?'

'We didn't make corned beef hash,' said Kathy. 'We made a meat pie using those tins of Irish stew Danny said he got cheap the other day.'

This announcement froze him rigid. After learning the devastating news of Andy's sudden departure he'd completely forgotten about the tins and what they truly contained. His day was going from bad to worse. So panic-stricken was he it never occurred to him to come clean. He had to get to that pie...

He needed to get in the kitchen by himself so

he could be free to do what he had to. In this small house, though, with three other people, it was nigh on impossible to be in any room on your own, except for the privy. Thankfully an idea struck him. 'While you're chatting, I'll make us all a cuppa.'

'I'll give you a hand, Danny,' Maxie offered. 'I need to make your sandwich anyway. You must be famished.'

His mind was whirling frantically. 'Oh, er ... to be honest, Maxie, I'm not really hungry. I'll wait for my dinner. I'm sure our mams have some more questions for you about your new job. You stay and chat with them.'

Before she could protest any further, he hurried off into the kitchen.

He found the pie in the larder under a tea towel. Feeling terrible guilt for what he was about to do, he picked it up, raised it high, then let it drop to the floor where it smashed into pieces, the tin plate it had been on clattering loudly against the stone slabs on the larder floor. Next thing he knew three faces were staring at him from the doorway. Danny eyed them all remorsefully. 'I'm so sorry, I don't know how it happened but I knocked the pie off the shelf.'

'Never realised I had such a clumsy clot for a son,' said Kathy, looking reproachfully at the remains of the pie splattered across the floor.

'Well, these things happen to the best of us,' said Ada in his defence. She turned her head and looked at Maxie. 'Looks like corned beef hash after all.'

185

CHAPTER TWELVE

'Oh, me head feels like a train's running through it,' moaned Ada pitifully the next morning.

'Well, I've a whole network of goods wagons running backwards and forwards through mine,' groaned Kathy. 'I wish you hadn't made me drink that last stout, Ada.'

'You didn't need no encouraging, gel. Anyway, it wasn't just Maxie's good news we were celebrating but the renewal of our friendship.'

'And we certainly did that, didn't we?'

'You both certainly did,' agreed Maxie as she entered the room to place a plateful of buttered toast on the table. She looked at them both, slumped in their chairs, looking very sorry for themselves. 'I was beginning to think you were both hell-bent on drinking the pub dry of stout.'

'We never did 'ote embarrassing, did we?' Ada asked her worriedly.

'Oh, we didn't, did we, lovey?' Kathy asked her, looking anxious.

She smiled at them. 'Not at all, you just thoroughly enjoyed yourselves. Are you sure you both don't want a cooked breakfast?'

'Oh, we're sure,' they both vehemently insisted.

'Another pot of tea then?'

'Make it an urnful, lovey,' said Ada. 'Those last two pots haven't gone anywhere near helping me back to normal.'

186

'What you both need is a blow of fresh air,' suggested Maxie. 'Why don't you go for a walk?'

'I don't think my legs would carry me as far as the yard, let alone any further this morning,' moaned Kathy.

'I'm not surprised they're giving you gyp after all that jigging about you did to the tunes that old boy was playing on the piano,' said Ada.

'You did yer fair share too,' Kathy responded.

'Yes, I did. And I'm proud that after all these years we can both still remember how to jitterbug. It might have been a very watered-down version compared to what we used to do twenty-odd years ago during the war, but it was still recognisable, wasn't it, gel?' she said proudly.

'Oh, it was that, Ada, and I was fair taken back to when we first moved in next door to each other just as our children were born. Every Thursday we'd wheel them up in their prams to the Assembly Rooms for the afternoon dancing, then while they slept we'd dance ourselves silly. Them were the good old days, weren't they, Ada? When we was young and didn't suffer no aches and pains in our legs and back after a spot of dancing.'

'Mmm,' she readily agreed. 'Like we're suffering for the spot we did last night. I just wish me head would stop thumping. A blow of fresh air does sound inviting. We could take chairs out and sit in the yard, I suppose,' she suggested. Then a thought struck her. 'A ride out is what we all need. Be just the ticket would that.'

'Oh, yes, just the job,' confirmed Kathy. 'I'll give Danny a shout and tell him to hurry up with his ablutions.'

'I'll have the dinner ready for when you get back,' said Maxie.

'You will not,' said Ada. 'You're coming with us. Me and Kathy can sit in the sidecar and you can ride pillion.'

'I wouldn't mind riding on the back with Danny,' said Kathy. 'I've always wanted to have a go at that.'

That sounded the best idea to Maxie. Not that she wasn't firmly of the opinion that Danny was a careful driver, but the thought of riding pillion herself frightened her to death. The sidecar wasn't the most comfortable way to travel – not that she had ever told Danny just how bone-shaking it actually was as the suspension on the old vehicle was not all that good. She would never intentionally hurt his feelings. Maxie was very aware that people of their own age sniggered behind their backs at such an old-fashioned means of transportation, but she never paid any heed as to her they were lucky to have a vehicle at their disposal when most of the mickey-takers were solely reliant on public transport.

Before Maxie could agree to Kathy's request to ride pillion, Ada said to her, 'Don't be daft, gel, yer too old and ... well, too well padded about the middle for that sort of carry on now, same as I am.'

'Mmm,' Kathy agreed. 'I s'pose yer right. I'll go and chivvy Danny up then.'

As soon as Ada heard her footsteps ascending the stairs, she said to Maxie, 'I keep meaning to ask yer, lovey, but it's not often I get to catch you on me own. Only ... how are things with you and Danny after we had our chat a while ago and I told yer what I did?'

'Well, since the part-time job he got himself as a forecourt attendant didn't work out, he hasn't mentioned getting another one. I'm glad as he works enough hours as it is and those extra ones in the garage just about killed him. He still keeps saying now and again that he's going to make my life better for me, but how he's going to do it he hasn't told me, and I don't probe any further because I'm happy the way I am. I couldn't wish for a better life than the one I have with Danny. But don't worry, Mam, I'll show him my support whatever he does, whether I agree with it or not.'

Ada smiled. 'Good gel, 'cos after my own experience I firmly believe that's the best thing a wife can do.'

Just then Danny appeared, followed by his mother. 'I believe we're all going out for a run?'

Maxie smiled tenderly at him. 'Seems we are.'

A couple of hours later, Danny expertly drew the motorbike and sidecar to a smooth halt outside their front door and jumped off to help Maxie alight.

Surprisingly, she had thoroughly enjoyed her ride, her arms wrapped tightly around her husband, the feel of the wind in her hair, and with a better view of her surroundings over his shoulder than the sidecar afforded her through its well-worn plastic windows. She inwardly scolded herself for letting fear get the better of her and not riding pillion before.

Danny was looking at her in concern. 'Were you all right, Maxie? Only I've always had a suspicion you weren't comfortable riding pillion, that's why

I've never suggested it before.'

So she hadn't fooled her husband like she thought she had! 'I did enjoy myself, yes, and wouldn't hesitate to do it again, but only because you're such a considerate driver,' she said sincerely.

With Maxie safely on the pavement, he proceeded to take the hood off the top of the sidecar and revealed the two beaming women inside.

'Thanks, Danny,' Ada said to him as he helped to heave her out of the front seat. 'That most certainly cleared my head. I feel human again after that. Could murder a cuppa, though.'

'That were grand, son,' his mother told him. 'It's hard to believe we've got such lovely countryside within a short distance of where we live. Such a pity lots more people haven't got their own transport, they never get to see and enjoy it. You ain't the only one who could murder a cuppa, though, Ada. Hurry and get the kettle on while Maxie and Danny help me out of here.'

As Ada bustled off Kathy continued, 'I can see why Ada insisted she sat up front. It's narrower in the back. Most undignified it's been for me, sitting all hunched up with me knees round me ears.' She gave a laugh. 'Good job me fancy man never saw me squashed in here with me dress round me waist or he'd have had every right to brand me a hussy!'

'Mother,' scolded Danny disapprovingly. 'You should have pulled your dress down. I hope no one saw you flashing your bloomers. And what do you mean by your "fancy man"?'

She gave a loud guffaw. 'As if I'd be sitting in

full view of the general public showing all me glory, yer daft beggar! Just like yer dad you are, he was gullible too. Give his last penny to the Queen he would have, if she'd told him she was broke. The only fancy man I ever had, or ever will have, was yer dad, God rest him.' Kathy's eyes twinkled in wicked amusement. 'He thought my bloomers rather fetching. Now, are you two gonna get me out of here or will you be bringing me dinner out to me?'

With Maxie supporting her under one armpit and Danny the other, they both heaved and tugged until eventually a chuckling Kathy was able to get her feet firmly on the sidecar floor to help push herself upwards. As arm-in-arm she finally waddled off with Maxie, hoping that by now the water in the kettle was well on its way to being boiled for her much-needed cuppa, Danny began to put the roof back on the sidecar and secure it in place.

Midway in his task he suddenly stopped and stared thoughtfully into space. His mother had thoroughly enjoyed her ride even though she'd joked about the tight fit. He knew there had been an element of truth behind her banter. His eyes ranged over the bullet-shaped container which was supposed to carry two passengers comfortably, providing they were not on the plump side as his mother and Ada were. Now his mother and Maxie's had reconciled their differences, in future there would be four to accommodate on their runs out on a Sunday afternoon. Anything more than a few miles would prove to be a trial to the sidecar passengers, and in bad weather

Maxie would suffer on the pillion. He had to buy a car, and soon. Getting the money for that was his priority now.

CHAPTER THIRTEEN

The next Thursday evening at approaching eight o'clock a very nervous Danny was standing at the bar of the Braunstone Gate public house, an untouched half-pint of lager shandy on the counter in front of him. He was very rarely in an environment such as this one without Maxie by his side – not that he would ever bring his beloved wife to such a seedy pub as this was – and felt lost without her company, as if part of him were missing. But then, he was only here in the first place because of Maxie, so in a sense she was with him.

Maxie had in fact accepted without question his excuse for a sudden uncharacteristic need to go out alone of an evening. Danny had claimed it was to offer his support and knowledge to a colleague at work who had bought himself an old motorbike and was fixing it up.

All he had in fact achieved in his last three nights on the prowl for a supplier was to learn what the inside of just about every pub in the area looked like, and the sort of clientele it attracted. All six had revealed virtually the same mix of characters. Single men and women meeting friends for a social drink, some obviously on the look out for a new romance; married men escaping their nagging spouses for a while; old men seeking company over a game of cards or dominoes; old women meeting their cronies for a gossip. And all the pubs had had their share of types who looked shifty to Danny. As naive as he might be in such matters, Danny had eventually realised that standing at the bar with an expectant look on his face would not bring him the sort of contact he was after. It certainly hadn't done so far. To date he'd been approached by three prostitutes touting for business; a poor old soul after the price of a pint whom he'd obliged; a scruffy, greasy-haired youth selling purple hearts at half a crown a pill; and several men his own age just wanting another to natter to while they supped their drinks. It was obvious to Danny by now that he needed to let it be known he was after a supplier of cut-price goods as it was very apparent one wasn't going to approach him. But to go up to anyone he suspected of being the sort he was seeking and be wrong could cause extreme offence, not to mention possible retaliation for his mistake.

The landlord of the run-down Braunstone Gate, a fat balding middle-aged man with an unhealthy pallor and cunning eyes, was eyeing his new customer with wary interest.

Standing before Danny, drying glasses using a filthy-looking cloth, he asked, 'First time?' His voice had the deep hoarseness of a heavy smoker's.

Danny looked at him quizzically. 'First time?'

'In the Braunny?'

'The Braunny? Oh, this pub. Yes, it is.'

'Who yer on the look out for then?'

'Sorry?'

'Come on, mate, it's obvious yer on the look

out for someone. Since yer've got here, all yer've done is check out my other customers.' Putting the grimy-looking if dry glass on a dusty shelf and flipping the cloth over his shoulder, he narrowed his eyes at Danny, a sneering glint in them. 'Copper, are yer? Think one of my regulars has done summat they shouldn't have, do yer?' His face turned even more ugly. 'Well, let me put yer straight, officer. I can alibi any of this lot in here now, and all my other regulars yet to come in, so whatever crime you're investigating, well, it definitely couldn't have bin any of my customers to blame 'cos they was all in here at the time, supping at my bar. Now, best you drink up and leave before any of this lot in here get wind of who you are and take matters into their own hands, if yer understand me?'

'I'm not a policeman. No, I'm a milkman,' Danny insisted, not liking the warning. He was so intent on putting the landlord straight he did not see that a man standing close by was listening intently to what he was saying. 'I work for the dairy on Gimson Road. My delivery round is the terraces between Hinckley Road, and Glenfield Road, from the Wingate Road crossroads to the start of King Richard's Road, and...'

'Okay, okay, son, I believe yer,' the landlord cut him short. 'Milkman, not a copper. My mistake. Yer are looking for someone, though, ain't yer?'

Danny looked at him thoughtfully. If anyone knew people with under-the-counter goods to sell it would be a pub landlord. 'Er ... well, yes, I am actually. I'm looking for someone I can buy stuff off to sell on, if you understand me?'

'Oh, I understand you all right.' He looked Danny over. 'You sure yer on the level? Only yer not the usual type that comes in here after what you are.'

'Oh, I am on the level, most definitely. I used to get my stuff through a mate who had his own contact only...'

'You're cutting him out 'cos yer sick of paying him his cut out of yer profits?' the landlord finished for him.

'No, it's not like that at all. My mate's gone away to try his luck in Blackpool, that's why I need to sort something out for myself.'

'Oh, I see. Come over here then,' he said to Danny, indicating a spot at the end of the bar that afforded them more privacy. When they were out of earshot of the others, the landlord leaned over the counter and in a low voice asked Danny, 'Got money, have you? Cash?'

'Oh, yes, plenty,' replied Danny, feeling excitement running through him. The landlord must be able to help him if he was asking these sorts of questions. 'And, yes, it's in cash.' He patted his jacket pocket. 'It's all in here.'

The landlord looked across the room at three men in a dimly lit corner, then turned his attention back to Danny. 'Well, it just might be your lucky night. The Guv's in. I wasn't expecting him as it's his birthday today and his wife's organised a big family party for him at the Stage in Oadby. Hang on here and I'll see if he's time to see yer. But don't get yer hopes up it'll be tonight, yer might have to come back.' Lifting up the counter flap, he passed through and headed

196

off across the room towards the dimly lit corner where the three men were sitting. Straining his eyes, Danny could just make out a burly bald middle-aged man with two younger thickset types flanking him. Moments later the landlord returned. 'Guv will give yer five minutes.'

'Oh, thank you,' enthused Danny. 'I'm very grateful to you, I really am.' His heart soared. Hopefully, oh, hopefully, he could strike a good deal with this man then tomorrow he'd have a pile of stuff to sell on his round and his plans would be back on track.

Hurrying across the room, he arrived at the table and sat down on a chair opposite the man the landlord had addressed. He looked pleasant enough to Danny, the kindly fatherly sort, and was very expensively dressed in a black dinner suit. 'Thank you for seeing me, Mr Guv. I appreciate you giving me your time, I really do,' Danny blurted out eagerly.

'Did the Guv'nor invite you to sit down?' one of the burly-looking men nastily enquired. Before Danny could answer he had risen, gone round the table and grabbed Danny by the scruff of his neck. He hauled him roughly to his feet and hissed meaningfully in his ear, 'Yer stand in the Guv's presence, got that?'

'Eh! Oh, I'm s–s–sorry,' stuttered Danny, reeling from the unexpectedness of what had just happened to him.

'You will be if yer don't show Guv respect.'

'All right, Frank, that'll do,' the huge man spoke up. 'I've got a birthday party I need to be at in half an hour and my wife won't be a happy woman if I show up late, so I haven't time for fun and games.' He fixed his eyes on Danny. 'Right, Bill's vouched for you and his word is good enough for me. What can I do for you – and make it quick?'

Danny gulped, beginning to worry just what he was getting himself into. 'Er ... well ... it's just that I'm wanting to buy some goods and the landlord seemed to think you could help me.'

'How much we talking?'

Danny stared at him blankly. Did he mean what amount of goods or how much money he had to spend?

'Money? Spondulicks?' Frank prompted. Turning to address his boss, he said, 'This man's thick, Guv.'

'I'll be the judge of that, thank you, Frank.'

'Yeah, sorry, Guv.'

Danny gulped. It was becoming rapidly apparent to him that Guv was not the kindly, fatherly sort at all.

'So how many pounds we talking?' Guv demanded again. Danny was feeling decidedly hot around the collar. 'Fif ... fifteen,' he falteringly responded.

Guv looked impressed. 'Oh, well, we can certainly do business. I've got all the top brands. Will you be wanting it all in fags, spirits, or a mixture of both?'

Cigarettes and spirits! Danny doubted the customers on his round would be wanting that sort of thing, but more importantly he himself didn't want to get involved in that trade. He gave a nervous cough. 'Well ... I ... er... was actually thinking more in the line of tea towels and other household goods, Mr Guv.'

The huge man looked at him incredulously for a second then he started to laugh. 'Oh, we've got a comedian, boys. He's not thick, Frank, he's funny! Not often I get a good laugh but I enjoyed that one. Give the keys of your van to Larry here and tell him where it's parked,' he told Danny, indicating with a nod of his head the man at the other side of him. 'He'll bring it back loaded up in about an hour. First, though, let's see your money.'

Danny was very aware that the items he was about to pay for were not bankrupt, fire-damaged or surplus stock. This stuff was illegal, and if he was caught with any of it he would face a lengthy prison sentence. He could definitely wave good-bye for good to Maxie if that happened as he could not expect her to live with the stigma of being married to a crook or to wait while he served his time. But these were the sort of men Danny was well aware you didn't mess about with. His heart thumped painfully and his legs started to tremble. He'd unwittingly got himself into this situation; the only way to get out un-harmed was to hand over his money. What he did with the goods afterwards, well, he'd decide that when he was away from here with all his body parts intact.

Thrusting his hand into the inside pocket of his jacket, he pulled out three five-pound notes and held them out to the Guv. 'Fifteen pounds. It's all there.'

Guv looked astonished for a moment, then his

face darkened thunderously. 'You on a fucking death wish or what?' he roared. 'I deal in hundreds, not singles. When you said fifteen, I took it you meant fifteen hundred. Fucking wasting my time! No one makes a monkey out of me, lad, not without deeply regretting it. Don't you know who I am?' He clicked his fingers at Frank. 'Get this idiot out of my sight, and make sure he understands not to bother me again.'

A surge of terror swamped Danny. The Guv'-nor was ordering Frank to maim him, maybe kill him. As Frank's huge hand clamped on to his shoulder, Danny cried out, 'No, please, listen to me! This has all been a mistake...'

'I said, get this joker out of my sight, Frank,' Guv cut in. 'Eh, and don't get blood on your suit. Remember, you're driving me to my party.' Then a questioning look crossed his face and he said, 'Hold on, Frank.' Glancing again at the petrified Danny, he said, 'It's me birthday, ain't it? Was this a set up? Yeah, it's got to be. No man in his right mind would do what you just have unless he'd lost the will to live. This is Roly Plant's doing. No ... no, it ain't. It's my wife that's behind this! She's paid you to do this, ain't she, as a birthday treat for me?' He gave a loud bellow of laughter. 'You should have said, lad! Bloody good, that, bloody good. She's always promised me she'd catch me out one day, and she sure has. Let him go, Frank.' Putting his hand in his pocket, he pulled out a wad of notes and peeled off a five-pound one which he poked inside the top pocket of Danny's jacket. 'I don't know how much my wife paid you, but here's a tip from me. It was

200

worth every penny. Now, joke's over, I've a party to get to.'

Danny didn't need another telling. Spinning on his heel, he fled from the pub and didn't stop running until he was round the corner where he stopped to collapse, panting, against a factory wall. Immediately he did so he almost leaped out of his skin when a hand unexpectedly clamped tight around his throat. He was yanked forwards then slammed forcibly back against the wall, so hard it knocked what breath he had left from his body.

A harsh voice said, 'So you're the bastard that's been nicking my customers.'

'What? I don't know what you're talking about,' Danny croaked, his eyes darting wildly.

'Fucking liar! I overheard yer in the pub, talking to the landlord. You're that milkman that delivers around the Hinckley Road. That's all my patch round there. I lost good business last week through you. Them all buying your goods meant they'd no money left to buy mine.'

'I ... I didn't know it was your patch. Honest, I didn't.'

'Well, now yer do. And if I get word you've sold even a matchstick on my patch again, you'll be very sorry, got that?'

'Yes, yes, I have,' Danny hoarsely agreed.

The grip around his throat was released but followed immediately by a hefty punch to his stomach that had Danny falling in agony to the ground.

'You better have 'cos next time I won't be so...'

Prostrate on the ground, despite the excruci-

201

ating pain he was in, Danny wondered why his assailant's voice had trailed off. It was then he heard the sound of footsteps running away and heavy plodding ones approaching accompanied by the patter of dog's feet. Next thing he knew a dog was sniffing at him and an old man was asking, 'You all right, son?'

Danny struggled to sit himself up. He smiled gratefully at the shabbily dressed individual addressing him. 'Yes, thank you, I'm fine.'

The elderly face looked unconvinced. 'Don't seem it ter me. That man I saw running away, had he just attacked you? Do you want me to get the bobbies?'

'No, no, I'm fine, honestly,' Danny insisted.

'Well, if yer sure, I'll leave yer to it.' He gave the dog's lead a tug and continued on his way.

Hunched in the gutter, a wretched Danny cradled his head despairingly in his hands. His venture into the world of buying and selling was over. He didn't need anyone else to tell him he was one lucky man, having narrowly escaped severe retribution from those hoodlum types in the pub, and further retribution from someone whose toes he had unwittingly stepped upon. He could have fared a lot worse than he had if that old man had not taken his dog for a walk. He was not equipped to handle the world he'd nearly found himself involved in, and there was no point him even thinking he was. Andy's contact, the man he'd been after, was still out there some-where, and others like him, but Danny being the man he was could end up dead trying to find him for himself. He couldn't abandon his goal, however, it was far too important to him. There had to be a way to give Maxie everything she deserved.

Awkwardly getting up, he brushed himself down as best as his still painful injuries would allow and made his way home.

Later that night as they were getting ready for bed Maxie looked across the bedroom at her husband. 'Is there anything the matter, Danny? Only since you got back tonight after helping your friend with his motorbike you've been rather quiet.'

Danny had been doing his best to change into his pyjamas discreetly as he knew he was bruised from the punch he'd received to his stomach and suspected by the painful tenderness he was experiencing that he was also injured on his back where he'd been slammed against the wall. The last thing he wanted was for Maxie to see his injuries and start asking him questions. He was telling her enough lies as it was without adding more.

Having successfully donned his pyjamas without her spotting anything amiss, he turned to face her as he folded up his trousers and laid them over the back of an old wicker chair an elderly neighbour had given them as a wedding present. 'Well, if I have it's only because you three women don't pause for breath long enough for me to get a word in.'

She laughed. 'Two women – I have the same trouble as you. I can't believe how much those two find to talk about! Oh, Danny, did you wince just then? Are you hurt?'

He had thought he'd managed to hide the stab of pain he'd received from his stomach as he climbed into bed. Obviously not well enough to fool Maxie's sharp eyes. 'Just a bit of a sore tum.' Which was true. 'I think I must have pulled a muscle when I was helping lift up the back end of the motorbike this evening so we could slip the wheel back on.'

Maxie didn't like the thought of Danny being in any kind of discomfort, however mild. 'I'll pop downstairs and fetch up the bottle of Helleman's lotion to rub on it. It might help ease it.'

'No need, Maxie, honest. It's just a twinge.' To change the subject he said, 'I'll pop around to our mams' houses tomorrow on my way home from work, see what progress has been made. I haven't been for a few days.'

She got into bed and snuggled up to him. 'It's funny, but although I can't wait to have our house back, I'll miss our mams. Now they're not bickering they're really good company.'

But Danny wasn't listening to her. His mind was fixed firmly on solving his money-making problem now the selling of goods was no longer an option for him.

CHAPTER FOURTEEN

Maxie placed a chunky drinking glass at the front of her desk containing a small posy of anemones she had bought from the local florist on the way back from her lunch break. Just a little gesture, costing a few pennies, but the deep purples and reds of the petals had been worth it. They added a welcoming touch to the reception room. It was medium-sized with white-painted walls and ceiling. Framed photographs of properties of all types hung at regular intervals around the walls; there were large shop-style windows at the front which allowed the daylight to stream through; and a seating area for clients to sit comfortably while they waited to see Matthew. His office was in a smaller room situated off reception, also painted white and with several filing cabinets lining the walls. Opposite his desk, above which framed originals of his university qualifications hung, were shelves crammed full of property manuals, law books relating to his trade and other paraphernalia. There was a small kitchen to the other side of the office which meant Maxie could provide beverages for clients and for themselves.

She felt it was an important part of her job to ensure that anyone who ventured in, either to browse through the properties they had on offer or to pursue a sale, should feel welcome and at ease on the premises. Matthew Holbrook had explained to her on her first morning that, after deciding on their partner in life, choosing where to live was the next most important decision people undertook. To him an estate agent's job was not only to help them decide on the right property for their needs, but also to make the process of buying it as smooth as possible. Until she had come here Maxie had had no idea how intricate the process of buying a property was or how many things could go wrong on the way.

A light began to flash on the small PBX switchboard on her desk, followed immediately by a ringing tone. Maxie sat down in her chair, picked up the receiver, flicked the relevant switch on the board and politely announced, 'Holbrook's Estate Agent, how may I help you? I'm sorry, Mr Holbrook is out on business at the moment but will return in about an hour. May I ask him to call you back? Yes, certainly I will. Thank you for calling Holbrook's, Mr Finch.' Replacing the receiver in its cradle, she picked up a pencil and wrote a neat message to give to Matthew when he returned, clipping it together with several others she'd taken for him while he'd been out. Despite having several clerical jobs to do she then leaned back in her chair, a contented smile on her face.

It was hard to believe that almost a month had passed since she had started her job as receptionist here. The time had flown by so quickly. Not that she wasn't missing her true vocation of working with children, but she was enjoying every minute of her new job. Matthew was proving to be a good boss to work for. He was a very easygoing man with a naturally pleasant disposition. No matter how clients behaved towards him, and some did display attitudes ranging from mild irritation to anger when matters were not proceeding as quickly as they felt they should be, Maxie had never seen him show anything but patience and understanding towards them. His attitude towards herself was exactly the same. The only thing that marred her contentment in her new role was that as yet Matthew had not mentioned to her whether he was happy with her work or not. She wasn't sure if this meant he was or he wasn't. Apart from several minor mistakes she'd made due to her ignorance of office work during her first couple of weeks, she herself felt she had given Matthew no major reason to regret employing her.

Matthew had been open for business not much longer than she herself had been working for him and still had a way to go before he was making the profit he hoped for, but so far he had concluded several successful sales. Those clients had been very happy with his services and, hopefully, as word spread and newspaper advertisements attracted notice, his gamble in opening in this area would prove to have paid off.

Her attention was alerted by the outer door opening. A young couple entered. They both wore expectant looks on their faces. Maxie smiled welcomingly at them as they approached her desk. 'Good afternoon. How may I help you?'

It was the young woman who responded. 'There's a house on Livingstone Street we're interested in. The board outside said you're handling the sale. We rent at the moment but have just been given notice to quit as we're in a slum clearance area. We was going to accept the council's offer of a flat but then my gran died. She left me some money and we've decided to use it as a deposit. The mortgage payments won't be much more than the rent we pay, we've checked. It'll be so exciting to own our own house! No one in my family ever has, nor in my husband's. The house we're after would be ideal for us. It's close to both our works and not far from both sets of parents. We've friends who live in the area too...'

Maxie knew the house they were showing an interest in as she made it her business to familiarise herself with the details of all the properties Matthew was handling. The house on Livingstone Street was a flat-fronted, three-bedroomed terrace – the third bedroom ideal for converting into a bathroom, should the buyers wish – with a decent-sized yard housing an attached outbuilding and toilet. It was in good structural condition for a house of its age, but needed a couple of damp patches attending to plus redecoration throughout. Matthew had typed up the details after his survey on special stencil paper – very slowly as he wasn't a trained typist – then it was Maxie's job to run copies off from it on the Banda machine.

'I'll fetch you a copy of the particulars, and I can make you an appointment to view it with Mr Holbrook tomorrow afternoon, if you wish?'

The couple looked at each other in dismay. 'Tomorrow?' the young woman said. 'Oh, but we were hoping to go and view it now. This house is the one we like the look of best and we both work all week. My husband,' she said, smiling proudly at him, 'managed to persuade his boss to give him the afternoon off today providing he works all Saturday afternoon to make up the time, and I'm on my lunch break. It's not possible to view in the evening as I'm a nurse and work until nine most nights. By the time we can arrange time off together again the house could have been sold.' She looked downcast. 'Oh, well, we're obviously not meant to have that particular one. We'll have to rush down to the agents in town who are handling house number two on our list and see if someone can show us around that.' She smiled at Maxie. 'Sorry to have bothered you.'

As Maxie looked helplessly on they turned to leave. She felt it was a shame to disappoint this young couple just because Matthew wasn't available to show them round. Then an idea struck her. Matthew might not be available but she was. She could show them round herself, couldn't she? In reality she would just be their chaperone while they ascertained whether the inside of the house suited them enough for them to take it further. All the keys for properties on their books were kept in a box on top of one of the filing cabinets in Matthew's office. Maxie could put the telephone on night service and pin a note to the outside door, telling possible callers that the staff were all out on business and would be back shortly, like she'd seen other businesses do. She wondered whether Matthew would be understanding about her decision to lock up for a short space of time while she obliged the couple, but she wasn't really being given time to ponder that as they were leaving. Maxie would just have to hope that he would.

Jumping up from her chair, she called over to them, 'Just a minute. I'll take you to view myself.'

Their delight at this news was readily apparent on their faces.

An hour and a half later Matthew returned. Stopping before her desk, he said to her, 'I'm sorry I've been away longer than I said I was going to be, Maxie, but the appointment took more time than I thought it was going to. Well worth the effort, though. Mrs Neville actually has four houses. She wants me to handle the rental side for all of them, not just the one as she led me to believe. Two have already got tenants but we should be able to fill the other two easily enough. The houses are in a good state and reasonable decorative order, much better than some I've seen landlords let out. This means, though, I'll have to see about employing a rent collector. Part-time to start, but hopefully as the rental side of the business builds we'll need someone full-time. Anyway, luckily I'm back with fifteen minutes to spare before my next appointment with Mr and Mrs Rose who want to pursue renting twenty-six Dunster Street.' He smiled warmly at her. 'How have things been here while I've been out?'

Mindful of what she had to tell him, she took a deep breath and said lightly, 'Oh, fine, Mr Holbrook. I've several messages for you to deal with.' She paused then added, 'And ... er ... well, I've something I need to talk to you about.'

A flash of concern crossed his face. 'Oh, I see. Well, why don't you come through to my office, bring the messages with you, and we can sit down there while you tell me what you need to.'

'Would you like me to bring you in a cup of tea?' she asked, knowing he must be ready for one.

He smiled gratefully at her. 'I'd appreciate that, thank you.' As he walked off to his office he called back, 'Like the flowers, Maxie. Nice touch that. In future I'll give you money out of petty cash for you to make it a regular thing.'

Having thanked her for the cup of tea, had a quick scan through the messages she had given him and ascertained they could wait to be dealt with until after he'd concluded his next appointment, Matthew leaned back in his chair and said to Maxie, 'I know you have something to discuss with me but first I should take this opportunity to ask you something myself. I've been putting this off, Maxie, I suppose because I might not like the answer but ... well, here goes. How are you enjoying your job? I have to say, I've not regretted for a minute asking you to come and work for me.'

'Oh, I really am enjoying what I do, Mr Holbrook, but I'm not sure whether you'll regret giving me a try out after I tell you what I have to.'

His handsome face fell. 'You're not thinking of leaving, are you, Maxie? Are you missing your nannying duties?'

'I can't say I don't miss having a child to look after, Mr Holbrook, but no, I wasn't thinking of leaving, not at all, but well, you might think it best I do when you hear what I did while you were out. I ... er ... shut up shop for an hour.' She shifted uncomfortably in her chair and took a deep breath before proceeding to explain why she had

211

done what she had.

When she had finished, he shook his head at her. 'Oh, Maxie, how can I fault you for using your initiative?'

Her face lit up in relief. 'So you're not angry with me, Mr Holbrook?'

He laughed. 'Not at all, Maxie. Just the opposite, in fact. Of course it's not ideal, leaving the office unmanned, but in the circumstances your decision was more than justified. Did you enjoy showing the couple around the house?'

'Oh, I did. I don't know whether it was presumptuous of me, but as we viewed each room I sort of got caught up in their ideas about what they'd do decoration wise and added a few suggestions of my own.'

'Well, you've impressed me even more, Maxie, because that's just what I would have done. It's called helping to sell the property to the customer. In my experience people welcome that sort of input. It helps open their minds to how the property could look with new wallpaper and a lick of paint, even alteration such as knocking certain walls down – providing, of course, those walls are not supporting ones.' He eyed her thoughtfully. 'It's just an idea, Maxie, and it depends on whether you agree, but when the business gets busier to the point where I need to employ more staff, I don't see why we can't make straightforward client viewings part of your job.'

She looked excited. 'Oh, really, Mr Holbrook? I like the sound of that, I really do.'

'Well, that's settled then. Did the clients give you any idea what they thought of the house on

Livingstone Street after they'd viewed it?'

'Oh, yes, Mr Holbrook, they did. They want to buy it! They've offered the asking price and I brought them back with me to the office and got them to fill in a form, the one you ask clients to fill in when they want to pursue a sale. I have it ready on my desk but I just wanted to tell you what I'd done before I gave it to you. I told them you would put their offer forward to the seller and let them know as soon as you could whether it had been accepted or not, then we could proceed from there. I hope I did right?'

'Well, if I was impressed with you before, now I'm ... amazed by you, Mrs Maws. Thank goodness I happened to be in that shop the same time as you were, that's all I can say. How does it feel to have made your first house sale?'

'My first sale? Oh, I have, haven't I? Actually, really good, Mr Holbrook.'

'When the sale goes through, and let's hope it goes smoothly for them as I think you have a good idea by now how many things can hinder the process, I shall make sure you get a bonus in your wages. It's the least I can do. Well done, Maxie.'

A proud glow filled her. Helping that young couple buy their first home was about as rewarding for Maxie as helping a child take its first steps.

The outside door was heard to open then.

She stood up. 'That'll be Mr and Mrs Rose for their appointment.'

'Please give me a minute to get their tenancy contract out of my briefcase before you show them through, Maxie,' Matthew said as he

213

reached down to the side of his desk. He put the case in front of him on the desk and clicked open the clasps. 'I took the blank forms home with me last night to type out there as I hadn't time during the day to do it yesterday.' He smiled at her and said jocularly, 'An estate agent's work is never done, especially those in business for themselves.' Then a terrible thought struck him and he said aghast, 'Oh, how stupid of me! I forgot to pick them up when I left home this morning. The forms are on the desk in my study. Oh, goodness, I'm not going to look very competent in front of these clients, am I, when we have to rearrange their appointment because of my stupid mistake?'

'Well, I could make them a drink while you go and fetch it,' she suggested. 'I could apologise for keeping them waiting, tell them you're having to finish some urgent paperwork for another client which has to go in the post tonight. You could slip out the back way.'

'That's a good idea, but better still, Maxie, by the time I've gone through all the tenancy rules and regulations with them and cleared up any points they might want to raise, to make sure they understand what's expected of them as tenants, you could be there and back with the forms and they'd be none the wiser. If anyone comes in while you're away or the telephone rings, I'll excuse myself and deal with it.' He fished in his pocket and pulled out a set of house keys which he handed to her. 'My wife didn't say she was going out today, but in case she has popped out to visit a friend or do some shopping you'll have to let yourself in. My study is the second door on the right.'

She felt honoured he trusted her enough to do this for him. Accepting the keys she said, 'I'll show through the Roses and be back as quick as I can.'

Matthew and his wife Melissa lived in a large four-bedroomed, pre-war semi on the affluent Sunnycroft Road, near the Western Park, a pleasant fifteen-minute stroll away from the row of shops that housed the agency. It could be achieved in seven minutes of dashing, she discovered. Arriving breathless at the front door, Maxie rapped purposefully on it using the ornate brass knocker. Receiving no reply after the second time she knocked, she let herself in and, mindful of the urgency of her task, didn't stop for a moment to appreciate the tastefully furnished entrance hall which was nearly as big as her own minute back room and tiny front parlour combined.

Following Matthew's directions, she went straight to the second door on the right and opened it. The room wasn't over-large but was light and airy due to French windows which opened out on to a large well-kept garden. Several boxes stacked by a wall told Maxie that Matthew still hadn't had time to unpack everything yet. She suspected all his time at the moment was filled with getting his business established and concentrating on his new wife. Going across to the desk, she immediately spotted the forms she had come to collect lying next to a portable Remington typewriter. Having had the foresight to bring with her a large brown envelope to protect them, she picked them up and slipped them inside. She had just turned to make her departure

215

when the unexpected sound of a key turning in the front door froze her for a moment. Obviously Mrs Holbrook had returned home from her outing. Maxie hoped she would not be shocked to see an unexpected intruder. She had almost reached the study door to announce her presence when voices reached her ears. Obviously Mrs Holbrook had bought a friend home with her. The friend, though, was a man. But it was what they were saying that stunned Maxie.

'You shouldn't have come back here, Derek. What if Matthew comes home for any reason?'

'So what if he does? You can tell him the truth then, can't you? That you married him on the rebound because you misconstrued a situation with your fiancé and another woman and were too stubborn to listen to reason.'

'I didn't misconstrue anything! You were kissing her, for God's sake.'

'*She* was kissing me, Mel. How many times do you want me to go over this? If you'd waited around long enough, you would have seen me push her away and explain to her that I was engaged to you and interested in no one else. She was drunk, Mel. It was a party we were at, after all. You never gave me the chance to explain. Just stormed off and refused to speak to me. When I telephoned, you wouldn't take my calls. I decided it was best I should go away while you cooled your heels. As you know, I was unhappy in my job and had been thinking of changing it for a while, so I gave in my notice and went.'

'Derek, normal people go to the country or the coast to get away for a few days. You went all the way to Australia! Can you imagine how I felt when I found out where you'd gone? I went to see your mother after you stopped calling me. I'd calmed down by then and realised how much I was missing you. I fully expected you to fall into my arms and beg my forgiveness for allowing that woman to molest you. When your mother told me she had no idea how long you'd gone for, or actually any idea when or if you were coming back, I had no choice but to believe our engagement was off. I can't tell you how distraught I was. When Rachael asked me to go and stay with her I jumped at the chance, if nothing else to get away from my mother who constantly told me that our break-up was all for the best because in her opinion you were all wrong for me. Anyway, Matthew was at the dinner party Rachael dragged me to and ... well, he was a welcome distraction that got out of hand. Before I knew it, I'd allowed myself to become Mrs Holbrook. But why Australia, Derek?'

'I've already told you, Mel – because my cousin had been asking us to visit him for long enough, and I thought with you being as you were, I'd be best by myself. I didn't intend staying long, just enough so that when I returned you'd have come to your senses. Then, out of the blue, I was offered a job and it was too good to turn down, Mel. The money I'm being paid ... well, it's a king's ransom compared to what I'd get in the same sort of job here.

'You should see the house I've bought for us! It's right on the beach. Imagine having your breakfast on the veranda every morning, watching the waves gently breaking. No more freezing snow or damp fog, the sun shines all the time there. It's paradise, Mel. The house itself and everything in it were bought with you in mind. A maid comes in daily to do all the work, so there's nothing for you to do unless you want to. You can live a life of leisure.

'As soon as I could get leave from my new job I took a flight back here, sure you'd have calmed down and be prepared to listen to my side of the story. I thought we'd get married by special licence and then I'd be taking you back with me. Can you imagine how I felt when I learned from your mother that you were married? And it gave her great pleasure to inform me, I could see. I begged her but she refused to tell me where you were living. I only managed to get the information out of your friend Nancy when I parked myself on her sofa and told her I wasn't leaving until she did. Anyway, I've gone over this same story so many times today, I'm getting fed up. Do you still love me or not?'

'Oh, I do, Derek, I do. I've been stupid and pig-headed, but it still doesn't change the fact that I'm married now, whether I want to be or not.'

'There is such a thing as divorce.'

'Don't you have to have a good reason to apply for one, Derek? Other women would find Matthew the perfect husband. He's kind, considerate, a complete gentleman, in fact. He's ploughed all his savings into buying this house for me, and now he's working all the hours he can to build up a profitable business to provide a good future for us. The only thing is ... he bores me! When I met him

218

I pretended to have all these things in common with him, but I haven't at all. Now I have to sit and listen to him going on about things I don't really care a jot about. But I can't see a judge finding a complaint of being bored enough to grant me a divorce, can you?'

'Then let him divorce you for desertion when you come with me to Australia. No one out there needs to know we're not married. You can un-officially call yourself Mrs Peterson, and when your divorce comes through we'll get married quietly. No one will ever be any the wiser.'

'Oh, we could, couldn't we? But what will I tell my mother? She'll never forgive me if I just walk out on Matthew for no good reason. My sister's already divorced and remarried and that nearly killed Mother. She really likes Matthew, says he's the best thing that's ever happened to me. He gets on so well with my father too. I can't bear the thought of neither of them speaking to me again over this. And what about Matthew? I might not love him or even care that much about him, but he deserves some sort of explanation from me. I need a little time to do this, Derek.'

'Mel, I was only granted seven days' leave. Nearly two days out of that was taken up travelling halfway around the world, then up here to Leicester, and the rest it's taken me to track you down. I have to fly back from Heathrow tomorrow or I can kiss goodbye to my job and the financial rewards it brings with it. If you don't come with me tonight then I know they'll all try and talk you out of doing this, especially your parents. I'm not flying halfway around the world a second time to come back and chase after you all over again.

'Look, while you're packing you can think of some good reason, I'm sure, to give your parents and Holbrook for what you're doing. Just write them a note each explaining, and either leave them here or post them from the airport, so you don't have to actually face everyone.'

'But I still need an excuse, Derek. My mother will never accept what I've done unless I have a good reason to give her such as well, Matthew treating me badly or having an affair or something like that which he isn't... Oh, yes, that's it! I've got the perfect excuse.'

'Great. Well, you'll have plenty of time to tell me all about it when we're on our way. I've to get back to my parents', pack my case and say my goodbyes to them. I'll meet you on platform two at London Road station no later than six-fifteen to catch the six-twenty-five to London.'

'I'll be there, Derek.'

From her frozen stance in the study, Maxie heard them kiss, then the front door open and shut and footsteps hurriedly ascend the stairs, followed not long after by the sound of something heavy being dragged along the floor which Maxie assumed was a trunk. She was still having trouble believing what she had overheard. Had Matthew's wife really married such a lovely man as he was on the rebound, not really loving him at all, her feelings belonging entirely to another? It was just so awful. How was she going to face him, knowing what she did? This news was going to devastate him, as from the way he always spoke of his wife, Maxie had no doubt he absolutely adored her. But she had to go back and face him now as he was urgently awaiting the documents she had come to collect.

Letting herself quietly out, she dashed back to the office.

As soon as she arrived Matthew hurried out of his own room to greet her. He had a worried expression on his face. 'Are you all right, Maxie? Only I was getting a little concerned you'd had an accident or something, you've been gone longer than I thought you'd be.'

'Oh, er … no, no, I'm fine, Mr Holbrook, thank you. It's just that the paperwork had somehow slipped down the back of your desk and it took me a while to find it,' she babbled, handing the envelope to him. It was an excuse she'd come up with during her race back because she could hardly tell him the truth about the delay.

'Well, I'd better get this signed and the clients sent on their way,' he said, hurrying back into his office.

As business intervened it was approaching five-thirty before Matthew finally managed to have another word with Maxie. Perching on the edge of her desk, he smiled warmly at her. 'Well, all in all it's been a successful day today, hasn't it? You securing an offer on the house in Livingstone Street, and me signing up those tenants for the flat on Fosse Road North and also securing the letting of Mrs Neville's four properties. Those people I've just shown out definitely want us to handle the sale of their house for them and I've arranged to do an inspection tomorrow. Thank you again for fetching those documents for me, I did appreciate it.'

Despite feeling inwardly terrible about what she knew was facing Matthew when he returned home tonight, Maxie managed to plant a smile on her face. 'It was no trouble really, Mr Holbrook. Oh, I haven't returned your house keys to you,' she said, picking up her handbag from under her desk and fishing inside for them. Just as she was holding them out for him to take, the outer door burst open and a woman charged in.

'I knew it!' she cried, marching across to stand before Maxie's desk, an angry accusing look on her otherwise attractive face. 'I suspected something was going on between you two by the way you're always singing your receptionist's praises, Matthew. Well, I no longer suspect, I have evidence now, don't I? What a cosy situation to find you both in.'

Matthew leaped off the desk and stood before her, an utterly bewildered expression on his face. 'Melissa, you have it all wrong. I'm just talking to Maxie in order to catch up on the day's events.'

'Oh, a likely story! I saw the way you were looking at each other. Any woman witnessing what I just have would draw the same conclusion.' She glared at the set of keys in Maxie's hand. 'Those are the keys to *our* house, Matthew. I don't wish to know why she's got them, I can draw my own conclusions about that too. You obviously found out somehow I was out for a while today and took the opportunity to have an assignation in our house. You went ahead, did you, to ready yourself for him?' she shot at Maxie.

222

Maxie was staring at her accuser, transfixed. So this was the idea Melissa had come up with to excuse herself to her parents for leaving Matthew and obtaining a divorce from him? Fabricate the story that he was having an affair with his employee. Maxie assumed she must have been waiting secretly outside, ready to seize her chance to do what she was now. The woman was despicable.

'But, Melissa...' Matthew pleaded.

She held up a hand in warning. 'I don't intend to stand here listening to you lie your way out of this. Our marriage is over, Matthew,' she announced resolutely. As she spun on her heel and marched towards the door, she called after her, 'You'll be hearing from my solicitor in due course.'

As the outer door closed behind her, Matthew stood staring after her, absolutely stunned. 'This ... but this is absurd. From us just having a chat, how on earth did Melissa draw the conclusion that we were... Oh, Maxie, I'm so sorry she would even think that you would do what she accused you of. Please accept my sincere apologies. I must go after her and sort this mistake out. The keys to lock up are on my desk and...'

'It's all right, Mr Holbrook. Just get off, I'll deal with matters here,' she urged him, despite the fact she knew he was wasting his time.

An hour later Ada and Kathy sat staring at her agog across the dining table.

'Oh, that poor man,' said Ada. 'That is so terrible of his wife, publicly telling him she was leaving.'

'It certainly is. Just wicked of her,' agreed Kathy. 'From what you've told us about him, Mr

Holbrook sounds a lovely man.'

While relaying her story Maxie had left out the part where Melissa Holbrook had accused Maxie and her own husband of having an affair as she didn't want to upset either Danny or their respective mothers with such blatant lies. 'He is,' she said now. 'There's plenty of women would cherish a man like him.'

From his armchair, Danny lowered the newspaper he was reading and flashed an extremely anxious look over at Maxie. He still feared that another man would come along and pursue her, someone better paid and more able to provide a comfortable life for her. He knew Maxie was fond of her boss by the way she spoke of him but had always assured himself that nothing more than an easy working relationship would ever transpire between them due to Mr Holbrook's married status. But the fact that Maxie's boss was about to become an unmarried man put a different aspect on matters for Danny. Holbrook would become just the sort he dreaded Maxie having close contact with.

'Don't you think it might be best if you left your job and got yourself another, Maxie?' he blurted out.

She stared at him, bemused. 'Why on earth would you suggest that, Danny?'

'Well, I ... just ... thought it might be a good idea, that's all.'

'Typical man you are, making suggestions yer can't substantiate,' said his mother dryly. 'There's no good reason why Maxie should leave a job she enjoys just 'cos the boss's wife has left him.'

Danny felt the need for some fresh air. This news and its possible consequences were deeply worrying for him. He could not sit here and listen to Maxie and their respective mothers sympathising with this man's plight when Danny suspected that, in his misery, that man could turn to his own wife for sympathy. He knew Maxie well enough to realise she would give it him, and then Matthew Holbrook would see for himself the many good qualities she possessed and try to lure her away.

Bunching up the newspaper, he thrust it down at the side of his chair and got up. 'I'm just off for a walk,' he announced.

They all looked after him as he left.

'That's good of him, leaving us to talk over this problem in peace,' said Ada.

'He's a thoughtful lad, is my son,' said Kathy.

Maxie smiled warmly. 'Yes, he is, and I'm so lucky to have him. I wouldn't swap him for anyone else.'

If Danny had waited around long enough to hear his wife's very complimentary comments about him then maybe his obsessional worries about the fragility of their future together would instantly have been vanquished. As it was, though, he was halfway down the yard out of earshot.

CHAPTER FIFTEEN

For the umpteenth time that morning, Maxie looked at her watch. It was nine-thirty. Matthew was obviously not coming in again today. The last time she had seen him was three days ago when he'd rushed off after his wife, and she'd heard not one word from him since. She was now extremely worried, not only for his welfare after such a devastating occurrence but as to how much longer she could continue to keep their clients at bay with excuses for Matthew's absence. Added to this was the deeply worrying fact that the agency was losing potential business as he wasn't there to secure it and Maxie lacked the necessary experience. She feared that if he didn't return to work in the very near future, he'd have no business to return to.

As matters stood it seemed to her she had no choice but to pay a visit to her boss at home to receive guidance from him as to how she should be proceeding in his absence.

The warm early morning showed great promise of turning into a glorious summer's day. Normally Maxie would have taken delight in what was going on around her as she journeyed along, but today her mind was too preoccupied with what she might find when she reached her destination.

As soon as she had brought the ornate brass knocker down against its plate the door burst open and Matthew appeared on the threshold, an eager look on his face which was quickly replaced by one of huge disappointment when he recognised the caller. Maxie's heart sank at the sight of him. Matthew was normally immaculate but she had seen down and outs look better turned out than he was at the moment. It was very apparent he had not washed or shaved since the last time she had seen him. Or slept either.

'Oh, Maxie, it's you,' he uttered. 'I thought... I was hoping...' His voice trailed off.

It was obvious to her he'd been hoping it was his wife returning. Did this mean, then, that he had no idea the woman who was the centre of everything for him was now on the other side of the world, in the arms of another man? Forcing a smile, Maxie said to him, 'I'm so sorry to bother you, Mr Holbrook, but I was very worried about you as I haven't heard anything from you since ... well, the other afternoon, and...'

He flashed a wan smile at her, scraping a hand through his already tousled hair. 'It's unforgivable of me, I know, to abandon you like I have. Look, I'll try and get in tomorrow or the next day ... as soon as I can anyway. I can't leave here until...You can keep things going meantime, can't you, Maxie?'

She wanted to say she would continue to do her best but her conscience wouldn't allow her to leave this man by himself in the state he was in. He was a relative stranger to Leicester, had no family of his own here, and Maxie guessed had not yet had time or opportunity to forge any close friendships to fall back on during his time of need. In the circumstances she felt she herself was more than likely the closest he had to a friend in his new home town, and if anyone needed the support of a good friend just now it was Matthew Holbrook.

'Have you eaten recently, Mr Holbrook?'

Her question threw him. 'Pardon?'

'No, I didn't think you had.' Without further ado, she pushed past him into the entrance hall. 'Kitchen this way?' she asked, pointing to a doorway at the back.

He was looking at her blankly. 'Look, I'm...'

She cut him short. 'Why don't you go and sit down while I see what I can rustle up for you?' Without waiting for a response from him, she entered the kitchen and took a look around. It was immaculate, not a dirty plate in the sink, not a crumb lingering on the modern work surfaces. The only evidence of recent use was that the kettle on the stove was hot and the teapot still warm, so at least she knew Matthew had been making cups of tea to help sustain him over the last three days. Going into the walk-in pantry, she was gratified to find it was well-stocked with tins and packets of dried food and the remains of a loaf. She gave it a squeeze, glad to find it hadn't yet gone stale thanks to the coolness of the larder. Selecting a tin of Campbell's condensed mushroom soup and the remains of the loaf, she made her way back into the main kitchen where, scouting around, she soon found a tin opener, saucepan and butter in a dish in the fridge.

His scratch meal now ready on a tray, she went in search of him. She found him sitting in an armchair in the lounge, staring blankly into space. He looked startled when she put the tray on his lap, having obviously forgotten she was there.

Sitting herself down in the armchair opposite, she coaxed him, 'Eat up, Mr Holbrook, before the soup gets cold.'

He looked at it for several long moments before saying, 'I appreciate very much your preparing this for me, Maxie, but I couldn't eat anything at the moment.'

'Well, it doesn't seem to me that you have since I last saw you, Mr Holbrook, and if you don't eat something soon you're going to make yourself very ill. Just a couple of spoonfuls is better than nothing. Please, Mr Holbrook.'

He stared down at the dish of soup again for a couple of moments before reluctantly picking up the spoon. Then something seemed to occur to him. Flashing an expectant look at Maxie, he asked, 'Melissa hasn't telephoned me at work, has she?'

Maxie shook her head. 'You've had many telephone calls, Mr Holbrook, but none from Mrs Holbrook.'

His shoulders sagged despairingly as he laid his spoon back down on the tray at the side of the soup bowl and looking over at Maxie, utterly bewildered.

'I can't understand this at all. Melissa's had time to reason this out, she must know now that this is purely a mistake blown out of all proportion. She knows how much I love her, the sort of man I am, and that I would never betray her in any way. I need to talk to her but I don't know where she is. I've tried all her friends that I know but haven't contacted her parents yet as what do I tell them? Besides, I know her mother would let me know out of courtesy if she was with them, whether Melissa wanted her to or not, as I get on well with her parents.

'I've called all the hotels asking if anyone is staying with them using the name of Holbrook or her maiden name of Grantley, the hospitals too, but nothing. But someone doesn't just disappear like this, leaving no trace, do they? She's got to be somewhere...'

Deeply bewildered, he gave a helpless shrug. 'Maxie, her leaving doesn't make any sense to me. I know she stormed off saying that our marriage was over but I was only a minute or so behind when I rushed after her to sort out the mistake. I didn't catch up with her on the way home, and when I arrived she wasn't here. I haven't left the house since so I know she hasn't come back at all, or telephoned either. Then, when I eventually checked, I found all her clothes and personal belongings had gone and her luggage was missing. Well, that must mean Melissa had packed before she came down to the agency and accused us, mustn't it? That she had all her belongings already with her? But until she comes back or contacts me this is all driving me mad, trying to work it out.'

Maxie was fighting her own inner turmoil. It wasn't really her place to tell her boss that his wife had left him for another man and was across the other side of the world with him by now, enjoying their new life together. But then, it wouldn't be fair of her to leave him in ignorance until a letter of explanation finally arrived from his wife. That could take a long while, depending on when she decided to write it and how long the post from Australia took to get here, during which time his state of mind and health were obviously suffering.

Taking a deep breath, she said, 'Mr Holbrook, I wasn't exactly truthful with you over my reason for taking so long fetching those documents the other day. I did find them exactly where you said they'd be, but as I was about to leave the study your wife returned from her outing and she had a man with her. I overheard them talking in the entrance hall.

'This man was her fiancé before she met you, Mr Holbrook, and they'd had a misunderstanding, it seems. Anyway, she was very angry with him and wouldn't take his calls or answer the door to him, so while she cooled off he decided to go off to Australia to visit his cousin. When Mrs Holbrook stopped hearing from him, she thought their engagement was over and was very upset. Meanwhile she'd met you and ... well ... you got married. Her fiancé – Derek, his name is – didn't know she'd got married and while he was out in Australia landed himself a really good job. He bought a house for them both and last week flew back here, hoping she'd calmed down by now and got over their misunderstanding. He thought they'd get married by special licence and then he'd take her back to Australia with him.'

Matthew's already ashen pallor turned a

ghostly grey. 'And that's where she's gone, back to Australia with this man?'

Maxie nodded. 'Since you haven't heard any word from her, I can only assume she has, Mr Holbrook. I heard her saying she was worried about not having an excuse to give her parents for leaving you, that she couldn't bear the thought of them never forgiving her for what she was planning to do.'

'So Melissa concocted the one about us having an affair? And she already had her belongings packed ready to go when she came to the agency?'

Maxie nodded.

His whole body sagged, face filling with hurt. 'Melissa never loved me at all, did she? That look on her face when we said her vows was just an act. She only married me on the rebound because she thought the man she really loved had abandoned her. I thought I knew her... I can't believe she could deceive me like this. When she asked me to marry her, I was so bowled over that the woman of my dreams wanted me as her husband, just beside myself that she didn't want to wait for us to become man and wife, I was happy to go along with whatever she wanted. She told me she'd been engaged previously but that it was all over as she'd realised her fiancé wasn't for her after all.

'I gave up everything for her, left my family and friends behind and a good job, to make a new life with her here. How could she do this to me when she knows how much I love her and would do anything for her?' His head dropped and he wrung his hands. 'I thought we were so happy,' he choked. 'But she could never have cared for

232

me at all if she could just throw me aside the moment this other man came back. And the way she did it... Surely I deserved at least being told to my face? Surely I deserved that at least?'

Maxie's heart went out to this man. His wife's callous, selfish actions had broken his heart, and Maxie could tell this wasn't something he was going to recover from easily, if ever in fact. She wondered what he'd do now she'd informed him of the truth.

He lifted his head and his bleak eyes met hers. 'Maxie, would you mind leaving me on my own? I don't know quite where I go from here, I need to think.'

'No, of course I don't, Mr Holbrook.' She picked up her handbag and rose to go, then looked at him worriedly. 'Look, I'm so very sorry I had to be the one to tell you all this.'

He flashed a desolate smile. 'Pity my wife never bothered to and saved you the trouble! I do appreciate how difficult this must have been for you.'

It was a very subdued Maxie who made her way back to the office to keep things operating there as best she could until Matthew returned.

CHAPTER SIXTEEN

Later that afternoon it was a very fed up Danny who left the premises of Drake and Son, builders. Having spotted a newly inserted card in the newsagent's window on his way home from the dairy, advertising a vacancy for a part-time labourer from two until six, he'd rushed straight round to apply for it, only to be told the job had gone an hour before.

After his experience at the Braunstone public house, Danny's hope of earning large amounts of money in a hurry in order to shower Maxie with luxuries had been forsaken. He'd given himself a good talking to, reluctantly revised his ambitions to just having a bit of spare money each week to hand over to Maxie for safekeeping. That way she would know he was honouring his promise to her, and as the weeks went by the sum would increase until she had enough to buy something useful for the house. Now, after yet another setback in a long line, his drive to assert himself as a man of worth was foundering, made worse by the fact he had convinced himself that it was only a matter of time before Matthew Holbrook started to make a move towards taking Maxie away. But, regardless, he would not let her go without putting up a fight and still hoped to find that elusive means of making extra money.

His route home from Drake's was taking him

down streets he didn't usually frequent. He happened upon a car scrapyard in a most unlikely location, sandwiched between two seemingly derelict factories amid terraces of empty houses. The council was clearing this area as part of the last stages of their urban renewal programme. Taken by surprise, he stopped for a moment to gaze through the rusting fence at the mounds of assorted vehicles piled haphazardly inside, all in varying stages of disintegration, while they waited their eventual fate in the large crusher Danny could hear in operation somewhere across the yard. As he stared through the fence he was wondering despondently if he would ever be in a position to afford a car at all, judging by the way things were going for him, even the price of a scrap one from here.

Inside the yard, leaning casually against a dilapidated two-berth caravan propped up on house bricks that served as his office, a scruffily dressed man, face and hands blackened by engrained engine oil and grease, stood smoking a roll-up while watching Danny closely.

'We've probably got the part yer after, mate,' he called over. 'Got most things, for most makes and models, or if not summat that would do as good. Yer won't find it standing out there so why don't yer come inside and have a look? Yer won't find no other scrappy in Leicester cheaper than us.'

'Oh, er ... I'm not looking for parts,' Danny called back to him.

The scrap dealer righted himself and sauntered out of the yard to join Danny. 'Well, car to do up then?' He gave a bellow of laughter. 'As yer can see, we've got plenty of those. Maybe it's a van yer after? Got a 1955 Austin A40 come in just yesterday that only needs a few quid spent on it to sort it out. Built ter last them vans are, and done up it'd do you for another few years. I can let you have it for a tenner. Come and have a look at it.'

Before Danny could stop him the man had grabbed hold of his arm and was herding him inside and across the yard to stand before a rusting brown van.

Danny was no expert but even he could tell that this twelve-year-old vehicle would be lucky to last the journey out of the yard and that it needed more than a few pounds spent on it to bring it up to scratch. He was just about to tell the man he was not interested in purchasing anything from the yard when his eyes fell on another vehicle close by. It was an ice cream van and the reason it had caught Danny's attention was because he felt sure it was the same one that until very recently had cruised the streets around where he lived, selling its wares. Maxie and he had often bought ice cream from it on a Saturday night to enjoy while relaxing before the television.

The beady-eyed dealer, ever on the look out for a sale, had not failed to miss Danny's interest in the recent acquisition. 'Good van that,' he said, walking across to it and clearly expecting Danny to follow. 'Bloke who owned it made such a fortune he's retired to ... er ... well, some place abroad I've never heard of.'

The words *made a fortune* registered like a thunderbolt on Danny. Scooting after the scrap dealer he said, 'Made a fortune? Really?'

'That's right, mate. So well off he could retire at fifty, and couldn't be bothered to sell on a perfectly good van but handed it over to me for scrap instead.' He banged his hand on the side of the van. 'Bodywork sound as a bell.'

Excitement was building within Danny and his mind began to whirl. Could this van, with its amateurishly painted pink-and-blue sign reading 'Don's Ices' on the panel above the front window, really hold the key to his future fortune? Was this the miracle he'd been praying for? Unlike the Austin A40 the dealer had just tried to palm off on him, this van did appear to be in good condition apart from small spots of rust on the wheel arches, but that sort of thing was easily remedied.

'So, er ... how does it all work?' he asked the dealer. 'I mean, what keeps the freezer box for the ice cream and lollies cold?'

'Simple, mate. Don't need to be Einstein to work that out. It's powered either by a separate generator at the side of the freezer, which you use when the motor isn't in use – overnight and such like, if you've any stock left over that needs keeping. When the engine's turning over, yer just flick a switch on the generator which cuts out its motor and the engine battery takes over. Yer have to remember to keep the generator topped up with oil same as yer do yer petrol tank. But the generator doesn't use much fuel, according to its last owner.'

Danny's whirling thoughts geared up a level. He'd never seen an ice cream van yet that didn't have a queue of people waiting to buy from it;

even in the depths of winter kids still demanded their ice cream or lollies. All you had to do was park the van in the middle of a street, play the tune announcing your presence over its speaker, and those who wanted your wares all came running. Buying the ice cream and lollies to sell posed him a problem but someone somewhere must supply all the other vans operating in Leicester, it was just a case of finding out who that supplier was.

In his mind's eye he saw himself handing loaded cone after cone, bowl after bowl, lolly after lolly, through the sliding glass window to the never-ending queue waiting to be served by him. The tin holding his money was overspilling, he could actually hear the tinkling of the coins as they landed on the van floor. Then he saw not one van but two, then a whole fleet of them being operated by people he employed, his name above each one: *Danny's Ices. Stop me and buy one.* Wouldn't Maxie be proud of her husband then, the once lowly milkman now the proprietor of a fleet of ice cream vans?

His thoughts were interrupted by the dealer asking, 'Look, are yer interested or not 'cos I've things to be getting on with?'

'Oh, yes, I might be,' he confirmed. 'Yes, I might well be. Is it possible to have a test run? Just up the street and back.'

'Er ... yeah, sure. The keys are in the ignition, help yerself.'

Seated in the driver's seat, Danny checked the gear was in neutral and turned the key in the ignition. Apart from a clicking sound nothing happened. Danny tried again. He got the same response.

The dealer poked his head inside the driver's window and checked the dials on the panel. 'Oh, damn, the battery's as flat as a pancake. I'll have to recharge it overnight.'

It was a disappointed Danny who climbed out to rejoin him. 'I'll come back tomorrow then, shall I, as soon as I finish my shift about two? Would that be convenient?'

'Depends what I've got on at the time. I have ter warn yer, though, it'll more than likely be too late by then as there's another bloke who's desperate to have it, yer see. He's coming back tomorrow morning with the cash. I can see yer really keen on it so if yer don't want to lose out then you'd better make yer decision now. First to pay me for it, gets it. I ain't fussy who that is. These vans don't come up very often, and rarely in this one's condition. Could be months or more before I get another in. Yer see 'em advertised in the paper sometimes but at prices way above what I'm asking for this one.'

'Oh, I see. As a matter of interest, how much are you asking?'

The scrap dealer sucked in his cheeks and eyed Danny closely. 'Make me an offer, and if it's more than the other bloke did you can have it, as long as we settle the deal tonight.'

Danny hadn't a clue how much the van was worth and was afraid of making a fool of himself. Whatever the other man had offered for it, Danny only had twenty-one pounds. As far as he knew the dealer might be thinking more like double or treble that. Even if he was lucky and the dealer only wanted that amount for it, he'd need money left over to buy his first load of stock. His heart sank as his dream of owning a fleet of ice cream vans faded away to join the one he'd had about selling knockdown goods to the housewives on his round.

Very subdued, he said, 'Well, I think I ought to tell you that I can only go to sixteen quid at the most. I'd need the rest to buy stock, so if it's more than that you're wanting for it or the other chap has offered you more than I can, I'll have to give it a miss.'

The dealer spat on his hand and held it out to Danny. 'Deal!'

'Really? You mean it? It's mine for sixteen pounds?'

'I've just said so, haven't I? I'm not a greedy man, and as I told yer, I got it for nothing so I'm happy with that.'

Thankfully, always on the look out for opportunities, Danny carried with him the profit he'd made via his association with Andy plus the five pounds he'd been tipped by the Governor. Was he glad now that he'd had the foresight to do that!

Grasping the dealer's proffered hand, he shook it vigorously.

'Well, if we settle up now, I'll have the van delivered to your address tomorrow morning,' the dealer promised him.

'Oh, will you? That's decent of you.'

'Just part of the service. Shall we retire to my office then?' said the man, heading off towards the rusting caravan over by the entrance.

A short while later, jauntily continuing on his way home, Danny decided that he would not tell Maxie or their mothers about his new venture but would surprise them with it when the van was delivered to their front door by the car dealer tomorrow after the battery had been charged. He was so excited! He couldn't wait to see their faces, especially the pride on Maxie's.

CHAPTER SEVENTEEN

The next morning, wondering if Matthew would show up today or whether the devastating blow she had delivered him yesterday would have distracted him, Maxie arrived prompt at the shop at eight-twenty to open up for business and was surprised to find him waiting for her, back to his normal well-groomed self. Standing next to him was a smartly suited, distinguished-looking middle-aged man. Despite being early for work she felt guilty that she had kept not only Matthew but a potential client waiting for her to arrive and open up.

'Morning, Maxie,' Matthew said to her breezily, none of the trauma he'd suffered recently apparent at all. 'I forgot I couldn't open up myself as you have my keys, haven't you? Anyway, this is Mr Inchman,' he introduced her to the stranger. Turning to the other man, he said, 'This is Maxina Maws, my very able receptionist.'

'Good morning. Very pleased to meet you, Mr Inchman,' she said to him politely.

'Likewise, Mrs Maws,' he responded cordially. Looking at Matthew he said meaningfully, 'Shall we get down to it then as we've a lot to get through?'

Maxie realised that in his way Mr Inchman was prompting her to hurry up and unlock the outer door. She already had the keys in her hand which she respectfully handed to Matthew so he could take charge.

As soon as they were inside, Matthew showed Mr Inchman into his office then came back out to address Maxie. 'Can you please make sure we aren't disturbed? And any telephone calls for me, please take a message. When Mr Inchman leaves, I'd like a private word with you.'

She thoughtfully watched him stride off into his office and close the door after him. She wondered what that private word could possibly be about?

It was getting on for three hours before they emerged, during which time Maxie had had to deal with a steady trickle of people coming in to enquire about properties to rent or buy, or wanting to make viewing arrangements or see Matthew about progress on matters already in hand. Some of them weren't pleased to learn he wasn't available and they would have to call back. She was deliberating as to whether she should take a tray of tea through then worried that such an interruption might not be appreciated. She decided Matthew would buzz her on the intercom should he require refreshments. Thankfully the office was now devoid of clients, the telephone silent, and Maxie, glad of the lull, was in the process of catching up with her clerical duties when the door to Matthew's office opened and he and Mr Inchman emerged.

'Well, best of luck, Holbrook. I'll be in touch,' Mr Inchman said.

Firmly shaking his hand, Matthew responded, 'I appreciate what you're doing.'

After seeing him out, Matthew flicked the snib on the outer door and flipped over the sign from Open to Closed. Making his way back to Maxie's desk, he said to her, 'Would you like to come through, Maxie?'

His manner was giving nothing away. Still with no clue what he wanted to speak to her about, she obediently followed him inside his office.

She sat down on a chair before his desk while he perched on the edge. His face took on an apologetic look. 'Maxie, there's no easy way to tell you this but I've decided to go back to Oxford.' The effect this news had had on her was very apparent to him but regardless he continued. 'With matters between Melissa and myself as they are, well, there's nothing keeping me here in Leicester.' His face clouded over sadly. 'You know what high hopes I had for my business, Maxie, but my heart's gone out of it now – I'm sure you can appreciate why. If the man at the helm doesn't care a jot whether the business succeeds or not, then it hasn't much hope, has it? Mr Inchman is a partner in an estate agent's based in town. I'm passing all my business over to him so none of our clients will suffer: they're a firm with a good reputation. Mr Inchman is also handling the sale of my own house for me. I did try to persuade him to give you a job as part of our negotiations but they're fully staffed at the moment.' He paused and looked at her regretfully. 'I am very sorry things aren't turning out as I led you to believe they would, Maxie.'

She smiled wanly at him. 'You don't have to explain to me, Mr Holbrook, I fully understand your need to go home.'

He gave a deep sigh. 'I was prepared to make this city my home, Maxie. It's not a bad place, far from it, with some good people in it.' She knew he meant herself by that and a warm glow filled her. 'I have no doubt you'll have no trouble finding yourself another job, and of course I will give you a good reference. I know nannying is your true forte, but you really should consider a career in an office. Based on your performance with me, I've no doubt that you'd go far. Meanwhile I would ask that you see out the remainder of the week with me, to help me pack up the office and tie up any loose ends. As a token of my appreciation for all your efforts and the fact it might take you a couple of weeks to get yourself settled in new employment, I will be giving you a month's wages on top of this week's.'

'That's very generous of you, Mr Holbrook,' Maxie said, choking back tears. She would miss working for this lovely man who in her opinion did not at all deserve what his wife had done to him.

She knew her family would be upset when she broke the news she was unemployed again because they all knew how much she'd enjoyed her new job. Arriving home, though, and seeing what was parked outside her house, she decided there were other matters to deal with first.

Entering the back room, she found Danny, Ada and Kathy sitting at the dining table engrossed in conversation. None of them had heard her come in and they all jumped when she crossly announced, 'What a cheek some people have got!

Have you seen what's been abandoned outside our front door? An old ice cream van. I suppose it'll be down to us to get it towed away to the scrapyard or it'll be there for ever, blotting the landscape.'

Danny had been desperate for Maxie to arrive home so he could tell her his exciting news. Jumping up from his chair to join her, he announced, 'No, Maxie, you've got it wrong...'

Before he could finish, Ada piped up, 'Yer sure have, gel. That van ain't been abandoned, it's Danny's new venture. He's going to be an okey-pokey bloke!'

'That's right, he is,' chipped in Kathy. 'He's just been telling us all about it. He's been dying for you to get home so he could tell you too.'

Maxie was amazed. 'You've given up your job with the dairy?'

Before Danny could utter a word, Ada said, 'No, he ain't, lovey. He's doing the okey-pokeying in the evenings and Sat'day afternoon, to earn some extra for yer both.' She looked at Maxie meaningfully. 'Very commendable of him, ain't it, ducky, wanting to make yer life better for yer and prepared to work hard to do it?'

'Yes, it most certainly is,' agreed Kathy. 'Yer landed lucky when yer landed my son, Maxie.'

'And he was lucky when he landed her,' Ada reminded Kathy.

'Well, 'course, that goes without saying,' Kathy replied sincerely.

Maxie was well aware of the hidden meaning in her mother's words. She was reminding Maxie to show her every faith in her husband now or suffer

246

the same fate Ada herself had with Maxie's father. She had been under the impression that Danny had forgotten his promise to make more money for them. Obviously she had been wrong.

Maxie had to admit that on the surface his idea had potential. She had never seen an ice cream van that didn't have a queue of people waiting to be served from it, whatever the weather, and the operators must make money from them or they wouldn't do it, would they? But although she couldn't fault him for wanting to do his best by his family, Maxie worried that doing this on top of his full-time job could prove as exhausting for Danny as his short-lived experience as a petrol pump attendant had. Her husband's health was far more important to her than a new suite or china dinner service to replace their everyday pot one. But her mother was right. As Danny's wife it was up to her to show her support for him. All she could do was keep her eyes peeled and check this new venture was not having an adverse effect on his wellbeing. Should she decide it was, then she'd deal with the situation in the best way she could and without damaging his pride in any way.

Maxie smiled at him proudly. 'Well, my husband a businessman. Isn't that something?'

The look on her face had sent his heart soaring. 'The man who had it before me made a fortune from it and was able to retire early,' Danny eagerly told her. 'It's the same van that delivered round here, so how much better could it be than having a ready-made round on my own door-step? All I've got to do is find out who supplies bulk ice cream and lollies and I'm away.'

'And the strawberry and chocolate sauce to go on top,' prompted Kathy. 'I like a squish of that on my okey-pokey. Oh, and them sprinkle things ... hundreds and thousands. And chopped nuts.'

'Oh, you're just a big kid, you are,' Ada jocularly chided her. 'My favourites are them 99s,' she said, licking her lips. 'It's a shame to me yer only get one flake and not two. Maxie likes strawberry Mivvis best, don't yer, ducky, so yer'd better get some of them as well, Danny. Oh, and do we get ours free, being's we're family?'

Before Danny could answer any of her questions, Kathy interjected, 'Knowing what a soft touch my son is, he'll be giving most of the kids in the street free cones.' She wagged a warning finger at him. 'Better start as you mean to go on, son. No free samples for anyone including family or yer'll never make a bean.'

'Yes, yer mam's right,' said Ada. 'We'll pay for what we have the same as everyone else.' Then she added as an afterthought, 'But if there's any going spare at the end of the day that's not worth keeping, you can always shove it our way.'

'I've always wanted to work on an ice cream van,' said Kathy wistfully.

Ada looked at her in surprise. 'Have yer really?'

'Oh, yes. It looks fun.' She gave a chuckle. 'Those customers yer like the look of, yer can stick a bit of extra ice cream on their cone or in their bowls, and those that yer don't yer can give less to. It's always fascinated me, watching the okey-pokeys making up them sundaes with all the bits of fruit and nuts and other stuff on. I've

248

always longed to have a go at it meself.'

'Well, yer can then now, can't yer?' said Ada. 'In fact, we both can. Me and yer mam will be yer servers, Danny, while you do the driving. We'll do it for love not money, won't we, Kathy?'

'Oh, most certainly,' she enthused. 'So when's our first outing then?'

Maxie pressed her lips together, hiding a smile. Whether Danny welcomed their mothers' help with the serving was immaterial, he would never hurt their feelings by turning them down.

'Well ... er ... as soon as I get the supplies, I suppose,' he replied thoughtfully.

'Well, sooner yer get cracking, the sooner you'll be raking it in,' said Ada. 'Tomorrow night then. When yer finish yer shift tomorrow yer can take the motorbike and sidecar down to the whole-saler's. As for finding a supplier, well, you can always ask in a local shop, casual like, where they get their supplies from, can't yer? In the meantime, when me and Kathy get home from work we'll give the van a good going over to make sure it's spotless. Won't we, Kathy?'

'Absolutely, Ada. And I'll have both our best pinnies ready for the off as soon as we've had our dinner.'

A thought suddenly struck Maxie then and she looked at Danny quizzically. 'As a matter of interest, where have yer got the money from to buy the van and your supplies?'

He looked blankly at her. It had completely slipped his mind that they would want to know the answer to this obvious question. Before the encounter with Terry that had set him on his

249

quest he'd always been scrupulously truthful with Maxie. For her to learn now he'd been keeping secrets from her regarding his extra money-making activities, and the fact that he'd been carrying twenty-one pounds in his pocket she had no idea about for the last couple of weeks, could cause her to start distrusting him. Regardless of how well he provided for her in the future, if she lost her trust in him, he could lose her that way. It was worth evading a truthful explanation of how he'd acquired the money to avoid that. But twenty-one pounds was a lot of money to explain away convincingly.

Unable to look Maxie in the eye as he did not want to see her face when she realised he'd been lying to her, Danny lowered his head and studied his feet. Swallowing hard, he took a deep breath and began, 'Well … er … you see…'

Before he could say another word, his mother matter-of-factly interjected, 'What's up with yer, son? Being a saver is n'ote to be ashamed of. That's how yer got the money together, ain't it? A few pennies here, the odd thru'penny bit, sixpence, shilling … well, it all adds up come time, don't it? When he was little he always had a piggy bank, and me and his dad always encouraged him to save half of anything he got to spend. Our teaching him to watch his pennies like this has paid off, ain't it? He wouldn't have had the money to buy this van otherwise and be about to do what he is, would he?'

Danny could have hugged the life out of his mother for solving his problem for him, despite the fact they all knew, though it must have slipped their minds and he hoped it stayed that way, that every penny of his savings had gone towards the wedding seven months ago, and on the wages he earned it was impossible for him to have saved up this much since then. He looked at Maxie, hoping vehemently the guilt he was feeling for his own lack of honesty wasn't apparent. 'I didn't tell you what I've been doing as I wanted to surprise you with it one day, give it all to you to buy something nice. To be honest, until I checked I didn't realise I had so much.'

An overwhelming rush of love for her husband filled her. Their tight budget didn't leave much room for saving, and he didn't have very much to himself each week for incidentals, so for him to have put some of that by, bit by bit, so he could surprise her one day... She felt awful that she hadn't managed to do something nice for him out of the housekeeping. 'Oh, Danny,' she uttered, choked. She took a deep breath and, smiling brightly at them all, said, 'I'd better get a pen and paper so we can make a list of the supplies we need and make sure we don't forget anything.'

Until they started making their list none of them had realised how many different items the vans carried in order to fulfil their customers' requirements. Three different-sized cones; small for children, large for adults, and double for those extravagant ones who wanted two different flavours of ice cream together. Wafers for making ice cream sandwiches. Chocolate flakes for the 99s. Catering-sized tubs of ice cream in vanilla, strawberry, chocolate and Neapolitan flavours, and scoops to serve them with. Small cardboard pots to hold the sundaes, and catering-sized tins of fruit cocktail to make them, along with sauces, chopped nuts and hundreds and thousands. Plus choc ices, Mivvis – which were ice cream on a stick covered by a layer of flavoured ice – and Orange Maid lollies.

As the list grew Danny worried he'd not have enough money to pay for it all, and also had no idea what quantities to purchase. Ada pointed out that it was better to play cautious and sell out of stock sooner than have lots left over. Kathy said she suspected the customers would be more of a trickle than a wave, until word spread a van was operating in their area again, and by that time he'd have a better idea of how much stock he needed to carry for each trip out.

As they were toasting the success of Danny's new venture with a cup of tea, a thought suddenly struck Ada. She looked at her daughter remorsefully. 'We've all sorted ourselves out with jobs but we forgot about you, ducky, didn't we?'

Maxie smiled. 'Oh, don't worry about me while you're out enjoying yourselves, I can find plenty to occupy me.' Like having some peace and quiet to study the Vacancies column again. She had decided not to spoil Danny's euphoria tonight by breaking the news about her own work situation. Due to Matthew's generosity she had a month to find herself another job.

CHAPTER EIGHTEEN

The warm evening was perfect for selling exactly the type of confectionery the van carried. Filled with a mixture of exhilaration and trepidation, Danny settled himself into the driver's seat, which wasn't that comfortable though he was far too preoccupied with other matters to be unduly concerned. Behind him in the body of the van, scrubbed clean by them both that afternoon, were Ada and Kathy, both wearing their best pinnies, ice cream scoops at the ready, champing at the bit to serve the customers. Maxie was on the pavement, ready to give them a cheery wave off.

As Danny's eyes settled on his wife, his reason for doing all this was sharply brought to mind. Tonight had to go well for him, it just had to.

'Come on then, son, let's get going,' his mother called to him.

'Yeah, come on,' echoed Ada. 'What are we waiting for?' Then she noticed a small boy peering up at her through the sliding glass window. 'Oh, hold on a minute, I do believe we've our first customer.'

Danny's heart soared. He hadn't even sounded the chimes announcing he was open for business yet and customers were coming. This business was going to prove everything he'd hoped it would, he just knew it.

'Oh, Ada, can I serve the lad? Please let me,' Kathy begged.

Ada desperately wanted to be the one to have the honour but her renewed friendship with Kathy overrode that. 'Oh, go on then,' she said generously, standing aside to allow her friend space.

'Thanks, Ada.' Leaning through the window, she asked the young boy, 'What's yer pleasure, sonny?'

He wanted a thru'penny cone and as she handed it down to him, the generous helping of strawberry sauce she had poured over it dripping down the sides, Kathy said to him, 'You enjoy that, sonny. And being's yer our first customer, you can have it free. Oi! But make sure yer tell all yer mates and yer parents it's the best ice cream yer ever had and that we'll be here same time every night, all right?'

Wide-eyed, he nodded. 'Oh, yes, missus. I will, I will! Ta ever so much.'

As Kathy righted herself, Ada nudged her in her ribs. 'I thought we wasn't going to be giving away?'

Kathy pointed over at the boy, now standing across the street surrounded by a group of friends. They watched as the youngsters dispersed in different directions. 'They've all gone to beg their parents for money for their own okey-pokies.'

Ada grinned. 'You ain't just a pretty face, are yer, gel? I see the method in yer madness.'

Just then front doors began opening and people of all ages and sizes started hurrying over. It took twenty minutes to satisfy the queue, and as each person was sent happily on their way they were asked to tell their friends and neighbours and each responded that they certainly would.

As the last customer departed, watched by a smiling Danny from his driver's seat, he asked, 'How did we do?'

Ada winked meaningfully at Kathy before she responded sarkily, 'Well, unless you've suddenly gone blind and deaf, lad, you could see for yerself how well we did. If we get half that response round the other streets we do tonight then I reckon we'll sell out and need to carry twice as much stock tomorrow.'

'And you sitting there with that Cheshire cat grin on yer face won't sell any more tonight,' said Kathy. 'So get that engine revved up and get a move on to our next port of call.'

Danny had been conscious that Maxie had been standing by the entry, watching proceedings with great interest. He turned to look at her and she gave him a big smile, a cheery wave, and mouthed the words, 'I'll have a cup of tea ready for you when you all get back,' before she turned and disappeared down the passage. He called to their mothers, 'Right, hang on to your hats! Oh, and remember to flick the switch on the generator when I've got the engine going.' Checking that the gear stick was in neutral, he turned the ignition key and frowned when nothing but a clicking sound was forthcoming. He tried again but got the same result. He inwardly groaned. It was just the same as last night when he had asked the dealer for a trial run. Obviously he had been wrong in his diagnosis of the problem. The battery didn't need recharging, it needed replacing as while it had been sitting here after being delivered it had lost its charge again.

'Got trouble, mate?'

He turned to see who was addressing him through the passenger side window and recognised Eric Barlow who lived several doors down and worked as a mechanic at a local garage.

'I think the battery's gone, Eric.'

'Might not, might just be a loose connection. I'll take a gander,' he offered.

Danny smiled gratefully at him. 'Oh, thanks, I appreciate that.

Ada's and Kathy's heads poked through from the back. 'What's the hold up?' Kathy asked him.

'Hopefully just a loose connection on the battery. Eric Barlow is being good enough to take a look.'

'Oh, well, while he is I'm just going to take advantage and pay a visit to the privy,' said Ada.

'Oh, good idea, me too,' said Kathy.

They both squeezed their way by the driver's seat to get out of the passenger door, then hurried off down the entry.

The bonnet of the van now up, Eric called out, 'The problem isn't with yer battery, Dan, it's with yer engine.'

His heart sank. 'The engine? Oh, no, it's not serious, is it, Eric?'

Slamming down the bonnet, Eric reappeared at the window. ''Bout as serious as it gets, mate. You ain't got one.'

Danny looked at him, stupefied. 'What do you mean, I haven't got one? I must have or how else did the dealer drive it round here this morning?'

Eric frowned. 'Just as a matter of interest, did you get this van from the scrap dealer's in the slum area by the canal?'

'Yes, I did. Why?'

He ruefully shook his head. 'I thought I recognised it! It's Sonny Beal's old van. I used to look after it for him until time came it wanted that much doing to it, it wasn't worth spending the money it'd cost and he decided to scrap it. He'd made his money and been thinking of retiring for a while, so that's what he did. The scrappy obviously had the engine removed and sold on for possible reconditioning or stripping of the good parts. Didn't you look under the bonnet before you bought it?'

A mortally embarrassed Danny shook his head. 'The dealer told me it was a good runner, Eric.'

'Then he certainly saw you coming, didn't he, mate? It's an old trick that, telling a potential buyer the battery is flat when he asks to have a trial run. Told you he'd charge it up overnight then deliver the vehicle to your address the next day, I suppose? He's towed it round here, and when you go and complain to him about the missing engine all he'll say is that it had one when he left it outside your door so what happened after that is n'ote to do with him. Well, Dan mate, you ain't the first to be screwed this way and yer won't be the last. Best thing I can advise you to do is have it towed down to another scrappy and hope he'll give you a couple of quid for its scrap value. Put the rest of your losses down to experience.

'Oh, and I'd keep an eye on the generator as

that was on its last legs too as I remember. Eh, and don't worry, yer secret's safe with me. If it's any consolation I had a similar thing done to me when I bought my first car to do up when I was an apprentice. I remember how stupid I felt when I realised I'd been had. Well, best be off. I'm playing snooker down the hall with the lads tonight and they'll be thinking I ain't coming.'

Through the windscreen Danny blindly watched Eric stride off down the street. Then his whole body slumped back against the seat as a flood of despair filled him. How pathetic he was to have allowed himself to be suckered by a devious scrap dealer! His mother was right about him, he was gullible, blindly believing anything anyone told him. Because he wouldn't dream of ever deceiving anyone else out of their hard-earned money, or out of anything in fact, he never stopped to consider they wouldn't hesitate to do it to him. This trait in his character had cost Danny dearly. Not only had he lost all his hard-earned spare cash, his family were now about to have it confirmed to them just what a loser he actually was as there was no other way to explain away the lack of an engine than to tell them the truth. After this, how could he expect any of them, especially Maxie, to look on him with even a modicum of respect?

A surge of sheer panic flooded through him as he saw his mother, mother-in-law and wife coming out of the entry and heading across to him.

Ada pulled open the passenger side door and they all looked at him expectantly.

'Eric sort the problem, did he? We're ready for the off?' his mother asked.

Danny gulped. 'Well, no, he didn't. It wasn't the battery connection after all.'

'What was it then?' Ada put in.

He gulped again. 'The engine. I haven't got one, you see.'

They all looked bemused.

'What do you mean, you haven't got one?' asked Maxie.

'Oh, my God! Yer mean, someone's stole it while we was all out this morning at work?' Kathy exclaimed.

'Never!' cried Ada. 'Is nothing sacred any more? Of all the low-down, rotten things to do. Well, I hope whoever stole it gets n'ote but trouble from it.'

Maxie was looking at him sympathetically. 'Oh, Danny, I'm so sorry.'

He couldn't believe it. Once again he'd been saved from mortal humiliation in front of the people who meant so much to him, by his own mother jumping to the wrong conclusion. But thank God for him she had!

'Yer don't think it was a spiteful act by someone jealous of the fact that our Danny was doing something for himself they hadn't had the brains to think of, do yer?' mused Ada, her face screwed up angrily.

'I can't think of anyone round here who would stoop so low,' said Maxie.

'Yeah, well, you wouldn't, me darling, 'cos you're like my son and see the good in everyone,' said Kathy. 'But some bloody-minded bugger

259

brazenly stole it, that's for sure.'

'Maybe someone saw who did this,' suggested Maxie. 'We should ask around.'

'That's a good idea,' agreed Ada. 'You and Danny take this side of the street and me and Kathy will do the other.' She looked inside the van at him. 'I can see what a shock this is to yer, lad, but sitting there like a stuffed dummy won't get that engine back. So come on, chop-chop.'

He felt terribly guilty for not putting them all right as to the truth of the matter, but overriding this was sweet relief at being spared the humiliation of his own stupidity becoming known.

A while later they all congregated back by the van.

'Well, no one saw 'ote on our side of the street,' said Kathy. 'Always the same, in't it? When yer don't want neighbours to spy on what yer up to, there they all are, curtains twitching. And the one time you hope they have, they've either all gone out or were getting on with their own business.' She looked at Maxie and Danny knowingly. 'I can see by yer faces that you got the same result we did.'

'Well, that's that idea up the spout,' said Ada sadly. 'And it was such a good idea too, Danny.' Giving him a sympathetic look, she patted. his arm affectionately. 'I can't imagine how gutted you must feel.'

'No, me neither,' said his mother, looking at him regretfully. 'I'm gutted for meself too as I was really enjoying being an okey-pokey. What will you do with the van now?'

'Well, buying another engine is out of the

question. I've no alternative but to scrap it, I suppose,' said Danny quietly.

'And don't forget about all the stock we've got. We can still sell that to the folks in this street until it's all gone. The generator will keep that frozen as long as we keep checking it's topped up with oil,' said Ada.

Maxie looked bothered. 'But I can't hear the generator running.'

Ada cocked her head towards the van. 'Neither can I.'

'Nor me,' said Kathy.

Neither could Danny. Kicking up his heels, he rushed around to the driver's door, clambering through into the back to stare down at the idle generator. He'd only filled it up with oil several hours ago, just before he'd gone off in the motorbike to fetch the stock. It couldn't have run out so soon. Leaning over, he pushed the starter button. It gave out nothing more than a splutter. He tried again and again but couldn't get it to fire. Turning to face the three women who were all peering at him questioningly from the driver's doorway, the look on his face gave them their answer.

Ada gave a deep sigh. As he rejoined them she said, 'Well, all I can say, lovey, is that you being an okey-pokey wasn't meant to be.'

'Don't look like it,' said Kathy. 'And such a shame, after all the hard work and your hopes for it too.'

Maxie was too choked with disappointment for her husband to be able to say anything.

A while later Danny sat on the closed toilet seat with his head in his hands. Back inside the house the three women in his life were sitting round the dining table commiserating with him over the failed venture which they thought was due to the callousness of another's actions, not to his own stupidity. All of the remaining stock had been shared around the neighbours, much to their surprise and delight free of charge, and it only remained for Danny to arrange to have the van towed to a scrapyard. This would put an end to any entrepreneurial visions he harboured as now he had nothing left with which to fund any opportunity that might arise in the future.

He gave a deep, demoralised sigh. He'd a few pennies less than ten shillings in his pocket, the proceeds from the sale of the ice creams and lollies to immediate neighbours before they'd given the rest of the stock away. At least five shillings of that was profit just on those few sales. He didn't want to think what he could have been sitting here with now, and what future profits and life-changing benefits would have resulted, if only he hadn't been stupid enough to be taken in by the devious scrap dealer. He couldn't really blame the man, though, as it was he himself who had fallen for the easy patter. All he was left with was the major problem of providing Maxie with a better life. Matthew Holbrook was possibly waiting in the shadows to do just that once he'd got over the trauma of his wife's betrayal of him. Put against a man like Holbrook, what chance did Danny himself have? He might as well give up now and wait for the inevitable to happen.

He envisioned a future without Maxie in it, sitting alone by the fire with her chair empty opposite his, left with only memories of her. To Danny there was no other woman like Maxie, none he could ever love as much, or who would suit him the way she did. A relationship with another woman was out of the question; it wouldn't be fair to her since he'd be unable to give her the love she deserved. Soon that bleak vision of his future would become reality. In Danny's troubled mind it was just a matter of time.

He jumped as a tap came on the privy door and a voice said, 'It's me, Danny. I was worried about you as you'd been gone so long. Are you all right?'

No, he was not all right. Far from it. How, though, could he tell Maxie he was suffering from the devastation of losing her? All that was open to him was to put on a brave face and enjoy what was left of their marriage. 'I'm fine,' he said lightly. 'I'll be out in a minute.'

Maxie knew he wasn't being truthful with her, but how could he be all right after the terrible blow he'd received? Opportunities to improve their lives like Danny had seized only came along once in a lifetime for people like them. Quite rightly he must be feeling very bitter and resentful towards the mindless person who'd put paid to his venture. She just felt honoured that he had wanted to make a success of the ice cream van for her benefit. She was a lucky woman to have such a thoughtful husband who wanted only the best for her. She so wished she could wave a magic wand to take away the pain of his disappointment, but all she could do was show him how proud she was of him, and hope her love would support him through this disappointing time.

CHAPTER NINETEEN

At four-thirty the following Friday everything that needed to be done had been, and Maxie was now standing in the empty premises waiting for Matthew to return from an errand. Why he should have needed to do anything now was beyond her. He had given her her wages plus the extra month's money he had promised her along with her P45 and reference. She had yet to read it but he had left her in no doubt that it was a very favourable one. There were no clients to see to as the 'Closed for Business' sign had been in place since he had told her he was going back to Oxford, and thereafter their time had been spent endeavouring to ensure all the clients' work in progress was handed over to Mr Inchman, with meticulous notes attached so he could easily carry on where Matthew had left off. There were no telephone calls to deal with either as the switch-board had been disconnected and reclaimed earlier that afternoon by the GPO engineer. There wasn't even a chair to sit on as Matthew had sold all the office furniture and equipment to a local firm who dealt with such matters.

As she stared around the empty space a surge of great sadness enveloped Maxie. She had been happy working here for the ever amiable Matthew Holbrook, and despite wondering what lay in store for her work wise now, was more concerned about him than herself. She sincerely hoped that once back in his home town amongst his family and friends he would be able to put his failed marriage behind him and find happiness again.

Just then he entered the office, carrying the biggest bouquet of flowers she had ever seen. He strode across to join her. 'Thank you for waiting, Maxie.' He placed the bouquet in her arms. 'These are for you.'

'For me?'

He smiled warmly at her. 'I couldn't have got through this week without your support, Maxie. You've been a treasure and kept me going. The flowers are a token of my appreciation.'

Blinking back tears, she said, 'You needn't have, Mr Holbrook. I've enjoyed every minute working for you.' She knew she was about to cry and thought it best she left before she made a complete fool of herself. 'Well, I expect you'll be wanting to get home to finish your last-minute jobs before the journey to Oxford tomorrow. All the best, Mr Holbrook.'

As she hurried towards the door, he called after her, 'And to you, Maxie.'

When she walked through the back door a short while later, Danny looked over at her from the sink where he was peeling potatoes for their evening meal and his eyes settled on the bouquet. 'Wow! I've never seen such a huge bunch of flowers. Who are they for?' he asked.

She smiled at him as she laid them gently on the kitchen table, then went over and gave him a kiss on his cheek. 'For me from Matthew.'

He felt the blood drain from his face. His fear

that this man could steal his wife away was proving to be true – and it had happened quicker than he'd expected. His legs felt weak and he clasped the edge of the sink for support. 'Oh, that was nice of him. Any ... er ... reason he would buy you flowers?'

'Yes, there is a reason, Danny.' Maxie looked shamefaced. 'I've something to tell you. I should have done it before but you were so upset about what happened over the van I didn't want to add to your worry. Are our mothers in? I might as well tell you all at the same time.'

Shivers of trepidation were running up and down his spine. 'Er ... no, they're not. I'm not sure where they are but they weren't in when I came back from work and haven't been in since.'

'Oh, well, never mind. I'll have to go over it again when they do come back. Come and sit down and I'll tell you all about it.'

Like a lamb to the slaughter he followed Maxie through to the dining room where they sat down on chairs facing each other.

Danny watched as Maxie clasped her hands and took a deep breath. 'Danny, Matthew is going back home to Oxford.'

He held his breath. He was in no doubt her next words would be to tell him that she was going too.

'So that means I'm out of a job again.'

His jaw dropped. He was wondering if he'd heard her right.

She mistook his stunned expression for worry as to what this would mean for their financial position.

'It's all right, Danny, Mr Holbrook has generously paid me a month's wages on top of this week's so we have some breathing space for me to find work. The flowers were a thank you to me for helping him get through this week after what his wife did to him. I only did what I would have done for anyone, really. But it was very kind of him to buy them for me to show his appreciation, wasn't it, Danny?'

An enormous flood of relief that Matthew Holbrook was being removed as a contender for his wife's affections left Danny virtually speechless. 'Mmm, it was,' he mumbled.

'I really enjoyed the work I did for him,' Maxie chattered on. 'He's given me a good reference but I know I haven't enough experience behind me to be taken on by another firm as a receptionist, and I have so missed having a child to look after that I'm going to try and get a nannying position again before I resort to anything else.' She paused then and looked at him, ashamed. 'I didn't intend to keep this from you, Danny, but I've already explained why I did. You aren't angry with me for not telling you as soon as it happened like I normally would, are you?'

He didn't reply. The back door opened and then Ada and Kathy bustled in.

Maxie looked bemused by the dishevelled state of both of them. 'Goodness me!' she exclaimed. 'You two look like you've just come off a building site.'

'As good as,' said Kathy, plonking herself down on the chair next to Danny's with Ada doing likewise next to Maxie. 'Any tea going?' she hopefully asked.

'Make mine an urnful,' said Ada.

'I'll mash you both a cup as soon as you tell me what you've been up to?' Maxie commanded.

'You tell 'em, Ada, I ain't got the energy,' Kathy wearily requested her.

Running a hand through her dust-filled hair and down the side of her grimy face, Ada leaned heavily on the table and said, 'I expect you'll both be glad to hear that you're getting rid of us both and yer house back to yerselves. When we came home from work today we found the landlord's agent waiting to tell us the repairs to our houses are now finished and we can move back in. 'Course, we wasted no time in going to make an inspection, and "building site" don't describe what we found, does it, Kathy?'

She shook her head. 'More like bomb site! Muck and dust everywhere. We set to straight away and we've given my house a good going over. We're doing Ada's tomorrow and reckon we'll be all ready to move back in on Sunday.'

Maxie smiled affectionately at them both. 'We'll miss having you here. It was hard to begin with, considering how you two were with each other, but since you've made up, well, it's been a pleasure having you both. I expect you'll be glad to get back to your own four walls, though. I'll come with you tomorrow and give you a hand with the cleaning.'

They both smiled tiredly at her. 'Thanks, lovey.'

'And I'll join you as soon as I finish work,' promised Danny.

'And don't forget what else we've to tell 'em,'

said Kathy to Ada.

'Oh, and what's that?' asked Danny.

'Shall I do the honours or do you want to, Kathy?'

'It's your turn, dear friend, as you let me serve the first ice cream.'

Ada drew a deep breath. 'Well, me and Kathy have decided that it's silly paying out rent on two houses when we get on so well so we're going to move in together. Trouble is, we can't choose which one of the houses it's to be, so we think you should decide for us by tossing a coin.'

'Oh, that's a wonderful idea,' enthused Maxie. 'You'll be good company for each other.'

Danny fished in his pocket and pulled out a penny. 'Okay, heads or tails?' he said, spinning it up in the air and expertly catching it, slapping his hand over the coin so neither of them could see which side it had landed on.

It was Kathy who won the toss and the rest of the evening was spent pleasantly deciding what furniture they would keep and what they would sell off for as much as they could to a second-hand shop, the profits to be used towards material for new curtains and cushion covers which Maxie offered to run up for them on her sewing machine.

As she nestled snugly in Danny's arms later that night, she said to him, 'I meant what I said: I will miss our mams living with us, but it will be nice to have the house back to ourselves, won't it?'

'Yes, it will,' he said, and meant to treasure every moment he'd got left with the love of his life before she realised she could do far better for herself than a common milkman.

CHAPTER TWENTY

Maxie couldn't believe her eyes the next Monday evening as she scanned the Vacancies column in the *Leicester Mercury*. 'Oh, Danny!' she exclaimed excitedly. 'Can you believe there's two jobs for nannies that would suit me?'

Receiving no response, she looked across at him. He was sitting in his armchair seemingly staring at the television screen although she had a feeling he wasn't watching it. She frowned to see him like that. Something wasn't right with her husband. He still didn't seem to have recovered from his shock over the theft of the engine and all it had entailed and was very down, regardless of how hard she had tried to play down the situation and chivvy him up. She supposed he just needed time as people did when they were recovering from a huge disappointment. Thankfully, though, since that fateful night he hadn't once mentioned his desire to give her a lavish lifestyle, or seemed to be doing anything about obtaining it for her. She hoped this meant he had now come to his senses and realised what her real priorities were.

'Danny, did you hear me?' she prompted him.

He'd been miles away, envisioning what might have been if just one of his ventures into making extra money had proved successful. One thing was for certain, he wouldn't be sitting here now, feeling like the weight of the world was resting on his shoulders, while he waited for the dreadful moment when Maxie told him their marriage was over.

He turned and looked across at her apologetically. 'No, sorry, Maxie, I didn't.'

She repeated what she'd said, adding, 'I shall write after them both tonight. Keep your fingers crossed I'm at least granted interviews. Oh, Danny, it would be great if I got one of them as that would mean we could use the extra money Mr Holbrook paid me for a trip somewhere, couldn't we?'

She hadn't meant her comment as a slight to him in any way, and before hearing Terry's damning words Danny wouldn't have taken it as such, but now he did and a wave of inadequacy washed over him. It was he who should be paying for that sort of thing, using money he had brought in, not the other way around. 'Mmm,' he mouthed absently.

Daphne Greencote smiled broadly at Maxie when she opened the front door to her large rambling house the following Thursday afternoon. In her early-thirties, she was a tall, slim woman with a cascade of thick straight blonde hair that flowed down to the middle of her back. She was dressed fashionably in hippy-style clothes, an ankle-length, brightly patterned peasant skirt and smocked, short-sleeved top. She wore sandals on her feet, and reminded Maxie very much of Nina, from the popular married duo Nina and Frederick for whose folksy style Maxie had a fondness.

'Ah, you must be Maxina. I've been so looking

271

forward to meeting you. Welcome to the mad house! I'm Daphne Greencote but please call me Daffy,' she said, standing aside to allow Maxie entry.

She led the way down a wide passageway, cluttered with furniture and children's toys which they constantly had to step over, and on into a huge farm-style kitchen which overlooked an overgrown garden and several outbuildings. Dominating the kitchen was a huge well-worn pine table, big enough to seat at least ten people. At the moment it was occupied by two young girls, the eldest no older than four, both absorbed in painting colourful pictures. A jamjar of water had tipped over, its contents dripping down on to the Cardinal-polished tiled floor which no one seemed to have noticed. Work surfaces were cluttered with kitchen paraphernalia, piles of folded washing and an assortment of discarded family belongings. A delicious aroma rose from a huge pan simmering away on the Aga. A fat collie dog lay snoozing on the floor beside it. The room seemed to welcome her in and envelop her. Maxie felt immediately at home here.

Daphne addressed her daughters. 'Girls, this is Mrs Maws who's come to see if she'd like to be your nanny. Say hello.'

Both girls had cherubic faces, blonde curly hair and bright blue eyes. They lifted their heads and smiled at her. 'Hello, Mrs Maws,' they said in unison, then immediately returned to working on their latest creations.

'They both take after me and their father, we're the creative type,' Daphne told Maxie. 'I'm a designer of children's clothes, have my studio in the attic. At the moment I'm working on a collection for a company who sell to Marks and Spencer, Liberty, Seifridges and such like, so I'm...'

A loud voice rent the air: 'Daffy, where's that new palette I bought yesterday?'

She tutted. 'That's my husband Brian. He's an art teacher at Guthlaxton College. He's working on scenery for the school play in his studio in the garden.' She went across to the stable-style back door and shouted through the open top, 'Where you put it! On the table by the door, under the bag holding the new pots of paint.' Coming back to join Maxie, she gave a rueful shake of her head. 'Why is it men don't look under anything? Would you like coffee or tea?'

'Tea would be nice, please.'

Just then a man entered by the back door. He was as tall and slim as his wife and had a shaggy mop of thick brown hair and a bushy full beard; he wore baggy brown corduroy trousers and a loose granddad-collared shirt, both smeared with paint. 'Daffy, I've looked where you said but I still can't find...' He stopped mid-sentence as he realised his wife had someone with her. 'Oh, you must be the new nanny,' he said, walking over to Maxie, a broad welcoming beam on his face.

She shook his proffered hand. 'Maxina Maws. I'm pleased to meet you, Mr Greencote.'

'Oh, please call me Brian. I have enough of that "Mr" from my pupils at school, it makes me feel very old.' He stared pitifully at his wife. 'I've looked where you said and I still can't find my new palette, Daffy.'

She tutted. 'What you mean is, will I come and find it for you?' She smiled at Maxie. 'I'd better do it or we won't get any peace for our chat. Won't be a tick. Girls, why don't you show Mrs Maws the pictures you've done?' She leaned towards Maxie and whispered in her ear, 'The one Charlotte has done … she's the youngest … with the big yellow blob in the middle of it, is supposed to be a sunflower. Katherine's, the red square with black on it, is supposed to be a bus.'

Maxie smiled at her appreciatively and mouthed 'thank you'.

When Daphne returned she was gratified to find her two children engrossed in a new picture Maxie was painting with them, and her chatter as she was doing it.

A short while later Daphne placed a mug of tea in front of Maxie along with a plate of assorted chocolate biscuits. After shooing off her children to play in their bedroom to afford her the peace to speak to Maxie, she sat back in her chair and said, 'My first nanny was a dear, became like one of the family and was so wonderful with the children. Unfortunately for us, but happily for her, out of the blue she met a lovely man and married him. They moved to live on the coast and run a caravan site. We then took on Miss Johnson. She came across as pleasant enough when I interviewed her, seemed very taken with the girls, but it soon became apparent to us that she wasn't like that at all.

'She made it very clear she completely disapproved of how we were raising our girls. Well,

274

children should be children is our motto, not made to sit still and be quiet, and if they dare to get a speck of dirt on them, well... Anyway, she made me feel like an intruder in my own home and Brian was never comfortable around her, so she had to go. I've been doing my best to look after the girls and do my work as well while we find the right replacement. We don't really need a live-in nanny as I work from home and we're here ourselves in the evenings and at weekends, so we're happy to have a nanny who's married herself if she's suitable. We just want someone like our first nanny was, who'll accept us for what we are, be like a member of the family, share the attitude that children should be allowed to be children and be heard and seen. I have to say, you come across as that type to me, Maxina.' She eyed Maxie keenly. 'Now it's your turn to tell me about yourself.'

Maxie did and when she had finished Daphne smiled, impressed. 'Well, I admire you for taking up the new challenge of office work when it was offered to you. Shows you aren't a stick-in-the-mud type, and at least you now know that nannying is really where your true vocation lies. Is there anything else you'd like to know about the job or have I gone over everything?'

Maxie thought for a moment. 'I think you've covered all I need to know.'

Daphne looked keenly at her. 'Can I ask if you like the thought of working for us?'

Maxie nodded. 'Oh, I do, very much.'

'I'm glad. Well, I've already seen three people and I do have another couple to see tomorrow, and obviously I'll have to check out your references ... no offence but you can't be too sure these days, can you? Not where children are concerned. But I'll tell you now that you are top of my list. I'll be in touch shortly.'

As Maxie walked jauntily down the tree-lined road she vehemently hoped she was the one chosen by Daphne Greencote to be her children's nanny. She would enjoy working for them as much as she had done the Carsons. She stopped for a moment to look at her watch. She had been longer at the Greencotes' than she had envisaged and if she was not going to be late for her appointment with Mr Marshall she had better hurry. She had been delighted to have been granted interviews by both of the advertisers but now, having set her heart on the job with the Greencotes, she wasn't as enthusiastic over the second appointment. But then, she reminded herself, she should not be complacent in thinking that the Greencote job was automatically hers. She should still do her best to be successful at the Marshalls'. As she arrived at the entrance to the short driveway of number twenty-two The Meadway, off the Letchworth Road, a white stucco-fronted gabled house with a well-kept front garden, it crossed her mind to wonder why her appointment was with a Mr Marshall and not Mrs as it was usually the mothers who interviewed for nannying jobs in her experience.

Her knock on the solid oak front door was answered by a tall, well-made man Maxie guessed to be in his mid-thirties. He was ruggedly handsome with a shock of well-groomed black hair.

He was dressed smartly in off-white slacks and an olive green cable pattern jumper, shop-bought not hand-knitted. But it was his eyes that caught Maxie's attention. They had the sad glaze of someone who had suffered unbearable grief at some time and never got over it.

'Mrs Maws, I presume?'

She smiled and nodded.

'Douglas Marshall. Please come in.' He stood aside to allow her entry, and after he had shut the door she followed him through a large reception room, thickly carpeted and tastefully furnished, and on into a connecting study whose walls were lined with books. He indicated for her to seat herself in a comfortable-looking brown leather chair before a large mahogany desk and asked, 'Can I get you any refreshment, Mrs Maws? Tea, coffee, a soft drink perhaps?' His manner was stiffly formal.

She shook her head. 'I'm fine, thank you.'

He proceeded around the desk to take his own seat in a leather-covered captain's chair. He looked at her hard for several long moments before he asked, 'How long have you been married, Mrs Maws?'

She was surprised that this was his first question to her. 'Oh, er ... eight months.'

'Is it a happy marriage?'

'Yes, very, Mr Marshall. I've known my husband all my life and he's been the only one for me.' She wondered why her marriage and its current state was so vitally important to him.

He seemed gratified by her answer and proceeded, 'My son is eleven months old. Thomas is

277

a good child, not much trouble. His mother...'
He paused and a look of pain crossed his face
fleetingly. 'She died not long after Thomas was
born. Neither she nor I had any family to call on
so I have had no choice but to hire a nanny for
my son. I noted from your application letter, Mrs
Maws, that you'd been with your first employer
for over five years, caring for their daughter, and
the reason you parted company was because they
moved from the area. So they were happy with
your work and conduct then?'

'Oh, yes, I got on with Mr and Mrs Carson very
well, and Felicity was a little treasure. I was very
sad when they moved, it was like losing part of
my own family. I have a reference from them, and
you can contact them personally to clarify
anything you feel you need to.' She placed an
envelope on his desk. 'My references and qualification certificates are all in there.'

He reached over and pulled it towards him.
'You further stated in your letter that you took a
job as an office receptionist. Why such a change
of direction?'

'Oh, well, I was offered the job out of the blue,
and as I'd not been able to secure a suitable
nanny's position at the time, decided to give it a
try. But Mr Holbrook moved back to his home
town of Oxford and that's the reason I'm looking
for another job now. I really enjoyed the work I
did for him but I do miss having a child to look
after and I know that being a nanny is really my
preference. There's also a reference in the envelope from Mr Holbrook, and he's happy to be
contacted as well if you want to clarify anything.'

Mr Marshall picked up the envelope she had passed him and took out the contents, carefully reading them. 'Well, they all seem to be in order.' Placing the paperwork on top of the envelope, he said to her, 'I would need you to start at eight and work until I get home about six. I'm not usually later than that, just very occasionally. Would that be a problem?'

She shook her head.

'I would also need an occasional evening's baby-sitting when I have a function to attend. Of course, at such times I would pay you extra. Would that cause you a problem?'

She shook her head. 'Not at all.'

'The care of Thomas is all I would expect of you, Mrs Maws. I have a lady who comes in daily in the mornings, a Mrs Sycamore, and she sees to the rest of the household chores. You'll find her very pleasant. Well, I think that's all. I'll check out your references and be contacting you shortly.' He rose and walked around his desk, holding out his hand to her. 'Thank you for your time.'

A surprised Maxie got up and accepted his hand, shaking it firmly. Was that it? she thought. It was the shortest interview she'd ever had. Apart from her marital status, he'd hardly asked anything else about her. There was one thing he'd said during the interview that bothered her, though. Mr Marshall had told her his wife had died not long after Thomas had been born, so who had been caring for him meantime? But she supposed it wasn't her business to ask. There was still one important matter that he hadn't dealt with and which Maxie felt she must raise before she left. It was definitely her business.

'Before I go, Mr Marshall, do you think I could meet Thomas?'

'Oh! Yes, of course. He's sleeping at the moment, in the nursery.'

She smiled. 'I promise not to wake him.'

He led her out of the study and up the stairs which opened on to a wide landing. The room he took her into was large and airy, decorated with yellow paper with a nursery-rhyme frieze running around top and bottom of the walls. The room contained everything that was needed for the care of a child, including a large chest which she assumed contained toys. A rocking horse stood by the window. Maxie tiptoed after Mr Marshall towards a cot standing alongside one wall. As he peered down into it, she caught sight of his face and was left in no doubt of the deep love he had for his son. Joining him, she peered down at the sleeping child.

Thomas Marshall wasn't the handsomest of babies. He possessed the very pale, almost deathly white skin of a red-head and his fine copper-coloured hair stuck up in a clump at the front; the rest of his head was almost bald. A large fat nose sat in the middle of an otherwise tiny face. His eyes were closed but she could tell they were big and would probably be blue, judging by the colour of his hair. Looking lost in the middle of the big wooden cot, he appeared so vulnerable to Maxie that a sudden deep sympathy rose within her for this poor little mite who'd never known his mother, never felt her comforting arms around him. She found herself choking back tears of sadness for his plight.

'You've a lovely son, Mr Marshall,' she whispered to him.

Still looking fondly down at his son, he whispered back, 'Thank you.'

As he closed the door on Maxie, Douglas Marshall breathed a huge sigh of relief. He had painstakingly sifted through all the applications he had received for the job but none of the candidates he'd chosen to interview before today had shown all the qualities he'd been seeking. This woman did. She was perfect for his needs. He had suffered dearly for his mistakes in the past but, finally, his search for the ideal woman was over.

On Friday morning Maxie sat back in a dining chair and stared thoughtfully across the room. Spread before her on the table were two letters, one from Daphne Greencote, the other from Douglas Marshall, both offering her the job of nanny to start the following Monday. Maxie had been highly gratified to be offered two jobs. The Greencotes were a lovely family, their house homely, their children a delight. She knew without a doubt that she would relish working for them. The job with Douglas Marshall was a different matter. He had come across as rather brusque. The house, although beautifully furnished, was very quiet and hadn't had a welcoming feel to it at all. She knew she wouldn't be made to feel part of Douglas Marshall's family. There would also be times when he would expect her to work late and occasionally throughout the evening, which she wouldn't have to do at the Greencotes'. Comparing them both, she found she was strongly drawn towards the job with the Greencotes.

She had a dilemma, though. Douglas Marshall was offering her two pounds a week more than the Greencotes were. Normally this fact would not have been an important consideration to her, but in view of Danny's recent behaviour it was. Admittedly since the episode with the van he had not mentioned trying to obtain another part-time job to top up their finances but he seemed uncharacteristically down and reserved. She knew it was just a matter of time, though. Soon enough he'd be embarking on another money-making scheme and then she'd be back to waiting for him to arrive home late at night, too tired himself to enjoy the benefits his extra money was bringing them. Her earning more in her weekly wage would hopefully stop that from happening. They could put away the surplus to save up and buy the things Danny had intended to provide for her. Her husband's wellbeing was the most important thing to Maxie... Her decision was made. She would accept the job with Douglas Marshall.

And there was another argument for this. The Greencote children had a mother to love and cherish them, nurture their growth into responsible adults. Thomas Marshall didn't. Although she would never presume to replace his mother, she could help give him the love and care only a woman could.

She immediately collected her handbag and set off for the telephone box to make two calls, one to the Greencotes thanking them profusely for

282

their offer but graciously declining it and the other to Douglas Marshall, thanking him for his offer and confirming she'd be starting the following Monday.

Danny's reaction to her news surprised Maxie. He made no comment about the higher wage she was being offered or her suggestion that they could save it, but seemed more interested instead in her new boss: what he looked like, was like as a person. If Maxie didn't know better, she'd have said Danny was worried that she had taken a fancy to her new employer and that's why she had accepted the job. But she knew it must be her imagination as Danny was well aware how much she loved and respected him, that she would never consider betraying him in any way whatsoever.

Maxie had not been wrong about Danny's fears, though. He lay in bed that night, his beloved wife sleeping peacefully beside him. Unlike him. Danny's mind was too preoccupied. A possible contender for his wife's attention had left the scene, only to be replaced immediately by another. Just like before, there was no way he could compete with this man or what he could offer Maxie. All Danny could do was live in hope that she didn't fall for her boss, bringing forward that haunting vision of his own cold, lonely future.

CHAPTER TWENTY-ONE

Hilda Sycamore was a homely middle-aged woman. Maxie graciously accepted the milky mug of coffee the housekeeper had made for her. Thomas was having his morning nap and Maxie had accepted an invitation to join Hilda in the kitchen for elevenses. She welcomed this as an opportunity to become acquainted with her fellow employee and hoped it was the start of a harmonious working relationship.

'He's a sweet little chap is young Thomas,' she said now to Maxie. 'Yer heart goes out to him, don't it, dear, him having no mother?'

'Yes, it certainly does,' agreed Maxie.

'Do you know what happened to her? Has Mr Marshall told you?' asked the older woman keenly.

Maxie shook her head. 'No, he hasn't.'

'Oh! Well, this is only my second week with Mr Marshall and I have ter say I don't find him very forthcoming... All I know is that his wife's dead, how I've no idea. He must have loved her, though, as he's put all the photographs of her away. He obviously can't bear to be reminded of her. Well, I haven't come across any while I've been cleaning, not even a wedding one. In fact, I haven't come across anything that would have belonged to his wife, like clothes or other personal belongings, so either he's packed the lot away or

284

else thrown it all out. Strange that, don't yer think?

'Mind you, people do strange things when they're grieving, don't they? I had a neighbour who for years after her husband died slept in his pyjamas, and was only persuaded by her daughter to stop when they'd worn so thin they'd virtually fallen apart! She still has the tattered remnants in her bottom drawer, though.' She paused long enough to take a sip of her coffee. 'What do you make of him yerself? Mr Marshall, I mean.'

'Oh, well, it's only my first morning so I haven't really had time to think about it, Mrs Sycamore.'

'Well, I don't know any more about him than when I first started. He's very ... what's the word? ... businesslike with me. If he was like that with his wife when she was alive, then God help her! Still, whatever he's like with me isn't important. I'm just here to do a job for him for which he pays me very well. And the reason we all work is money, ain't it, lovey?

'I'll give him his due, he always thanks me for what I've done for him, and that's all we menials can ask: recognition for a job well done. I do know he's a wine importer and has his own office in town. I saw some paperwork on his desk last week when I was cleaning it and he was working at home, looking after his son while he found a nanny. He must do well out of his business to afford the upkeep on a place like this and pay our wages. So what does your husband do, ducky?'

Maxie smiled at the thought of him. 'My Danny's a milkman,' she said proudly.

Hilda looked impressed. 'Milkman, eh? That's a

responsible job. You must trust him with all those housewives he has to deal with on his round!'

'Implicitly. I've known my husband since we were babies in our prams together as our parents lived next door to each other. He's never given me cause to doubt him.'

'Ah, that's nice to hear. Too many of you young things these days are in too much of a hurry to wed the first chap who looks in your direction. Nothing's been the same since the last war. It changed things in so many ways... But I'd better not start on that or we'll be here all day, and I have to prepare His Nibs's dinner for when he gets home tonight. Going to make him a nice fish pie all ready to heat up. Mr Marshall has told me you're to be in charge of Thomas's meals but I'll leave a sandwich out for yer lunch when I go at twelve-thirty.'

Swallowing the last of her coffee, Maxie rose, saying, 'Thank you, Mrs Sycamore, I appreciate that.'

Douglas Marshall had told her she would find his housekeeper a pleasant woman and it seemed he was right. The weather was warm and sunny so Maxie planned to take Thomas for a walk in the park that afternoon. She decided that while he was still sleeping she would take the opportunity to look through his wardrobe and familiarise herself with all his clothes, making a note of any new ones he needed so she could inform his father.

She heard her boss's key in the lock promptly at six that evening. Gathering Thomas in her arms and holding him protectively, Maxie took him down from the nursery to greet his father. They found Douglas Marshall hanging up his coat in the small cloakroom off the hallway.

'Good evening, Mr Marshall. Thomas is already bathed and ready for bed but I didn't want to put him down until you'd had chance to say goodnight to him.'

'That was very thoughtful of you, Mrs Maws,' he replied stiffly. As he took his son from Maxie, he asked, 'How has he been?'

'No problem at all, Mr Marshall. He ate all his porridge at breakfast, a boiled egg for lunch, and mashed carrots and potatoes for his dinner this evening. He's ready for his milk before bedtime – I hope it's not presumptuous of me but I left that for you to give him.'

'Again, that was very thoughtful of you, Mrs Maws.'

She wished he would address her as Maxie to make things less formal between them. 'We went for a walk in the park this afternoon, didn't we, Thomas?' she said to him, gently touching his cheek with the tips of her fingers and smiling warmly at him. 'You enjoyed it, didn't you, sweetie?'

'I expect you'll be wanting to get home to your husband, Mrs Maws.'

Mr Marshall's brusque manner was leaving her in no doubt that he meant to keep their relationship on a purely business level. 'I'll just collect my handbag and see you in the morning then, Mr Marshall,' said Maxie evenly. She turned her attention to his son then and her voice softened.

'Goodnight, Thomas. Sleep well, and I'll see you too in the morning.'

As she made her way home, she knew it was far too early to make a judgement as to whether she would come to like this job as much as she had her one with the Carsons or know without a doubt that she would have done better with the Greencotes, but she felt she would rub along well enough with Hilda Sycamore and had certainly spent a rewarding day with her new charge. She felt that already she was getting an insight into his personality, his likes and dislikes. Thomas was a dear little thing and had proved no trouble so far. They were going to get along well together, and to Maxie that was more important than his father's brusque manner towards her which she only had to cope with for a few minutes twice a day, when she arrived and departed.

A couple of days later, an unusually cold snap for August had cooled the weather so much that it ruled out the usual walk in the park, so Maxie decided instead to take Thomas for a visit to Ada and Kathy, who she knew were both keen to meet her new charge. It was past two o'clock so both of them would be home from work and have had their lunch.

Ada was delighted see Maxie pushing the pram into her back yard. Hurriedly wiping her hands on a towel as she had been washing up, she rushed out to greet her daughter.

'Oh, is this him then?' she gushed, sticking her head inside the pram and saying to Thomas, 'Hello there, young man.' Without further ado

288

she picked him up. 'Let's go and see if Auntie Ada can find you a biccie.' With him cocooned in her arms, she began making her way inside.

Maxie rushed after her. 'Oh, Mam, I don't want his appetite spoiling for his dinner...'

Ada was in the kitchen now, trying to lift the lid off the biscuit tin one-handed. 'Oh, one biscuit won't hurt him. It never hurt you, Maxie. Tek this lid off for me, will yer, lovey? I was an expert when you was little at doing things one-handed but I'm out of practice now.'

Maxie relented, and Ada selected a plain Arrowroot which she gave to the baby. Maxie smiled tenderly as her mother sat down at the kitchen table, settling Thomas comfortably in her lap. While he was munching – more sucking – on it he was looking up at her wide-eyed, the expression on his face clearly asking, Who's this stranger?

'He's a good little thing,' said Ada, smiling down at him. 'Most kids his age would have howled the place down at a stranger picking them up. So, what's yer new boss like?'

Maxie was busying herself making a pot of tea. 'I don't see much of him, Mam. A couple of minutes in the morning when we hand over, and the same in the evening.'

'Well, that's good, isn't it? Better than having him breathing down yer neck all the time, watching everything you do and sticking his oar in. Gives you free rein to do what yer best at, and that's caring for his son.'

Putting cups on the table along with the milk jug and sugar bowl, she said, 'Yes, I suppose you're right. I'm just finding it so different after

289

being in a more usual family situation.' She smiled fondly at Thomas. 'I did enjoy working for Mr Holbrook but it's good to be looking after a child again, Mam. I find it very rewarding. I know I've only been in the job a couple of days, but Thomas looked really happy to see me when I arrived to take over from his father this morning.'

'Poor chap,' mused Ada. ''Tin't right, a man being left with a young babby to raise. Have you found out how his wife died yet?'

Maxie shook her head.

'And the woman who does for him doesn't know either?'

'No. Mr Marshall seems a very private man, but his wife's death must have affected him badly as there are no photos of her around at all and Mrs Sycamore ... she's his part-time housekeeper ... well, she told me she's never come across anything belonging to a woman when she's been cleaning, so he must have packed everything away. Obviously can't bear to be reminded of her.'

Ada pulled a knowing face. 'Ah, well, grief affects people in different ways. But he'll have to get the photos out one day to show this little man what his mother was like. I'm glad to hear yer settling in well, though, Maxie.' She tickled Thomas under his chin. 'And you, my lad, are very lucky to have my daughter looking after you.'

They both laughed as Thomas, chuckling himself, took the biscuit out of his own mouth and stuffed it in Ada's.

Tea now made, Maxie put the pot on the table – well out of reach of Thomas – and sat down herself. As she poured milk into the cups, she asked her mother, 'Where's Danny's mam, by the way?'

Wiping her mouth free from soggy biscuit Ada told her, 'Oh, she's next door having a gossip with the new neighbours that've moved into my old house. A Mr and Mrs Salmon. Elderly couple. I haven't met him yet as he works nights as a watchman for a factory down Tudor Road. She seems pleasant enough. I feel sorry for her as she lost both her sons during the war. And talking of sons, I haven't seen Danny since me and his mam moved back. Is he all right?'

'Yeah, he's fine ... well, no, he's not exactly his usual self, Mam, if I'm honest. He's still down after what happened over the van.'

'Oh, is he? Poor love. Well, that's understandable. It was a big blow for him to get over after putting all his savings into it and having such high hopes.'

'Yes, I know, Mam. I feel guilty, though, because a part of me is glad about what happened. I appreciate Danny wants to buy me expensive things and take me to nice places, but I'd sooner do without and have him home with me.'

'Well, now you're bringing a bit extra in he won't feel under such pressure, will be? I bet he was pleased when yer told him what yer new wage was?'

'Well, that was the main reason I took the job, Mam. But Danny seemed more concerned with what Mr Marshall was like.'

'Oh, well, that's 'cos he wants to be sure he's the sort to treat yer the way you deserve to be treated, Maxie.'

She looked surprised. 'Oh, I never thought of it like that. I got the impression Danny was worried I'd take a fancy to Mr Marshall and run off with him.'

Ada laughed. 'Don't be daft, lovey! Danny knows how much you love him, that you'd never look in another man's direction, and the same with you for him. If ever I was sure two people were destined to spend the rest of their lives together, it was with you and Danny. Me and Kathy said as much when you were babies, and neither of us was surprised by how inseparable you became as you grew up nor when you announced you intended to get married.' She gave a sudden sniff. 'Oh, dear, I think this young man has filled his nappy. Fetch his clean one and I'll change him for yer.' She gave her daughter a mischievous wink. 'Give me a bit of practice for when my own grandkids came along. Oh, and while I'm doing it, you'd better fetch Kathy else she won't forgive me if she knows you've been here with this young man and she never got introduced and a chance to coo over him herself.'

Maxie smiled at this show of consideration as she went to the pram to collect the spare nappy. No one who met the two women together now would suspect that several weeks ago, and for over ten years previously, they'd been sworn enemies. Maxie knew she was lucky with her mother and mother-in-law as neither of them talked incessantly about wanting grandchildren like most young married couples had to suffer from their parents, despite the fact that both Danny and she were well aware that neither woman could wait for such a time. In the future they planned to oblige their mothers, but not for a couple of years yet. The two of them wanted to enjoy the early stages of their marriage before they shared each other with the children they hoped to have.

CHAPTER TWENTY-TWO

Dashing out of the entry into the pouring rain to leave two pints of milk on Bernice Frasier's back doorstep, Danny nearly jumped out of his skin when the door burst open and Bernice herself, dressed in a tight-fitting short red skirt and low-cut pink blouse, leered suggestively at him. 'Not selling yer label-less tins anymore? Well, not to me at any rate.'

As he had been delivering that morning all Danny's thoughts had been centred on Maxie – in fact, it wasn't often his mind was on anything else these days. She'd been in her new job for two weeks now and thankfully had given him no reason to suspect she was looking at her new employer in any other light. He vehemently hoped it stayed that way, but regardless it didn't stop him worrying himself witless that the situation would change as time passed and they started to see each other differently as they grew more familiar.

'I don't sell anything anymore, Mrs Frasier, apart from milk.'

'Oh, that's a blow. I was hoping yer'd make another cock-up and I'd get me milk bill paid again. Never mind, I'll come up with another way ... like blackmailing the coalman. I'll say I'll tell his wife he keeps asking me out on a date. The beggar *does* keep asking me out an' all, so if he doesn't cough up a few quid I will tell her and

294

it'll serve him right.'

She poked her head out to look up at the thick black clouds relentlessly dispensing their load. 'Pissing weather,' she grumbled, then gave a raucous laugh. 'Pissing weather ... get it?'

She sniffed disdainfully at Danny's sombre expression. He was finding it difficult these days to raise a smile with what was preying on his mind. 'Miserable sod you are these days, Dan Maws. Yer never used to be so miserable. Your cheery whistling used to drive me mad when yer first took over this round from Sid Clapper. Oh, well, with you in this mood, at least I don't have to put up with that every morning.' She poked her head out of the door again. 'It don't look like it's going to go off today so I reckon I'll give work a miss – spend the day putting me feet up. My lot will have to make do with bread and chips for their dinner 'cos I ain't risking a soaking getting to the shops just to feed their fat faces. Well, I'm off back in for a cuppa.' She eyed Danny up and down as she provocatively ran her tongue over her top lip. 'Join me, if yer wanna. Me old man's out at work. I'll put that smile back on yer face, promise yer I will.'

At her suggestion Danny did an abrupt turn and hurried off to the sounds of Bernice's bellowing laughter echoing down the entry.

The milk float was parked a few houses away. As he ran over to it, above the pounding of the rain against the pavement the sound of someone sobbing grew louder and louder. He stopped abruptly and, wiping rain from his eyes, peered around in search of whoever it was. But apart from himself and a woman in the distance, weighed down by heavy shopping and struggling to keep an umbrella over her head, the street was otherwise empty. Someone was crying, though, hysterically, but where they were he hadn't a clue. Despite the oilskin cape provided by the dairy for the protection of their deliverymen in such weather, standing here was only getting the parts of him the oilskin didn't cover more soaked by the second. Rain was trickling down his neck, the bottoms of his trousers were sopping and his work shoes squelched.

Whoever it was he had heard crying seemed to have stopped. He could no longer hear anything and resumed his rush to the float. Arriving behind it, he put down his metal bottle-holder, whipped out the empties and went to replace them with full bottles for his next delivery. He suddenly stopped as out of the corner of his eye he caught sight of a battered suitcase propped against the front end of the float. He stared over at it, wondering what it was doing there and more importantly who it belonged to. Then the sound of sobbing began again and realisation struck him. It was coming from inside the cab. Going over, he was taken aback to see a woman sitting on the floor, her knees bent, head resting on them, arms wrapped around the top of her head as she sobbed uncontrollably.

His own worries flew from him as concern for this woman took over. Rushing around to the driver's side, Danny slid into the seat then reached over and laid one hand gently on the soaked shoulder of her coat. 'Are you all right?'

he asked her, knowing this was a stupid question as it was obvious she wasn't but he didn't know what else to say.

At the sound of his voice her head jerked up and tear-blurred, red-rimmed eyes looked at him wildly. 'I'm ... I'm ... so sorry, but I saw the cab was empty and I had nowhere else to shelter.'

Danny frowned. He really should ask this woman to be on her way as he had to complete his deliveries before customers started to complain, but regardless of the risk to his job he could not bring himself to treat her with such disregard in view of the state she was in. He smiled at her kindly. 'Oh, well, I'd have done the same in your position. Only ducks would be glad of this weather. Er ... fancy a cuppa? I've a flask of tea,' he said, reaching under his seat for his haversack. Taking the flask from it, he unscrewed the cup and then the screw top and poured out a measure of steaming tea. 'It's got sugar in. I hope you don't mind?'

She flashed him a grateful smile as with a shaking hand she accepted the cup from him. 'You're ... so ... so ... kind,' she faltered.

As she sipped the hot tea, Danny appraised her. She seemed to be in her late-twenties or early-thirties at a guess. It was difficult to tell the colour of her hair as it was sopping wet and plastered to her head. Her wet coat was crumpled, as if she'd been sleeping in it, but regardless seemed of a better quality than was to be had from the market. Despite her extremely distressed state, Danny could tell she was an attractive woman. He wondered what had brought her to this situation. Something terrible, he assumed.

He knew it was against company rules and he'd be in big trouble if he was caught but he felt he had no choice but to offer her help. 'Have you far to go? If it's local I'll drop you round there in the float, if you like?'

At his offer her face crumpled and a fresh flood of tears ran down her face. 'Thank you so much for your offer but I haven't anywhere to go. Nowhere at all.'

'Nowhere? Everyone's got somewhere.'

'I ... I haven't.' She drained the cup and handed it back to him. 'I really appreciated that, thank you so much.' She smiled weakly. 'First hot drink I've had for a couple of days, since my money ran out. Well, I've taken up too much of your time. I'd best go, let you get on with your job.'

He looked at her with concern. 'But if you've nowhere to go, what will you do?'

Her head lowered, she uttered softly, 'I don't know.' Then she looked up and asked, 'Do you know of a place that takes in women with no money?'

He was aware of hostels in town that catered for drunks, down and outs, the sort of homeless people he didn't think this woman belonged with, but even they asked the price of a bed, as little as it was. He shook his head. 'No, I don't.'

Her whole body sagged in despair. 'It's hopeless, isn't it? With no permanent address I can't get a job, and I can't get an address with no money to pay the rent as I've no job.' She wrung her hands despairingly. 'Can you direct me to the river from here, or the canal will do?'

'Oh, well, you go...' His voice trailed off and he stared at her. To Danny there could only be one reason why she was asking for directions to those places. She was contemplating throwing herself in! 'Oh, er ... no, I don't. It's miles ... miles from here,' he blustered.

His mind raced wildly. His conscience would not allow him to part company with this woman now that he knew what she intended to do to herself. He'd spend the rest of his days worrying about what had happened to her, never knowing whether she'd succeeded or not, and consumed with guilt that if she had, he'd done nothing to try and prevent her. He could offer to give her the few shillings he had in his pocket to pay for a bed for a couple of nights in a women's refuge, but that few shillings wouldn't go far and very shortly she'd be in this position again. There was only one real option Danny felt was open to him. He felt sure Maxie wouldn't have any objection in the circumstances, and she'd maybe have more of an idea what they could do for this woman than he had, being a woman herself. From what his stowaway had told him she must be starving and he felt sorry now he'd already eaten his two shrimp paste cobs so he'd nothing to offer her by way of food.

'Look, er ... if you don't mind waiting while I finish my shift, I'll take you home with me. I'll make you something to eat while your clothes are drying. My wife Maxie will be home from work about six-thirty. I'm sure she'll be able to come up with some ideas about what you can do. I'll put your case behind the crates on the back of the float.'

The woman looked totally stunned by his suggestion, then her face crumpled and she buried her face in her hands as a fresh flow of tears burst from her.

Danny took her response to mean she accepted his offer.

Maxie was glad to be home that evening. She stripped herself out of her sopping coat and dried her legs off as despite the shelter of an umbrella, the driving rain had managed to strike her where the umbrella offered no protection. She sniffed appreciatively at the delicious aroma of the shepherd's pie she had prepared the previous evening. Danny had put it in the oven to cook.

Her day had been a trying one. Due to the discomfort of cutting his back teeth, Thomas had been very irritable and grizzly all day. Nothing Maxie had tried to aid or distract him with – teething gel, a hard rusk to gnaw on, reading to him, playing games – had taken his mind off what he was suffering. Her heart had gone out to the poor little soul. Thankfully, after his nightly warm bath and bottle of milk, exhaustion had overtaken him and he had fallen into a deep sleep just before his father returned home.

Mr Marshall might be very formal in his manner towards her but it was obvious to Maxie how much he loved his son. He had shown deep concern when she had relayed the events of the day, taking her advice on what to do for Thomas should he wake up suffering during the night, and sincerely thanking her for her care of him that day.

As she hung up her coat, an unfamiliar one hanging from the drying cradle suspended from the ceiling caught Maxie's eye, but before she could wonder who it belonged to Danny had arrived in the kitchen to greet her home.

Kissing her cheek and taking her wet coat from her, he asked, 'Had a good day?'

'Not really. Thomas is teething so he's been mardy all day, but it's not his fault, bless him.' She smiled warmly at her beloved husband. 'I shouldn't be complaining about my day as at least I've been inside while you've been out in this, delivering your milk. I hope your customers appreciate you.' As he let down the drying cradle to put her coat on it she caught sight of the unfamiliar coat again. 'Have we got a visitor, Danny?'

'Er ... yes. Yes, we have.'

'I don't recognise the coat. Whose is it?'

'Well, I ... er ... don't actually know her name. Look, why don't you go through and sit down and have a warm by the fire while I finish hanging your coat up. I'll pour you a cuppa. I mashed a fresh pot just before you came in. I'll tell you all about her then. Well, what I know, that is.'

Maxie looked even more bemused. 'Isn't she, whoever she is, in the living room?'

'No. Look, I think it'd be best to explain things from the beginning so go through, I won't be a minute.'

Maxie couldn't wait to hear who their mystery visitor was, and more importantly where she was. As she curled up comfortably in her armchair, glad that despite its being summer Danny had lit a fire to take the chill off the room caused by the unexpected cold snap, her eyes caught sight of a battered suitcase propped against the leg of the dining table and she frowned. The mystery of their visitor grew deeper.

Bringing her mug of tea with him, Danny had hardly settled himself into the armchair opposite before she was demanding, 'Well, come on then. Who is this visitor of ours?'

Taking a deep breath, he explained to Maxie the events of that morning.

When he had finished she looked at him worriedly. 'You really think this woman was planning to do away with herself?'

'Well, why else would she want to know the way to the river or canal, especially after she told me she'd nowhere to go and no money?'

'And she's upstairs now, having a sleep on the spare bed?'

He nodded. 'When I got her back here, I made her a sandwich and she gobbled it down like she hadn't eaten for a week. She had three cups of tea. I didn't like to ask her anything about herself until she'd finished. I was just about to when I noticed she was having real trouble keeping her eyes open, so I asked her if she wanted to go and have a lie down on the bed upstairs for an hour.'

'And she's been asleep since?'

'Well, I assume so as she hasn't come down.' He looked at her questioningly. 'I had no choice but to bring her back here, did I, Maxie?'

'Oh, you certainly did the right thing, Danny. You couldn't let her go off, not when you sus-

302

pected she was going to try and do that.' Maxie frowned. 'I wonder what happened to her? Someone must be missing her, Danny. Everyone has someone, haven't they? If not family then friends, one at least. Was she wearing a wedding ring?'

He shrugged. 'I never noticed.'

She smiled at him knowingly. 'I bet you can't tell me what colour dress or skirt she was wearing either?'

'No, I can't, but is that important, Maxie?' he asked seriously.

She grinned. 'It just proves a point. It's quite true what they say, men don't notice the same things as women do. Well, I suppose there's nothing we can do but wait until she comes down then hopefully she'll tell us what's happened to her and we can try and help her somehow.'

'I told her you would be able to help.'

'It's good to know you have such faith in me, Danny, but we've no money to give her and I don't actually know what else we can do for her. We could give her a decent meal, though. She can have my share of the shepherd's pie and I'll have something else.'

'She can have my share, Maxie,' Danny said resolutely.

Her husband was such a good man, she thought. Most others finding themselves in the position he had done that morning would have shied away, sent the woman packing for someone else to deal with and not given it another thought. Not her Danny. He had a conscience and a good heart, and that was one of the reasons Maxie loved him so much. She smiled at him tenderly.

303

'We'll eke it out between the three of us.'

They sat there all evening, the television turned low, their mystery visitor's share of the pie keeping warm in the oven, waiting anxiously for sounds above to notify them that she was up and about. As ten o'clock approached with still no sign of life from her, they decided there was nothing else for them to do but retire to bed themselves and see what the morning brought.

Danny having left the house three hours before, Maxie rose early the next morning not quite knowing what to expect, whether the woman had already risen and would be waiting for her or if she had departed during the night. She arrived in the back room to find no sign of her or any evidence she had been up during the night, but she hadn't left the house as her battered case was still propped against the leg of the dining chair. Creeping back up the stairs, Maxie inched open the spare bedroom door just far enough for her to poke her head inside. A lump under the covers and the soft sounds of breathing told her the woman was still sleeping. Her ordeal, whatever it was, had certainly drained her if she needed to sleep this long under a strange roof and Maxie felt disinclined to disturb her. Sleep was a healer. Whatever had befallen this woman, it might not seem so unbearable looked at in the fresh light of a new day. She herself, though, had to go to work. Leaving a note propped on the table telling the woman to help herself to something to eat and informing her that Danny would be home around two that afternoon, Maxie quietly locked the back door behind her and set off.

Unfortunately she had little time to dwell on thoughts of their mystery visitor as Thomas was again letting her know that his gums were sore, though thankfully according to his father, in their brief handover before he left for work, he had slept soundly through the night, not waking once. Thankfully, too, the typical British weather had about-turned and clear skies and an increasingly warm sun were replacing the previous day's deluge. Maxie took the baby on a long walk down to the Abbey Park. Once there the antics of the wildlife on the lake and a gentle push on the children's swings helped distract him from the discomfort he was experiencing.

Her route took her past the row of shops on the Hinckley Road where Matthew Holbrook had rented his premises. As she approached her former workplace she thought of him, wondering how he was faring, sincerely hoping that by now he was well on the way to coming to terms with what his wife had done to him and starting to rebuild his life without her in it. She made to steer the pram around a young woman who was blocking the pavement, staring into the shop that had once been Holbrook's Estate Agents, a look of extreme annoyance on her face. The woman spun round to face Maxie, addressing her peremptorily.

'Excuse me, I was told there was an estate agent's here. Has it moved or have I got the wrong address, do you know?' Her face became quizzical. 'You look familiar. Do I know you?'

Maxie smiled at her. 'Yes, you do. I'm Maxina Maws. Maxie. You moved in at the end of our street. I never got a chance to wish you well

305

before you moved out again. How are you, Gail?'

'Oh, I remember you now.' She glanced Maxie up and down and looked pityingly at the plain navy blue pleated skirt and white short-sleeved blouse she was wearing along with her serviceable flat black shoes. 'You never told me you were a nanny. Oh, I don't know how you could do what you do! You poor nannies have a rough time of it, don't you, having to wear such unflattering clothes? But then, if I remember right, you were dressed old-fashioned the night I invited you over. You should try modernising yourself, it would do wonders for you. And a new hair cut too... A Mary Quant bob would suit you. I have an eye for these things, you know.'

Maxie wasn't at all insulted by Gail's opinion of what she should or should not wear. She felt comfortable with the conservative way she dressed and styled her hair, which was to please herself and not follow what the fashion designers of the day dictated to sheep like Gail and so many other women in their age group. 'Well, thanks for your opinion, Gail, but I happen to like myself the way I am,' Maxie said evenly.

Gail stared at her, taken aback. 'Do you really? Oh well, each to their own, I suppose. Anyway I'm fine, thank you, or would be if I could find where this bloody estate agent's is.'

'Oh, you can't because he's no longer in business.' Maxie eyed the woman quizzically. 'Are you and Terry looking to move back around this area again?'

Gail gave a scoffing laugh. 'Most certainly not in the street we were in, and not with Terry either!

I've moved on to better things. Terry lost his job just after we moved because his boss decided he wasn't management material after all. He's gone back to Coventry. I haven't a clue what he's doing now, and to be honest I don't care. I wasn't going to go back to living in a pokey flat and having no money to spend on new clothes and going out enjoying myself.' Her face took on a superior expression and she said proudly, 'My new chap has his own business. He's older than me ... well, a lot older ... and divorced, but I don't care because he looks after me far better than Terry did.' She held out her hand to Maxie. 'See this ring? Diamond and sapphires. It cost a packet and there's plenty more where that came from.

'I've told Cedric I'm not happy living in the house he shared with his wife and given him an ultimatum: either we move or he finds himself someone else. It's not a bad house – in fact, it's quite posh – but I knew he'd agree to me putting it on the market and finding somewhere else of my choice. Talk about besotted! I've got that man wrapped around my little finger. Anyway, I fancy living in one of those huge houses around the Western Park, and after hearing about a local estate agent, thought he'd know best what was going around there. Oh, well, if he's no longer in business then I'll have to use the agents in town.'

She looked at her dainty gold wrist watch and issued a sigh. 'Hell, look at the time. I wanted to get the house business moving today which I won't have time to now as I've an appointment with the beautician at eleven-thirty.' She took a hurried glance around her. 'Hell again. I can't

307

remember where I've parked my car. You haven't passed a bright yellow Mini coupé, have you?'

The latest model cars that the media dictated were must-haves else you weren't living a proper fulfilled life, had never held any particular interest for Maxie, like the latest fashions in clothes or hair styles. She wouldn't know a Mini coupé if she was standing beside it. She shook her head.

Gail gave her a look as if to say, Fat lot of good you are. 'Well, I'll be seeing you then.' Before she rushed off she took a glance inside the pram and said, 'That poor child must be such a disappointment to his mother. He's not been very blessed in the looks department, has he?'

Maxie gazed after her as she hurried off on her impossibly high platform sandals. To Maxie, all children were beautiful. Smiling fondly at Thomas, sitting as good as gold in his pram, taking in the goings on around him, she said, 'I think you're handsome, sweetie, so don't you listen to what that naughty lady said about you.'

Maxie was anxious to be home promptly that night to find out if there were any further developments regarding their guest. Danny was cutting chips when she walked though the back door, panting and out of breath as she had run all the way home. He immediately stopped what he was doing to go over to her and kiss her cheek, asking how her day had gone.

'Better today. I took Thomas to the park and it helped take his mind off his sore gums. Hopefully he's over the worst now. Anyway, I'm more interested in our guest. Is she still here?'

He nodded.

'So what have you found out?' Maxie asked him eagerly, although mindful to keep her voice low in case they could be overheard.

'Nothing yet. She's still in bed.'

'Oh! Well, she must have been exhausted to have slept for over twenty-four hours.' Then a terrible thought struck Maxie. 'Oh, you don't think she's taken ill, do you, Danny? I'd better go and check.'

Dashing into the back room, she stopped short as she realised someone was coming down the stairs. Her eyes fixed on the door at the back of the room as it slowly opened and a woman appeared. She was dainty as a doll, with porcelain skin and honey-blonde hair which still had the untidy look to it of someone who'd just risen from their bed. Her small heart-shaped face was undeniably attractive but the pale blue eyes looking at Maxie seemed almost frightened.

Maxie smiled warmly at her. 'I was just coming to check if you were all right. We were getting bothered about you, as you'd slept so long.'

'Oh, I'm so sorry to have worried you. I couldn't seem to wake myself up.' Her voice was soft and refined.

'Well, you're awake now. I bet you could do with a cup of tea and something to eat?'

The woman's face lit up. 'Oh, I could, thank you so much.'

Maxie walked towards her, holding out a hand in greeting. 'I'm Maxie, Danny's wife.'

'Danny? Oh, the milkman who was so kind to me.' Accepting Maxie's hand she gave it a light shake as if anything more strenuous would snap her delicate wrist. 'It's so kind of you both to offer me somewhere to stay until I get myself sorted out. I can't tell you how much I appreciate what you're doing for me.'

Maxie stared at her blankly. As far as Danny had told her all he had offered this woman was a hot drink and a meal. Someone had got their wires crossed. 'Er ... please make yourself at home while I go and tell Danny there'll be three of us for dinner. I hope you like egg and chips?'

Their guest flashed a wan smile. 'Sounds like a banquet to me.'

Back in the kitchen, closing the door behind her, Maxie hurried over to Danny and in a low voice said, 'She's awake now and in the back room. Seems to think you said she could stay here with us until she gets herself sorted out?'

He looked bewildered. 'I didn't. I'm sure I didn't. Just a cup of tea, something to eat and a chat with you when you came home, to see if you could help her more than I could.'

'Well, I haven't the heart to put her right. She looks like she's the weight of the world on her shoulders. We'll just have to play it by ear. I still don't even know her name. She never offered it when I introduced myself to her.'

A while later their visitor looked appreciatively at the plate of food Maxie put before her. As she sat down herself, she said, 'Help yourself to bread and butter.'

They ate in silence for a few minutes before Maxie asked, 'The meal okay for you, is it?'

The other woman looked at Maxie and said

310

softly, almost timidly, 'It's lovely, thank you.'

'I'm glad.' From under her lashes Maxie watched her eating for several moments before saying, 'Er ... you know I'm Maxie and my husband is Danny but we didn't catch your name?'

She paused mid-forkful and a remorseful expression filled her face. 'Oh, I'm so sorry for not introducing myself. Ellen. . . my name is Ellen.'

'We're pleased to meet you, Ellen. More tea?'

The offer was eagerly accepted. Maxie was running out of small talk and desperately wanted to get down to more in-depth conversation, namely what had brought Ellen to be sitting at their table. Trouble was, she didn't appear at all willing to volunteer any information about herself. Maxie worried that whatever had happened to her was too traumatic and private to relay to strangers. But then, if she didn't unburden herself, how could anyone offer to help her? Or maybe she didn't feel comfortable talking about her problems in the presence of a man. Yes, maybe that was it. As soon as the meal was over she would privately ask Danny to make himself busy in the kitchen while she tried to coax Ellen into opening up to her. Maxie had noticed she was wearing a wedding ring.

The table cleared, and Danny having assured Maxie he would leave the way clear for her to have a woman-to-woman talk with Ellen, she closed the kitchen door and settled herself in the armchair opposite the visitor's.

'Oh, this is the best part of the day for me,' she said casually. 'A good day's work done, dinner past, and a few hours to yourself to relax. Well, I

311

suppose I should be doing some darning but it won't hurt for Danny to have holes in his socks for another day,' she said jocularly. 'By the state of them sometimes, I think he does his round without his work boots on. So, Ellen ... what part of the day do you enjoy best?'

She gave a heavy sigh. 'Oh, I used to enjoy every minute. Now ... well, I'm not sure I'm even glad to be alive, if you want the truth.'

Maxie gasped at this response. Danny had been right: Ellen had been contemplating ending her own life. Leaning forward she asked softly, 'What's happened to you to make you feel like that?' She didn't care if Ellen thought she was prying. She wasn't doing it out of simple nosiness but from a desire to help a woman who seemed to need help urgently.

Her shoulders immediately sagged. Her whole face contorting, in a voice that was choked with emotion, she began, 'When I was under the impression I was happily married, is ... is my husband throwing me out of our house, knowing I'd hardly any money in my purse, a good enough reason for me to feel like my life has ended?'

Maxie gazed at her. 'Oh, I see. Why, though, Ellen? Why did he do that? What reason did he give you for what he was doing?'

Her face crumpled. Jumping up from her seat, she proclaimed, 'I'm sorry, I can't talk about this now.'

She made a bolt for the door leading to the stairs and Maxie heard her feet pounding up them, followed by the sound of the spare room door shutting.

She got up and went into the kitchen.

Danny looked at her expectantly as she entered. 'Did you manage to find out anything?'

'Only that her husband threw her out with hardly any money. She said it was all too painful to talk about just now and ran upstairs.'

'Oh! Oh, dear. Well, maybe after she's calmed down she'll come back and tell us more.'

'Hopefully,' said Maxie. 'Oh, Danny, she doesn't come across as the sort who would do something so bad her husband would feel the need to throw her out with no money. She seems such a nice woman. I feel sorry for her. I just hope we can help her in some way. I'm not sure how, though. Anyway, it looks like she's stopping with us for another night, doesn't it? That's helping her, isn't it? Our spare bed is better than her sleeping rough.'

Ellen did not show her face again that night, and neither had she by the time Maxie left for work the next morning. As soon as she arrived home that night she asked Danny, 'Have you found out any more about Ellen?'

He shook his head. 'She only came down about five minutes ago. I gave her a cup of tea and left her to drink it in peace.' He gave Maxie a helpless look. 'I don't know what to say to her. Thought I'd leave that to you. You women are better at this sort of thing. I excused myself by telling her I had things to do in the kitchen. It is sausage and mash tonight, isn't it?' Receiving Maxie's nod he said, 'Leave me to it then. You go in and sit with her. After her sleep she might feel more like talking today.'

Maxie smiled welcomingly at Ellen who was curled up in the armchair she usually sat in, nursing a mug of tea, a distant expression on her face. Maxie sat down in the armchair Danny usually occupied, curling her own legs under her and relaxing.

'So, Ellen, how have you been today?'

She looked at Maxie for several long moments before she said softly, 'Well ... I'm afraid I slept all day again.'

Maxie smiled sympathetically at her. 'You obviously needed to. Anyway, sleep's a healer. Problems don't seem so serious when you've slept on them, do they?'

'Don't they?'

'Well, when you're tired you can't think straight, can you?'

Ellen heaved a deep sigh. 'Tired or not, my situation is still the same.'

Maxie looked at her searchingly for several long moments before gently probing. 'Did you have a row with your husband and he threw you out in the heat of the moment?'

'No. We'd had no row.'

'Well ... what made him throw you out then, Ellen?'

She took a deep breath, her grip on the mug of tea tightening till her knuckles gleamed white. 'He ... he came home from work one night and as soon as he got in told me he didn't want me as his wife anymore. He didn't love me, simple as that, he said. Told me I'd five minutes to pack my things and get out.'

Maxie was staring at her agog. 'What?'

314

'I thought he was having some sort of joke with me so I laughed and said I didn't think he was being funny. He grabbed my arm and dragged me out of the kitchen. He pushed me towards the stairs and repeated I'd five minutes to pack my things or I'd leave with nothing. I ... well, I thought he'd had a brainstorm or something. I told him as much. He just looked at me with such an expression of disgust on his face! He ran up the stairs himself and came back down almost immediately with my case packed, hardly any more in it than a change of clothes. He grabbed my coat and handbag which he looked inside first and took out my house keys. Then he opened the front door and threw everything outside, ordering me out too. I was so shocked I couldn't move. So he came over to me, grabbed my arm again and dragged me over to the door. He pushed me out, telling me he didn't ever want to see me again, then shut it. I heard him shoot the bolts across.

'It all happened so quickly. I stood there for ages, staring at the door. I couldn't believe what had just happened. I tried to talk to him through the letterbox but he completely ignored me. I was still of the opinion he'd had some sort of brain seizure or something and that's why he was acting so strangely. It was obvious he wasn't going to let me back in that night so I had no alternative but to go and get a hotel room. Thankfully I had a few pounds in my purse left over from my housekeeping.'

Maxie was staring at her, dumbstruck. 'Oh, you poor thing. Had you no family to turn to?'

Ellen sadly shook her head. 'I've only an aunt

still alive, and she lives where I originally come from, up north.'

'What about friends, Ellen?'

'I haven't any close ones I know well enough to turn to in circumstances like this. I met my husband two years ago when he stayed in the hotel where I was working as a receptionist. He was attending a conference. He asked me to join him for a drink that night.' Her eyes glazed over distantly. 'I couldn't believe he was asking me to do that. He was the handsomest man I'd ever seen. I think I fell in love with him the moment I saw him. Everything seemed to happen so quickly after that night. I'd always wondered what people meant by being swept off their feet. Then I found out. I almost didn't realise what was happening to me. Before I had time to catch my breath, we were married by special licence and I was living down here. I'd often pinch myself, couldn't believe I'd got everything I'd always dreamed of. Other women might see this as strange but I didn't feel the need for friends; my husband was my best friend.'

Maxie could fully relate to that. Danny had always provided everything she'd expect of a friend: trust, loyalty, a confidential ear, sharing fun things together. She'd never felt the need to expand her circle to include anyone else, and as far as she was concerned she didn't lack for anything.

Ellen's face puckered miserably, her eyes began to fill with tears. 'I thought we were so happy. I had no reason to suspect my husband wasn't until the night he threw me out.'

316

'Have you been back since to try and talk to him?'

She nodded. 'Twice. He wouldn't even answer the door to me. The last time I went he threatened to call the police and have me charged with causing a public nuisance.' She put her mug down on the hearth and jumped up from her seat. 'I'm so sorry, I can't bear thinking about it.' With that Ellen ran up to her room once again.

Maxie rose from her seat and went to join Danny in the kitchen. He listened intently to what she relayed to him.

When she had finished she asked him, 'If her husband won't even talk to her it's obvious he's not considering taking her back, isn't it?'

He gave a shrug. 'Seems that way.'

'Oh, Danny, I feel so sorry for her. Ellen seems a lovely woman. She's in such shock over all this and I can fully understand why. From what she's told me she had no idea at all her husband didn't love her anymore until he threw her out. I feel so bad that I can't think of a thing to suggest to her, not if he won't even speak to her.'

Danny privately felt he had enough to contend with in his own marriage without taking on the problems of someone else's.

'Maybe she'll just have to accept it's over and go back home ... up north, was it, you said she told you she came from?'

'Mmm ... as matters stand it doesn't seem like she has any other choice, does it? But maybe I should suggest she has a last try at getting her husband at least to speak to her. She deserves to be given a bit more of an explanation for him wanting to end their marriage than he has given her so far. If he still refuses then ... well, let's hope he's had time by now to realise what a mistake he made and is wanting to put it right.'

'What if ... er ... well, what if her husband has met someone else he thinks suits him better than Ellen does? Gives him a better life?'

'Oh, I hadn't thought of that. Well, let's hope he remembers he promised to stick by Ellen through thick and thin when he made his wedding vows to her, not cast her aside as soon as the promise of someone better came along.'

'Oh, I hope you will do too, Maxie,' Danny blurted out.

She looked at him strangely. '*What* did you say, Danny?'

'Eh? Oh, I meant, if that's the case, then I hope he does too,' Danny blustered. 'Do you want a cuppa?' he asked her by way of changing the subject.

Maxie gave a heavy sigh. 'I don't often feel the need for a strong drink but I do just now. Since we haven't got anything in, a cuppa will have to do. You go and sit down. I'll make it as you cooked dinner and washed up. Fair's fair.'

As she busied herself mashing the tea, all her thoughts were for the woman upstairs in her spare bedroom. Maxie couldn't begin to comprehend how desperate she must be feeling. She tried to imagine how it would feel to come home from work one evening and be told by Danny he no longer loved or wanted her anymore, that she had five minutes to pack her bags and clear out. Maxie shuddered. It didn't bear thinking about.

CHAPTER TWENTY-THREE

Once again Ellen had not risen by the time Maxie left for work in the morning and she decided to pay a visit on her mother and mother-in-law that afternoon. As worldly women themselves, maybe they could come up with alternatives to Ellen's terrible predicament, other than the one Maxie had thought up herself. She didn't feel she was betraying Ellen's confidence as she had not asked Maxie to keep her business private, and besides, Ada and Kathy did not know Ellen or they her.

She didn't get the opportunity to pay that visit, though.

Arriving at work, she found an extremely anxious-looking Douglas Marshall just about to leave the house with an hysterical Thomas in his arms. Mrs Sycamore hovered close by, looking worried.

'I'm so glad you've arrived promptly, Mrs Maws,' Douglas Marshall said to her in his usual brusque manner. 'I need you to come with me to the hospital with Thomas. He wouldn't settle at all last night and now he's running a temperature.'

Maxie went across to them, looking closely at Thomas who was wriggling uncomfortably in his father's arms. She noted the red blotches on his cheeks and felt his forehead. It was hot to the touch admittedly, but not burning. 'I'm sure he's just teething, Mr Marshall. It's nothing more serious than that,' she said with confidence. 'Cutting teeth, especially back ones which Thomas is doing now, affects some children worse than others. Poor little Thomas is one of those children, bless him,' she said, looking at the child with deep sympathy. 'I haven't tried the old remedy of rubbing ice on his gums yet. Maybe that will help ease the soreness more than the other things have.'

'With all due respect, Mrs Maws, you're not a doctor. Thomas is really ill, I know he is. Now please hold him,' Mr Marshall snapped at her, putting the squirming, screaming child into her arms, 'while I fetch the car out of the garage. As I said, I'll need you to accompany me.'

Several hours later, back at home, Douglas Marshall looked awkwardly at Maxie. 'It seems I owe you an apology, Mrs Maws. I feel very foolish for having insisted the doctor carry out all those tests on Thomas. You were right, he is just suffering from cutting his back teeth.'

'I didn't take offence, Mr Marshall. It's better to be safe than sorry, isn't it?' She chose to forget the derogatory way the doctor had looked at her when Douglas Marshall had introduced her as his son's nanny, as though to say, Well, if you're qualified, how come you haven't recognised the obvious symptoms?

Douglas Marshall seemed to appreciate her restraint. 'Well, I'd better get off to work for what's left of the afternoon. I've a special shipment of Italian wine coming in today and want to check it's arrived safely. I've customers waiting for it.' His

320

face suddenly softened and he flashed a smile at her, adding, 'I'll leave Thomas in your capable hands now that the ice the nurse rubbed on his gums seems to have done wonders, which ... er ... was what you suggested, wasn't it? Thank you for ... er ... well, thank you.' He flashed her a quick smile before grabbing his briefcase and heading for the front door.

Maxie stared after him. He was warming towards her, she felt sure he was.

It was too late to take Thomas out now to visit Ada and Kathy, so unless Ellen had solved her problem herself while Maxie was out at work, she would visit them tomorrow to ask their advice then.

She arrived home that evening and was surprised to find no sign of Danny. He hadn't mentioned he'd be late home for any reason and she wondered where he was. Ellen, though, was up and sitting in an armchair. Her dainty figure looked lost inside it. She jumped when Maxie said to her, 'Hello, Ellen. Do you know where Danny is?'

'What? Oh, I'm sorry, I didn't hear you come in, I was miles away.'

Maxie didn't need to ask where her thoughts had been. She was just about to repeat her question when she heard the back door open and Danny was entering the room to greet her with a kiss on the cheek. He looked very tired.

'Danny, there you are,' she said, her voice betraying her relief to see him. She returned his greeting and asked, 'Where have you been?'

Stripping off his work jacket, he laid it

temporarily over the back of a dining chair then sat down to ease off his work boots. 'They were short-staffed at work today, some bug going around, and Mr Stibbins asked if I'd stay on after my own shift finished and help out in the bottle-sterilising department.'

Danny had jumped at the chance to earn extra money and knew exactly what he was going to do with it when he received it in his pay packet the following week. It wouldn't be enough to take Maxie out for dinner and dancing at a night club as he'd promised to do several weeks ago, but he could take her for a meal at the new Chinese restaurant that had opened recently at the bottom of the Belgrave Road in town. It would give her a chance to doll herself up in the new dress he'd bought her which she hadn't yet given an airing. But before he mentioned his plan to her he would wait until the following pay day to make sure he had the money to pay for it.

'How was your day?' he asked.

'I'll tell you later or we'll never get any dinner tonight, but one good thing happened today. My boss is finally showing signs of getting to like me.'

Danny looked at her sharply, a glint of fear in his eyes. 'What do you mean? What did your boss do to make you think that?'

She frowned at him, taken aback. 'He said thank you to me and actually smiled. I'm beginning to think that maybe there's a nice man lurking somewhere under that stiff manner of his. Anyway it's nice when your boss shows he appreciates your efforts, don't you agree?'

'Er ... yes, 'course I do.' As long as her work was

all her boss was appreciating about Maxie, he thought, resentment building inside him against the man he was having to share his wife's attention with.

Maxie realised Ellen was looking at them both intently and smiled across at her. 'I've been most rude and haven't asked you how you've been today, Ellen?'

She gave a heavy sigh. 'Oh, well, I've been sitting here wondering what to do. I'm trying to will myself to pay my husband another visit in the hope he might have relented and be willing to speak to me now.'

Maxie went over and perched in the chair opposite, looking at her keenly. 'Well, actually, Danny and I were talking after you went up last night and we were going to suggest that very thing to you. It's worth a try, Ellen.'

She looked worried, wringing her hands nervously. 'I don't know if I've got the nerve, though. I don't know what I'll do if he still refuses to speak to me.'

'But you won't know if you don't give it a try,' Maxie coaxed her. 'Your husband doesn't know where you are so it's not like he can come and see you, is it? Now he's had time to think over what he's done, I'm sure he's deeply regretting it.' Maxie dearly hoped he was, for Ellen's sake. 'Look ... would you like me to come with you for support? I don't mean to come inside the house with you, but for company on the way. I'd wait outside.'

'Oh, I couldn't expect you to go to that trouble. You're doing enough for me, more than enough already.' She flashed a weak smile over at Danny. 'Both of you. I'll never be able to repay your kindness.' She paused and thoughtfully gnawed her bottom lip for several moments before announcing, 'I will go to see him again. Tomorrow night after six, when I know he'll be home from work.'

Maxie leaned over and reassuringly patted her knee. 'If you change your mind about me coming with you, just let me know.'

Ellen flashed a grateful smile at her before saying, 'If you don't mind, I'm going up now. I'm tired.'

After she had departed Maxie said to Danny, 'I don't like it that she spends so much time on her own in her room. At least if she stayed down here and watched a bit of television it would help take her mind off things. And again she's had no dinner. I'll take her some up on a plate and hope she's tempted by it.' She gave a sigh. 'Oh, I hope her husband at least speaks to her tomorrow. That poor woman doesn't deserve to be treated in this way.'

As she rose to make a start on the dinner Maxie noticed the door to the cellar wasn't shut properly and went across to do it, saying to Danny, 'You never shut the cellar door properly after you. I worry that any mice down there will get in here if we don't keep it closed.'

'I haven't been down the cellar recently,' he said. 'Anyway, when I do I always make sure I shut the door properly behind me.'

She smiled warmly at him. 'Yes, I know you do. Well, maybe the catch is faulty. Can you have a look at it when you get a minute?' She went over and shut the cellar door. 'It's shutting all right now. One of life's little mysteries, eh? Right, dinner coming up.'

Maxie decided to resurrect the visit to see Ada and Kathy that she had been unable to take due to Thomas's trip to hospital. Despite the fact that they had both taken a shine to the baby and clucked over him like two broody mother hens, they needed to be advised about her and Danny's house guest so she didn't come as a surprise when they next came round. It was imminent as they hadn't visited since Ellen had arrived on the scene a couple of days ago and usually never more than two or three days at the most went by without either Ada, Kathy, or both together popping in to see them, plus the fact Maxie still wanted to ask their advice on what she could suggest Ellen do to repair her marriage. It was Sunday the day after next and as the weather was favourable a ride out in the motorbike and sidecar would be on the cards. If Ellen was still with them then accommodating five people was out of the question, and it wouldn't be very charitable of them all to go off enjoying themselves, leaving her at home on her own.

Douglas Marshall had been extremely cordial to her again as he had departed for work that morning, actually telling Maxie he hoped she had a good day. She felt that her humiliation in front of that doctor at the hospital was well worth it if it had brought about such a change in her boss.

Ada and Kathy were as usual delighted to see her. As soon as she arrived Kathy scooped Thomas out of his pram. Now he was perched comfortably on her lap in an armchair in the living room and she was keeping him entertained with a tin of old buttons.

Maxie was sitting beside her mother on the sofa.

'Really! Oh, I say,' an appalled Ada was saying as Maxie related the story behind Ellen's coming to be with them. 'Her husband did what?' she exclaimed when Maxie got to the part where Ellen's husband had bodily thrown her out.

'Can you speak up, Maxie lovey, and repeat that last bit? I missed it as Thomas was giggling,' said Kathy. 'No, Thomas, not in your mouth. There's a good boy, that's right, throw them on the floor for Auntie Ada to pick them all up.'

When Maxie had obliged, Kathy too gasped in shock. 'He did what? Oh, that poor woman! Eh, up, Ada. Elsie Hopwood's husband did that to her, if you remember, when our two were just nippers. It was quite a scandal at the time.'

'Yes, well, in fairness to Arthur Hopwood he did have good cause to as he had caught Elsie in bed with the gasman,' Ada responded, pursing her lips disapprovingly. She fixed her attention back on her daughter. 'From what you've told me this Ellen doesn't sound the sort that'd do anything like that.'

'She's a lovely woman, Mam. Very polite and well-mannered. To be honest we hardly know she's there. She's so grateful to us for doing what we can for her. You can tell she's completely bewildered by what her husband's done. Can't understand it at all.'

Ada looked at her thoughtfully. 'Well, the only hope I can see for her is that this husband of hers has had time to think on what he's done while she's been gone and now regrets it.'

'Yes, seems that way to me too,' agreed Kathy.

'That's what we hope, Mam. Ellen's going to go and see him tonight. I've offered to go with her for support but she said she didn't want to put me to the trouble as she felt we'd done enough for her already. I've told her to let me know if she changes her mind.'

Ada affectionately patted her daughter's knee. 'Not many youngsters these days would have taken a strange woman into their home and offered her what you two have. I'm proud of you and Danny, ducky.'

'Me too,' echoed Kathy.

'Right,' said Ada, easing herself up, 'it's my turn with that babby, Kathy. So give him here while you go and mash us another cuppa.'

Meanwhile Danny was just arriving home after finishing his shift. He found Ellen in the back room immersed in looking through the stack of LPs on the radiogram.

'That's Maxie's favourite,' he said to her as he sat on a dining chair to take off his boots. 'Put it on, if you like.'

She jumped, spinning round to face him. 'Oh, I didn't hear you come in!' She looked worriedly at him. 'I hope you don't mind me looking through these?'

'Not at all. As I said, the one in your hand is

327

Maxie's favourite. Put it on if you want to listen to it.'

She looked at the cover of the Andy Williams LP for several moments before she replaced it on top of the pile of other records, then walked over to the table and sat down opposite Danny. 'I need to concentrate my mind fully on facing my husband tonight and music will distract me. I'm just hoping he's willing to speak to me. I couldn't sleep last night for worrying that he still won't be. I don't know what's going to become of me then, I really don't.'

'I'm sure it'll be fine,' he said to her reassuringly.

She sighed heavily. 'I hope you're right. Er ... Danny?'

In the process of rising to put away his boots and hang his jacket up, he stopped and looked at her. 'Yes?'

'Well ... oh, it doesn't matter. It's just me being silly.'

It was obvious to him she had something on her mind she wanted to speak about. He smiled kindly at her. 'What were you just being silly about, Ellen?'

Her face took on an anxious look. 'Well ... it was just something last night I happened to notice. When Maxie told you her boss was starting to act nicely to her, well, I just thought that he ought to because Maxie is a lovely woman. But I saw the look on your face and ... well, I don't think I'm wrong when I say you looked very worried, like you were bothered that her boss was maybe starting to appreciate her for more than just the

328

work she does for him.'

This woman might have a lot on her own mind but she didn't miss much, thought Danny. 'And do you think, from what she said, that he is?' he urgently demanded.

'Er ... no. No. I'm sure it's just what Maxie said it was and he was thanking her for a job well done,' Ellen stressed. 'It's just that ... well, after I went to bed I remembered that incident and it got me thinking and ... my husband has a secretary. When we first got married he hardly spoke about her and I knew nothing much about her except that she was about my age and married herself. But it's striking me now that recently he'd been talking more and more about her. Just casual things like the fact that she had looked pretty that day in a new dress or was wearing a new pair of shoes or she'd had her hair done to be honest, the sort of things men don't usually notice about a woman unless they're interested in her. Then I caught him looking worried one night as we were eating dinner and asked him why. He said he was just bothered about his secretary as her marriage had broken up and she'd gone back to live with her mother. Her husband was hounding her to go back to him and she didn't want to and it was upsetting her. I thought at the time he was showing concern for her as her boss but now I'm wondering...

'Well, it's well known, isn't it, that people who work closely together can end up falling for each other? I wonder if that's why my husband doesn't want me anymore, because he's fallen for his secretary over the time they've been working together.' Her face crumpled. 'Oh, I so hope that's not the reason he doesn't want me anymore,' she uttered, distraught. 'I love him so much and couldn't bear to think that he'd replaced me with someone else. And what about...' Her voice trailed off and her eyes blazed wildly.

'What about what, Ellen?' Danny asked her.

'My ... my... Oh, I must go and get myself ready, look as nice as I can, to go and see him and my ... my... Oh, he must be missing me, surely he must be? Whether my husband still loves me or not, he'll have to let me see him, won't he? He can't stop me doing that. He wouldn't be so cruel.'

Danny was looking at her, puzzled. Her ramblings weren't making any sense to him. But before he could ask her to explain herself more clearly she had rushed to her room.

Maxie came home to find Danny sitting at the dining table staring into space. As soon as he realised she'd arrived he jumped up from his chair and asked, 'Your boss, Maxie. Was he ... well, how was he with you today?'

She gave a nonchalant shrug while at the same time looking at him, puzzled. 'Very pleasant, which I much prefer to the way he was when I first started. Why?'

'Oh, just wanting to make sure he was treating you with the respect you deserve, that's all.'

Her mother was right. She'd been silly to think Danny was worried that she might take a fancy to her new boss and run off with him. He must know she'd never do that to him, but was concerned she should be treated properly by any man she came into contact with. After all, Maxie wouldn't like it very much if Danny's boss treated him badly, and it was only right that he should feel likewise. When she had worked for the Carsons he had known how well she was treated by them so he hadn't needed to ask. Not many men bothered themselves about their wife's welfare at work, most were just interested in the money they brought home every pay day. She had a husband in a million, she knew that.

Maxie suddenly felt another presence. She glanced across towards the door to the stairs and saw Ellen standing watching them.

When the other woman realised that Maxie had noticed she was lurking there, she came fully into the room. 'I'm sorry, I didn't want to interrupt anything so I waited until you'd finished. I hope you don't think I was eavesdropping?'

Maxie hoped she hadn't been as the conversation she and Danny had just had would only have brought forcibly home to her that Maxie had a husband who cared very deeply for her whereas Ellen had been utterly rejected by hers.

She smiled warmly at her guest. 'Are you still going to see your husband tonight? You haven't changed your mind, have you?'

She shook her head. 'No. I'm not looking forward to it but it's something I have to do. I'm going now.'

'What about something to eat first?'

'Thank you, but I'm not hungry.'

'Well, maybe you'll feel like something when you come back ... if you come back,' she added optimistically. 'My offer to come with you still stands.'

Ellen looked gratefully at her. 'Thank you, but you've just arrived home from work and will be wanting your dinner, and I ... well, I want to get this over with before I lose my nerve. I'll see you both later then. Wish me luck?'

'Oh, we do,' they both said in unison.

Worried about what Ellen was possibly facing and sincerely hoping a pleasant reception awaited her at her destination, neither Maxie nor Danny was very hungry so they settled for beans on toast. The second they had cleared away a tap sounded on the back door and it opened to a call of, 'Cooee, it's only us!' Ada and Kathy bustled in, each clutching a capacious black handbag and a tapestry knitting bag.

A very distracted Maxie, her mind fully occupied by Ellen's plight, was wiping the stove top but she smiled happily to see them. She was always glad to see these two women but especially tonight as they would be a welcome distraction. 'This is a nice surprise. I'll put the kettle on.'

'Well, we'll just make our own way through then while you mash it,' said Ada.

'Danny's running the Ewbank over the fireside rug. He'll be pleased to see you and it won't take me a tick to...' Maxie suddenly stopped her flow and looked at them both knowingly. 'Oh, I see, it's not me and Danny you've come to see, is it? You want to meet Ellen.'

'Don't be silly, dear, 'course we've come to see you and Danny,' said Kathy, then added as an afterthought, 'well, maybe Ellen as well, if we're honest. But don't worry, we'll keep a check on ourselves not to let on you've told us anything

332

about her troubles.'

'There's no need to as Ellen's not here. She's gone to see her husband.'

'Oh,' they both mouthed, looking at each other in disappointment.

'Well, good job we came then. If Ellen's husband hasn't had a change of heart, no disrespect to you, dear, but that poor gel will need a more mature woman's advice on the matter, like mine and Kathy's,' said Ada self-importantly. 'And you musta thought so too or you wouldn't have come seeking it from us this aft'noon.'

'No, you wouldn't have,' said Kathy. 'Now, we've both brought our knitting so while we're waiting for her to come back we can be getting on with the jumpers we're knitting for you and Danny. Oh, and *Maigret* is on the telly at seven-thirty. I'll tell Danny to get it tuned in ready, shall I? Well, unless of course there's something else on you was both planning to watch?' Both women were looking at Maxie as if to say, I hope not because we like *Maigret* and aren't keen on missing an episode.

She hid a smile. '*Maigret* will be fine with us. It's mine and Danny's second favourite detective programme after *The Saint*. You both had a way of making sure we all watched it when you were stopping with us.'

By the time nine o'clock came and Ellen had not returned, both mothers conceded defeat and began winding up their wool ready to put their knitting away.

'We can't wait around any longer,' sighed Ada. She'd been looking forward to meeting her daughter's and son-in-law's guest and dispensing her own worldly wisdom.

'No, we can't,' said Kathy, equally as disappointed for the same reason. 'Work beckons in the morning and we need our beauty sleep, don't we, Ada?'

'Well, you more than me,' she responded to her friend tongue-in-cheek.

'Do you think the fact Ellen hasn't come back yet is a good sign?' Maxie asked them both.

'Oh, I think it has to be,' said Kathy. 'Don't you, Ada?'

'Oh, yes, most certainly. I mean, it's a nice night for taking a stroll but if yer upset then it's a shoulder to cry on yer'll be wanting. If that was the case for Ellen she'd have been back to cry on yours and Danny's by now.' She eyed them questioningly. 'Yer still both coming for yer tea tomorrow afternoon, ain't yer? I'm making a trifle. At the outside chance Ellen's still with yer then she's invited too.'

'Don't forget Sunday?' Kathy prompted her.

'Oh, yes, about Sunday. We forgot to tell you this afternoon when you popped in but our conversation was dominated by more important things, wasn't it? If yer was planning to take us both out for a spin then we're sorry to disappoint yer but we're booked on a day trip out. Saw it advertised in the *Mercury* last Tuesday night, didn't we, Kathy? And we thought, Oh, that'd suit us just smashing, a day trip out to Skeggie. And best of all it were on special offer. Nineteen shillings and a tanner instead of thirty bob. Years since I've been to the seaside.'

'Me too,' said Kathy. 'Anyway, we can't wait to have a paddle, can we, Ada?'

'No, we can't. And we'll bring you both a stick of rock back,' she said, looking excited.

Maxie and Danny hid their smiles as they both conjured up the comical vision of their mothers, clutching their dresses, showing their legs and possibly the tops of their long knickers, and giggling like school girls as they enjoyed their paddle.

Maxie hoped they were right and Ellen and her husband were making up and putting the last few days behind them to begin afresh. To be on the safe side, though, when they went to bed they left the back door unlocked so Ellen could let herself in. But on discovering her bed hadn't been slept in the next morning when she popped her head around to check, Maxie was positive that the next time they saw Ellen it would be to collect her belongings and say her goodbyes to them as she was back where she belonged with her husband.

CHAPTER TWENTY–FOUR

'It's all right for me, I only work part-time, but I bet you're glad it's Saturday and you finish at one today so you can rest up a bit tomorrow. You've had a bit of a hectic few days of it, haven't you, with young Thomas suffering like he has been?' Mrs Sycamore was chatting to Maxie as they sat sharing their elevenses at the kitchen table the following morning.

Maxie finished chewing the last of one of Mrs Sycamore's delicious scones, which had been thickly spread with best butter, before she responded. 'Everyone looks forward to the weekend, don't they? For me it means I get to spend more time with my husband.' She paused, wondering if there would be three of them this weekend or if, as it did look like, Ellen had resolved her marital problems and she and Danny now had the house back to themselves again. 'Have you anything planned, Mrs Sycamore?' she asked the older woman.

'Just the usual, dear, for me. Doing my weekend shopping in town this afternoon, church tomorrow morning, straight back after to see to the Sunday dinner, then whether I get a rest or not depends on whether either of my daughters or both of them bring the grandkids for a visit. If they do they usually expect their tea. Weekends can't be easy for Mr Marshall, can they, him being on his own?'

'Well, he's not on his own, is he? He's got Thomas keeping him company.'

'I meant another adult. Anyway, I have to admit that there's been a bit of a change in our lord and master recently, ain't there? He ain't quite so uppity with us now. More mellow. I can actually confirm he's got teeth, I saw them for meself when he smiled at me this morning. He even stopped long enough in the kitchen to have a chat with me before his handover with you, told me how much he was enjoying the meals I prepare for him. He's still not what you'd call comfortable around women, to my mind, but at least he's a bit more amenable than he was. And it all makes for a pleasanter life, don't it, ducky?'

'It certainly does,' agreed Maxie. 'I was saying as much to my husband last night.'

The older woman pursed her lips thoughtfully. 'I wonder if he's had a bad experience concerning a woman and that's why he's so wary around 'em. Well, you and me at any rate. Possibly with his wife. Maybe she led him a dog's life and her death was a relief to him. Maybe that's why there ain't no evidence of her existence around the house, like he wants to erase all memory of her. If it wasn't for Thomas you'd never know there had been a Mrs Marshall, would yer?'

Maxie had to agree with that. His wife must have done something really terrible for him to have resorted to such measures. Was Mr Marshall's story the same as Matthew Holbrook's: had his wife betrayed him with another man before she had died? Mrs Sycamore's mention of her charge made Maxie look at the clock. She drained her cup and rose to her feet. 'Those scones were delicious, Mrs Sycamore. I'd best get back up to the nursery and check on Thomas, see if he's awake from his nap.'

One o'clock came and went and there was no sign of Douglas Marshall returning home to relieve her. It was half-past two before she heard him enter by the front door. Scooping up Thomas with whom she'd been playing on the nursery rug with building bricks and a selection of toy cars, she took him down to greet his father.

Douglas looked up apologetically at Maxie as she descended the stairs. 'You have my sincere apologies for my lateness home, Mrs Maws,' he said to her. 'I had a puncture and the wheel nuts proved so stubborn to shift it took me nearly an hour to do the job. I am conscious that it's really your time off now and will compensate you.'

She smiled at him. 'There's no need, honestly, these things happen, Mr Marshall.'

'But I insist. Would you just give me a minute to wash my hands before I relieve you of Thomas?' Maxie followed him through to the kitchen and while he washed his oily hands he commented, 'Thomas seems to be in good spirits today.' He turned his head to look over at his son in Maxie's arms and smiled tenderly. 'Hopefully his teething troubles are over for the time being.'

'He allowed me to have a check around this morning and the ones he was bothered by have definitely broken through. Hopefully you're in for a peaceful weekend. Thomas really is a lovely natured little man, except when he's teething,' she added jocularly.

Having dried his hands Douglas joined Maxie and relieved her of his son, kissing the child's forehead. Thomas responded by grabbing hold of his father's bottom lip and pulling at it.

The boy's actions were obviously proving painful to Douglas but regardless he gently eased his son's grip off his lip then gave him a tickle on his tummy. 'No, no, Thomas, Daddy's lip isn't for pulling. Toys are for playing with but fathers you have to treat gently.'

Maxie smiled warmly at this touching scene. There was no doubt in her mind how much this man loved his son. She did wonder, though, why all evidence of the child's mother had been removed.

After enquiring from Maxie how she had kept his son occupied that morning, and wishing her a pleasant rest over the weekend before once again apologising for his lateness, Mr Marshall let her take her leave.

As Maxie hurried off in the direction of home, she was mindful of the time. Since their marriage she and Danny had gone together into town every Saturday afternoon to do the weekend shopping so he could help her carry the heavy bags home, which she always appreciated him doing. Due to her lateness today, by the time they'd caught the bus the afternoon would really have worn on and it was possible she would have missed some of the shops as they closed at four. Plus she would be left with only the substandard fruit and vegetables left on the market after the earlier shoppers had had the best pick. But more important than that, their mothers were expecting them for tea and it would cause a fuss if they arrived late. Maxie would avoid that if she could help it. She made a spot decision. Danny would understand when she explained to him why she had decided it was best for her to do the shopping herself that afternoon. Turning around, she headed for the bus stop.

Danny was caught between being glad that Mr Stibbins hadn't needed him to do any extra hours today because he liked to accompany Maxie to do the weekend shop, and disgruntled because he would have welcomed the extra money. His workmates took the mickey out of him for accompanying his wife to do the shopping on a Saturday afternoon. They saw his actions as unmanly. To them shopping was solely for women, unless they were shopping for something for themselves that they didn't trust their wives to get for them. Danny didn't care what they thought and ignored their jibes. It was his opinion that women were best at shopping and he was generally happy to leave it to them, but it wasn't fair that they should then have to struggle home with it alone when a lot of the stuff inside those heavy bags was for their men's benefit.

It would be nice, just Maxie and himself being alone again. As their mothers were off on their own outing tomorrow, he would suggest to Maxie that he take her out to Dovedale for the day for a picnic. That was her favourite place, and he knew she'd had an arduous week. Hopefully the tranquillity of the countryside would help recharge her energies for the week ahead. But, regardless, whatever Maxie wanted to do, he was happy to go along with.

Hurrying around the corner of his house, he stopped so abruptly he almost toppled over, shocked to see an unexpected figure crouched on his back doorstep. It was Ellen and she was obviously in great distress. There was a large suitcase beside her.

Going over, he knelt down on his haunches and lightly touched her shoulder. 'I ... er ... take it things didn't go according to plan last night?'

She miserably shook her head.

Standing up, he gently took her arm. 'Come on, let me get you inside and a cuppa down you, then you can tell me all about it if you want to. Or Maxie should be home any minute if you want to wait for her.' Which Danny was hoping she would do as he had a good listening ear but when it came to advising women, he felt other women were best left to it.

Without a word she allowed him to help her up and inside, along with the suitcase. A few minutes later he handed her a mug of tea. 'I've put plenty of sugar in as I'm always hearing the women in my life saying that sweet tea is good for ... well, times like this.' He glanced at the 1930s-style clock, a gift from a neighbour for their wedding, ticking away on the mantelpiece. 'Maxie's a bit later than she normally is but she shouldn't be long now. Er ... can I get you something to eat? I don't think we've any bread as we've yet to do the weekend shopping but I'm sure we've some Jacob's crackers in the cupboard and a noggin of cheese left.'

Sniffing hard, Ellen smiled weakly up at him. 'Just the tea is fine, thank you, Danny. You're so kind, you really are.' Then with her bottom lip trembling, sorrowful tears glinting in her eyes, she uttered, 'My husband did talk to me.'

'He did?' He presumed that the outcome hadn't gone the way she had hoped considering the state she was in, and didn't know quite how to respond. He was saved from his dilemma as after sighing she continued talking.

'He said he'd give me just long enough to get it through my head that he meant what he'd said, our marriage was over. I told him I didn't understand why. I wished I hadn't then as he told me he'd grown tired of me, I didn't suit him anymore and he wanted to be free to be with someone who did. I can't tell you how humiliated he made me feel, that I was utterly worthless. I knew it was pointless begging him to give me another chance because ... well, he took such delight in telling me that that special someone had come along much sooner than he'd expected. She's working for him, he let on that fact. He's going to see his solicitor about dissolving our marriage so he'll be free to pursue matters with her.

'Oh, Danny, it must be his secretary! While I thought we were happily married, he's been carrying on behind my back with her.' Clutching her mug of tea so tightly her knuckles shone white she continued, 'I didn't want to but I didn't see I had any other choice. I told him I'd do what he wanted and go away if he'd let me have the baby and all our things, then he'd be rid of us both and could get on with his life.'

Danny was stunned speechless by her revelation. Ellen had a child! So that's what she had been talking about when he hadn't understood her.

'He laughed at me,' she continued. 'Said the baby was the only good thing to come out of our marriage. I'd have a fight on my hands to get custody, though. No judge in the land would see fit to hand over a child to be raised by a single, homeless women, which is what I am now. My husband knows I have no money to take him to court. I pleaded that a child needs its mother, and he laughed again and said he had another mother lined up already. Someone who loved children and would be a better mother to my baby than I ever was. But I was ... am ... a good mother, Danny,' she insisted. 'My baby and my husband were my life. Everything I did was for them both. He had that case packed ready with the rest of my clothes and threw it out to me.' Jumping up from her seat, dropping her cup on the hearth rug and spilling its contents, she cried out, 'I can't bear this!' before rushing from the room and seeking refuge in the spare room once more.

He stood staring blindly after her, feeling utterly helpless. What could you say to a woman who had been stripped of her whole reason for living through no fault of her own? From what she had told him it didn't appear she had any option left but to accept her fate. This was a situation for Maxie and he hoped she arrived home soon to deal with it.

At just before six that evening, when Maxie finally struggled through the back door laden down with shopping, she was preoccupied by the fact that her trip into town had taken much longer than she'd expected. It seemed that half of Leicester had decided to shop later than normal that day and she had had to join lengthy queues for everything she had wanted. She knew Danny would be worried about her whereabouts if he hadn't realised what she had done, plus the fact they were dreadfully late for tea with their mothers. She wasn't at all prepared for him to rush up to her without his usual warm greeting.

'Oh, Maxie, Ellen's back! Her husband is divorcing her, but that's not all. She has a baby, and he won't let her have it back. He's someone else ready to take her place as his wife and the baby's mother, can you believe that?'

Staggered by this unexpected announcement, she dumped her heavy shopping on the kitchen floor and exclaimed, 'What? Ellen has a baby and ... and... Oh, Danny, this is so awful,' she said in genuine distress. 'I just can't begin to imagine what she's going through. What must she be feeling like? Where is she now?'

'Upstairs.'

Sinking down on a kitchen chair, Maxie rubbed her hands over her face. 'What do I say to her?' she implored, looking at him in the hope that he could give her some guidance.

He gave a helpless shrug. 'I was hoping you'd know.'

Just then there was a tap on the back door and

Kathy and Ada bustled in, managing just in time to stride over the abandoned shopping bags and not fall over them. Both of them looked worried.

'When you didn't turn up for tea we knew summat had happened,' said Ada to them.

'And we can tell by yer faces summat has,' said Kathy.

'What is it?' they both demanded in unison.

Maxie did the honours. When she had finished both women looked extremely grave.

'Oh, dear,' mouthed Ada.

'Oh, dear indeed,' said Kathy.

'I should go up and speak to her,' said Maxie. 'But I don't know what to say.'

'Nothing you can say,' said her mother. 'You can't tell her everything is going to be all right, can yer, 'cos it don't sound to me like it will be for her. It seems her husband has made up his mind.'

'He seems to have, from what you've told us, ducky,' agreed Kathy.

'What about if I offer to speak to him, see if I can…'

'Don't even think of it, lovey,' cut in Kathy. 'Yer can't interfere between husband and wife.'

'Kathy's right,' said Ada. 'Anyway, it's not like this man knows you, is it? And I don't think I'd welcome a stranger barging into my home, sticking their nose into my business.'

'Soon tell them to sling their hook, wouldn't you, Ada? And so would I,' said Kathy.

'So what do I do?' Maxie asked them both.

'As yer mam said to you before, lovey, there's nothing you can suggest to her if her husband's determined that their marriage is over. Anyway, it's not like Ellen is a close friend ... or you know her all that well, in fact. She's only under your roof in the first place 'cos it was Danny's float she picked on to shelter in, not someone else's. You're already doing far more for her than others would in the circumstances.'

'Yes, you certainly are,' Ada confirmed, looking at them both proudly. 'You've offered a roof over their head to a stranger in trouble, and fed her as well ... given her sanctuary really. Now look, she'll need a shoulder to cry on sometime or other and she'll let yer know when she's ready. The best thing you can do is carry on as normal meantime. Let's get this shopping put away, then come around to us as yer'd planned to do and have yer tea. You can leave Ellen a note on the table saying where you are. I would think she needs to be on her own after the shock she's had, to gather her thoughts and see where she goes from here.'

Maxie nodded and smiled at her. 'You're right, Mam.'

CHAPTER TWENTY-FIVE

When they arrived back from tea with their mothers, having feasted on cheese-and-pickle and tongue sandwiches followed by trifle, there was no evidence to suggest that Ellen had come out of her room, even to make herself a drink.

'Do you think I should make her one and take it up?' Maxie asked Danny.

He looked dubious for a moment before advising, 'Yes, she must be thirsty, but just tap on the door and tell her it's outside.'

'I will, and I'll let her know we'll be up for a bit if she wants to come down for some company.'

Ellen did not show her face again that evening, but when she went to bed Maxie did notice she had collected the mug of tea along with the sandwich she had left for her.

On Sunday they rose to discover that Ellen had got up before them and gone out. They could only hope that she had gone to try and reason with her husband again but it was a worry. In the circumstances they didn't feel they could go off on a jaunt in the countryside and therefore spent a fraught day at home, worrying about Ellen and what she might do next.

They were trying to enjoy their tea when the back door opened and they were relieved to see Ellen walk in. That was immediately replaced by worry for her when they noticed her harrowed expression, the defeated stoop to her shoulders.

'We're just having tea, you're welcome to join us,' Maxie said tentatively.

Their guest shook her head. 'Thank you, but if you don't mind I'd like to be on my own.'

'Of course we don't mind.'

Maxie and Danny watched helplessly as she made her way upstairs. After they had heard the click of her bedroom door, Danny said, 'I wonder where she's been all day?'

His wife gave a heavy sigh. 'I'm just glad to see her back here in one piece, Danny. I thank God she hasn't harmed herself. Anyway, let's finish our tea.'

As he resumed his meal Danny's mind reverted to his own consuming worry. He jumped when he realised Maxie was talking to him. 'Sorry, Maxie?'

'You were miles away then, Danny. You had a look on your face like ... well, like the world was about to end any minute and you didn't know what to do about it. You're not worried about anything, are you? Well, apart from Ellen, that is.'

'No, what have I got to worry about, Maxie?' he said heartily.

As Maxie was relieving Douglas Marshall of his son the next morning he asked affably, 'So what have you planned for Thomas today, Mrs Maws?'

Straddling her charge comfortably on her hip, she replied, 'Thomas seems to enjoy the park and it looks set to be another lovely day today so I plan to take him there after lunch. Mr Marshall, there was something I wanted to ask you about...

I noticed as I passed by the other day that the church on the Hinckley Road holds a coffee morning twice a week. When I went past one morning I saw several women going inside with children around Thomas's age. It would be good for him to mix with other children and I wondered if you had any objection to me taking him along? There's one on this morning, in fact. The notice did say everyone was welcome.'

'Well, if you think it's a good idea that's fine by me.' He smiled tenderly at his son. 'Have a good day and I'll see you tonight.' He made to depart then stopped. 'Oh, I have something to ask you, Mrs Maws. I have a wine merchants' sales conference to attend next week in Hunstanton in Norfolk. It's an evening affair so I wondered if you'd be able to stay with Thomas for the night? I also wondered if you'd consider something else.

'Thomas has never been to the seaside and I thought that if we travelled up early it would be a good opportunity for me to spend some time with him on the beach during the afternoon, weather permitting. I would still need someone to be with him, though, while I attend the evening affair. I'd pay for everything and you'd be free to do what you wanted when you weren't required to be with Thomas. If your husband can get a day off from his job then he could be my guest too.'

'That's very generous of you, Mr Marshall. I'm sure my husband would have loved the chance to spend a day at the seaside. Unfortunately it's not possible for him to take odd days off as holidays.'

When Maxie had accepted this job she had also

agreed to cover the very odd occasion when Douglas Marshall would need an overnight stay away. This proposal would mean a night away from Danny for her which did not appeal at all, but these circumstances were exceptional. She thought it just wonderful of her boss to want to spend time with his son in a location many children never got the chance to visit and was glad to be able to play a part in bringing this about.

'Of course I'll come and care for Thomas while you attend your function,' she said.

Mr Marshall looked pleased. 'Good, then I will make the arrangements.'

Maxie would look forward to their trip to the seaside, but not nearly as much as she would have done if Danny had been accompanying them. Smiling fondly at Thomas, she said to him, 'Well, young man, we have a big day ahead of us so we'd better get on with it, hadn't we?'

Danny's day had been uneventful so far. None of his customers had grumbled about him being late; no old dears had asked him to help them with a chore they couldn't manage by themselves; Bernice Frasier had not embarrassed the life out of him by propositioning him; no babies had needed rescuing from runaway prams; he'd found no strange women sheltering in his float, and no mishaps had happened to the vehicle itself. He was, though, still only halfway through his round and therefore not in the clear yet.

As he drove up to the end of the road to turn into the main Hinckley Road on his way to the next side street, he noticed a woman with a pram standing on the edge of the pavement ready to cross. Out of courtesy he slowed down to allow her safe passage. As he drew closer he realised that it was Maxie. She noticed that the driver of the milk float was her husband and gave him a cheery wave. After stopping the float – making sure that the hand brake was on – he jumped out and rushed over to join her.

'Where you off to?'

'Me and Thomas are going to the coffee morning at the church hall, aren't we, Thomas? So he can mix with some children of his own age,' she said, including the child in their conversation. He happily chuckled back at her, waving the golliwog that he had clutched in his tiny hands.

'So you're Master Thomas?' Danny addressed the youngster, bending his head to look at him at eye level. 'I've heard a lot about you, young man. Well, I'm your nanny's husband so I'm trusting you'll look after her well.'

Thomas responded by hitting him in the face with the golliwog.

Maxie laughed. 'So now you know what he thinks of you!'

Danny laughed too. 'Well, I'd better get on with it before I start getting complaints.' He kissed her on her cheek. 'See you later.'

He made to depart but was stopped by Maxie grabbing his arm. 'Oh, Danny, I know it's a long shot but is there any chance, do you think, that Mr Stibbins would let you have a day off next week?'

'I shouldn't think so, doubt it very much in

351

fact, unless it was for a family funeral. Why?'

She looked dejected. 'Oh, it was just that Mr Marshall has a wine merchants' do on at the coast next week and has asked me to go along to look after Thomas while he attends. He's invited you along as his guest too, and plans to spend the afternoon we get there with Thomas on the beach so we could have had that time together. I know what your firm's rules are about taking holidays but I thought it was worth asking, just in case you might have been able to wangle it.'

Danny looked disappointed. 'Oh, I would have liked that. No way Mr Stibbins will give me a day off to go frolicking at the seaside, though. If I just took it off, I'd get the sack.' He suddenly looked questioningly at her. 'Will this mean an overnight stop for you?'

Maxie nodded. 'You don't mind, do you?'

Of course he did. He would miss her, feel lost in bed without her by his side. To say nothing of the fact that recently he viewed every man she met as a possible contender for his wife's affections and didn't at all like the thought of Maxie being in the company of her boss in a social setting. This outing was work-related, though, and therefore he couldn't raise any objections to Maxie's going.

'Oh, it would have been good if you had been able to come along, Danny,' she was saying to him now. 'I'll bring you a stick of rock back.'

'Just bring yourself back to me, Maxie.'

As he returned to his float, she glanced quizzically after him, wondering what he had meant by that. Who else would she return to?

Danny tried to put Maxie's impending trip to the seaside out of his mind. On returning home he was hungry for his lunch and hoped their house guest wasn't in as he was looking forward to a short nap before he checked to see what household chores needed doing. He had hardly closed the back door behind him when a voice called out.

'Oh, Danny, thank goodness you're home! I need to speak to you urgently.'

He looked across to see Ellen standing in the back room doorway, a look on her face that had him demanding, 'What on earth has happened, Ellen?'

'You'll need to sit down for this, Danny,' she said, going back inside the room.

Mind racing, he dashed after her to find her sitting at the dining table. Sinking down into a chair opposite, he demanded again, 'Ellen, what is it? Is it something your husband has done? Has something happened to your baby?'

She took a deep breath. 'I told you my husband had another woman lined up to take my place, didn't I? His secretary, or so I thought. Well, I was wrong. It's not her at all. It's ... oh, Danny, I have a terrible feeling ... no, more than a terrible feeling, that it's ... well, it's Maxie.'

He was staring at her, stupefied. 'Maxie! My Maxie? But she doesn't know your husband.'

'She does, Danny. She's working for him. She's my son's nanny.'

His jaw dropped open. When he'd recovered himself he stammered, 'Mr Marshall, Maxie's boss, is *your* husband?'

353

Ellen nodded. 'I made a decision yesterday, while I was out walking. I walked for miles, I couldn't tell you where exactly ... as I expect you can appreciate, I had a lot on my mind.

'Douglas has left me with no choice but to accept that our marriage is over and I'll never get my son back. It's time for me to go back to my home town and try and get on with my life as best I can. I know my aunt will take me in for a short while once I've explained to her what has happened to me. I was going to tell you and Maxie all this and say thank you to you both before I went, naturally. Anyway, I decided that before I left I just had to see my son one last time. I had to, Danny, you can appreciate why.

'My husband has his own business and can work from home for long periods but he has to go to his office to check on things as well. With me gone I had assumed he'd moved his secretary in at home by now. It was my plan to beg her to take pity on me and allow me to see Thomas, say my goodbyes to him with my husband out of the way.

'I arrived at the house this morning just in time to see my husband getting into his car. He had his briefcase with him and I knew by the way he was dressed that he was going to work. Well, someone must be looking after Thomas, I thought, and it must be Julia ... that's the secretary's name ... as I couldn't think who else it would be. I hid myself across the road behind a tree, working myself up to facing her, when I saw the front door opening. First the pram came out and then ... well, I couldn't believe it when I saw who was pushing it!

Not at all who I was expecting it to be but Maxie. I made to rush across to her then I realised... Oh, Danny, you see what this means, don't you?' she implored. 'It's *Maxie* my husband was talking about as a replacement for me, not his secretary. I didn't even realise that Maxie was a nanny, let alone that she was working for my husband. It's never come up in conversation, has it? He told me the woman he had lined up to take my place loved children, and obviously Maxie does. It must be her, it must be!'

An ashen-faced Danny was staring at her, dumbstruck. Terry's prophecy, his own worst fear, was coming true. His heart was hammering painfully, a rushing noise dinning in his ears. He felt faint.

'I never realised that my husband was so devious, Danny,' Ellen continued. 'I thought he was such a good man until this. But if he can do this to me, I feel he's capable of anything. He's obviously not at all bothered about breaking up your marriage to get what he wants. I'm worried that if Douglas has set his sights on Maxie as his next wife and my baby's mother then she more than likely won't realise what's happening to her until it's too late and he's completely won her over, like he did me. And what if he does to her then what he's done to me after growing tired of me?'

'But ... but you could be wrong. It still might be his secretary not Maxie that he's after?'

Ellen looked sympathetically at him. 'I wouldn't be telling you this if I wasn't sure of my suspicions, Danny.' She took a deep breath. 'The same thought crossed my mind. I went across to knock on the door. If Julia replied then I had my answer, didn't I? But it wasn't Julia that answered the door but an older woman who said she was the housekeeper. When I asked to speak to Julia she said there was no one of that name living there. I apologised, telling her I had obviously called at the wrong house. Then I thought that to be doubly sure Julia wasn't going to be moving in unbeknownst to the housekeeper, I'd ask her to her face. I knew where she lived as Douglas had mentioned it once when he was talking about her.

'No one was in but the next-door neighbour was cleaning her step. After I told her I was an old friend of Julia's looking her up, she told me that Julia and her husband had recently had problems and were making another go of it in Peterborough. Whether she ever had an affair with my husband or not I'll never know, but she obviously isn't now. I even checked if he had a new woman working for him but when I rang and asked for Mr Marshall's secretary, I was told he was in the process of finding a replacement for one who'd just left.

'This means, Danny, Maxie is the only one Douglas could have been talking about when he said he'd found someone to take my place, someone who worked for him.'

Stricken-faced himself now, Danny stared at her for several long moments. 'I saw Maxie this morning. She was taking your son to a coffee morning at the church so he could mix with children of his own age. She told me then that your husband had asked her to accompany him to a wine merchants' do next week at the seaside. But he invited me along too ... he wouldn't have done that if he was trying to lure Maxie away from me, would he? I can't go, though, because I wouldn't be able to get the time off work.'

Ellen pulled her chair close to Danny's, laid her hand on his arm and looked at him earnestly. 'Douglas isn't stupid, Danny. He would have known you couldn't take up his offer when he invited you along. Look, listen to me, I know you're having trouble believing what I'm telling you but why would I lie to you? You and Maxie are lovely people and have been good to me. I'd hate to see Douglas destroy your marriage for his own selfish reasons. If he wants Maxie he'll get her, believe me.'

Danny would do anything to prevent that. He beseeched Ellen, 'Will you tell Maxie all this when she gets home tonight, make her see what kind of man she's working for and what you think his intentions are? Make her believe you, Ellen.'

'I'll do my best, Danny. But why wait? Let's go and tell her now, then when Douglas comes home this evening she can tell him she no longer wants to work for him and have done with it. At least I can go away knowing that, though he might have destroyed my life, he won't have destroyed yours and Maxie's.'

If Maxie ever left him for a good man who could give her more than he could, Danny knew he loved her too much to stop her. But knowing what a despicable man Douglas Marshall really was and the callous deception that was in his mind,

Danny could not stand idly by. He vehemently prayed that Maxie would listen to what they had to tell her and leave the man's employment before he managed to seal her fate and Danny's own.

He jumped up from his chair and urgently cried, 'Yes, you're right. We'll go now, Ellen.'

Fired with a consuming need to get his beloved wife away from Marshall before it was too late, Danny raced through the streets with Ellen to her former home. They were disappointed to find no one there when they knocked on the door but decided to do the same as Ellen had done that morning, hiding across the road, a little further down, to await Maxie's return.

CHAPTER TWENTY-SIX

Their wait seemed to last for ever, during which time Danny's need to deal with this potentially disastrous situation intensified to fever pitch. He now perceived Douglas Marshall as the devil incarnate and Maxie as the innocent victim, being offered up to him for sacrifice.

Finally, at just gone four-thirty, they saw her coming up the road. Danny made to rush over and confront her but Ellen grabbed his arm, pulling him back. 'No, wait until she's inside. We can't tell her what we have to in the street.'

Danny knew she was right but it took all his will-power for him to contain himself.

When Ellen felt enough time had elapsed to give Maxie time to settle Thomas and be free to devote her attention to what they were about to say, she told him, 'I'm not looking forward to this, Danny, but let's go and get it over with.'

Maxie was most surprised to see who the callers were when she answered the door to their urgent knocking. Before she could utter a word, Danny got in with, 'We need to talk to you, Maxie.'

She was looking very confused, wondering what on earth was so important they had to disturb her at work. Why had Danny such a frantic look on his face, and why was he acting so jumpily? 'But ... but ... couldn't it wait until I get home?'

'No, it can't. We need to speak to you about this now.'

'About what, Danny? And, Ellen, why are you here?' If something had happened to one of their mothers then surely Ellen wouldn't have come ... but what on earth besides that could possibly be so important?

'She needs to be sitting down for this,' Ellen advised Danny. 'The lounge would be best. Where's Thomas?' she asked Maxie.

'Thomas? He's in the nursery, playing in his playpen while I prepare his tea. But why do you want to know where he is?'

His hand gripping her arm, Danny was urgently propelling her towards the lounge. 'Because you need to listen to what we've got to tell you, Maxie, without any distraction. It's best he's occupied so you can listen calmly.'

A feeling of deep foreboding was filling Maxie now. She perched on the edge of Douglas Marshall's brown leather Chesterfield, Danny sitting beside her, and demanded, 'Just tell me, for God's sake!'

He took a deep breath and began, 'Well, it's Mr Marshall, your boss ... he's Ellen's husband.' He flashed a glance over at the other woman who was standing just inside the doorway. 'He is, isn't he, Ellen?'

She nodded. 'Believe what Danny is telling you, Maxie.'

Maxie looked utterly astonished. 'Mr Marshall is your husband? *He's* the one who's done all that to you?' She wanted to ask if this was some sort of joke but then thought better of it. It was certainly

360

no joking matter. 'But ... but ... Mr Marshall told me and Mrs Sycamore that his wife was dead.'

Ellen gasped. 'He's telling everyone that, is he?' she cried, mortified. 'Oh, how could he, how could he? He's rotten to the core, evil.'

'How can his wife be dead, Maxie, when she's standing right over there?' Danny implored her.

Maxie still couldn't believe what she was being told. Was she really working for a man who could be so cruel as to throw his own wife out of her home and then tell everyone she was dead? But she had witnessed him with his son. Surely no man who loved his child as much as Douglas Marshall obviously did would deprive him of a mother like that? But there was the troubling fact that there were no photographs around the house to show a wife had ever existed. It had always puzzled Maxie, the way he allowed no memento of his child's mother to feature in the house. But though she might not know him on a personal level, she still couldn't believe that Douglas Marshall was the sadistic monster who had been described to them. But then, she had to believe it as Ellen was standing large as life only feet away from her, swearing it was true.

'That's not all, Maxie,' Danny was saying to her. 'He's planning to make you his next wife.'

She stared at her husband, sure she had mis-heard him. 'What? That's ridiculous. The most ridiculous thing I ever heard.'

'He is, Maxie, he is,' Danny insisted. 'He told Ellen he'd found someone to take her place who suited him much better than she did. The woman worked for him, he said, and she loved children.

361

Apart from his elderly housekeeper, you're the only woman who works for him, Maxie. And he's offered to take you with him next week to the seaside. When he asked me to come along he knew I wouldn't be able to get a day off. He wanted you to himself, Maxie, so he could start working his charm on you, sweep you off your feet like he did Ellen. It's true, isn't it?' He looked across for Ellen's support and frowned to see she was no longer there.

Just then the sounds of a child's cries became audible, swiftly followed by the slam of the front door.

Maxie and Danny looked at each other for a second, frozen, before she jumped up from her seat with a look of pure horror on her face. 'Oh, God! Oh, God!' she cried. Rushing to check, she shouted, 'I think Ellen's taken Thomas. Oh, please, no, please don't let this be true.'

Reaching the front door, she yanked it open and ran down the drive into the street. There was no sign of Ellen or Thomas. Running back inside, praying she was wrong, she saw Danny coming down the stairs. The look on his face told Maxie all she needed to know.

'He is her baby,' Danny said as Maxie joined him in the hallway.

'But I'm responsible for him, Danny,' she shouted, panic-stricken. 'Oh, God, what am I going to do, what am I going to do?' she implored. 'Did you know she was going to do this?'

'No, Maxie, I had no idea, honest I didn't. We just felt you needed to know what kind of man you were working for and what he had in mind to do about you. But I'm stupid, aren't I? I should have twigged that was why she had to see you here and wouldn't wait until you came home tonight.'

'Oh, hell! I don't know whether to fetch the police, but you're right – Thomas *is* Ellen's baby. In the circumstances I can't blame her for doing what she has. She had no other choice, did she, to get her son back? But all the same, Mr Marshall will think we're involved in this as she has been staying with us. He won't believe we didn't know she was his wife. Oh, Danny, this is a dreadful situation we're in. What are we going to do?'

As her eyes darted wildly Maxie caught sight of a white envelope propped against an ornate vase on the occasional table Danny was standing by. There had been no envelope there when she had returned from her visit to the park or she would have seen it. She went over to pick it up. It was addressed to her boss. 'It must be from Ellen, explaining what's she's done,' she told Danny.

Just then a key sounded in the lock and Douglas Marshall walked in. He didn't seem to notice Danny's presence at first. Catching sight of Maxie, he said to her as he put down his brief-case and took off his coat, 'I'd dealt with all I had to at the office and thought I'd take the opportunity of finishing earlier so I could bathe Thomas and put him to bed, let you go home early.' His coat draped over his arm ready to hang in the closet, he turned to face Maxie fully, then saw she had company and simultaneously noticed the frozen expression on both faces. 'Has something happened to Thomas, Mrs Maws? And who are you?' he asked Danny.

Facing this despicable man, who had not only treated his own wife appallingly but had planned to steal Danny's as well, a rush of fury erupted within him. Before he could stop himself he had gone up to Douglas Marshall, poking the dazed man in the shoulder and announcing angrily, 'I'm Maxie's husband, that's who I am. The man whose wife you intended to steal away. Well, we know your game and it's up, mate. Telling everyone your wife's dead when she's very much alive and has been sheltering with us as she's nowhere else to go after you'd kicked her out with hardly a penny to her name! And how could you be so cruel as to prevent a mother from seeing her son? What kind of man are you, eh?'

Douglas was completely confused. Finding his voice at last, he demanded, 'Have you gone insane, man? My wife is dead.' He stared at Maxie in bewilderment. 'What is going on here?'

'I've told you what's going on, Mr Marshall,' Danny erupted before Maxie could find her voice. 'There's no point carrying on your game anymore 'cos you've been sussed.' He turned to his wife. 'Give him the letter and let's get out of here,' he ordered.

'What letter? From who?' Douglas demanded.

Danny grabbed the envelope from Maxie's hand and thrust it at him, crying, 'From your wife, that's who. Now tell us again she's dead. Dead women can't write letters, can they?'

He ripped open the envelope with shaking hands. 'For God's sake, man, I've told you – my wife is dead.'

'But she can't be, Mr Marshall,' spoke up Maxie. 'Danny's told you, she's been staying with us. Although I didn't know who she actually was until a few minutes ago...'

'Listen to me, will you?' Douglas Marshall shouted. 'Whoever that woman was, she is *not* my wife.' Having opened the letter he glanced down at it. As he read, his face paled. The coat draped across his arm slid off to fall at his feet, the letter fluttered down after it. 'Thomas!' he cried and raced up the stairs, Maxie and Danny staring after him. Seconds later he came back down, declaring, 'She's taken my son. She's demanding a ransom for him. Oh, God!'

Maxie and Danny were both unable to comprehend what he was saying. Why would Ellen ask a ransom for her own son?

Douglas grabbed hold of Maxie's arms and frenziedly shook her. 'What did this woman look like?' he demanded.

Danny grabbed hold of him, fighting to pull him away from Maxie. 'Let go of her,' he shouted, incensed. 'You're hurting my wife.'

Releasing his grip, Douglas blurted, 'I'm sorry, Mrs Maws. Very sorry. But whoever that woman was, she's kidnapped my son. If she doesn't get her money she says she won't tell us where she's hidden him but will leave him to die.' He bent down and snatched up the letter, waving it at them both. 'Read this if you don't believe me.'

Danny took the letter and scanned it. Then, stricken, he looked at Maxie. 'Oh, God, Maxie, it's true. Everything Mr Marshall is saying. This is a demand for twenty thousand pounds for Thomas's safe return. If she doesn't get her money, she'll never reveal where she's hidden him. She'll be waiting by the children's paddling pool in the Western Park at six. She said she wants you, Maxie, to bring the money and when you've handed it over then she'll tell you where Thomas is. No money, no Thomas. A minute past six and she'll be gone, leaving him to die wherever he is. She's also warned us not to get the police involved as even if she's captured by them she'll never reveal where Thomas is.'

He struggled to look at Douglas, too ashamed to meet his eye. The woman who had written this ransom demand obviously had no regard whatsoever for a child's life. She had completely fooled them into believing she was this man's wife, badly wronged by him. Danny felt himself pathetic to have been so easily taken in by her and didn't know what to say.

Douglas was frantically pacing up and down. 'Where am I going to get twenty thousand pounds from? I haven't got money like that. Why should this woman think for one minute that I have?'

Maxie didn't pause to consider that or to question why she herself had been so easily fooled. There was a frightened child out there somewhere whose life was in danger. Without further ado she dashed to the telephone and picked it up.

Douglas stopped his pacing and cried out, 'What are you doing?'

'Calling the pol–'

Before she could finish, the telephone receiver

366

was snatched from her hand and slammed back into its cradle. 'No police! Didn't you hear what the letter threatened? If there's any sign of them we'll never find out where Thomas is!'

He began pacing again. 'Where can I get the money from at this time of evening? Who do I know who'll lend it to me? But it's a fortune... No one I know would have a sum like that, let alone lying about at home.' He spun round to look at Maxie and Danny. 'You must know more about this woman... Who is she?'

'Believe us, Mr Marshall, all we know is what she told us. That her name was Ellen and her husband had thrown her out. He wouldn't let her see her baby and said he wanted a divorce from her,' Maxie told him. 'We thought we were helping out a woman in trouble, like anyone would do.'

'She only told me about an hour or so ago that she was your wife,' Danny said. 'Up until then we had no idea there was a connection with you.'

'What does she look like?' he demanded.

'Not as tall as I am. Petite. Blonde hair. Very pretty. She came across as such a lovely woman,' Maxie told him. 'We had no reason to disbelieve anything she was telling us.'

At Maxie's description of the woman Douglas's face became a death mask. He covered his eyes with his hands and gave out a despairing groan. 'Oh, God, I thought I'd seen the last of her when I sent her packing.'

'You do know this woman then?' Maxie asked him.

Sighing heavily, he nodded. 'Yes, I knew her as

367

Susan.' Then realisation filled his face. 'Now I see why she's demanding twenty thousand pounds. She must think I continued keeping it in the safe in my study... But I didn't. No one in their right mind keeps a sum of money like that in the house. Anyway, I can't get my hands on it at all as it's no longer mine.' Maxie and Danny stood by helplessly. At least it was starting to make sense to him – which was more than it was to them.

'This woman is mad. Believe me, I know. She will do what she says in the letter. She told me she'd pay me back for what she felt I'd done to her.' His face crumpled then, fat tears filling his eyes. 'Oh, Thomas...' he wailed. 'He must be terrified, poor little mite. If a single hair on his head is harmed... Oh, I can't bear it!' He began pacing again. 'I've got to do something, I've got to find him. I need to think of some way to get that money.'

A deeply worried Maxie glanced over at the hall clock. It was gone five-thirty. The banks had shut at three-thirty. Even if Mr Marshall did miraculously think of someone who could lend the money to him, there was barely time to arrange it. They had to stall Ellen ... Susan ... somehow, plead with her to give them a better chance to raise the money. But what if she wasn't prepared to give them any more time? Oh, it didn't bear thinking about.

A picture of Thomas's little face swam before Maxie. She looked at his distraught father, pacing frantically backwards and forwards, desperately trying to find a solution to his problem.

368

There must be something she could do. Think, woman, she ordered herself. Then an idea came to her. Susan had fooled them completely with her lies. Could Maxie fool her likewise? Had she got it in her to pull this off? She wasn't a natural liar and what she had in mind was going to take a performance worthy of an accomplished actress. But there was a child's life at stake here. Time was running short for Thomas. Of course she'd got it in her!

Spinning on her heel, she rushed off to the larder where she grabbed an empty brown carrier bag. Stuffing several items inside, the first that came to hand, she then rushed back into the hallway, dashing past the two men towards the front door. As she opened it to leave Douglas shouted after her.

'Where are you going, Mrs Maws?'

'Hopefully to get Thomas back,' she shouted as she ran down the driveway.

CHAPTER TWENTY-SEVEN

The woman Maxie had known as Ellen discreetly trailed her quarry as Maxie hurried through the park towards the designated meeting place. She was glad to witness the bulky carrier bag. From her hiding place behind a tree, she watched Maxie stand by the paddling pool for several long moments, looking around, her face wreathed in anxiety. Smiling wickedly, she emerged from her hiding place and walked purposefully over.

As the two women came face to face, Maxie firmly reminded herself what was at stake here. She must save a little boy's precious life. She dearly hoped the other woman could not hear the thumping of her heart or witness the trembling of her legs.

'Mrs Maws, how lovely to see you again,' Susan said, smiling at her, looking the picture of innocence she'd always portrayed herself as to Maxie. 'I've been watching you so I know you haven't been stupid enough to involve the police. Mind you, I couldn't have wished for a more gullible couple to help me with my plan! I have much to thank Douglas for in choosing you as his new nanny. Couldn't have wished for better, in fact. And your husband takes top prize in the stupidity ratings.'

Fury boiled inside Maxie at this woman's derogatory comments about her beloved husband, but she reminded herself again what was at stake and kept her own counsel.

'I've never met anyone like him, so easily manipulated into believing anything you want him to believe,' Susan continued. 'Did you think I sheltered in his milk float by chance? It was no accident. Nothing about our association was accidental in the least. I'd been watching to see who Douglas took on as his next nanny and once I knew I followed you home. When I knew you were both out, I paid a visit to one of your neighbours and had a chat. Women never change. Given a chance they love to gossip, don't they, and because of what she told me about you both, I felt like I'd known you all my life. Maybe you should have a word with her, ask her not to be so free with her information about you to strangers in future. Anyway, men are always suckers for a crying woman so I decided your husband was my best way in. Boy, did he fall hook, line and sinker for my sob story! As though I'd *ever* contemplate killing myself over a man. Your husband believed I would, though.

'Once inside your house, with you two believing you were giving sanctuary to a wronged woman, I was free to decide which one of you would best aid me with the rest of my plan. It quickly became clear to me that although you'd both be easy targets, Danny was still my best bet. Oh, by the way, my real reason for wanting to be on my own so much in my bedroom was to get away from you two. You're so bloody boring, the pair of you, so wrapped up in your own twee little world! Don't you ever do anything more exciting than watch the television or go for a spin on that clapped-out motorbike of yours? I'm so glad you never insisted you took me out in it as I would have died from embarrassment. You really should drag yourselves into the twentieth century, especially your clothes. My mother used to dress like you when she was your age, but at least it was modern then. And your taste in music ... exactly the type my mother likes to listen to as well. You two would really get on.'

A highly charged Maxie really didn't care what this repellent woman thought of her and Danny, she just desperately wanted to manoeuvre her into giving away Thomas's whereabouts. But it was obvious Susan wanted to brag about her accomplishments. The last thing Maxie wanted to do was antagonise her, so she had no choice but to listen.

'I had no trouble at all convincing your husband that Douglas was planning to take you off him,' she continued. 'Did you know your dear husband is terrified someone will steal you away from him? Well, I did,' she said smugly. 'I saw that straight away when you came home one night and told him Douglas had been more pleasant with you that day. It helped me see how I was going to get inside the house and take that brat, to make his father pay for what he'd done to me.' Her face turned ugly. The innocent creature Maxie had always seen her as was gone. Before her stood a scheming, wicked stranger.

'Nice man, Douglas Marshall ... that's what you think, Maxie, isn't it? Let me tell you, he's not at all. He led me on. Made me believe he wanted me as much as I did him. I would have been a good wife to him and mother to his kid ... well, as affectionate as you can be to an ugly thing like he is. But it turned out Douglas didn't think I was good enough for him. He said I was mad, a lunatic. But is it madness or lunacy to know you'd be the perfect wife to a man badly in need of one? He should have been honoured I chose him. He was the mad one for turning me down. I warned him I'd make him pay... Twenty thousand should do the trick. Right, I've had enough of the chat, hand over the bag,' she demanded.

Maxie gulped. Now she had to give the performance of her life and prayed she would for Thomas's sake. Without a word, she handed the carrier bag over to Ellen.

With a smug smile of satisfaction on her face, she accepted the carrier and opened it. When she saw what was inside her eyes blazed furiously. 'What's this?'

Maxie took a deep breath to calm her jangling nerves. 'Well, I thought you might be hungry on your journey wherever it is you're going,' she said evenly. 'Most people like cake and biscuits. I'd have made you some sandwiches but I never had time before your deadline.'

'What!' Susan exploded. 'Are you taking the mickey? Don't forget I'm the only one who knows where that kid is. I want that money or his death will be on your hands.'

Maxie smiled sweetly at her. 'I should have told you before that we have Thomas safe and sound. He's with his father, having his bath before he goes to bed.'

Susan was sneering at her. 'Liar! You're bluffing. You think I'm that stupid? You haven't got him! You haven't had time to work out where I've put him. I never gave you enough time. Just enough for Douglas to get the money out of his safe and for you to get here.'

Maxie was fighting with all her might not to lunge at this evil woman and beat the information out of her. 'Well, you underestimated me. I realised straight away where he was. You're not so clever as you think you are. Danny went to fetch him while I came here. Anyway I can't hang around, I need to get back as Danny will be wanting his dinner.'

She forced herself to turn and begin walking away. And if she hadn't prayed hard enough that her plan would work before, now she pledged her very soul for it.

She almost cried out in relief when she felt a hand grab her shoulder. She was roughly pulled around and Susan's frenzied face was pushed into hers.

'I know you're fucking lying, you bitch!' she was screaming. 'I know you are. You're bluffing, I tell you.'

Maxie played her trump card. Taking a deep breath, she said, 'I love children, you know that, Susan. I must do, mustn't I, to do the job I do? Would I be walking away without begging you to tell me what you've done with Thomas if I didn't already know where he was and that he was safe? I'm not a liar like you, remember, and neither would I ever risk a child's life for any reason, let alone to line my own pockets.'

The other woman's eyes were dancing wildly and Maxie could tell she was wavering as to whether to believe her or not. 'But ... but ... you'd never have guessed to look down there for him,' she blurted. 'Even if you had had time to go back and check around, the whisky in the milk and sugar I forced the brat to drink will have knocked him out for hours. You'd never have heard him crying to guide you to him, and he's well hidden so even if you had looked down there you'd never have found him, not unless I told you where exactly. I made sure of it.' Then she swung back her hand and slapped Maxie's face hard. 'Now give me my money or that brat dies! This is your last warning.'

The blow had caught her unexpectedly but Maxie was heedless of the pain. All her thoughts were centred on what Susan had just told her. 'Down there', she had said. She had hidden him 'down there'. But down where? What was down? What did you have to do to go down? Stairs, obviously. Then suddenly a memory flooded back to her. She remembered the cellar door not having shut properly and Danny telling her he hadn't been down there recently. Nor had she. But she knew where Thomas was now. Or prayed she did.

Maxie raced back the way she had come, leaving a thwarted Susan gazing after her impotently.

CHAPTER TWENTY-EIGHT

Several hours later Maxie jumped as she heard a key in the lock and the front door open. She was standing by the chesterfield, stiff with anxiety, not knowing what lay in store for her and Danny after today's events and their role in them. Douglas Marshall walked in and immediately asked her, 'How's Thomas?'

'He's sleeping soundly. The doctor called back again and said he was satisfied there'd be no lasting effects from the alcohol bar a headache tomorrow, and obviously he won't be acting himself. He advised me to get as much fluid down Thomas as possible. He's had enough for tonight, though. It was difficult to get drinks down him, with him being so drowsy, but I managed.'

Douglas looked mortally relieved as he made his way over to an armchair and sank down into it, sighing heavily. 'She's been charged with kidnap and extortion. The police said they would need to see you for your statement of events, but tomorrow will do. Thank goodness we both followed you to the park although we hadn't got a clue what you were up to and therefore kept our distance. Knowing you hadn't got the ransom to pay over, I couldn't imagine what your plan was. But when we saw you running off after your confrontation with her, I could only think ... hope ... that you'd found out from her where Thomas was. All that was important to me then was to catch you up and go with you to get him. I didn't realise until the police called here and asked me to accompany them to the station that your husband had accosted Susan before she could get away and forced her down to the station. How did you manage to get out of her what she had done with Thomas?'

'I took a big gamble, Mr Marshall. I knew you had no hope of getting that money in time, if at all. It occurred to me that if she could fool me and Danny so convincingly with her lies, why couldn't I do the same to her?' Her voice became low. 'I daren't think of the consequences if I had failed.' If Susan had been diligent enough to close the cellar door behind her after her inspection of it, Maxie feared she might not have guessed so quickly where Thomas was hidden. She was just so grateful for this laxness in an otherwise well-executed revenge plan.

Douglas flashed a grateful smile at her. 'You didn't fail, Mrs Maws. Let's be grateful for that. I'll be eternally indebted to you for doing what you did. I was so consumed with trying to think of a way to get hold of the money in time that any other way of resolving the situation never occurred to me.' A look of utter bewilderment filled his face. 'I can't believe that woman nursed such a grudge against me that she was willing to sacrifice my son's life to get her own back.'

A distant expression then replaced the one of bewilderment. 'She came across as kind, caring, very amenable, doting towards Thomas. Just the type I needed around me after my wife died.' He gave a deep sigh. 'My wife Ellen was killed in an accident while driving her car, Mrs Maws. Thomas was barely weeks old when she went out to do a spot of shopping while I watched him one Saturday afternoon. She was involved in an accident with a lorry and killed outright. The driver escaped unhurt and it was never proved whose fault it was, but my wife was a careful driver, that's all I can say. I loved her dearly, she was my life. Thomas's arrival completed our family but we planned to have more children in time. When she died I had no choice but to find someone to take care of Thomas while I kept the business running to provide for him.

'I found Susan through an agency in London, picked her from several nannies who were sent to me for interview. It was my intention to employ a housekeeper too, but when I took Susan on she told me she would be happy to combine the two jobs. I was so grateful for her offer as it saved me the trouble of finding a suitable woman. I was grieving at the time, terribly, but conscious nevertheless that Ellen would have wanted me to make the woman who was helping me care for her son feel comfortable in her new surroundings. I encouraged Susan to treat the house as her home and invited her to eat with me in the evenings rather than from a tray in her room. I had no idea she was getting ideas above her station. There were occasions when I suspected my private things had been disturbed but I put this down to not being my proper self, still not thinking straight after Ellen's death.

'Susan had been working for me about six

months when I returned home from work one night and walked in here. The first thing I noticed was that the silver-framed wedding photograph that usually sat on the table was missing. I assumed Susan must have accidentally broken it when she was doing the housework. Then I noticed that all the photos that had shown Ellen had gone. I couldn't understand why. I went upstairs to say goodnight to Thomas and decided afterwards I'd ask Susan what had happened to them. When I pushed open the nursery door, she had Thomas in her arms and I was so shocked to hear her saying to him, "Say goodnight to Mummy then, Thomas. Hopefully Daddy and I will have another baby soon to join you."

'I rushed in then and demanded she join me downstairs. As soon as she did, I asked her what she was thinking of, saying things like that to my son? She looked surprised that I would be angry and just said, "Well, I was only telling Thomas the truth. You do want more children, don't you, darling? Soon as we're married we'll make a start on that." I was stunned. Asked her what on earth had got into her, to make her think we were anything other than employer and employee. She said I had led her to believe I cared about her by the way I treated her. I said that was just because I wanted her to feel welcome in this house, nothing more than that, and I was sorry if she had read my intentions wrongly. Then I asked her what had happened to all the photographs of Ellen.

'She told me she had burned them all as she didn't wish to be constantly reminded of my

379

former wife when she had become my new one. And she had gone through the house and got rid of everything else she knew had been Ellen's, for the same reason. I was outraged that she would take it upon herself to do such a thing. Incensed, I shouted at her that she had no right to do what she had or be thinking as she was. She started ranting at me then. Like a madwoman she was. Screamed at me that I had led her on, then started accusing me of casting her aside as I'd obviously found someone else I thought would suit me better. She was going on about suing me for breach of promise. I'd had enough by this time. I told her to pack her bags and leave. Then she started begging me to give her another chance. Told me she loved me, would die without me, and looked at Thomas as her own. It was awful ... horrible. I went to her room and did her packing for her, while she was all the time begging me to reconsider, then I marched her out of the house. As I shut the door on her she was yelling at me that she would get me back for what I'd done to her. I was just too upset about Ellen's things and too glad she was gone to take any notice.

'The next day I called the agency in London and told them about her. I decided also that my next nanny I would hand pick myself and thoroughly check out before I took her on, but most importantly she would be a happily married woman. My new housekeeper too. I'm sure after what I've told you, Mrs Maws, you will appreciate my reasons. That's why I questioned you so thoroughly as to the state of your marriage when I interviewed you, and haven't been exactly warm

380

towards you since you've been here, to make absolutely sure there was no way I could cause any further misunderstandings.

'A couple of weeks after I'd complained to the agency about Susan's behaviour they contacted me to say they'd done what they should have done when she first registered with them for work and made enquiries about her. It was discovered she wasn't actually the Susan Atkinson she claimed to be but an impostor. The real Susan, a fully qualified nanny, thought she had lost her qualification certificates three years previously but it now appeared they had been stolen from her, obviously by the woman masquerading as her. Since then the impostor had secured several jobs with different agencies in various parts of the country, only accepting assignments with widowed men. She had left all of them abruptly, and all her employers complained to the agencies afterwards about her behaviour which had been the same as she had shown with me. Her aim was obviously to get herself a husband, but what a way to go about it. The woman is definitely deranged.

'What her real name is the police don't know as she isn't talking to them yet. Well, not before I left the station she wasn't. There are no reports of children being kidnapped and held to ransom by their nanny so the police seem to think I'm the only employer she has done that to, and probably because she had known of the existence of that twenty thousand pounds.

'Ellen had been left the money by her own mother, her only surviving relative, who died only months before she herself did. Only the day before her death we had drawn out the money in cash because we'd seen a house we wanted to buy. It was in the countryside with views over Bradgate Park and had extensive grounds, perfect for bringing up a family. The type of place we'd not have been able to afford if it hadn't been for Ellen's inheritance. We negotiated a price of twenty-one thousand, a good price for what it was and its prime location, but the owner said he'd knock off a thousand if we gave him cash. As soon as Ellen returned from her shopping trip we were off to seal the deal.

'With all I was going through afterwards I'd forgotten about the money sitting in the safe in my study until about four months later. Anyway, one day I remembered about it and, after thinking long and hard as to what Ellen would have wished me to do with it, I decided to put it in trust for Thomas for when he came of age. I was checking it and filling in the deposit slip ready to take to the bank the next day when Susan walked in to inform me that Thomas was ready for bed. When she saw the money piled up she commented what a huge amount it looked, at a guess about fifteen thousand. I corrected her by telling her it was twenty and said as soon as I'd put it back in the safe, I would join her in the nursery. Obviously she assumed I always kept that amount in the safe, hence the ransom demand for the return of Thomas.' He suddenly looked at Maxie remorsefully. 'Oh, dear, I have gone on, haven't I? But you do deserve to know what brought about this sorry situation.'

He gave another heavy sigh. 'Your husband left

the police station the same time as I did so I expect he's waiting for you at home, Mrs Maws. Please thank him again for his gallant action. At least we know ... well, whatever her real name is ... is under lock and key and no longer at liberty to carry on her antics. I think I'll take a day off work tomorrow to stay with Thomas, I'm sure you understand my need to, so you take a day off too and enjoy it, Mrs Maws. I'll see you on Wednesday.'

Maxie was surprised to hear this. 'You aren't going to sack me then?'

He looked at her askance. 'Why would I want to fire a perfectly good ... no, excellent ... nanny for my son?' Then he looked extremely worried. 'You're not thinking of leaving me, are you?'

'No, not at all. It's just that ... well...'

'Oh, I see,' he interjected. 'Look, Mrs Maws, it wasn't just you and your husband that woman fooled with her lies, but me and her other employers and the agencies she used to get her jobs too. Far less trusting people than you and your husband are. So please put your mind at rest on that matter. And I'll never forget or be able to repay your quick thinking ... okay, it was a gamble you took but one that paid off and it saved my son's life. You took that gamble at a risk to yourself as you had no idea if his kidnapper was violent or not; all you were concerned for was my son. What better nanny could I hope to have for Thomas than one whose top priority is him?' He paused and gave a wan smile. 'I just know that one day I will lose you, when you have children of your own, and selfishly I hope that time comes later rather than sooner.'

The shrill of the telephone, followed by a wail of protest from Thomas, made them both jump.

'Would you–'

Pre-empting Douglas's request, Maxie interjected, 'Of course.' And immediately rushed off.

As Douglas replaced the telephone receiver, Maxie joined him again, holding a miserable-looking Thomas protectively in her arms.

'Wrong number, would you believe,' said Douglas.

'Well, I suspect you could be in for a long night,' she responded, as she ran her hand gently over the top of Thomas's clumps of fine red hair.

Smiling tenderly at his beloved child, Douglas relieved Maxie of him. 'Let's see if a cuddle from your old dad will help settle you again.' He gazed lovingly into his son's face. 'Shall we see Mrs Maws safely off, and then how about me and you settling into the rocking chair and having a look at the stars through the window?'

As she looked on, Maxie conjured a vision of the wonderful scene he was creating and saw herself with Danny doing the same for a child of their own one day.

Several moments later, outside on the doorstep, Maxie turned to say her goodbyes. 'Thomas has already had his bedtime milk but some more won't do him any harm, in fact it would be just the ticket to get him back to sleep,' she advised her employer.

'I shall heed your advice this time, Mrs Maws,' he responded gratefully. 'A bottle of warm milk coming up, eh, son,' he said to Thomas.

Thomas giggled, grabbed his father's cheek with his tiny fingers and unexpectedly proclaimed, 'Dadda.'

Douglas's face lit up and he exclaimed excitedly, 'Did you hear that, Mrs Maws, Thomas said "Dadda". He did, didn't he? It was "Dadda", wasn't it?'

She laughed. 'It certainly was.' She reached over and ran her fingers tenderly down the side of the child's face. 'Who's a clever boy, then? You'll soon be chatting away. Oh, I can't wait to start helping you pronounce your words.'

Douglas reached over and placed a hand on her arm and, eyeing her fondly, said, 'As I said before, I couldn't wish for a better person than you to help me raise him.'

Meanwhile Danny had returned home from the police station, after giving his statement, to find the house empty. Knowing Maxie was either still at the home of her employer or on her way back, he immediately set off to meet her, needing to reassure himself she was not suffering any ill effects from her ordeal earlier. He arrived at the entrance gate at the exact moment Douglas placed his hand on Maxie's arm and completely misconstrued what was being said. His heart thudded painfully and his whole body sagged at the realisation that the events of earlier had brought employee and employer closer together and his worse fears had come to fruition. He was looking into the face of the man he felt would, in just a matter of time, steal his beloved wife from him.

Spinning on his heels, a completely defeated Danny fled home.

Maxie made to depart but Douglas stalled her. 'Oh, just one more thing ... would you mind if I called you Maxie? After what we've just been through it doesn't seem right that I keep addressing you so formally. And will you please call me Douglas?'

A warm glow filled her. She had been happy and content with the Carsons but had had a feeling that this job was going to prove even more rewarding to her. She smiled happily at her boss. 'I'll be delighted to, Douglas. I'll see you on Wednesday, eight sharp.'

CHAPTER TWENTY-NINE

Maxie arrived home to find the downstairs rooms empty and frowned to hear movement from their bedroom. Danny surely couldn't be getting himself ready for bed without waiting to greet her home, especially after what they had both just been through? This wasn't like him.

Making her way up, she was totally confused to find him packing a suitcase.

'What on earth are you doing?'

Not having heard her enter, he jumped and spun round to face her, staring at her, frozen.

'Danny, why are you packing?' she asked him, mystified.

'Well, I just thought I might as well get it over with.'

'Get what over with?' She pulled a face.

His own clouded over miserably. 'You and me going our separate ways.'

His words stunned her. 'What! You're leaving me? Why, Danny? Why?' she implored.

He gave a miserable sigh. 'It's not that I want to, Maxie. It's the last thing I want, in fact. But I can't go on like this anymore. I might have been good enough for you when we married, but how much longer could we hope to last before you saw me for what I really am? Especially after today.'

'Eh?' she exclaimed.

'I'm just a milkman, Maxie, I can't provide the sort of life a woman like you deserves. Terry was right about me.'

Her face twisted for a moment as she struggled to remember. 'Terry? Terry who? Oh, you mean that chap who moved into number one with his girlfriend and invited us across that night? What do you mean, he was right? Right about what?'

'Me being a loser, Maxie. I overheard him, you see, when I was trying to get rid of your drink in the rubber plant. They'd gone into the other room together. He was angry that Gail had invited my sort into his house, bothered I'd ruin his reputation if people saw he was mixing with the likes of a milkman. He told her to hurry up and get rid of us. Gail told him she thought you were all right, and he just said how could you be if you'd saddled yourself with the likes of me? But then he said it was a shame that he was with Gail. He wouldn't mind having a go at seducing you as he found you attractive.

'I also saw your face when you were looking around their house, Maxie, and heard what you said to Gail. You said you'd do anything to have a house and furniture like they'd got, and I felt so inadequate because I couldn't pay for a house and stuff to go in it like they had.'

Maxie was so shocked by what Danny was spilling out to her that she was rendered speechless.

His shoulders sagged despairingly. Throwing the pile of clothes he was holding into the suitcase, he sank down on the bed and looked up at Maxie defeatedly. 'What I heard him say got me so worried. I wasn't surprised Terry found you attractive. You're beautiful, Maxie, but not only that. I know you've got so many other good qualities, ones any man would be glad to have in a wife, like I am. But what if Terry hadn't been with Gail, and had made a play for you, and you had found him attractive back and realised you'd be better off with his sort because he could do so much more for you than I could? Thankfully for me Terry was spoken for, but I worried how long it would be before someone else like him came along and made a play for you? The thought of losing you terrified me, Maxie. I didn't know what to do about it. I couldn't stop you being attracted to another man who was better looking than me, could I? But then I thought, if I bought you nice things to make our home a better place to live in, and took you to nice places, maybe you wouldn't look at another man so easily.'

Maxie was completely astonished. 'So that's why you were so desperate to bring extra money in, because you thought I'd leave you if you didn't for someone who could?' she gasped.

He nodded. 'I couldn't even do that, though, could I, Maxie? Everything I tried, I failed at. I made a right muck up of the job as petrol pump attendant. I was that bad the owner wasn't prepared to give me the time to get better at it.'

'But you were tired after finishing your full-time job by the time you started that one, Danny. The owner knew it was too much for you.'

'I suppose,' he said, unconvinced. 'I managed to sell some tea towels then, out on my round, so I suppose I made a success of something. But then there was that business over the tins. I mean, how could I not have known it wasn't Irish stew but dog meat in them? I was so gullible to believe what Andy told me. That's what a stupid husband you've got, Maxie. I could have been responsible for poisoning people if there'd been something in that dog meat that didn't agree with humans. We nearly ate it ourselves as our mothers made a pie with the two tins I brought home. Thank God I managed to destroy it before we did eat it! I even got blackmailed by one of my customers who found out what really was inside the tins. She gave me no choice but to settle her milk bill out of my profits or she'd have spilled the beans and had me lynched by the other purchasers.

'Then I nearly got myself mixed up with the criminal world when I tried to find someone to provide me with goods after Andy went off. I just thank God that Guv bloke thought my approach to him was a joke played on him by his wife as a birthday present, else I might not be sitting here now with all my limbs intact.

'The business with the van was the final straw. I was really excited about that, Maxie. Thought at long last I'd found a foolproof way to bring in the amount of money I needed to buy you all the stuff I wanted to. I put every last penny I had into that.'

Maxie couldn't believe he had kept so many of his efforts at money-making secret from her, but from what he was telling her she could see why. Sitting down beside him, she looked at him earnestly. 'But how can you blame yourself for

390

someone stealing the engine?'

'Maxie, no one stole the engine. There wasn't one in it when I bought it! The bloke from the scrapyard told me it was in good nick and I was stupid enough to believe him. He had it towed around when we were all out. Then I wasn't even honest enough to own up to the truth but let you all believe it'd been stolen as I just couldn't bear the thought of you seeing me for the failure I was.

'Anyway, I'd lost any means I had of doing something by myself so I tried to get another part-time job, but the better paid ones were always gone by the time I applied for them and the others weren't paying anywhere near enough to do what I wanted so all that was left for me to do was make the best of what time I'd got left with you. Well, I can't expect you to respect me any longer and want to stay married to me, Maxie, not when it was me who brought that awful woman into our home. You deserve better than me, Maxie. Staying tied to me is hindering you from finding someone who would look after you better. The best I can do for you is to free you.'

Maxie jumped up from the bed and glared at him angrily. 'Oh, you've got it all worked out, it seems, Danny. But aren't you forgetting one thing?'

He looked at her. 'What?'

'That I love you. I couldn't ever love anyone more than I do you. You're a decent man, Danny, and I wouldn't swap you for anyone, not even a millionaire. I can't believe you would ever think I could. That Terry had no right to say those things about you! If anyone's a loser it's him. If it's any

391

consolation, I saw Gail recently and she told me that he'd been sacked from his manager's job because he was no good at it and she'd dropped him like a ton of bricks to take up with someone else who'll keep her in luxury – that's how loyal *she* is! You know I'm not that sort, Danny, and I'm annoyed you let that Terry make you believe I was. Your job as a milkman is an honest job, the dairy only employ trustworthy men to collect their money. Men like you, Danny. The likes of that Terry wouldn't last five minutes in a job like yours, but then the likes of him would never take it in the first place. And I only said what I did about their house and furniture because I felt obliged to. In truth I was thinking how lucky I was not to have to clean such a place while I was still working.

'Oh, Danny, what an idiot you've been! You should have told me what you'd overheard Terry saying about you and I would soon have put you right. I couldn't understand why you suddenly decided to do all those things for me. I've never given you the impression I wasn't happy with our life, because I *am* happy, more than happy. I spoke to my mother about what you were up to, at least what I knew you were up to at the time, and she told me she thought it was admirable of you to want to better our lives and as your wife I should encourage you or risk you thinking I considered you incapable. I could see the wisdom in that, but if I'd known what was really behind it I'd have put a stop to you killing yourself with overwork straight away. Your health is the most important thing to me, not what you can buy me.

'Danny, I know that crooked scrap dealer would never have fobbed you off so easily with that van if you hadn't been so fired up by the fact you thought you'd found a way to earn money from it that you never took time to check it over properly. Those sorts make their living from conning people out of their hard-earned money, they're experts at it, spot a trusting man like you a mile off. Well, I'd sooner have a man like you any day than one like him. That idea of yours was an excellent one. If we'd had the money to replace the engine, well, who knows? We hadn't so there's no point dwelling on it.

'As for you bringing that woman back here, well, that's because you're kind, Danny, and how were you to know it was just an act she was putting on, to use us in her plan to get back at Mr Marshall? I never saw through her, and neither did lots of other people she had dealings with either. Anyway, it's only down to your heroic actions that she's now going to pay for what she's done and not be free to carry on.

'Now, I'm not blaming you, but the reason I took the job with Mr Marshall in the first place was because it offered more money than the other one and I felt I should take it as you seemed hell-bent on bringing more in. I felt it only right as your wife to do what I could to help you. If you hadn't got this silly notion in your head that I could leave you for a richer man, we'd never have been mixed up in that woman's plans in the first place.'

She threw her hands in the air in frustration. 'Danny, I don't care if we're never any better off than we are now. I don't care that our furniture is second-hand – it's just something to sit on and sleep in. I don't care that we drive around in an old motorbike and sidecar left to you by your father. It's transport and takes us to places other people never get to see and enjoy. I don't care what other people think of us. I'm not changing the way I am and nor do I want you to, just so we can fit in with what they think we should be like.'

She looked at him tenderly, the love she felt for him brimming unashamedly from her eyes. 'Oh, Danny, I'm the luckiest woman in the world that you're mine. How many husbands would care about their wives so much they'd do anything to stay married to them? I just want you as you are, Danny. The good, kind, lovely person I fell in love with when we played together as babies and always knew was the one for me in every way. Please don't ever change, ever, not a fraction,' she begged him.

He threw his arms around her to hug her fiercely, relieved and happy tears pouring from his eyes. 'Oh, Maxie,' he blubbered. 'It's been like a nightmare for me. I am stupid. Why did I let what that man said get to me so much? I won't listen to anyone else in future, Maxie. If I do have any worries...'

'You'll talk to me about them, same as I would you, and like we always used to?' she cut in, pulling away just enough to fix him with her eyes and let him see she meant business.

He nodded. 'I promise,' he vowed.

'So can we go back to how we used to be before we met Terry, and move onwards? I'm not bothered about the upwards, Danny, leave that to those who feel they haven't got a life unless they've expensive things around them to brag about and are seen in the best places.'

'Yes, Maxie, yes,' he vehemently agreed.

They hugged each other again. Wrapped protectively in each other's arms, both were in no doubt that all the money in the world would not make either of them happier than they were now and always would be. They felt sad for all those people who were under the impression that money bought happiness. It might to a degree, but they both knew riches couldn't buy love, not the deep love they shared, the long-lasting, respectful, trusting sort that saw those who shared it through all the obstacles life put before them. Their strength as a couple had been tested by another's interference but they had survived and would use this experience in a positive way, becoming stronger, even more united, as they continued their life's journey together.

The publishers hope that this book has given you enjoyable reading. Large Print Books are especially designed to be as easy to see and hold as possible. If you wish a complete list of our books please ask at your local library or write directly to:

Magna Large Print Books
Magna House, Long Preston,
Skipton, North Yorkshire.
BD23 4ND

This Large Print Book for the partially sighted, who cannot read normal print, is published under the auspices of

THE ULVERSCROFT FOUNDATION